'Marianne, this is Lydia,' Jill introduced her friend. Smiling, her heart fluttering, Marianne shook the beautiful young girl's hand.

'Pleased to meet you,' Marianne replied warmly. Turning to Jill, she smiled sweetly. 'So, how are you?'

'I'm fine! I wanted you to meet Lydia because . . .' Jill uttered the trigger word.

Already? Marianne thought with some surprise as she stared into space, her arms limp, her body still.

'There, what did I tell you?' Jill giggled. 'She's hypnotized, and she'll do anything we ask!'

'That's incredible!' Lydia gasped as she stood before Marianne and squeezed her firm breasts. 'With the power we have over her, we could do absolutely anything to her!'

'Exactly! Let's get her to strip off. Right, here goes – Marianne, take your clothes off!'

Also by Ray Gordon in New English Library paperback

**Arousal
House of Lust
The Uninhibited
Submission!
Haunting Lust
Depravicus
The Splits
The Degenerates**

Enslaved

Ray Gordon

NEW ENGLISH LIBRARY
Hodder and Stoughton

Copyright © 1997 by Ray Gordon

First published in 1997
by Hodder and Stoughton
A division of Hodder Headline PLC

A New English Library paperback

The right of Ray Gordon to be identified as the Author of
the Work has been asserted by him in accordance with the
Copyright, Designs and Patents Act 1988.

10 9 8 7 6 5 4 3 2 1

All rights reserved. No part of this publication may be reproduced,
stored in a retrieval system, or transmitted, in any form or by any
means without the prior written permission of the publisher, nor be
otherwise circulated in any form of binding or cover other than that
in which it is published and without a similar condition being
imposed on the subsequent purchaser.

All characters in this publication are fictitious and any resemblance
to real persons, living or dead, is purely coincidental.

British Library Cataloguing in Publication Data

Gordon, Ray
Enslaved
1. English fiction - 20th century
I. Title
823.9'14

ISBN 0 340 67230 7

Typeset by Avon Dataset Ltd, Bidford-on-Avon, Warks
Printed and bound in Great Britain by
Cox & Wyman, Reading, Berks

Hodder and Stoughton
A division of Hodder Headline PLC
338 Euston Road
London NW1 3BH

Chapter One

'So I failed!' Marianne tossed her long blonde hair over her shoulder and smiled wryly at Barry.

'You failed *miserably*!' he elaborated, reclining on the sofa, eyeing his girlfriend's red miniskirt, her long shapely legs, her red stilettos. 'All that time and money – wasted! You never listen to me, do you? I told you that going on a hypnosis course was a stupid idea! You've been away all bloody week, and for what? Nothing! Hundreds of bloody pounds wasted on a stupid bloody course! Hypnotism doesn't work, Marianne! Get it into your head that all this fancy stuff you see on the TV, on the stage, is fixed!'

'It's not fixed! Anyway, I'm going to ring Jill and tell her about the course,' Marianne countered. 'At least *she*'ll show some interest!'

Standing in the hall silently cursing Barry, Marianne was about to ring her friend when she had an idea. Recalling the course lecturer talking about trigger words, she gingerly lifted the receiver but didn't press any number keys. Glancing at the open lounge door, she grinned, knowing that Barry could hear her every word as she pretended to talk to her friend.

'I muffed it, but it was worth trying,' she articulated loudly. 'The lecturer? Oh, yes, he was very good! It wasn't his fault that I made a hash of things. Actually, to prove that hypnosis works, he placed a trigger word in my subconscious. Whenever I hear the word, I fall into a hypnotic state and will do anything that's asked of me! What is it? Well, if I tell you, you will keep it to yourself, won't you? No, I haven't told Barry! God, there's no saying what he'd get me to do if he knew about it! I'd end up giving him breakfast in bed every morning and God knows what else if he realized the power he could wield over me! OK, the word's *'juxtaposition'*. Exactly – that's why the lecturer chose it, because it's hardly ever used. Not the sort of word to crop up in everyday conversation. No, he was going to erase it from my subconscious but he was taken ill this afternoon, the last day of the course. Yes, OK, come round for coffee and we'll have a chat about it. Right, I'll see you tomorrow, then. Bye, Jill.'

Returning to the lounge, Marianne sat in the armchair and crossed her slender legs, wondering whether Barry had taken in all she'd said. Would he try and use the magical word? He frowned as he brushed his thick black hair away from his forehead and gazed into her misty blue eyes. 'So, what will you do now?' he asked nonchalantly.

'I don't know. I suppose I could try reflexology. Or aromatherapy, perhaps? I really would like to set up something from home, Barry. Now that I've been made redundant, I want to try working for myself. The spare room's all ready, but for what?'

'Well, my job will keep us going financially, so there's no immediate panic,' he smiled.

Averting his gaze, Barry took a deep breath. This was it, Marianne knew, as she waited in anticipation. 'Juxtaposition,' he whispered, quickly locking his eyes to hers. Marianne stared blankly across the room, her hands limp in her lap, her face serene. 'Stand up,' Barry ordered, his dark eyes blinking in disbelief as his girlfriend obediently rose to her feet. 'Are you really hypnotized?' he asked. His words were slow, unsure as his human marionette stood silently, her eyes still staring blankly. 'Come on, Marianne! You can't fool me!' Barry laughed. 'There's no such thing as hypnosis! It's a stage act, a con!'

Her arms hanging meekly by her sides, Marianne did her best to contain herself as Barry stood up and walked towards her. Determined to fool him, to put a halt to his continual sarcasm, his perpetual cynicism, she decided to go along with whatever he asked her to do.

'It's no good!' he laughed as he kissed her cheek. 'I know you're bluffing!' Marianne remained perfectly still, praying that she wouldn't giggle and give the game away as he gently squeezed her firm breast through her flimsy summer blouse. 'All right, I'll put you to the test!' he announced. 'Jump up and down!'

Bouncing on the spot, Marianne was sure that she couldn't keep up the pretence for long. But if she could, she thought wickedly, she could have some *real* fun! 'Stand still!' instructed her master. 'I still don't believe this! I need a *real* test, a foolproof test. I've got it – take off your skirt!'

As though in a trance, Marianne tugged her short skirt down her slender legs and kicked it across the room. She experienced a sharp pang of excitement – arousal. *This is going to be interesting!* she thought, wondering how far Barry would go in his effort to expose her as a fraud.

'Take your panties off!' he ordered excitedly as he resumed his spectator's seat. Slipping her panties down her shapely thighs, Marianne revealed her trimmed blonde pubes, her pinken girl-slit, to his doubting eyes. Kicking her shoes off, she stepped out of her panties and stood with her feet wide apart, awaiting her next instruction. 'This isn't a real test,' Barry sighed. 'I know, take *all* your clothes off! Then I'll put you to the ultimate test!'

Her hands trembling, her clitoris stirring, Marianne unbuttoned her blouse and slipped it off her shoulders. Unclipping her red lace bra, she began to realize the fun she could have if she could convince her boyfriend that she really *was* under his spell. The potential was amazing, she mused as her stomach somersaulted delightfully at the prospect of sex.

Peeling the bra cups away from her firm young breasts, she felt her nipples extend, hardening in her rising arousal. Watching Barry from the corner of her eye, she stood naked before him, wondering what the ultimate test would demand of her. She was centre stage, the leading lady – and loving it! The sense of power was exhilarating. *Who's the real master?* she mused happily as her vaginal muscles tightened.

'You've a beautiful body,' Barry praised, his voice deeper, husky now. 'I love your cunt!' he added crudely – to shock her, she realized. 'I really do love your sweet cunt!'

Their sex life had always been good, but nothing out of the ordinary, she was well aware. Several times Barry had asked her to masturbate while he watched, but she'd never found the courage to realize his fantasy. He'd even gone so far as to buy her a vibrator, but she'd never been brave enough to use it. Many times he'd complained that she wasn't adventurous enough in bed, but she hadn't been able to relax, to open up and really enjoy herself, her curvaceous young body.

But now, in her feigned hypnotic state, her inhibitions were falling away like autumn leaves, leaving her naked, exposed – free of guilt and embarrassment. Whatever he asked of her, she would comply. After all, she concluded, she wasn't to be held responsible for her actions. In her wanton abandonment, she would be completely innocent.

'Go to the fridge and get a nice juicy cucumber,' Barry ordered her. Another pang of arousal jolted her womb as she realized that she was discovering Barry's darker side, his secret fantasies. *God, a cucumber!* she thought, knowing exactly what he would demand she do with it.

Obediently, she fetched the long, cool green phallus and stood dutifully before her master. 'Lie on the floor and push it right up your cunt!' he commanded. His words were alien to her. This was the other side of the man she loved. Did she really want to discover what lurked in the dark depths of his male mind? *Everyone has a darker side*, she mused as she stretched her naked body full length on the carpet. A good side and a dark, evil side, she remembered reading somewhere.

Her hands trembling, she began to wonder whether her little game was such a good idea after all. 'Push the cucumber right up your lovely wet cunt!' Opening her legs wide in response to her boyfriend's cold, unfamiliar words, Marianne presented the rounded end of the phallus to her gaping crack, wondering what it would feel like as she gently twisted and pushed the green shaft into her tightening pussy. As the fruit opened her, stretched the soft walls of her secret garden to press against her cervix, she shuddered. Wondering what Barry was thinking as he watched her wicked act, she allowed her hands to fall by her sides once she'd fully inserted the fruit, parting her legs further to display her stretched pussy lips, the long green shaft emerging from her bloated sex valley. 'That's very good!' Barry praised. 'But I still don't believe that you're hypnotized! I want you to masturbate, to frig your clitty to orgasm while I watch.'

She'd never before brought herself off in front of Barry. Hadn't touched herself, in fact, since moving in with him a year previously. She'd masturbated before on the odd occasion but it was wrong, or so she'd been led to believe by her mother. Beautiful, but wrong. The overwhelming sensations and immense relief the act had brought her when she was young had been incredible, but she'd never been able to free herself of the racking guilt. *Never again!* she'd resolved remorsefully each time she'd pulled her navy-blue school knickers up after her secret pleasure. But now? Either she complied with Barry's demand and massaged her clitoris to orgasm, or she blew the game – spoiled the chance of any future fun. 'Go on – if you're really under hypnosis you'll frig yourself off!' he laughed as she drifted in her quandary.

This was it – the ultimate test! With the cucumber cooling her inner vaginal flesh, her pussy lips tightly encompassing the thick green shaft, her arousal was already riding high. *What the hell!* she thought as she slipped a finger between her swelling girlishness and located her stiffening clitoris. *This will prove it!* she smiled inwardly as she began her gentle massaging – her slow, rhythmical female masturbation.

Strangely, there was no feeling of humiliation, no degradation. To her surprise, her vaginal muscles responded immediately to her intimate caress. Tightening, crushing the solid phallus, her young pussy spasmed, contracted, as her clitoris swelled. Emitting involuntary gasps of pleasure, she realized that her climax was quickly approaching as she massaged her cumbud faster.

'I'll spunk over your lovely tits after you've come!' Barry laughed. Although his words heightened Marianne's arousal, they worried her. This was so unlike Barry. Normally soft, gentle, loving in his sexual coaxing, this coarse language was so uncharacteristic. 'You can wank me off and I'll come all over your nipples!' he chortled. *Undoubtedly Barry's darker side!* she mused as the incredible pleasure emanating from her clitoris caused her to arch her back.

Her stomach rising and falling, her firm rounded breasts heaving as her climax neared, she grabbed the cucumber with her free hand and began thrusting the fruit in and out of her hot vaginal sheath. The new and exciting sensations rocked her young body, reaching out to every nerve ending, tightening every muscle. With Barry watching her most intimate and obscene act, she was discovering hitherto unknown sexual pleasure.

'God, I'm coming!' The treacherous words bubbled from her full red lips before she could halt them, before she could conceal the immense pleasure her wanton act of masturbation was bringing her. 'Come . . . coming! Ah, ah, yes!' Now she was discovering her *own* darker side, a side she'd never dreamed had existed, and she was determined never to reveal her trickery. The game was new and exciting. It would add something to their relationship, rather than take away from it. *Wouldn't it?*

Kneeling between her open legs, Barry grabbed the cucumber and thrust it deep into the girl's gripping sex-sheath as her young naked body convulsed in response. 'You love being fucked by a cucumber, don't you?' he asked in his wickedness. 'You'd like me to fuck your arse with it, wouldn't you?' His words shocked Marianne as her climax waned, leaving her breathing deeply, her head rolling from side to side in the aftermath of the most spectacular orgasm she'd ever experienced. *Fuck your arse with it.* They weren't Barry's words. *Or were they?* she wondered.

Her blue eyes closed, she listened as her boyfriend tugged his zip down and pulled his hard penis out. Watching through her eyelashes as he knelt astride her head, his massive member hovering threateningly above her pretty face, she knew that she was about to be instructed to do something she'd never done before. Something he'd often asked of her but that she'd never been able to bring herself to do.

'Open your pretty mouth and suck my knob!' he demanded crudely as he gripped his veined shaft and pressed his swollen glans to her pursed lips. The cucumber, the masturbation, hadn't been the ultimate test after all, she thought anxiously as she parted her red lips. 'Come on, you fucking bitch! Suck the sperm from my cock!' Barry ordered harshly.

Marianne allowed his glans to slip into her hot mouth and rest against her tongue as his loveless words echoed in the confusion of her mind. She was driven now not by her sexual arousal, but by her curiosity. How far would he go to satisfy his cold lust? To what extent would he use her for debased sex – use her body, the body of the girl he professed to love so much?

Now, with his darker-than-dark side emerging fully, she thought about her relationship. Was this the man she really wanted to marry? she wondered as his knob slipped further into her wet mouth. He'd always been so kind, loving and gentle with her, making sweet love with her – not lust. But now?

'Ah, that's good! You've a succulent mouth, a fuckable mouth!' Barry gasped as his knob came to rest at the back of her throat, his broad shaft absorbing the inner heat of her wet mouth. 'Suck it, bitch! Wank me off and drink my come!' he cried as he leaned forward, resting his weight on his hands, his heavy balls rolling in anticipation.

Barely believing the blunt demand, the crudely uttered words of cold lust as she took her boyfriend's shaft in her hand, Marianne began her wanking movements. She was tempted to reveal her feigned hypnotic state and expose him for the heartless pervert she now knew him to be. 'Coming!' he gasped as she was about to pull his penis from her bloated mouth and tell him what she thought of his loveless act, his cruel violation of her young naked body. But she wanted to learn more about his inner self. She'd put a halt to the games. But not yet, she decided.

His sperm suddenly jetted from his throbbing knob, filling

her mouth, bathing her tongue as she wanked his rock-hard shaft. To her surprise, her first-ever taste of male come aroused her, sending electrifying quivers of sex deep into her very core. Salty, creamy, she savoured the taste and texture of the male liquid, only swallowing hard when her cheeks had filled and she began to cough and splutter. Running her tongue over his silky glans, she felt her clitoris throb, her vaginal lips swell around the massive cucumber, her stretched pussy-hole ooze with her juices of lust.

'That's it, lap it all up – slave!' Barry ordered as his flow stemmed. 'Swallow my spunk – tart! I'll fuck your mouth every day now that I know your secret word! And I'll fuck your bum! That's something I think about when I wank. You didn't know that I wank, did you? Well, you do now! I have to, you see. You're so bloody mean when it comes to your cunt, your mouth, that I have to wank almost every day! But now that you're my sex slave, you can pleasure me on demand!'

As the sex fiend pulled away and ordered his puppet to slip the cucumber from her pussy and hide it under the sofa for the next gruelling sex session, Marianne could barely believe the change in him. But this wasn't change, she decided – it was the *real* Barry!

'Get dressed now, and I'll fuck your arse for you later!' he laughed, zipping up his jeans. Confused, Marianne climbed to her feet and retrieved her clothes. Cupping her firm breasts in her red lace bra, she decided to pretend that the trigger word didn't work anymore. And to announce the end of her relationship with the man she'd thought she'd known so well. Holding back her tears as she finished dressing, she followed her boyfriend's orders and sat in the armchair as he retook his position on the sofa.

Wondering how he'd bring her out of her *hypnotic state*, she breathed a sigh of relief as he clicked his fingers and ordered her to wake up. *Naive bastard!* she thought as she looked around the room, trying not to catch his eyes. *Bloody bastard!*

'Coffee, love?' he asked softly, rising to his feet.

'Er... yes, OK,' she half smiled, her tears streaming down her flushed cheeks as he left the room. His salty sperm lingering on her tongue, she had to admit that she'd enjoyed him coming in her mouth. Oral sex was nice, it brought a certain closeness, she mused. But his words, his cold, loveless words had destroyed something. The way he'd used her, her young body to satisfy his debased craving for perverted sex had taken away the love she'd thought they'd shared.

As he brought the coffee in and placed her cup on the table, Marianne began to think that she'd been too harsh. *He is a man, after all,* she thought, smiling up at him. *What normal man wouldn't take advantage of such a situation?* But his cruel words of depraved lust still pained her. Did he want her for the woman she was – or only her body?

'So, what have you been up to all week?' she asked, picturing him lying in their bed masturbating while she'd been away.

'Working at the office every day,' he replied, sipping his coffee. 'And I've spent most evenings with John, working on his bloody thesis. It's still nowhere near finished!'

'How's he getting on at the uni?'

'Not bad at all – fitting in quite well, considering that he's a total nutter! He says it's hard going, but he's enjoying it. Better than working for a living, he reckons! And as for the girls there! Well, you know what John's like when it comes to... the less said about that the better, I think!'

'God, he's not coming round this evening, is he?' Marianne asked agitatedly as the doorbell rang, wondering what the young man would think if he discovered the hot, girl-wet cucumber beneath the couch – the evidence of Barry's debased inner self.

'He did say that he'd call round, yes. But he won't stay for long, so don't worry.'

Jumping up, Barry left the room to answer the door – and Marianne to ponder on her wicked game. She was in two minds now. Wondering whether Barry really would slip his penis deep into her bottom-hole, her stomach somersaulted at the thought of being penetrated, fucked there. *I'd be completely innocent,* she concluded, wondering what other debased fantasies he'd live out whilst she was supposedly hypnotized.

'Go into the lounge and I'll bring you a coffee,' Barry said, opening the door.

'Ah, Marianne!' John greeted her. 'How for art thou?'

'I'm fine, John! More to the point, how are you?' Marianne laughed as he sat on the sofa, the girl-wet phallic fruit only inches from his feet.

'Bearing up under the strain of being surrounded by dozens of nubile young women! How was the hypno' course?' he asked as he ran his fingers through his blond hair and perched expectantly on the edge of the sofa.

'It didn't work,' she sighed despondently. 'I failed miserably!'

'Oh, that's a shame. I thought you'd be giving us a demo or something.'

'A demo?' she echoed anxiously.

'Yes – you know, getting Barry to prance around the room like a prize prat!'

'No chance, I'm afraid! Still, at least I tried.'

'Better to have tried and failed, as they say – whoever *they* are!'

'There you go, John,' Barry grinned as he closed the door with his foot and passed his friend a cup of coffee.

'Ah, thanks!'

Feeling a wetness between her legs, Marianne made her excuses and left the room to cleanse her drenched pussy. Her thoughts still swaying between Barry's alien words, his uncharacteristic behaviour, and her incredible sexual arousal, she decided not to come to any conclusions until she'd enjoyed another session of wanton sex with him – and discovered what else lay hidden in the murky depths of his subconscious. *Shame to spoil the game now,* she mused as she closed and locked the bathroom door, again wondering whether Barry wanted her for the woman she was – or craved only her young pussy.

'It's a shame Marianne wasted all that money on the course!' John remarked as Barry sat beside him.

'It wasn't wasted.' Barry's lips furled into a grin. 'She can't hypnotize people, but the course instructor has planted a trigger word in her subconscious – and I know the word!' he chuckled.

'A trigger word? What do you mean?' John asked, his eyes frowning.

'A word that sends her into a hypnotic state. When I say the word, she'll do anything I ask – and remember nothing about it afterwards.'

'That's crap! You're having me on!'

'No, I'm not! I'll prove it to you when she comes back.'

'Trigger word, my foot!' John mocked.

'Shush! Here she comes!'

Sitting opposite the men, Marianne sipped her coffee and asked John about his thesis. He grinned, turning to look at Barry as he waited for him to utter the magical word and send the pretty girl off into some strange robotic state. 'Juxtaposition!' Barry articulated loudly and clearly.

Marianne's heart leaped, her hands trembling as she realized she was required to perform before John. *Perform what?* she wondered uneasily. Still holding her coffee cup, she awaited Barry's instructions, praying that he'd not ask her to masturbate. *If the bastard does, I'll have to expose myself as a fraud!*

'Stand up!' Barry ordered. Placing her cup on the table, Marianne stood before her audience, her heart banging hard against her chest as she wondered what she'd have to do to prove to John that she really was hypnotized. 'Do a little dance!' Barry laughed gleefully.

Leaping around the room, Marianne was relieved that a dance was all that was required of her. 'That proves nothing!' John jeered. 'You're both having me on! What do you think I am, brain-damaged?'

'All right!' Barry replied. 'Marianne, stand in front of us and lift your skirt up over your stomach!'

Frozen to the spot, the girl wondered whether to fake an illness or something, anything to halt the humiliation. 'Go on, *do it!*' Barry ordered impatiently as John scoffed at the very idea of trigger words and hypnosis. Thankful that she'd washed her pussy and changed her panties, she stood before her spectators and lifted her skirt, revealing the tight pink material following the contour of her swollen vaginal lips, the neat dividing groove between her warm hillocks of girl-flesh.

'There, proof enough?' Barry asked triumphantly.

'That proves nothing!' John returned, much to Marianne's horror. 'We've all seen a pair of pussy-bulged knickers before! That proves nothing, other than that Marianne's a gorgeous bird!'

'Bloody hell!' Barry groaned irritably. 'What do you want, blood? Er . . . Marianne, keep your skirt up, and pull the front of your panties down.'

There was to be one ultimately humiliating test after

another, it seemed! Her hands now visibly shaking, Marianne knew that the time had come to end her game of deception. As she made her decision and lowered her skirt, Barry repeated his instruction with a hint of exasperation in his voice. 'Pull your bloody skirt up and your knickers down – and show John your pubes!'

The devil emerging? Or had Barry changed? Marianne wondered as she tentatively lifted her short skirt again. He'd always been so possessive, so jealous – but here he was, asking her to display her feminine intimacy to another man! Wondering just how far he'd go, she decided to play along, if only to discover the full depravity of the monster she now thought her boyfriend to be.

Her thumb between the tight elastic of her panties and her smooth stomach, she held her breath, wondering how she'd feel by exposing her blonde pubes, her pink crack, to her voyeurs. Barry was a bastard, but she'd get him! Somehow, the tables would turn and the day would soon come when the whole thing would backfire on him, she promised herself.

Pulling her panties down, her eyes blank, her face expressionless, she felt her womb flutter as John gasped. 'God, she must really be under!' he finally acknowledged as she pulled the flimsy material down a little further to reveal her inner lips protruding from her pussy-slit.

'What did I tell you?' Barry quipped smugly.

'Fuck me! Will she do anything? I mean, absolutely anything?'

'You should have seen what I got her to do earlier! Christ, you should have seen her! I'll tell you what . . . No, it's not fair to use her like this,' Barry smiled, sending a wave of relief rolling through Marianne's racked mind. 'Pull your knickers up and lower your skirt and then go and sit down, love,' he said softly.

Which is the real Barry? she wondered as he clicked his fingers. Picking up her coffee cup, she smiled sweetly as if nothing had happened. She'd passed the ultimate test! she thought happily, praying that, in the future, Barry would only use the word when they were alone together. The game was going well. Not only had she convinced John, but Barry was now completely under her spell.

But, ultimate test or not, she realized that Barry wouldn't stop there. His conscience had obviously won the day, and he'd not asked her to masturbate in front of John – but would it always win? Would his darker side demand that he humiliate her again and again? If that happened, then all she had to do was pretend that the trigger word no longer worked, that it had worn off.

Sipping her coffee, Marianne became aware of her vaginal juices seeping into her panties. To her horror, she realized that displaying her young pussy to another man had sexually excited her. Her vagina aching, her clitoris stiffening, to her surprise she began to wish that Barry *would* order her to masturbate with the cucumber while John watched.

'You all right, love?' Barry asked, noticing her face flush.

'Yes, fine!' she smiled as her womb fluttered. 'I'm just a little hot, that's all. I'm going to ring Jill again. There's something I forgot to tell her.'

'OK, see you in a minute.'

Phoning her friend for real this time and with the lounge door closed, Marianne slipped her hand between her thighs and gasped. 'God, I'm wet!'

'Sorry?' Jill asked.

'Oh, hi, Jill – it's me, Marianne.'

'Hi! Who's wet?'

'I was talking to Barry about the . . . about the kitchen floor. Anyway, how are you?'

'I'm okay. How was the course?'

'It was fun! I failed, but it was fun! Listen, the course lecturer has given me a trigger word which . . .'

Her words tailed off as she realized that if anyone twigged that she was playing games, especially the indiscreet young Jill, Barry would eventually find out. Not wanting to ruin her fun, she decided to say nothing about the word. Too late!

'A trigger word?' Jill asked.

'Er . . . yes, he . . .'

'That's where someone becomes hypnotized when they hear a certain word, isn't it?'

'Yes, that's right.'

'So, the lecturer has implanted a word in your subconscious, then?'

'Yes, no . . . Look, I don't want Barry to know about it, Jill. If he knew the word, there's no saying what he'd get me to do!' *Why am I saying all this?*

'What's the word? I promise I won't tell him!'

'I'd rather not . . . Oh, I might as well tell you – it's "juxtaposition".'

'Does it work?'

She'd have to concoct lies now – lies to cover lies.

'Yes, the people on the course all had trigger words, and we all had a good laugh making each other do this and that! But I don't want anyone to know that the word still works. The man running the course became ill and went home before he could erase the word from my subconscious.'

'I'll pop in tomorrow and you can tell me all about it!'

'Okay, great! But remember, tell no one about the word.'

'Don't worry, I won't. Oh, someone's at the door – I'll see you tomorrow. Bye!'

Returning to the lounge, Marianne sat down and smiled at Barry, wondering why she'd lied to Jill. *If I carry on like this, I'll convince myself!* she reflected as the phone rang.

'I'll get it,' Barry said, jumping up from the sofa and dashing into the hall. Marianne looked at John, her full red lips half smiling. She knew only too well what he was thinking, what he was picturing! But, she reminded herself, she was completely innocent.

'Sod it!' Barry cursed as he opened the door. 'That bloody job I've been working on, it's gone wrong!'

'Which job?' Marianne asked.

'That advertising job I was doing for Brooke-Smith. The editing boys have fucked up the video tape! I won't get the next contract unless Brooke-Smith is kept happy. I'll have to go down to the studio and see if I can salvage something. If I can't, Saunders will fire me!'

'It's not your fault, Barry!' Marianne complained.

'As far as Saunders is concerned, *every*thing's my bloody fault! I'll be a couple of hours, if not more, I'm afraid. Sorry to dash off, John. I'll ring you.'

'Okay, I'll just finish my coffee and then I really must be going – I've got my bloody thesis to finish! Fucking bore that it is!'

The atmosphere was tense as Barry left the house and closed the front door behind him. Marianne knew what John was thinking, she knew that the picture of her young pussy was indelibly etched in his mind, and she prayed that he'd hurry up and leave so that she could relax and contemplate the evening's events in peace.

'Barry works too hard!' John quipped, rolling his coffee cup between his palms as he moved forward, perching himself on the edge of the sofa.

'Yes, he does. This is always happening! They think that they can ring him at any time of day or night and he'll go dashing to their rescue!'

'Perhaps he should say no once in a while.'

'That's what I've told him, but he won't listen. Anyway, John, I'm tired after travelling back from the course so, if you don't mind . . . ?'

There was a pause. Marianne sensed an awkward silence as John shifted on the sofa. What was he thinking? she wondered. But worse, what was he planning? He knew the word. Surely, he wouldn't . . .

'Juxtaposition,' he breathed softly as he looked down at the floor. Her heart missing several beats, Marianne stifled a gasp as the word reverberated through her aching mind. *Juxtaposition*. This was ridiculous! she thought, keeping perfectly still as she wondered what the hell to do. Surely, John wouldn't . . .

'Marianne, you sexy little thing – I want you to stand up.'

Desperately trying to think of a way out of the incredible situation, she stood up and turned to face him, her eyes staring blankly at the wall. Unless she played the game, John would tell Barry – and she'd be exposed! She wanted to continue the game with Barry but, she decided, there was no way she'd follow John's instructions!

'Take your skirt off, Marianne!' he ordered firmly. *No, no!* her subconscious screamed. Her stomach churning, alarm bells ringing, she realized that her arousal was rising fast. But she couldn't bring herself to strip before John! Or worse, masturbate as he watched! 'Come on, take your skirt off!' he repeated indignantly.

The protesting voice in her subconscious fading, losing the battle, her clitoris swelling, urgent in its demand for attention, she knew that she was quickly falling prey to her darker side. Tugging her short skirt down, she decided to put a halt to the proceedings should things go too far – to take her deception a little way down the dangerous road, and then turn back.

Kicking her skirt aside, she stood before her *master*, her bulging panties wet, stained – blatantly on display. Her mind reeling, she was all too aware of her demanding clitoris now, her sex-juices seeping between her engorged inner lips.

'Panties!' John said firmly. 'Come on, take your panties off! I'm enjoying this! I want to see your wet snatch!'

Her heart fluttering, her hands trembling, she knew that *this* was the ultimate test! Was it worth it? she wondered. To fool Barry and continue with her games, to discover his secret fantasies, his inner desires – was it worth revealing her feminine intimacy to John?

John was in his late teens, at least four years younger than Marianne, which gave her a sense of control. He was good-looking, well-spoken, and he'd been friends with Barry for several years. They were like brothers, she reflected – surely he wouldn't use Barry's girlfriend like this and risk destroying the friendship? She knew only too well that, if she were to comply with his request, he'd come back for more and more. Who was *really* in control?

'I knew you were conning me!' John scoffed. 'You might be able to fool Barry, but you can't fool me! I don't know why you're playing this game with Barry, I don't know what you're up to – but I'll tell him that you've taken him in, tricked him. Trigger word, my arse!'

Pulling her panties down to her knees, Marianne sensed John's eyes on her swelling pussy lips. His amorous gaze was burning into her very femininity, piercing the sexual centre of her very being. But this was all part of the big con, all part of the game that had started as a joke and had quickly got out of hand. Marianne's thinking was blurred, her mind confused as she tried to think what was driving her to display her young pussy to another man – what goading monster lurked within her mind.

'Your knickers are stained with your cunt juice!' John observed crudely. 'Fuck me, you really are under hypnosis!' Her face flushing, her womb fluttering, Marianne's thoughts swayed between her dangerous game and the compelling need between her inflamed vaginal lips. What the hell would John ask of her next? she wondered. *Christ, if Barry were to walk in!* But, she consoled herself again, she was the innocent party, blameless, guiltless – impeccable in her innocence.

'Take your knickers right off, and then undo your blouse,' John ordered as Marianne's conscience eased a little. Complying, her stomach somersaulting, she kicked her panties aside and unbuttoned her blouse, revealing her full, straining bra. 'Okay, blouse off, and then your bra,' he said, picking her panties up and examining the stained crotch. 'There's nothing I like more than a bloody good pair of tits!'

Marianne watched as he held her warm panties to his face and breathed in her girl-fragrance. But, strangely, she felt no embarrassment now – only a dangerous inner desire for sexual satisfaction. As she freed her firm breasts, her nipples grew, hardening as her arousal continued to soar to frightening heights. Her areolae darkening, she stood completely naked before her new master, wondering what obscenity he'd demand of her.

'Come closer to me and open your cunt lips,' he demanded crudely. Were all men like this? she wondered as she took two steps forward and peeled her fleshy girlhood open, revealing her intimate inner sex-folds to his sparkling eyes. Perhaps Barry and John were no different from any other men? If that were the case, she mused wickedly, by playing her hypnosis game she could have any man she wanted eating out of her pussy! If word got round, she'd be inundated by men offering her this and that and . . . But no. The game had been devised to fool Barry, and now John, it seemed. Two men were more than enough!

'Finger your wet cunt!' John ordered as he moved nearer to the edge of the sofa, his eyes wide, his penis straining within the confines of his tight jeans. Marianne slipped her middle finger into her hot vaginal sheath as John watched with bated breath. Her stomach somersaulting again, she thought of the cucumber, wondering whether to *accidentally* kick it across the carpet and expose the phallus to her master. *Christ, what the hell am I doing?* she wondered as the cold reality of her wanton behaviour hit home.

'You've a nice body,' John breathed. 'I like your tits, and your cunt's beautiful! Would you like me to finger your cunt for you?' Things were going too far, she decided. Getting out of hand! 'Slip your finger out, and *I'll* finger-fuck your tight cunt for you.'

Standing with her feet slightly apart and her hands hanging limply by her sides, she closed her eyes as John's finger circled the entrance to her young vagina. As his finger gently slid into her hot duct, her womb convulsed, her mind swirling with sex, lewd sex. She'd taken her game so far now that there was no turning back. With another man's finger invading her once-sacrosanct vagina, there was no back-tracking.

'You're very hot and wet!' John remarked, chuckling like an excited schoolboy as he massaged her inner flesh. 'Just think, I can call round when Barry's at work and do what I like with your beautiful body! God, I can have a beautiful naked girl follow my every command whenever I want – with no strings!'

The notion excited Marianne and, again, she told herself that none of this was her doing. If ever she was caught committing her wanton act of infidelity, she'd be completely blameless. She smiled inwardly as the amazing thought struck her. *If anything, Barry's to blame!*

Slipping his finger from her tightening vaginal cavern, John ordered his sex slave to get on all fours. 'On your hands and knees like a dog!' he laughed as she submissively took her position. 'That's it, knees wide apart so that I can see your pretty cunt lips hanging below your arse-crack!'

Never had Marianne so crudely and blatantly exposed the centre of her femininity to Barry, let alone another man! Her mind reeling with images of her distended vaginal lips, her exposed bottom-hole, her clitoris throbbed. Jutting her bottom out in her new-found devilry as uncharacteristic thoughts besmirched her mind, she half hoped that Barry would return and discover her debauchery. *That would teach the bastard a lesson for exposing my pussy to John!* she gloated. *If anyone's to blame, it's Barry!*

'I really don't know how far to go, Marianne,' John debated as he gazed at her invitingly swollen pussy lips, her yawning dividing groove. 'I'd like to shove my cock right up your hot cunt and fuck you but . . . I don't know, it doesn't seem right.'

Please, fuck me! she found herself thinking in her sexual delirium as her juices seeped from her pussy and trickled down her inner thighs. Never had she felt so sexually alive! Never had she dreamed that she'd crave lewd sex like this!

Moving behind her, John slipped three fingers into her drenched pussy-hole and explored her inner femininity. His penis straining for relief, for her gripping young cunt, he knew that he could hold back no longer. 'Oh well,' he sighed lustfully as he slipped his wet fingers from the girl's hot duct. 'Barry will be ages, and you'll know nothing about it – so I might as well give you a bloody good fucking!'

Squeezing her eyes shut as she sensed John's purple knob between her hot vaginal lips, Marianne gasped as he rammed the entire length of his broad shaft deep into her quivering body. Grabbing her hips, he thrust into her with the urgency of a young man discovering the joys of sex for the first time. His heavy balls swinging, his belly slapping her buttocks as he took her closer, higher to her illicit sexual heaven, he moaned his debased appreciation for her young body.

'You're a bloody good fuck, you filthy little whore!' he gasped, increasing his rhythm. Never had Marianne heard such coarse words. Barry's sexual mutterings had always been of love, satisfaction and appreciation – until now. But John's obscene words excited her beyond belief, roused something deep within her subconscious – something that had been lurking, sleeping.

'I'm going to spunk up your cunt!' John breathed as he sensed his climax approaching. 'Ah, God, you're fucking good! I'm going to come round every day and give your tight cunt a damned good fucking!' he promised. Marianne quivered, her body shaking uncontrollably as her orgasm neared. John's crude words playing on her mind, she wondered at herself, her wanton infidelity, her uncharacteristically lewd behaviour. Barry had once asked her whether she'd mind him talking dirty to her. She'd shunned the idea, telling him that it sickened her. But now she was revelling in John's expletives, his vulgarity.

'Coming!' John cried as his sperm gushed into her spasming vagina. 'Coming up your tight cunt!' Marianne shuddered as she sensed her master's sperm pumping, filling her young sex-duct to the brim. Her orgasm ripping through her naked body, taking her to terrifying depths of depravity, she prayed that John *would* return every day and use and abuse her.

Her arms collapsing, she rested her head on the carpet, her buttocks projected up and back, the open centre of her naked body now blatantly displayed to her master. Looking back, watching his balls swinging between her legs as her mind-blowing orgasm gripped her, she realized what she'd been missing – the depraved sex, the tremendous pleasure on tap from uninhibited debauchery. Her mind reeling, she imagined men coming to the house in their droves, all using the magical word – and her naked body for the satisfaction of their base sexual desires.

'God, that was good!' John gasped as he withdrew his wet shaft from the girl's inflamed love-hole and sat back on his heels. 'I'd better clean your cunt before you dress, you're dripping with my spunk and your come-juice!' he laughed as he zipped up his jeans.

Marianne gasped as John's tongue ran up her bottom-crease, tasting the sensitive brown flesh encircling the private entrance to her bowels. Never before had she allowed anyone to pay intimate attention to her smaller hole, and she shuddered as the exotic sensations permeated her very being.

What would her sex life with Barry be like after this? she wondered. But now, he'd always use the magic word. Never again would he make love to her as he had in the past – not now that her body was his for the abusing at the drop of a word. Not now that she was a submissive sex slave.

Moving his attention down to her distended, glistening pussy lips, John sucked on her soft girl-flesh. Her body quivering again as his tongue entered her pinken hole, she prayed that he'd engulf her glowing clitoris in his hot mouth and take her to another mind-blowing climax. Lapping the juices from her sex-groove, his tongue sweeping over the sensitive tip of her swelling clitoris, Marianne cried out, whimpering as her second orgasm stirred within her womb, shaking her perspiring body.

Lying on the floor with his head between her knees, John pulled her down, settling her open vulva over his mouth.

Sucking on her clitoris, he brought out her shuddering orgasm, sustaining her incredible mind-blowing pleasure, delighting in the girl's dreamlike state, her complete and utter abandonment. As her climax subsided, she crumpled and rolled onto her back, stretching her trembling body out across the carpet. Gasping, her head tossing from side to side, her long blonde hair matted, concealing the blatant satisfaction plain in her expression, she rested her sated body.

'You'd better get dressed,' John smiled, gazing at the naked girl, the gentle rise of her mons, her inflamed pussy-crack gaping between her ostentatiously spread thighs. 'I'll come round again in the morning and fuck you rotten!'

Dressing, Marianne suddenly sensed a terrifying remorse. Guilt filtering into her mind, she began to realize just what she'd done. Her relationship with Barry would never be the same, not now that she'd been unfaithful to him. Their sex life would be incredible, but only when Barry used the word. Never would they be able to make love together normally. Nothing would ever be the same again – unless she pretended that the word had gone, been erased from her subconscious for good. But even that wouldn't erase the vile act of lust she'd committed with John.

As she flopped into the armchair, John retrieved her from her *hypnosis* and smiled at her. 'Thanks for the coffee. I'd better get going now or I'll never finish my bloody thesis!'

'Yes, all right,' Marianne replied softly, imagining him gloating over the sight of her open body, her bottom-hole, her gaping pussy lips. 'I hope Barry won't be too long.'

'I'll stay until he gets back, if you want.'

'No, no, it's all right. You go and finish your thesis.'

Seeing John out, Marianne closed the front door and breathed a sigh of relief. 'God, what the hell have I done?' she gasped, recalling John's words. *I'll come round again in the morning and fuck you rotten!* 'What the bloody hell have I started?'

Climbing the stairs, her vagina spilling out its cargo of illicit spunk, she slipped out of her clothes and crawled beneath the quilt. Praying that Barry wouldn't return and whisper the treacherous word in her ear, use her aching body for an hour of depraved sex, she closed her eyes. *I'll come round again in the morning and fuck you rotten!* As sleep engulfed her, she relaxed, her curvaceous body calm, her breathing slow. Her satiated vagina empty – for a while, at least!

Chapter Two

Marianne had thought that the cold reality of her promiscuity had hit her the night before, but when she woke and turned her head to see Barry sleeping beside her, she realized the full horror of her debauched behaviour. Her wanton infidelity had changed everything, ruined her future.

They'd planned to marry in the autumn – the honeymoon in Barbados had been booked and paid for. But now Marianne knew that she couldn't go through with the wedding. Her discovery of Barry's sexual depravity was of lesser consequence now that she knew that John, and possibly all men, were the same beneath their chivalrous exteriors. What *did* worry her was her *own* darker side, the *real* Marianne hiding behind what she now realized was a façade.

'All right, love?' Barry yawned as he opened his eyes and turned his head to face her.

'Yes, I'm all right,' she replied softly as he rolled over and put his arm around her waist.

'I didn't get back until three!'

'I know – I heard you come in.'

'At least I was able to salvage most of the video. Sorry you had to go to bed alone.'

'That's okay, it couldn't be helped.'

'I've got a busy day ahead, I'm afraid. I'll probably be

bloody late home tonight. What have you got planned, anything interesting?'

I'll come round again in the morning and fuck you rotten!

Marianne cringed, her blue eyes wide as John's words drifted through her racked mind. Even though she tried to console herself with the thought that it had been Barry's fault, her guilt was rising fast. *God, Jill's coming round!* she remembered. Aware of a warm stickiness between her thighs, and Barry's solid penis pressing against her leg, she threw the quilt back and slipped her bathrobe over her shoulders.

'I've nothing planned,' she replied, praying that Barry wouldn't use the word – use her defenceless body. 'Jill's coming round for coffee this morning, but I've nothing else planned,' she added as she slipped out of the room. She made a dash for the bathroom before Barry's penis demanded that he use the word and slip his solid knob deep into the welcoming warmth of her wet cunt – or her accommodating mouth!

Cleansing her young body in the shower, she gazed down between her pert breasts at her rubicund pussy lips and smiled. 'You'll get me into trouble!' she giggled, massaging perfumed soap between her soft sex-folds. 'My bloody word will get me into trouble!' Rinsing the lather from her gentle curves, her female crevices, she stepped out of the shower and slipped into her gown before returning to the bedroom.

Barry was dressed and ready to leave, to Marianne's relief. 'I didn't realize what time it was!' he groaned, kissing her cheek. 'No time for breakfast, I'm afraid! I'll see you later, love!' he called as he bounded down the stairs.

That's one potential problem out of the way, she thought happily as the front door slammed shut. Slipping her gown off, she gazed at her reflection in the full-length mirror, wondering at the potential of her young body. Again, she imagined several men discovering her secret word and calling at the house to use her for debased sex. *If only I had my own flat!* she found herself thinking, all too aware now of her sexuality. *God, the fun I could have if Barry wasn't around!*

Monogamy – the word had taken on a new meaning for Marianne. Monogamy, once so precious, bringing security – but now it was synonymous with such horrifying words as chains, prisoner – slave. *Barry has power over me,* she mused dolefully. *But no, I have power over him! He thinks that he's using me, but I'm using him!* The sudden realization pleased her. In Barry's eyes, she was the innocent party – but in reality, she was the perpetrator! But she was fearful of herself, the Marianne she hadn't known existed – the unknown Marianne waking within her.

As she ran her fingertips around her stiffening nipples, darkening her areolae, her mind became torn again. Her thoughts lurching between her new-found dangerous games of lust and the real world, she wondered whether to pretend that she was out when John called. Playing the game with Barry was one thing, but with John – and with whoever else might discover the word?

Her fingers wandering over her smooth stomach, she closed her eyes as she located the top of her sex-groove and remembered John's massive penis buried deep within her hot vagina as he shafted her to orgasm. Circling her swelling clitoris, she breathed heavily. 'God, I can't masturbate *now!*' she gasped, grabbing her clothes and quickly dressing before she fell prey to her insatiable clitoris.

Eyeing the clock as she sat at the kitchen table sipping her coffee, Marianne wondered when John, her master, would arrive for his debauched sex session. She also wondered whether he'd told anyone else. *God, he might turn up with half a dozen friends!* To her horror, and her delight, the thought sent a thrill up her spine – a quiver through her womb.

Imagining several young men attending her most intimate needs, she desperately tried to take a grip on herself.

The doorbell rang as if signalling that her time had come, and her heart leaped. 'What shall I do?' she whispered as she stood up and walked through the hall, the word *master* looming in her racked mind. Remorse came again, flooding her mind, gnawing away at her soul. 'I should never have allowed John to . . .' Recognizing Jill through the frosted glass, she opened the door and breathed easily again.

'Thank God it's you!' she smiled, closing the door and leading the attractive nineteen-year-old into the kitchen.

'Why, who else are you expecting?' Jill asked.

'Oh, no one special. Coffee?'

'Thanks. So, you reckon that this trigger word of yours works, do you?'

'I *know* it works!'

'I was thinking about it after you'd phoned last night. You're not pretending, are you?' Jill asked suspiciously.

'Pretending?' Marianne echoed nonchalantly. 'Pretending what?' *I'm innocent!*

'The trigger word. It occurred to me that you could pretend to have had a word implanted in your subconscious so that you could trick Barry.'

'Why on earth would I want to do that?'

'For fun! I was thinking about it, the fun you could have if he thought that you were hypnotized. Don't you see the potential? You could play all sorts of games. He might even turn you into his sex slave! You might discover a host of sordid sexual fantasies that Barry secretly harbours!'

Strange how people unwittingly hit the nail on the head! Marianne reflected, gazing into the girl's dark eyes. *Some people, and in particular Jill, seem to have the uncanny knack of seeing through the wool.*

'The word works, Jill,' Marianne replied firmly. 'There's no pretence, I can assure you! Anyway, I enjoyed the course. I met some interesting people,' she smiled, desperate to change the subject. 'There was this awful woman from Hull who . . .'

'Juxtaposition.'

Stifling a laugh, Marianne feigned her hypnotic state, expecting Jill to order her to hop on one foot and sing a song or something as equally ridiculous. Her eyes staring blankly, her pretty face expressionless, she was beginning to master the fine art of deception.

'So, you reckon that you're in some sort of hypnotic trance, do you?' Jill asked mockingly. 'Let's put you to the test. Show me something, something in the house that you'd rather I didn't know about – a secret. It could be a court summons, a letter from an admirer – anything!'

Thinking quickly, Marianne remembered the vibrator that Barry had bought her. Leaving the room, she climbed the stairs and grabbed the pink cylindrical device from the bedside cupboard, grinning as she wondered at Jill's reaction to her sexy secret. Returning to the kitchen, she placed the plastic phallus on the table, wondering why she'd never experimented with the sex-toy. Her panties moistening at the thought of masturbating, bringing her clitoris to orgasm with the vibrator, she awaited her mistress's instructions.

'A vibrator!' Jill shrieked. 'Now that *is* something I'll bet you don't want me to know about! Oh, and it has batteries fitted!' she giggled, switching the device on and sensually brushing the buzzing tip across her cheek. 'Show me how you use it. Show me how you make yourself come with your vibrator.'

Marianne froze, praying that her friend was joking. But, joking or not, this was another test – and one that she daren't fail. *How many tests will there be? And how many people will put me to the test?*

Jill was infamous for letting secrets out, deliberately putting her foot in it to shock people – to embarrass people. Marianne recalled the time when she'd first met Barry, and Jill had delighted in continually talking about Steve, an older, married man whom Marianne had once become entangled with. Although Barry hadn't been on the scene at the time, his jealousy had quickly surfaced and he'd demanded to know whether she'd finished with Steve or not – even accusing her of lying when she swore that it had been over for some time. Unless Marianne passed the test, Jill would revel in enlightening Barry, delight in telling him of Marianne's hoax. If she was exposed, then John would know that . . .

She *had* to go through with the test, or at least be seen to go through the motions. The minute Jill realized that she was going to slip her panties down and use the vibrator, Marianne consoled herself, her mistress would stop her. *This will be three people I've convinced,* she mused as she lifted her skirt up over her stomach, wondering exactly when Jill would halt her.

'You might as well take your skirt off,' Jill said softly, to Marianne's dread. Her voice was low, husky – sensual. 'We don't want it getting in the way of your masturbating, do we?'

Was she bluffing? Marianne wondered as she unzipped her skirt and wriggled the garment down her long legs. There had always been rumours concerning Jill, her sexual identity. Until now, Marianne had laughed off the accusations, the jokes about Jill being a lesbian. She'd never had a boyfriend and she lived alone in her small flat, but that didn't make her a lesbian, did it?

'And now your panties!' Jill giggled as Marianne stepped

out of her skirt. The magical word was certainly revealing the darker side of those around her! Having discovered one or two of Barry's secret fantasies, and John's blatant lack of morals and respect, she was now learning something about Jill!

'Come on, take them off, Marianne!' Jill coaxed. 'I've always fancied you, your beautiful body!'

Always fancied my body? Her mind aching, her hands trembling, Marianne was shocked. *Always fancied my body?* Was there to be no end to the shocking revelations? she wondered as she gazed at Jill through her eyelashes. The time had come to put an end to the dangerous games!

There had been a time when Barry had taken rather too much interest in Jill. Marianne recalled questioning him, accusing him of cheating on her, lying to her. Little had she known that Jill's roaming eyes had homed in on *her*! Barry had laughed off Marianne's accusations, condemning Jill as a rampant lesbian who'd never take any interest in men. *God, how right he was!*

'I don't think you're hypnotized!' Jill said accusingly as she sat before the girl and gazed at the swell of her red panties. 'If you were, you wouldn't hesitate – you'd follow my orders and slip your knickers off. I don't know much about hypnosis, but I *do* know that you're faking it!'

Swallowing hard, Marianne peeled her tight panties away from her soft mound, determined now to take her deception further – to fool all those who discovered the mystical word. She had nothing to lose, she convinced herself as she slipped her panties down her shapely thighs, revealing her sparse blonde pubes, her pink pussy-slit, to her young lesbian friend.

No one would know what she'd done. As far as Jill was concerned, even Marianne, in her hypnotic state, would know nothing. *Only Jill will know about this,* she thought as she slipped her panties over her ankles and kicked them aside. *Hopefully, only Jill will sense the stab of guilt.*

'Let's go into the lounge,' Jill suggested, clutching the vibrator as she led her slave through the hall. 'You'll be far more comfortable on the sofa.' Marianne followed the other girl, her heart thumping hard against her chest, her hands trembling, her womb fluttering as she imagined lying on the sofa with her sexuality bared to another woman, the vibrator taking her to orgasm.

Although she'd never used the sex-toy, the thought of doing so *had* crossed her mind once or twice. She recalled the morning when Barry had sucked her clitoris into his mouth and fingered her inner vaginal flesh, and the phone had rung – destroying her climax, their planned lovemaking. He'd rushed off to the office leaving her on a sexual high, desperate for orgasm. But she'd not found the courage to use the vibrator to bring her the much-needed relief she craved.

'Lie on the sofa with your legs open wide,' Jill instructed, breaking Marianne's reverie. Marianne sat down, reclining and parting her thighs as the girl settled between her feet and gazed appreciatively at Marianne's gaping vulva.

All thoughts of Barry and John faded as she sensed Jill's fingers probing between her swelling pussy lips. All thoughts of the real world, of right and wrong, drifted into obscurity as, for the first time in her life, a female finger penetrated her young sex-sheath, absorbing the inner heat of her spasming vagina.

Her head back, her legs spread wide, Marianne opened the feminine centre of her young body, offering herself completely to Jill. Her racked mind seemed to settle now, to calm and accept the incredible situation – this lesbian coupling. As Jill's finger massaged Marianne's fleshy sex-duct, inducing torrents of creamy fluid to secrete from her inner nectaries, Marianne closed her eyes, surrendering to complete and utter submission.

'I've dreamed of doing this to you,' Jill confessed softly as she slipped a second finger into Marianne's quivering body, stretching her glistening vaginal flesh open. 'Many times I've thought about you, imagined your pussy, with me fingering your beautiful pussy-hole. But I'd never dreamed that I'd be able to send you into a hypnotic trance at the drop of a word and have your beautiful body all to myself like this!'

Marianne had never dreamed that she'd be deceiving people like this, let alone offering her young vagina to another girl! As the sensations of lesbian sex welled, she opened her mouth, her full red lips dry as she gasped and her womb contracted. Her mind ran amok again, confusing her, torturing her. *This is so right! No, this is wrong! Not a lesbian! No, no – yes!*

As she heard the vibrator softly buzz, her heart leaped and she opened her eyes a little, spying on the fresh young girl wielding the beautiful humming phallus, moving the pink tip ever closer to Marianne's yawning sex-groove – her stiffening clitoris.

Whatever John had had in mind for today, whatever sexual delights he'd planned for Marianne, she'd never thought that she'd be lying with her pussy bared, open and swollen with sex, blatantly on offer to Jill! Her act was forbidden and yet, strangely, so right. She was finding an uncanny comfort with another girl, a bizarre acceptance of the young lesbian now exploring between her thighs. She was discovering a frightening sexual deviance in the murky depths of her own subconscious.

Her body jolted as the tip of the vibrator brushed gently against her blossoming clitoris. The electrifying sensations transmitting deep into her spasming cunt, reverberating through her womb, she gasped, whimpering as every muscle tensed and every nerve ending tingled with sexual pleasure.

'You're going to enjoy this,' Jill assured her softly, her fingers still locked within Marianne's tightening vagina as she deftly circled the girl's clitoris with the buzzing phallus. 'You're going to be a good girl and come for me!'

Marianne's senses momentarily returned and she gazed around the lounge through her eyelashes. The TV she'd enjoyed watching with Barry, his book and empty coffee cup on the table, the newspaper he'd left in the armchair, his paperwork spilled on the floor... This had been *their* lounge, *their* domain – but now it was a sex den that belonged to Marianne, to John, and to Jill. No longer would she be able to make love with Barry by the fire or on the sofa without images of John looming, thoughts of Jill's probing fingers excavating her love-hole.

Her pussy, her body, her very being, had belonged to Barry – it had been his to enjoy, and his only. *Times change!* she mused as her clitoris throbbed and the beginnings of her orgasm welled, causing her to arch her back and quiver in her ecstasy.

'There's a good girl!' Jill praised, all too aware of her slave's impending orgasm. 'Just relax and let it come.' Marianne did relax, and her climax did come. Wave after crashing wave of orgasmic pleasure erupted from her vibrating clitoris and ripped though her nervous system. Crying out as she dug her fingernails into the sofa and parted her thighs as far as she was able, she shook violently, her mind awash with sex, her body afire with lesbian lust as she imagined herself taking Jill in turn to such an incredible orgasm.

Now, even the familiar lounge, the furniture, the memories, faded into oblivion. It didn't matter who was working intimately between her legs, male or female, it was of no consequence. Her concentration, her thoughts, her entire being centred on her burning cunt, her exploding clitoris.

'Keep coming, my angel – keep coming!' Jill's words drifted, floating somewhere above Marianne's consumed body. 'Keep coming, and then *you* can make *me* come!'

At last, the vibrator moved away from Marianne's aching clitoris, allowing her orgasm to subside, her mind to return to her quaking body. As she lay exhausted on the sofa, her juices decanting from her fiery cunt-hole as Jill slipped her wet fingers from her open body, Marianne gasped in her incredible pleasure.

She was enjoying her first lesbian affair, and she was delighted to think that there were more firsts to come, more new sexual experiences to encounter. Suddenly, Jill's darting tongue lapped, probing between Marianne's rubicund sex-lips, cleansing her there. The thought that this was a female tongue heightened the girl's arousal, lifting her high on another swirling cloud of orgasm. Her clitoris receiving attention now, she whimpered, stifling her orgasmic screams as her perspiring body shuddered uncontrollably and her thighs gripped her partner in lesbian lust. On and on her climax rolled as Jill mouthed and sucked on her erupting clitoris, the incredible sensations ripping through her mind, shaking her perspiring body.

Again, Marianne was released from the velvet grip of her come, leaving her panting for life-giving breath, desperate for her body to calm. As Jill finished her licking, cleansing Marianne's inner sex-folds with her wet tongue, lapping up the product of her orgasm, Marianne became aware of an urgent inner desire – a desire to reciprocate. Imagining lapping between the teenage girl's young pussy lips, fingering her young cunt, Marianne gave a final shudder of pleasure.

'You did well!' Jill praised as she licked her full red lips, savouring Marianne's slippery cuntal cream as she sat back on her heels, admiring her slave's open sex-groove. 'When you've recovered, I'll take your place and you can attend my pussy with the vibrator – and your lovely wet tongue!'

As Marianne's senses returned, she realized that she was about to be put to the most demanding test yet – to lick another girl's clitoris to orgasm! The thought had aroused her, but now? *There's no way out of this one!* she mused, wondering what it would be like to bury her face between Jill's hot, wet sex-folds. What would another girl taste like? What would it be like to have another girl's clitoris throbbing in orgasm in her mouth?

When the doorbell rang, Marianne breathed easily again, praying that Jill would order her to dress and answer the door before she was forced to commit the forbidden act, the lesbian licking.

'Who the hell's that?' Jill groaned despondently as the caller persisted. 'Quick! Get your skirt and panties on!' she instructed, dashing into the kitchen. Following her mistress and hurriedly dressing, Marianne sat at the table, the bell still resounding around the house as Jill sat opposite and told her to wake up.

'I wonder who that could be?' Marianne smiled sweetly, innocently, as she rose to her feet, sure that it was John. 'Oh, didn't I make you a cup of coffee?'

'No, you . . . you were just about to. See to the door, and I'll fill the kettle,' Jill smiled nervously, guiltily.

'Okay, I won't be a minute,' Marianne replied as she left the room, her sex-duct oozing with her vaginal come, her mind tortured with guilt.

Opening the door, Marianne was stunned to find Barry standing on the step. 'I forgot my bloody briefcase!' he complained, holding his head. He looked older in his anguish, drained of life – unlike the youthful Jill. 'My door key, papers, bloody everything's in my briefcase!'

'Oh, no! You've got a head like a sieve!' Marianne laughed nervously, imagining him arriving to find Jill vibrating her clitoris to orgasm – or John screwing her from behind! 'I'm just having a coffee with Jill, do you want one?'

'Yes, I might as well, now that I'm here. God, Saunders is going to string me up by my balls for this! Oh, by the way, Brooke-Smith is coming to dinner this evening.'

'What? Why the hell didn't you tell me?'

'Because I've only just found out myself! Saunders rang me on my mobile, wanting to know where the hell I'd got to, among other things. Anyway, he suggested that, to keep my client sweet, I invite him to dinner.'

'Couldn't Saunders have invited him to dinner?'

'No, I've been dealing with Brooke-Smith for the last year. He's *my* client so it's all down to me, I'm afraid.'

'Oh, that's great! I've nothing in, Barry!'

'Then go shopping! You've got all bloody day! Christ knows, you do sod-all every day!'

'I don't have work at the moment, do I? Anyway, calm down and come into the kitchen and I'll make the coffee.'

Frowning at Jill, Barry sat at the table and sighed. 'God, life stinks at times!' he complained.

'Life's wonderful!' Jill beamed, the taste of Marianne's love-juices lingering on her tongue, her thoughts on the next session of lesbian lust with her pretty slave.

'Is it?' Barry returned, rubbing his forehead.

'What you need is a housekeeper – someone to do the shopping, the household chores. It would leave you both free to get on with more important things – don't you agree, Marianne?' Jill goaded. 'You need a slave, someone who will do this and that, someone who will follow orders and . . .'

'Oh, what a bloody good idea!' Marianne interrupted. 'Who do you suggest we employ as a slave?'

'I don't know. Perhaps you have an idea, Barry?'

'Oh yes, I know plenty of slaves! The slave trade is booming at the moment! What the hell are you talking about, Jill? A slave? This is nineteen-ninety—'

'I was only joking, Barry! Anyway, I'll leave you two love birds to have a row. I'll ring you, Marianne. It was nice . . . Er . . . I'll come again! I'll see myself out.'

Barry groaned despondently as Jill left the room and closed the front door behind her. 'Bloody stupid lesbian! A slave, for Christ's sake!'

Lesbian! God, what have I done? 'She was only joking, Barry!' Marianne returned as she placed his coffee cup on the table, aware of her vaginal lips swelling, her clitoris calling for attention again.

'Yes, I know but . . . Juxtaposition.'

Marianne stood still, praying that Barry wouldn't demand sex as she felt her panties moistening, absorbing her slippery love juices. Staring blankly across the room, she anxiously awaited her master's instructions.

'I want a good spread this evening!' Barry ordered the girl. 'You'll wear that tight black dress you bought – you know, the one that you said was far too short. Red stilettos, hold-up stockings, no bra . . . I want to impress Brooke-Smith, not only with you coming up with a bloody good meal, but . . . You'll flirt with him, do you understand? You'll give the dirty old bugger the come-on. I'll leave the room for a while, and you'll flash your tight knickers, pull them aside and show him a bit of cunt lip. I need this contract, Marianne! You're my slave, you're my key – and you'll help me get it if you have to open your legs and fuck the old fart! This hypnosis thing is going to work well for me, I can see that. What with you being under my control, it's going to bring me all I ever wanted – contracts, money . . . Right, I must hurry! Now, wake up!'

Her hands trembling, Marianne gazed out of the kitchen window, wondering what sort of man Barry really was. *Flash your knickers. Show him a bit of cunt lip. Fuck the old fart.* Was this contract worth more than her? Would he really use her body as some sort of commodity to get his bloody contract?

'You all right, love?' Barry asked, his voice now gentle, soft, loving.

Bastard!

'Don't worry too much about tonight, I'm sure you'll play the part of a hostess extremely well!'

Play your bloody slave extremely well! 'Are you, Barry? What makes you so sure? What if I fuck up?'

'Of course you won't! All you have to do is prepare a nice meal and smile at the old bugger. Everything will be fine, you'll see. Shit, there goes my bloody mobile! If it's Saunders, I'll . . .'

As Barry answered his phone and did his yes sir, no sir act, Marianne pondered on his hurtful words. *Open your legs and fuck the old fart.* Her mind aching, she couldn't believe what he was proposing she do to help him. *I mean nothing to him,* she reflected sadly. *All he's interested in is his contract and making bloody money!* As Barry slipped his phone into his jacket pocket and made for the door, Marianne couldn't face him. Stunned, all she could do was gaze out of the window.

'See you this evening, love!' he called as he left the room. 'We'll get here around seven!' he added, closing the front door. Where was the love? she wondered. What had happened to the love and affection? Gone!

John didn't turn up, much to Marianne's relief – no, her disappointment. Spending most of the day wondering about Barry and Jill, her mind became awash with confusion. The last thing she could do was go shopping and then prepare a banquet for Barry and his bloody client!

Her thoughts continually swirled around Jill, the pretty teenage lesbian. The intimacy, the previously unknown closeness, had been nice. Somehow, being another female, there had been a gentleness, a lovingness that Marianne had never experienced before. Barry had always been soft and gentle with her, but in a manly way. Jill's intimate attention, her feminine fingers, her feminine tongue, had felt so right. *I'm not a bloody lesbian!* Marianne desperately tried to convince herself. *Christ, this hypnosis thing is fucking me up!*

As the afternoon wore on, Marianne began to realize the implications of her dangerous game. Barry was obviously out to use her for whatever he could get. Jill wanted rampant lesbian sex sessions, and John . . . This was like a bad dream, she reflected, wondering how one evening could change her life, turn everything upside down. Within a few hours of returning home from the course, her life had changed dramatically!

I'll beat the bastard at his own game! she decided as she slipped into her tight black dress – knickerless and braless. Flattening the silky material over her smooth stomach with her palms, she felt a pang of arousal snake its way through her pelvis. *Use me, would you? I'll bloody well teach you a thing or two – you fucking bastard!*

Rolling her hold-up stockings up her long legs and slipping her red stilettos on, she decided that she'd follow Barry's instructions to the letter. *A bit of cunt lip!* she smiled inwardly. *I'll show the old pervert more than a bit of cunt lip!*

Her long golden locks shining, her make-up impeccable,

the dining room table laid, she waited for the Indian takeaway to arrive by taxi. Her plan formulating well, she grinned, imagining Barry leaving her alone with his client for a while. *Flirt with him. Give the dirty old bugger the come-on.* Barry's words swirled in her mind as she imagined bending over, her taut buttocks on display, her pouting vaginal lips swelling invitingly below her bottom-crease.

She was driven by a terrifying thirst for revenge now. Barry's words had hurt her deeply, they'd stirred emotions – scorn, hatred. *I'll teach you a lesson – you fucking bastard!*

Barry's key in the front door lock sent a shiver up Marianne's spine. Her stomach churned, her heart raced. *I can't go through with it!* she decided, wondering what had happened to the old Marianne – the old Barry! Leaping to her feet as Barry entered the room and introduced Brooke-Smith, she smiled amicably, tugging her dress down to conceal her knickerless pussy.

'Pleased to meet you, Mr Brooke-Smith. Would you like a drink?' she offered.

'Please, call me Jonathan,' the middle-aged man grinned, eyeing the long nipples pressing through her tight black dress. 'Scotch and water, please,' he added, perching himself on the arm of the sofa.

'If you'll excuse me for a moment?' Barry said, catching Marianne's eyes. 'I have a phone call to make.'

Marianne sensed Jonathan's amorous gaze on her shapely thighs as she stood with her feet apart and bent over to take the glasses from the cabinet. Suddenly mustering up the courage, her long legs straight, she bent over further, praying that he'd spy her full vaginal lips nestling between her unblemished thighs.

What the hell am I doing? she wondered as her guilt, her shame stabbed her conscience. Displaying the most intimate part of her young body to Barry's client was despicable! Her mind racked with confusion again, her heart racing, her clitoris stirring, revenge loomed. *Barry's a complete bastard!*

'You've a nice place,' Jonathan remarked. Marianne's stomach somersaulted as she took a deep breath and almost touched her toes, exhibiting her full womanly glory to the client's wide eyes. 'Very nice, indeed!'

'Yes, we like it,' she replied, standing up and pouring the whisky. Smiling, she turned and passed him a drink.

'Barry's a very lucky man!' he enthused, eyeing her shapely thighs.

'It's not that nice!' she laughed. 'We'd like a bigger place really, but . . .'

'No, I meant that Barry's a lucky man to have you.'

Her arousal, and her annoyance with Barry, increasing, Marianne decided to play the game to the limit. *Might as well go for it!* she thought wickedly, sitting in the armchair with her legs parted, her naked pussy-crack smiling between her firm thighs.

She didn't like Brooke-Smith – she sensed an air of haughtiness about him which she found belittling. Wearing a pinstriped suit, crisp white shirt and tie, he reminded her of an authoritative boss. But who was in control, who *was* the boss? As he gazed between her naked thighs, she realized the power she had over him. Whatever he was, he was a man, a man who appreciated the female form, she mused as she parted her legs a little further.

'Sorry about that,' Barry apologized as he entered the room. Glancing at Marianne's blatantly exposed naked pussy, his mouth hanging open, he frowned. 'Er . . . how's the meal coming on? Do you . . . do you need a hand?' he asked hesitantly, making odd facial expressions that she took to mean that he wanted to speak to her in the kitchen.

'I'll go and check,' she smiled, rising to her feet, deliberately leaving her dress hoisted up to reveal her beautiful pussy-crack.

Taking the curry from the simmering oven, Marianne concealed a grin as Barry closed the kitchen door and breathed the magical word. She stood still, her expression blank as she awaited his instructions. 'Go and put your panties on!' he ordered her with a hint of anger in his voice. 'When I said *give him the come-on*, I didn't mean . . . Just go and put your bloody panties on, you dozy bitch! Now, wake up.'

Taking the plates from the shelf, Marianne asked Barry how long he thought Brooke-Smith would be staying. 'I don't want him here to the early hours,' she said. 'It's not easy being nice to someone you don't like!'

'He won't stay too long, he's a busy day tomorrow,' Barry replied. 'Here, I'll do that – if you need to go upstairs?' he added, wondering why she hadn't immediately followed his instruction.

Leaving the room, Marianne knew that she'd got one over Barry. Far from her being unable to go through with the plan, it was Barry who couldn't cope with it! Jealousy was his weak point, and she was determined to play on it, she decided as she entered the bedroom, lifting her dress and gazing at her proud vaginal lips reflected in the full-length mirror. 'No, no panties!' she affirmed wickedly. 'This is what he wanted me to do, and this is what I'm *going* to do!'

Returning to the kitchen, Marianne bent over to take the naan bread from the oven, deliberately exposing her taut buttocks, her bloated vaginal lips to Barry's wide eyes. She could feel his seething anger, his rising jealousy, as she wantonly exposed the very centre of her femininity.

'Juxtaposition!' he breathed through gritted teeth. Marianne stood up, her dress high over her rounded buttocks, revealing her dark dividing crease. 'Put your bloody panties on, woman!' Barry spat. 'I'll do the food – you go upstairs and put your bloody panties on!'

As he brought her out of her *hypnotic trance*, Marianne grinned inwardly. She was winning the game, beating Barry at his own game – and she was loving every minute of her sweet revenge! 'Will you deal with the food?' she smiled amicably. 'I'm just going upstairs for a minute.'

Entering the lounge, she smiled at Brooke-Smith. 'I hope you like curry?' she asked as she sat in the armchair.

'Very much!' he replied, holding his empty glass up.

'Here, let me get you another drink. So, what's this contract all about?' she asked, tossing her long golden locks over her shoulder and taking his glass.

'An advertising campaign. We're launching a new product this autumn and . . . Well, to be honest, I really don't think your husband's company is up to the job!'

Husband? Husband-to-be – not to be! 'Oh, why's that?' she asked nonchalantly.

'They've made too many cock-ups in the past, I'm afraid. It's a competitive business – there are plenty of other companies out there only too willing to . . .'

'Oh well, I'm sure Barry's not bothered one way or the other,' Marianne smiled, standing before him and passing him the glass.

'But I thought that he . . .'

'Barry doesn't really care one way or the other!' she laughed wickedly, wondering why she was trying to ruin Barry's chances of getting the contract. Revenge was one thing, but to destroy Barry? 'To be honest, he's had enough of the job!'

'Oh, I see. I hadn't actually decided to go elsewhere, it was just that . . .'

'Don't worry about it, Jonathan! If you give the contract

to Barry, fine – if you don't, it's not a problem!'

'You're quite a woman, aren't you? I thought that you'd be grovelling at my feet, playing the little hostess, doing your best to . . .'

'No, no way! Look, why not decide what you're going to do about the contract? Get it over with now so that we can enjoy the evening.'

'The contract's his! I was only bluffing when I . . .'

'Yes, I know you were!' she grinned, parting her thighs again as she projected her hips forward, her tight dress hugging the contour of her young mound. 'Don't tell Barry just yet – let him sweat for a while!'

'But I thought he wasn't bothered?'

'I was bluffing, too!' she replied, an impish glint in her sparkling eyes. 'I'll go and see how he's getting on.'

Barry's forehead was lined, his face anguished as he turned to see Marianne in the kitchen doorway. 'Everything all right?' she asked.

'No, not really. I don't like the way things are going,' he replied angrily.

'What do you mean?'

'I don't know. This bloody contract is . . .'

'Where is the contract?'

'I left it in the bloody office. I should have brought it home but, in my panic, I forgot.'

'Why don't you go and get it? Surely it would be better to get him to sign it this evening, if he agrees, that is?'

'What about the food?'

'You'll only be half an hour. We don't have to eat yet. Stick it back in the oven – I'll entertain him while you're gone.'

'Entertain him?' Barry echoed suspiciously.

Jealous, Barry? 'Yes, entertain him – look after him. You

go and get the contract, and I'll keep him happy.'

'I don't like this, Marianne!'

It's your own doing! 'Why ever not? What's the problem, Barry? You seem very worried, what's the matter?'

'He's a randy old sod. I don't want to leave you alone with him.'

'Don't you trust me? What do you think I'll do, flash my pussy at him?' *After all, that is what you wanted me to do!*

'I . . . I don't know. Of course I trust you, it's just that . . . Juxtaposition.'

Here we go again! Marianne thought excitedly, amazed by the unfathomable depths of Barry's jealousy. 'You'll not go anywhere near him!' he ordered. 'Don't even show him a bit of leg, and don't let him touch you! And put your bloody knickers on, you disobedient little bitch!' *Whatever happened to the bit of cunt lip?* she wondered sinfully.

'OK,' Barry smiled as he brought Marianne round. 'I'll go and get the contract. I'll be as quick as I can.'

'Right, I'll go and keep Brooke-Smith happy. I'll tell him that you've had to . . .'

'Don't say anything about me, just chat to him. Oh, and try and get him to . . .'

'I'll get him to give you the contract, Barry – don't worry! I know how to handle . . .'

'Handle what? What are you up to?'

'Nothing! I don't know what's bothering you, I really don't! Go and get the contract and I'll deal with Brooke-Smith.'

Concealing a grin as Barry frowned and moved towards the door, Marianne was delighting in the game. His jealousy eating away inside him, she knew that he was regretting ever using the word – regretting ever trying to use *her*!

'Another drink?' Marianne asked Brooke-Smith as she entered the lounge. 'The food will be a little while yet.'

'Thanks,' he smiled, eyeing her thighs again, wondering, no doubt, why she wasn't wearing panties. 'Where's Barry?'

'Organizing things. He's good in the kitchen – shame he's not good in the bedroom!' she laughed, stunning her guest – and herself!

Jonathan shifted uneasily on the sofa, obviously wondering what sort of girl his hostess really was as she reclined in the armchair, blatantly exposing her pinken pussy-crack. Her stomach somersaulted and her heart fluttered as he focused his disbelieving eyes on her young slit.

'Are you married?' Marianne asked.

'Yes,' he replied, his eyes widening as they feasted on her open girlhood.

'We were going to get married, but ... Well, there's no rush. Besides, I'm not sure that I really want to settle down just yet.'

'Oh, I'm sorry, I thought that you were married?'

'No, no.'

'Do you work?' he asked, his gaze still glued to her creamy vaginal crack.

'No, I'm not working at the moment – I was made redundant. I'm hoping to start a business from home.'

'What sort of work did you do?'

'Secretarial work for an export company.'

'I'm looking for a new personal assistant, if you're interested?'

'Really? Well, I suppose ... Where are you based?'

'Just outside town – Greenways Industrial Estate. You'd have a company car, of course.'

'Oh! Er ... I don't know what to say!' Marianne smiled, closing her legs and tugging her dress down to conceal her girl-crack. *I shouldn't have come across as too tarty!*

'Say yes! What have you got to lose?'

Marianne's opinion of Brooke-Smith was rapidly changing. *Perhaps he's not the pompous git I thought he was?* she mused as she rose to pour herself a vodka-and-lime. 'Sounds interesting,' she smiled, imagining roaming around his office – knickerless. 'The thing is . . .'

'Is there a problem?' he interrupted, handing her his empty glass.

If only he knew about the word! 'No, no, it's just that . . . As I said, I was hoping to start something from home.'

'You could do that later – you're only young, you've all the time in the world!'

'Yes, I suppose I have.'

Passing him his drink, Marianne wondered at Barry's reaction to her working for Brooke-Smith. He'd be assured of future contracts, which was all he seemed to be interested in! Perhaps he'd react favourably? He'd probably delight in having her on the inside, gleaning inside information about his competitors.

'What's this new product you're launching?' she asked. 'I really don't know anything about your company – Barry doesn't talk about his clients, you see.'

'I'm in soft drinks. The television advertising campaign is to launch a new orange drink we've developed. We've called it Golden Pip.'

'What's the salary?'

'Negotiable! I'm sure we could come to an amicable agreement – if you know what I mean?'

Marianne *did* know what he meant! *So, it's my body he's after!* she thought excitedly as she relaxed, allowing her thighs to fall apart again. 'I'll give it some thought,' she smiled as she heard the front door closing. 'I'll just see how Barry's getting on. I won't be a minute.'

Frowning as she entered the kitchen, she asked Barry why

he was back so soon. 'The bloody contract was in my car!' he swore. 'I saw it on the passenger seat as I drove round the corner!'

'You're getting worse! Anyway, I've secured the contract for you.'

'What? But how...'

'I'll tell you later. It's about time you joined him, you've hardly spoken to him since he arrived! Get him to sign the contract, and I'll sort the food out.'

'What did you do to make him...'

'I'm a woman, Barry – we women have our ways!'

Marianne sat quietly during the meal. Barry did his boring arse-licking piece, sucking up to his client, which annoyed her but, exasperating though the evening was, she was thankful that Brooke-Smith didn't mention her working for him. That was a subject she wanted to broach when she was alone with Barry.

After the meal, the men retired to the lounge, leaving Marianne to clear away the dishes, and to think about the job offer. *He's obviously attracted by my naked pussy!* she mused as she loaded the dishwasher, praying that Barry would tell him about the word. *God, I'm turning into a tart! What the hell? Money's money! And a car!*

Making the coffee, Marianne's thoughts turned to Jill, the wanton act of lesbian sex she had enjoyed with the young girl. Recalling the vibrator, Jill's hot mouth engulfing her clitoris, her fingers massaging her inner vaginal flesh, her thoughts then lurched to Brooke-Smith. *God, I flashed my pussy at him!* she recalled excitedly, wondering again at the incredible change she'd gone through.

'He's got to go, Marianne,' Barry said as he popped his head round the kitchen door. 'He had a phone call and...'

'Okay, I'll come and see him out.'

The pleasantries over, Barry closed the door, frowning at Marianne as she gave a sigh of relief. 'Thank God that's over!' she gasped.

'How on earth did you get him to agree to . . .'

'I'm not just a pretty face!' she laughed. *A pretty pussy, too!*

'But how did you . . . I mean, he wasn't at all interested in our offer until . . .'

'I talked to him, said that your company was the best to handle his advertising campaign. And, don't forget – I'm an attractive woman!'

'You didn't do anything else, did you?'

'Anything else? What do you mean?'

'Nothing. I'm just a little surprised, that's all.'

'You don't seem to trust me anymore, Barry. What's happened?'

'Nothing.'

'You've been nervy all evening.'

'I'm just tired, that's all. I like the dress, by the way. It's a bit short, but I like it.'

'Oh, guess what! I've been going around without my panties! God knows how I forgot to put them on! I hope he didn't see anything!'

Barry cringed as Marianne lifted the front of her dress, displaying her sparse blonde pubes, her swollen pussy lips and very wet crack. 'Come to think of it,' she smiled innocently. 'I had my panties on before Jill came round, and I don't remember taking them off so . . .'

'How long was the lesbian here?' he asked suspiciously.

'Not long. It's funny, I felt very wet between my legs after she'd gone. Perhaps my being away from you for a week has left me sex-starved!'

'You told Jill about the course, didn't you?'

'Yes. What's that got to do with it?'

'Nothing. I'm going up to bed. Have you told anyone else about the . . . the course?'

'No, only Jill. Oh, and John knows, of course!'

Chapter Three

Barry had left for work by the time Marianne woke up. Her hands running over her young naked body, her gentle curves, her feminine crevices, she didn't want to reach out from beneath the warmth of her quilt and answer the phone, but the caller was annoyingly persistent.

'Hallo,' she sighed dreamily as she brushed her hair from her face and pressed the receiver to her ear.

'Marianne, it's John.'

'Oh, hi, John. Barry's already left, I'm afraid.'

'Yes, he called me just now. He hasn't said anything to you about me, has he?'

'What do you mean, *said* anything?'

'He rang me and asked if I'd been to see you.'

'I'm sorry, John, I've only just woken up – I'm not with you.'

'Barry asked me whether I'd been to see you or not. I just wondered why he'd asked.'

'I've no idea. Are you sure you didn't misunderstand him?'

'Yes, quite sure. I just thought it rather odd.'

'It *is* odd! Perhaps he thinks we're having an affair!' *God, I shouldn't have said that!*

'No, of course he doesn't!'

'You hadn't arranged to come over, had you?'

'No, no, I'd arranged nothing with him. Are you in this morning?'

'Er . . . Yes, I suppose I am – why?'

'I thought I'd come round for coffee, if that's OK?'

For sex, more like! 'All right, John. You'll have to give me time to get up, though – I'm still in bed. Was there something in particular you wanted to see me about?'

'No, I've a free morning so . . . I'll see you soon. Actually, Barry asked me to come and see you.'

'Why?'

'I'll tell you about it later.'

'OK, John, bye.'

Marianne lay back on the pillow, grinning as she imagined Barry ringing John in his jealous desperation and tentatively questioning him, anxiously probing. *Poor Barry!* she mused. *He displays my pussy to John, asks me to flash a bit of cunt lip to his client, and then not only gets cold feet – but regrets the whole thing! But why ask John to call round?*

As she climbed out of her bed and slipped her gown on, Marianne decided not to dress. *Might as well be prepared!* she thought wickedly, allowing her gown to fall open, revealing her pert breasts, her erect nipples. Descending the stairs, wondering whether Jill would call round for coffee, for lesbian sex, she pondered again on the incredible change she'd been through.

From a secure and comfortable relationship with Barry, to opening her thighs and allowing Jill to bring her to orgasm with the vibrator – having John screw her, use and abuse her . . . And all within a couple of days! 'I'm enjoying this!' she giggled in her new-found sexual deviance, her gown flowing behind her as she breezed into the kitchen, her blatant nakedness arousing her.

Sitting at the kitchen table gazing out of the window,

Marianne felt sure that she'd caught a glimpse of someone skulking in the bushes at the end of the garden. Turning her head to one side, she noticed Barry from the corner of her eye. 'What the hell's he doing hiding out there? He's supposed to be at work!' The stark realization suddenly hit her – he was spying on her!

As the doorbell rang, she was in two minds about letting John in. Barry was obviously going to wait until John was screwing her, and then burst in and . . . *And what?* she wondered. *If John uses the word and takes advantage of me, then that's Barry's fault!* But why the hell did he ask John to come round knowing full well what would happen?

The situation was ridiculous! *All this because I pretended to have a secret word and had a laugh with Barry!* she thought. *Now he's set me up! And he's spying on me!* Again, another side to Barry was coming to light, but what was he up to? 'To hell with it!' she cursed, dashing through the hall and opening the front door to John.

The kitchen, she mused. *Might as well give Barry a good view!* 'Come through, John, I'll put the kettle on,' she invited, her gown provocatively revealing her full, rounded breasts.

'I hope you don't mind me calling round like this?' he smiled anxiously, following her into the kitchen. 'Only, Barry's call worried me.'

'Worried you – why?'

'First of all he asked me whether I'd been to see you, and then he said that he didn't like you being alone in the house all day. He suggested that, if I had the time, I come and keep you company. In the end, he almost begged me to come round!'

'Why didn't you tell me all this when you rang?'

'I suppose I didn't want you thinking that Barry had sent me here to check up on you. Has he always been so concerned about you?'

'No – I can't think why he's suddenly so worried! I wonder what he thinks I get up to?'

Glimpsing Barry hiding in the bushes, Marianne wondered again at his peculiar plan. But the question wouldn't leave her mind. *Why? Why set me up with John?* If he firmly believed that the word worked, which he did, then what would he gain from catching her red-handed with John? She prayed that John would use the word so that she could discover what was behind Barry's curious plan, apart from sheer madness! Turning to face John, her gown open, revealing her blonde pubes, her pinken slit, she smiled.

'Barry left early this morning, and he probably won't be home until very late. I suppose I do get lonely sometimes,' she said, allowing her gown to fall further apart. 'But I can't think why he's suddenly so concerned about me!'

'Juxtaposition!'

Her face serene, her hands relaxed by her sides, Marianne gazed into space. 'Take your dressing gown off!' John ordered her firmly. Rising to her feet, concealing a wicked grin, she slipped the robe over her shoulders and let it fall to the floor. With Barry watching the bizarre proceedings, her submissive obedience, she felt a delightful gush of desire surge through her contracting womb.

'Kneel at my feet!' John ordered. Complying, Marianne was thankful that her naked body was in full view through the backdoor glass. Barry would be watching her every move, she knew as she gazed at John's bulging jeans. 'Undo my belt and pull my jeans down!' her master commanded unashamedly.

John's penis was big, too big, Marianne thought as the rampant organ sprang to life before her wide eyes. The silky-smooth purple plum glistening invitingly, her vaginal juices began to flow in torrents as she imagined sucking on the young man's knob, drinking his jetting sperm. She also imagined Barry bursting in through the backdoor and throwing a fit!

'Before we go any further,' John murmured pensively, 'stand up and find me something to tie your hands with.' Marianne rose to her feet and glanced around the room, her stomach somersaulting at the prospect of bondage. Taking one of Barry's ties from the pile of washing, she passed it to her master. Standing compliantly with her hands behind her back, she allowed him to tie her wrists together.

'Now, on your knees again – slave!' he ordered excitedly. His hard penis wavering before her wide eyes, she opened her full red lips, following John's orders and engulfing his hard knob within the moist heat of her mouth. John sighed as Marianne swept her tongue over his smooth glans, causing his penis to balloon and twitch. Her juices flowing freely from her hot hole and coursing down her inner thighs, she mouthed and sucked fervently, delighting at the prospect of drinking John's gushing sperm while Barry watched.

Wondering when Barry would make his dramatic entrance, bounding through the back door and exploding with rage like a madman, she sensed an incredible feeling of complete and utter submission. She was John's slave! Her hands tied behind her naked body, kneeling before her master, sucking his solid knob – she was his sex slave!

Was she discovering another side to herself? she wondered. Was having her hands tied, her young body crudely violated, a latent inner desire she'd unknowingly harboured? As she sucked on and mouthed the twitching knob so impertinently forced upon her, she felt a terrific pang of depraved sexual excitement rock her womb. This was to be her role in life, she knew. From now on, to play the part of a slave – a sex slave – was her role.

'Lick my balls!' John ordered. 'Lick my shaft and my balls!' Marianne swept her tongue over his hairy balls, watching as his penis jerked and his knob swelled. Running her tongue up his veined shaft, she desperately wanted to engulf his knob in her mouth, to drink his jetting sperm. Giving in to her passionate desire and sucking his glans into her mouth, she breathed heavily through her nose. 'No, don't do that!' he reprimanded. 'You'll do exactly as I say, when I say! Now, lick my balls!'

Slipping his glans from her mouth, Marianne wondered at her new role of sex slave. Licking her master's heavy balls, she realized the immense pleasure gained from playing the submissive role. 'Lick all over!' he demanded. Her tongue dutifully licking, wetting his rolling balls, his veined shaft, she closed her eyes. She felt completely in his power, totally under his control. She had relinquished all responsibility, as far as John and Barry were concerned, anyway! The guiltless feeling, the sense of total freedom, brought her a strange sense of satisfaction, gratification. She was under orders, at the mercy of her master. Now, her sense of being in control had gone.

'Now lick my knob! Don't suck it, just lick it!' Snaking her tongue around his throbbing purple glans, she prayed for his spunk to gush. 'Lick all over my knob!' he cried as his sperm jetted, splattering her blonde hair, her pretty face and running down her chin. 'Now! Now! Suck it now!'

Moaning through her nose, she took his pulsating knob into her mouth and sucked as his come filled her cheeks. Salty, the aphrodisiacal nectar aroused her, made her young clitoris swell. 'Ah, that's good! Keep . . . keep sucking!' His knees sagging, John held Marianne's head, thrusting his throbbing shaft deep into her hot mouth, draining his heavy balls until, shuddering and gasping, he finally pulled away.

His spent penis glistening, hanging half-erect before Marianne's eyes, she wondered whether her sex session was over or not, and why Barry hadn't burst in. *Perhaps he's enjoying this?* she wondered, catching a glimpse of her boyfriend as he peered out from the bushes.

'Stand up and bend over the table!' John ordered as he pulled his jeans up, completely unaware of his audience. Marianne complied, bending over the table with her hands tied behind her back, her feet apart, her bottom-crease yawning. The view from the back garden would be perfect, she was only too aware as she jutted her buttocks and parted her feet even further, displaying her tightly closed anal-ring, her wet, glistening vaginal lips.

But why hadn't Barry made his entrance? So jealous, so possessive, she'd imagined that he'd have come bounding in the minute she'd slipped her gown off and knelt before John's stiff penis. What the hell was he playing at?

'And now for your punishment for disobeying my instructions, you dirty little whore!' John bellowed, rolling up a tea towel. Whipping her taut buttocks with the towel, he administered his punishment, causing the whimpering girl's young body to jolt, her buttocks to tense, her tears to stream. 'Your errors need correcting, my girl!' he warned. 'If you're to be my sex slave, you'll have to mend your ways!' Was Barry into bondage and whipping? she wondered as her taut flesh burned, stinging with every lash.

Biting her lip as he discarded the towel and parted her crimson buttocks, Marianne imagined him entering her there, sliding his huge tool into her young body and fucking her velveteen bottom-sheath.

His fingertip caressing the sensitive brown tissue surrounding the portal to her bowels, Marianne gasped with the electrifying sensations. But what was Barry up to? she wondered again as John's finger invaded the privacy of her bottom. What the hell was Barry thinking? Massaging her inner anal flesh, John groped between her legs with his other hand and slipped two fingers between her swollen cunt lips and deep into her drenched vagina.

'Ah, ah, God!' she cried involuntarily as her sheaths tremored, tightening around John's massaging fingers. Her face resting on the pine tabletop, her mouth open, gasping, the very centre of her femininity crudely pillaged, she'd never known such sexual pleasure, such beautiful abandonment.

'You like having my finger up your bum, don't you?' John asked in his rising wickedness, stretching her tight brown hole open and delving further into her anal tube.

'Yes, yes, I love it!' Her words of confession fell from her full red lips as she quivered and writhed on the table.

'Ever had a cock up there?' John persisted in his ever-increasing quest for lust.

'No, I've never had a ...'

'Do you want my cock up your tight arse? Do you want me to fuck your tight arse?'

Her body alive with lust, Marianne desperately wanted John to use her there, to fill her tight anal tube with his throbbing penis and fuck her – fill her bowels with his sperm. But she didn't reply. She was the submissive slave following orders, not begging for this or agreeing to that. As his finger delved deeper into her bottom-hole, bringing her electrifying sensations of depraved sex, she almost gave in and pleaded for him to thrust his penis deep into her bowels and fill her with sperm.

'Well, do you want my cock up your arse?' he repeated.

'I ... I ...'

'Whether you want it or not, you're going to get it!' he chortled, slipping his finger from her hot, tight hole.

Turning her head to one side, Marianne gazed though slitted eyes towards Barry, lurking behind the bushes, spying. What was he thinking *now*? What was his plan? Was he masturbating? she wondered, recalling his confession. Was he delighting in watching his girlfriend endure sexual abuse at the hands of another man as he wanked himself off in the bushes? If this was Barry's darker side, then he had severe problems! she concluded as she felt John's solid knob stab between her splayed bottom-cheeks.

'You're going to enjoy this!' John sniggered as he pressed his purple plum past her yielding anal sphincter. 'You're going to love this, you dirty little whore! I know I am!'

Gasping as her virginal hole was stretched wide to accommodate her master's bulbous knob, Marianne grimaced. A finger was one thing, she thought apprehensively, but a massive male organ? As inch by inch of solid fleshpole drove into the hot depths of her bowels, she lost her senses, tossing her head, whimpering, gasping for more.

Grabbing her hips, John began his fucking, driving his shaft deep into her rectum and withdrawing only to impale her again on his massive organ. Grunting expletives with every thrust, he finally rammed his penis in to the hilt. 'Coming! God, I'm coming already!' he gasped as his sperm discharged from his weapon-head. Marianne could feel the male come lubricating her anal cylinder, filling her velveteen sheath. 'God, you've a tight arse!' he praised her as he withdrew and thrust deep into her again with alarming vigour.

As the flow of semen ceased and John stilled his pistoning cock, Marianne squeezed her eyes shut. Desperate for her hands to be released now, she prayed that her beautiful ordeal was finally over. Her bottom-hole felt painfully bloated, her pelvis strangely inflated, and she wondered at her wanton act of depravity – her complete loss of morality.

Sobbing with pleasure as John slowly withdrew his weapon, Marianne glimpsed Barry again. He'd set her up with John, used her. But what had become of his raging jealousy? He seemed to change with the wind, she mused as she was ordered to stand up. As John released her hands and helped her into her gown, she decided to finish with Barry. With John and Jill knowing about her magical word, she'd not be short of company – or a rampant and fulfilling sex life.

'Sit at the table and wake up!' John ordered.

'Oh! I feel strange!' she cried as she sat down and looked up at John.

'Strange? How . . . how do you mean?' he asked nervously.

'I don't know. I feel . . . Oh, never mind. As I was saying, I can't think why Barry's suddenly so concerned about me being alone in the house.'

'No, neither can I. Look, I'd better be going – I've just remembered that I'd promised to help a friend with . . . I'll call round to see you again – if you want me to, that is?'

'Yes, please do! It's been nice seeing you, John. I'm in most mornings so . . .' *God, what am I suggesting?* 'Yes, come round again.'

'I will. I'll see myself out. Bye.'

'Bye John – and, please, do come again!'

Wandering out into the garden, her bottom-hole wet, her buttocks sore, Marianne walked across the lawn towards Barry's hide. Wondering whether to pretend to suddenly discover him, to ask him what he was doing, she turned and made for the house. He'd come in by the front door and question her, she was sure as she closed the back door. There was no way he'd be able to refrain from questioning her, but what about? He could hardly confront her!

As she'd predicted, Barry arrived by the front door and breezed into the kitchen. 'Hallo, love!' he smiled. 'I've an hour or so between clients so I thought I'd come home.'

'I'm pleased you did,' she replied. 'God, is that the time? I had no idea! I'm not even dressed yet! Where on earth has the time gone?'

'Time flies when you're enjoying yourself!' he quipped, with a hint of sarcasm, she decided.

'But I've only been . . . What have I been doing all this time?'

'You must have gone back to sleep. Anyway, how do you feel?'

'How do I feel? How do I feel about what?'

'How do you feel about . . . Juxtaposition.'

Ah, now I might learn something! she thought as Barry asked her to remove her gown and stand naked before him. 'I was watching you from the garden,' he began. His voice was stern, accusing. 'I watched you sucking John's knob, you filthy little tart! I saw John whipping you and fucking your arse. Did you like it, Marianne? Tell me, are you really such a whore that you enjoy having another man fuck your arse?'

Frozen to the spot, Marianne couldn't believe Barry's words, his condemning words. He'd been the one who'd set her up! she thought angrily. What the hell was he playing at by accusing her of whoredom? But, she reflected, this was his jealousy surfacing. He was so jealous that he'd lost all reason! No doubt he regretted setting her up and was now trying to blame her for his mistake.

'I quite enjoyed watching you,' he continued. 'In fact, I've never been so turned on in all my life! Watching my supposedly loving, faithful bloody girlfriend swallowing sperm from another man's cock was a bloody good turn-on! The thought of you going with someone else has always sickened me, but when I actually watched you . . . Funny thing, jealousy. The very idea of you with another man has always . . . Anyway, it's given me an idea. I've decided to . . . No, there's little point in telling you anything whilst you're hypnotized. Bend over the table, as you did for John, and open your buttocks for me. I want you to act like the filthy little tart that you really are!'

Taking her position, Marianne reached behind her quivering body and splayed her crimson bottom-orbs with her slender fingers, opening the sperm-drenched entrance of her anal sheath to her boyfriend's appreciative gaze.

'Don't mind if I fuck you there, too, do you?' he asked as she sensed his solid knob pressing against her wet, brown flesh. 'After all, being the filthy, two-timing whore that you are, that's what your holes are for – for fucking! Now, hold on to the table because you're about to be fucked as you've never been fucked in your entire life!'

Marianne didn't understand Barry's thinking, his logic, or lack of it! But worse, she wondered about the future, *her* future if she were to stay with him. Having decided to end the relationship, she was now in two minds again. She'd enjoyed Barry watching as John had used and abused her body. She'd enjoyed the experience so much that she didn't want to put an end to the games. But would Barry stop there? Would he bring men home and sit and watch as they fucked her? Would he fall deeper and deeper into his murky well of voyeurism until he drowned in his own vileness? *Where will it all end?* she wondered as she felt his huge shaft drive into her already stretched and inflamed rectal sheath.

'Ah, God! I should have done this to you ages ago!' he cried as he drove his weapon in to the hilt, her tight brown ring painfully gripping the broad root of his penis. 'I'll invite John round again this evening. Yes, I'll get him round and then I'll pretend to go out. Perhaps I could set up a hiding place somewhere inside this time? That's it!' he laughed as he withdrew his shaft and crudely impaled her again. 'That's it, I'll spy on you from the dining room, through the serving hatch!'

Marianne sensed her clitoris swelling at the thought of Barry watching again as John fucked her, ordered her to suck his knob and drink his sperm – as he bound her wrists and whipped her naked buttocks. 'Ah, ah!' she cried as Barry grabbed her hips and thrust into her with such force that the table glided across the floor. 'Ah, no! No, it . . .'

'Shut up, tart! This is only the beginning of your new life! You've no idea what I have planned for you, no idea at all!'

Praying that Barry would quickly discharge his sperm and withdraw his massive cock from her sore duct, Marianne squeezed her blue eyes shut, wondering what the hell had happened to her life, her warm, loving, cosy relationship. Barry was, indeed, a monster – but she was beginning to crave the cold, crude perverted sex. She was even beginning to pray that he'd bring several men to the house to simultaneously use and abuse her.

Suddenly picturing Barry screwing another woman, shafting another woman to orgasm with his hard penis, Marianne wondered not only where his love for her had gone, but her love for him. The love had been transformed into cold lust, she concluded, wondering now if they'd ever shared real love at all.

'Your arse is so tight!' Barry gasped as his climax neared. 'Christ! It's so . . . so fucking tight!' Marianne shuddered as the beginnings of her own orgasm stirred within her swirling womb. Reaching between her thighs, she massaged her neglected clitoris, whimpering as Barry's body suddenly became rigid and his sperm gushed.

'Right up your hot arse!' he cried as Marianne's clitoris erupted in the most exquisite orgasm her young fingers had ever managed to elicit from her sex-nodule. Her body jolting with every ramming thrust of Barry's hard cock, her cunt spasming, yearning for a cock of its own to grip on, she knew in her heart that her life would now be a life of cold sex.

Barry was of no consequence now, he meant nothing to her. He was just another man with a penis she'd use for her debased pleasure. He was her voyeur who'd bring her untold pleasure by spying on her, watching her lewd games of depravity.

Her thoughts turning to Jill, she wondered how Barry would react if he were to see the girl licking between Marianne's pussy lips, or Marianne sucking an orgasm from the young lesbian's pulsating clitoris. *It could easily be arranged!* she thought as Barry's shaft drove deep into her bottom-hole, pumping the last of his sperm into her bowels.

As the final ripples of pure sexual ecstasy drifted through her body, she decided to give Barry – the voyeur, the bastard – the most exciting, the most lewd, lesbian show ever. *I'll show him that I don't need him and his bloody cock!* she mused as he slipped his flaccid tool from her brimming anal sheath. *I'll use not only Barry, but all those who discover my word and use me for their perverse filth!*

'You're a bloody good fuck!' Barry praised her as he zipped his trousers. 'Did you enjoy John whipping your lovely arse? You seemed to, from what I saw – so I'll give you a damn good whipping and see just how much you like it!'

Spying through slitted eyes, Marianne wondered where Barry was going as he left the room. The tea towel was still rolled up ready for the thrashing, so where had he gone? Returning with several lengths of rope, he grinned wickedly as he bound her ankles to the table legs. Taking her hands and spreadeagling her arms, he tied her wrists to the far table legs. Her limbs outstretched, her buttocks splayed, her abused anal hole exposed, she wondered fearfully at his plans for her.

'Right!' he boomed. 'I'll show you what I do with cheating, two-timing whores!' The first lash of the rope caused Marianne to cry out with the stinging pain. Pink weals appearing across her already burning buttocks, Barry ignored her cries, giving her no quarter, thrashing the girl with all the strength he could muster.

To Marianne's astonishment, she felt a terrific pang of arousal run through her pelvis. With every stinging lash, she felt her clitoris respond by transmitting minor orgasmic pulses through her quivering body. Her cries of sexual gratification driving Barry on, he continued the thrashing, losing himself in his wanton debauchery as he reddened the girl's taut, twitching flesh.

'Enough!' Marianne finally cried. Her buttocks fire-red, her stinging flesh burning, she could take no more. As Barry discarded the rope and sat on a chair gazing at his handiwork, she breathed a sigh of relief. The thrashing had brought her immense satisfaction, but she'd been afraid that the pain would eventually outweigh the pleasure.

'I don't know what you'll think when you see your arse!' Barry laughed, thrusting two fingers deep into her dripping vaginal sheath. 'You should see your bum! God, you look as if you've been horsewhipped a thousand times!'

What next? Marianne wondered as Barry's fingers manipulated her hot, creamy vaginal walls. Would he invade the privacy of her tight rectum again once his penis had recovered from the anal fucking it had just given her?

'I've got to get going,' Barry sighed despondently as he slipped his fingers from her tethered body. 'Shall I leave you tied over the table until I get back? No, I'd better not!' he laughed as he released her. 'There'll be lots more crude sex,

Marianne!' he warned brutally. 'Lots more wonderfully vile and crude sex and debauchery before I've finished with you, my girl!'

Not even bothering to instruct his slave to conceal her perspiring body with her gown, Barry hid his bondage equipment and snapped his fingers. 'What . . . what am I doing naked?' she asked, grabbing her gown. 'God, my bum really hurts!'

'How do I know what you've been up to?' Barry returned indifferently. 'I've been upstairs. Look at your buttocks! What the hell have you been doing to yourself?'

'I . . . I really don't know! God, I must have hurt my bum somehow! It's stinging like hell!' she complained, covering her naked body with the gown.

'I must get back to work,' Barry snapped as he left the room and closed the door behind him.

'Already?' she asked as he walked through the hall and slammed the front door shut. He'd gone, used her, fucked and whipped her – and gone.

Alone at the table, Marianne recalled Barry's words. *I'll invite John round this evening. I'll spy on you from the dining room, through the serving hatch!* 'He's a fucking bastard!' she hissed through gritted teeth as she rubbed her sore buttocks. 'He's a fucking perverted bastard!'

A tear rolling down her flushed cheek, she wondered what she'd become, what sort of person she really was. Although she wished she'd never begun the pretence, never thought of the ridiculous idea of a trigger word, she couldn't deny the immense sexual pleasure she'd derived from her exploits. *If only I had a word to use on Barry,* she mused as the phone rang. *A word that really worked!*

'It's me, Jill!' came the bubbly lesbian's voice as Marianne answered the phone. 'I was just wondering what you were doing this morning?'

'Er... nothing much, why?'

'Fancy coming over to my place for a... for a chat?'

Shaking her head and biting her lip despairingly, Marianne was about to decline the offer. She'd had more than enough sex for one day! But, hearing another girl giggling in the background, her heart leapt at the thought of being attended by two young lesbians.

'Give me half an hour or so,' she replied. 'I'll have a quick shower and then come over.'

'Great!' Jill responded excitedly. 'I've a friend here I want you to meet.'

'Really? Who's that?'

'Just a girlfriend. See you soon, and be quick!'

Somewhat anxious to see me! Marianne laughed inwardly as she replaced the receiver, wondering again what it would be like to have two young girls attending her naked body. *Anxious to see me naked!* Suddenly remembering Barry saying that he'd ask John to call round that evening, Marianne held her hand to her mouth and gasped. 'I'm nothing more than a sex object! God, this is getting way out of hand!'

Arriving at Jill's flat wearing a red suede miniskirt and loose-fitting blouse, Marianne found herself torn, yet again, between her new way of life, the incredible sex, and her old boring but comfortable and secure existence. But when Jill opened the door, her pretty, angelic face beaming, her firm young breasts pert, ballooning her tight top, Marianne knew that she had to enter the flat and experience a lesbian three-some. *I might never have the chance again,* she mused as she followed Jill into the lounge. *Opportunities don't always come twice.*

'Marianne, this is Lydia,' Jill introduced her friend. Smiling, her heart fluttering, Marianne shook the beautiful young girl's hand. In her late teens, with long black hair and deep, dark eyes radiating a child-like innocence, the girl appealed to Marianne – certainly her curvaceous body appealed to Marianne.

Lydia's legs were long, shapely, her thighs unblemished in youth. Her red leather microskirt barely covering the swell of her panties as she stood with her feet apart, jutting her hips forward, she radiated an uncanny sexual charisma that Marianne had never encountered before. But were the dark mirrors of her soul reflecting innocence? Marianne wondered, gazing into the girl's eyes. Or was there a powerful sexual desire twinkling there? A lesbian sexual desire lurking?

'Pleased to meet you,' Marianne replied warmly. Turning to Jill, she smiled sweetly. 'So, how are you?'

'I'm fine! I wanted you to meet Lydia because . . . Juxtaposition.'

Already? Marianne thought with some surprise as she stared into space, her arms limp, her body still.

'There, what did I tell you?' Jill giggled. 'She's hypnotized, and she'll do anything we ask!'

'That's incredible!' Lydia gasped as she stood before Marianne and squeezed her firm breasts. 'With the power we have over her, we could do absolutely anything to her!'

'Exactly! Let's get her to strip off.'

'How do you know she's not pretending to . . .'

'She's not pretending! She's not like us, she's only into men, so there's no way she'd consciously allow me to do what I did to her the other day.'

'She's very pretty, isn't she? Very sensual, very sexy,' Lydia grinned.

'She is, and she's got a lovely hot, wet pussy! Right, here goes – Marianne, take your clothes off.'

Her excitement rising, Marianne unbuttoned her blouse, revealing her red lace bra to her wide-eyed spectators. Again, a powerful feeling of complete submission engulfed her. Although enacting the role of obedient sex slave perfectly, she was the totally innocent participant, she reminded herself.

Her firm breasts thrusting proudly from her bra cups as she unclipped the flimsy garment, she gazed at her brown milk-buds, delighting as they grew and stood erect from her areolae. But the most exciting part of her unrobing was yet to come. As she unzipped her tight skirt and wriggled the garment down her shapely thighs, a thrilling wave of arousal rolled though her contracting womb. Kicking her skirt aside, she stood before the girls with only her thin red panties concealing her most intimate place.

Lydia moved closer to Marianne and sucked her nipple into her hot mouth, causing her sex slave to gasp with delight. 'Suck the other one!' Lydia cried, turning to Jill. With her nipples simultaneously sucked into hot female mouths, Marianne closed her eyes, revelling in the beautiful sensations of lesbian lust.

'I'll rip her panties off!' Lydia giggled excitedly as she slipped Marianne's teat from her mouth and knelt before the girl. 'Keep biting her nipples – bite them hard!' she instructed Jill. Lydia was obviously the dominant partner, Marianne thought as Jill sank her teeth into her nipple, causing her to wince with mingled pain and pleasure.

Her young womb quivering, sending electrifying tremors through her pelvis as her mistress tugged her panties down, Marianne breathed heavily. Never had she known such sexual stimulation, such terrific heights of arousal, such a craving to have her body intimately attended by two young girls – two lesbians.

'What's she like at eating pussy?' Lydia asked Jill impishly. 'As good as you, I hope!'

'I don't know, I didn't get that far with her. Anyway, if she's no good, we can always train her!'

'I'll do the training! God, she's got beautiful, fleshy cunny-pads!' Lydia shrieked, squeezing each outer vaginal lip in turn. 'When we've got her worked up and begging for it, I'll order her to give me a good licking!'

The words of sapphism echoing through her mind, Marianne realized that, as a sex slave, she would not only have her naked body intimately attended, but she herself would be called upon to attend her mistresses' innermost needs. The realization sinking in, she tried to imagine slipping her tongue between another girl's vaginal lips, lapping up another girl's slippery cuntal lubricant.

As Lydia's finger slipped between Marianne's inner lips and drove deep into her hot sex-sheath, Marianne gasped, her legs sagging as the pleasure crept over her trembling flesh to bathe her entire body in lust. A second finger slipped into her wet vagina, stretching the pinken flesh, sending another wave of lust through her naked body.

'Undress me!' Lydia demanded as she slipped her fingers from Marianne's hot sheath and stood up. Her voice was harsh, almost menacing, Marianne mused fearfully. She was, indeed, a dominant young lady! Moving to the sofa, Jill grinned, watching as Marianne followed her instructions and pulled Lydia's T-shirt over her head.

'God, look at her bum!' Jill shrieked, noticing the crimson flesh, the pink weals fanning out across her taut bottom-cheeks. 'She's been whipped!'

'Must have been her boyfriend!' Lydia laughed. '*I'll* give her a bloody good spanking later! I'll spank her so hard that she'll wet herself! And now, slave, take my bra off!' Unclipping the garment and peeling the cups away from the girl's pert breasts, Marianne gazed in awe at her elongated nipples, her dark areola discs.

'Well, aren't you going to take my skirt off?' Lydia goaded. Kneeling before her mistress, Marianne tugged the girl's leather skirt down, exposing her bulging pink panties. 'Well, go on, then!' Lydia urged as she stepped out of her skirt. 'Behave like a dirty little lesbian for me! Pull my knickers down!'

Taking the elasticated waistband between her fingers and thumbs, Marianne peeled the silky material away from Lydia's mound, her eyes opening wide as she realized that the girl had shaved her pubic hair. Further she pulled the material down, exposing Lydia's soft, silky-smooth pussy lips, her opening sex-groove. A little more, and the girl's pinken inner lips came into view, emerging from her sex-valley like two small tongues.

'You're doing well for a beginner!' Lydia purred as Marianne pulled her panties down to her ankles. 'Now, I want you to kiss me, kiss my pussy,' she grinned, standing with her feet as wide apart as she could, her pussy-slit opening to reveal her glistening inner flesh.

Tentatively moving closer to her mistress's gaping vaginal crack, Marianne planted a kiss on the soft swell of her warm mound. Breathing in the heady scent of the girl's moistening groove, she moved down and kissed each puffy outer lip in turn.

'Lick me, slave!' Lydia ordered as Jill stood up and slipped her skirt down. 'Do as I say and lick me all over, my pussy lips, my thighs – lick me all over!'

Hesitantly pushing her tongue out, Marianne tasted the girl's soft mound. Working down, she licked the smooth skin of her vaginal lips, the creases at the tops of her thighs. As

Jill moved behind her and cupped her buttocks, Marianne felt a jolt of excitement run through her pelvis. The time had come to lick her mistress's sex-groove, to push her tongue right out and taste her lubricious vaginal offering.

As Jill's finger located Marianne's tight bottom-hole, encircling the sensitive tissue, tantalizing her there before the inevitable penetration, Marianne peeled open Lydia's creamy sex-groove with her thumbs and licked from the bottom to the top of her yawning cunny-slit. Her taste buds alive with her first-ever sampling of girl-juice, she lost herself in her debauchery, lapping fervently at the flesh-folds, savouring the aphrodisiacal female nectar.

Jill's finger twisting, pushing, entering her tight anal sheath, Marianne gasped, mouthing and sucking on her mistress's wet cuntal flesh, breathing in her maiden-fragrance, taking her ever-closer to her orgasm with her darting tongue.

'You've a lovely tight bottom!' Jill breathed as her finger drove deeper into Marianne's rectum, waking sleeping nerve endings there.

'She's got a nice tongue, too!' Lydia gasped as her clitoris swelled in response to the sweeping female tongue. 'Ah, yes, that's it! Lick me just . . . just there!' she stammered as her budling throbbed deliciously in her slave's fervent mouth.

Suddenly, images of Barry loomed in Marianne's swirling mind. *If only he could see me now!* she giggled inwardly as she worked on Lydia's flowering clitoris. She knew that she had Barry to thank for her new-found sexual deviance and, again, she promised herself that she'd give him the lesbian show of his life.

'Come . . . coming!' Lydia cried in her shuddering as her clitoris ballooned. The rock-hard nodule pressing against her hot tongue, Marianne sucked and licked until the girl sang out in her lesbian coming. 'Ah, ah! Oh! Oh, God!' she wailed, her body shaking violently in the grip of her multiple orgasm.

Marianne sustained the girl's pleasure by fingering her spasming vaginal sheath and licking her pulsating clitoris faster and harder. Her own clitoris swelling in response to Jill's beautiful anal fingering, Marianne could barely believe that she was locked between two naked lesbians. But there was better to come, she mused, picturing a girl licking between her own sex-folds as she reciprocated. *Lesbian sixty-nine!* she thought excitedly as her neglected cumbud grew ever nearer to its climax, yearning for a caressing female finger – a female tongue.

Lydia finally collapsed to the floor in a shuddering heap, whimpering, writhing as her pleasure receded. Slipping her finger from Marianne's bottom-sheath, Jill ordered the girl to lie on her back with her limbs spread. Complying, Marianne sensed her clitoris tingling with anticipation, her vaginal muscles tightening in readiness to grip on a thrusting feminine finger.

'God, she's good!' Lydia gasped, her hands between her thighs, her fingers toying with her inner lips, twisting and pulling on her sensitive rubicund sex-folds.

'I told you we'd have some fun with her!' Jill replied. 'This trigger word of hers is going to bring us as much lezzie sex as we want! And *when* we want it!'

'Why not get a man round so that we can watch her being fucked?' Lydia laughed wickedly.

'That's a good idea! Yes, that's a brilliant idea! But for now, we have her to ourselves, so let's get on with it.'

'Jill,' Lydia murmured pensively, a wicked glint in her eyes as if she'd just dreamed up the most depraved act they could commit on their naked slave. 'Let's shave the bitch's cunt.'

'Shave her? But she'd . . . she'd have to explain it to Barry, her boyfriend! She'd realize that someone had used the trigger word and . . .'

'So? It would be a laugh! Imagine her discovering that her pubes have gone! Anyway, you'd like her pussy shaved, wouldn't you? You like my pussy shaved so . . .'

'We have to be careful, Lydia! You can't be too naughty with her! Try and control your . . .'

'I'll decide what we do or don't do, Jill!' Lydia reprimanded angrily.

'All right. Go and get your cream and we'll do it. God knows what she'll think when she discovers that she's naked between her legs – but we'll do it!'

Marianne lay on the floor listening to her mistresses talking about her as if she was no more than an object, a soulless naked body to be used for their lesbian pleasure. But the thought of having her pussy shaved excited her immensely. Imagining her mound, her vaginal lips devoid of hair, smooth and soft. Her heart fluttered.

Barry would blame John! she concluded. Again, Barry's sinful behaviour would backfire on him! But would it? she wondered. Barry delighted in watching his girlfriend, once his true love, being sexually abused by another man, so he'd probably be turned on by the thought of Marianne being shaved. But would his jealousy finally win the day? When he saw Marianne's naked love lips and the reality of her debauched infidelity had sunk in, would his jealousy soar out of control? *Sod Barry!* she thought as Lydia settled between her outstretched legs and smeared the depilating cream over her mons, her veil of blonde curls.

The cooling cream, the massaging feminine fingers, sent a satisfying tingle up Marianne's spine. As Jill knelt astride her head, Marianne gazed longingly at the girl's gaping crack through her eyelashes. Lowering the open centre of her body,

Jill settled her full vaginal lips over her slave's mouth and began to rock her hips, sliding her wet inner girl-flesh over Marianne's face. Pushing her tongue out, savouring the copious flow of pussy juice, Marianne lapped between the pinken folds, swallowing the vaginal offering.

'Ten minutes should do it!' Lydia giggled as she covered the last vestige of veiling pubic hair with the white cream. 'Ten minutes, and she'll be transformed!'

Gasping as Marianne's tongue snaked into her vaginal entrance, Jill didn't reply. Reaching down and peeling her swollen pads of pussy flesh wide apart, exposing her erect clitoris, her yawning hole to Marianne's probing tongue, Jill shuddered as the birth of her lesbian-induced climax stirred within her young womb.

Joining the sex games, Lydia pushed her finger between Marianne's buttocks and located the sensitive portal to her anal duct. Rudely forcing her way past the girl's defending sphincter muscles, she drove her finger deep into the hot, creamy rectal tube before slipping another finger between Marianne's inner pussy lips and delving deep into her spasming cunt.

Massaging her ducts, bringing Marianne immense sexual pleasure, Lydia began her thrusting, finger-fucking the girl, causing her to gasp for more through mouthfuls of Jill's cuntal flesh. 'Don't stop! Ah, ah! Harder!'

Jill shuddered and writhed, grinding her open cunt into Marianne's hot mouth as her climax shook her very soul. Decanting her love-juices, gyrating her hips, she wailed her appreciation in sympathy with Marianne's muffled gasps of orgasmic pleasure. The three-way lesbian coupling brought Marianne untold sexual gratification, taking her higher to her sexual heaven, deeper into the murky depths of wanton debasement. Never would she forget the incredible threesome, never would she find such sexual satisfaction as now.

Finally slipping her open cunt from Marianne's mouth, Jill lay on the floor, her stomach rising and falling, her pert breasts heaving as she rested in the wake of her climax. Still finger-fucking Marianne's love-holes, Lydia massaged the last ripples of sex from her slave's young quivering body, delighting in her wanton act of female masturbation.

At last, Lydia allowed Marianne to rest, slipping her fingers from her ducts, leaving her holes inflamed, closing to fill the void, leaving her naked body quivering, perspiring with sex. Was this the end of her sexual ordeal? Marianne wondered as the incredible sensations receded and her breathing slowed. Or was she to be taken to another climax, ordered to lick and mouth another orgasm from her lesbian mistress's insatiable clitoris?

'I'll clean her fanny and see what she looks like without her pubes,' Lydia finally said, dashing to the bathroom and returning with a warm flannel. Wiping her intimate flesh, the girl cleansed Marianne, exposing her smooth naked skin, her full vaginal lips. 'She looks wonderful!' the girl cried as she wiped away the residue of white cream and fallen curls. 'God knows how she's going to explain this to her boyfriend!'

'She'll have to admit to shaving herself!' Jill laughed as she rolled over and gazed lovingly at Marianne's swollen sex-hillocks. 'God knows what he'll think!'

Ordered to dress, Marianne's stomach somersaulted at the thought of showing Barry her blatant nakedness. She'd appear to be stunned, she mused – totally shocked, mystified. What he'd say, she had no idea – but she didn't really care. All this was Barry's fault so he could hardly complain!

'Bring her out of her trance now,' Lydia said as the girls finished dressing. 'We'll use her again and again! Next time, I'll give her a bloody good thrashing!'

'Wake up, Marianne!' Jill ordered, sitting on the sofa and relaxing, nonchalantly gazing at a magazine.

'Oh! What . . . what happened?' Marianne asked as she looked around the room, feigning disorientation.

'Nothing happened,' Jill smiled. 'Anyone for coffee?'

'Please,' Lydia replied.

'Er . . . Not for me,' Marianne said softly, aware of her silky panties against her smooth pussy lips, her soft mons. 'I . . . I think I'd better be going.'

'So soon!' Jill returned surprisedly. 'You've only just got here!'

'Yes, I know, but . . . I don't feel too well. I'll see myself out. It was nice meeting you, Lydia. I'll see you again, I expect.'

'Yes, you can be sure of that!' Lydia smiled, turning to Jill and winking.

'Sorry to dash off, but I feel quite strange,' Marianne said as she left the room, leaving the lesbians to laugh and chat about their incredible experience.

Out in the street, Marianne breathed in the flower-scented summer air, happy with her new-found life, her lesbian relationships. She'd gone so far down the road of trickery now that she could never turn back. But, she decided, she didn't *want* to turn back.

Her sexual identity now confirmed, her lustful craving for sex divided equally between male and female, she looked forward to many beautiful encounters, many wondrous orgasms. But there was Barry to confront. That evening, she'd slip her clothes off, pretending that she was about to have a shower, and he'd notice her nakedness. She'd look down, horrified, gasping with amazement.

'Life's good!' she mused as she walked down the road, her vaginal juices seeping between her swollen, hairless pussy lips, draining into her panties. 'Life's bloody good!'

Chapter Four

Surprised to find Barry at home at three in the afternoon, Marianne asked him why he wasn't working. He'd already spent half the morning skulking in the bushes, watching John screwing her, so what was he up to now?

'I've got the afternoon off,' he replied, eyeing her short skirt, her naked legs as he filled the kettle. 'Where have you been?'

'Out for a walk,' she smiled, aware of her naked pussy lips, her clitoris, as she imagined his reaction when she displayed her hairless girlhood to his disbelieving eyes.

'You've been gone a bloody long time!' he returned accusingly. 'I've been back for well over two hours so . . .'

'It was a long walk, OK?' she replied, annoyed by his disbelief, his mistrust – his jealousy.

'Where did you go, exactly?'

'Down to the park, round the pond and . . .'

'Juxtaposition!'

Ah, the magical word! she mused as she feigned her hypnotic trance, realizing that he would not only breathe the word to use her for sex, but to try and prise the truth out of her.

'Now, tell me exactly where you've been!' he demanded, sitting at the kitchen table.

'Jill's,' Marianne whispered.

'And what happened at Jill's?'

'I . . . I didn't stay for long. I . . .'

'I know that she's aware of your secret word because I heard you telling her about it on the phone. Did the lesbian order you to strip?'

'I . . .'

'I don't suppose you'd remember anyway. On second thoughts, subconsciously you'd remember – somewhere deep inside your mind you'd remember all that had happened. I know that much about the subconscious!'

She knew that Barry was right. Subconsciously, she'd recall all that had happened to her and, if genuinely hypnotized, she'd reveal all. *It wouldn't do any damage to tell him exactly what had happened at Jill's place – it might even be fun!* she thought wickedly.

'I arrived at Jill's and she had a friend with her, a young girl – Lydia. They told me to take my clothes off . . .'

'You stripped naked?'

'Yes, and then they took their clothes off and we all had sex – lesbian sex. They did this to me.'

Lifting her skirt up over her stomach, Marianne pulled the front of her panties down and displayed her hairless pussy-crack. 'God!' Barry gasped. 'They've shaved your cunt! Actually, you look beautiful like that! Just right for Dave this evening!'

Dave? Marianne pondered, concealing her naked crack. *Who the hell's Dave?* Barry had obviously planned something awful for her. *Something wonderful!* she guessed, imagining a stranger using her, fucking her as Barry watched. *God, how I've changed!*

'I intend to use you, Marianne,' he said pensively as she flattened her skirt over the slight swell of her stomach with her palms. 'I'm thinking of giving up my job and earning a fortune from you, from your body – your cunt.'

So, this was the *real* Barry! she pondered. She'd thought there was more to his darker side, but she hadn't expected him to sell her for sex, to use her as a prostitute, to live off her immoral earnings!

'I intend to sell video tapes, too – videos of you masturbating with a vibrator and candles, being fucked by several men at once, used by lezzies, tied down and whipped. I'll rig the camera up so that I can video you and your lezzie friends licking each other's cunts out! Now that I know I'm secure, that our future together is secure now that I have power over you, I'm off my jealousy trip – thank God. I'll make more money from you and your cunt than I'll ever make from the dirty mags I import.'

Dirty mags? Marianne thought, totally perplexed. There was *indeed* far more to Barry than she'd ever imagined! How long had he been importing dirty mags? Who did he sell them to, and where did he keep them?

'I've a nice little business going,' he enlightened the stunned girl. 'I've a few hundred regular customers who'll be delighted when I announce that I'm now selling dirty videos too – *really* dirty videos! There's so much crap around at the moment – blurred, shaky pictures, cunts that you can hardly see, dubbed sound . . . Yes, I'll earn a fortune from you, Marianne – from your shaved cunt!'

Her head spinning as she stood quietly listening to the incredible revelation, Marianne held back her tears. *Marriage!* she thought. *My God, I was actually going to marry the bastard!* Although more sexually aware, alive, than ever before, she couldn't bring herself to feign hypnosis and allow Barry to film her masturbating, being fucked by strangers. The game, and her relationship with Barry, had to end now, she decided. She could still enjoy playing the hypnosis game with Jill and Lydia, and John, perhaps – but not with Barry.

'I've some bloody good ideas for the videos!' he chortled. 'I'll make up a wooden pillory to bind you to – you know, like they had in the old days. Yes, I'll design something to strap your naked body to so that your cunt and your arse are exposed to the camera, your holes open for fucking. But for now, I think I'll have a little fun, try out one or two ideas – a rehearsal, so to speak.'

If Marianne gave her game away now, word would soon get back to Jill and Lydia – and John. It was no good owning up to her deception: the only way was to leave Barry, end the relationship by walking out. But he'd follow her, she mused. He'd not understand why she should suddenly up and leave without an explanation. Besides, she owned half the house, half the furniture. If she were to carry on her games with the others, she'd have to plan the end of her relationship with Barry carefully.

'Take the wooden spoon from the drawer,' Barry instructed. Images of her mother spanking her with a wooden spoon loomed in Marianne's mind as she opened the drawer. Was he going to thrash her naked buttocks? she wondered as she passed him the spoon. 'Pull your knickers down and bend over the back of the chair,' he ordered, placing a chair in the centre of the room.

Slipping her panties down, Marianne lifted her skirt and leaned over the chair, exposing her crimson buttocks to her boyfriend's wicked eyes. Tensing her muscles in readiness for the thrashing, she gasped as the long, thin spoon handle slipped deep into her rectal sheath.

'Yes, that's good!' Barry laughed. 'But I need something bigger. Wait there while I search the garage. I want to see just how much I can stretch your tight arse open!'

The spoon handle bringing her heavenly sensations, Marianne pondered on the situation. She'd play along with Barry for the time being, allow him to experiment, to stretch her bottom-hole open – but she'd put an end to the debauchery well before he set up his video camera.

'This is ideal!' Barry said triumphantly as he entered the kitchen, holding up a length of plastic drainpipe. 'I'll shove it up your cunt and have a look at your cervix before I stick it in your arse!' he laughed, leaving the spoon in place as he pushed the pipe between her bulging pussy lips.

The two-inch diameter pipe opening Marianne's vaginal sheath, Barry pushed and twisted until the end pressed gently against her cervix. 'Ah, that's good!' he cried, kneeling behind her. 'I can see right up your cunt! God, you're wet, all pink and creamy! I've never seen a cervix before. I wonder whether I could use a bigger piece of pipe and really open you up?'

Quivering as Barry slipped the pipe from her spasming vagina, Marianne felt her clitoris swell. But her fear outweighed her pleasure as he slowly withdrew the spoon handle from her bottom-hole and pushed the end of the pipe between her buttocks. 'Sod it, it's the wrong shape!' he complained. 'I need something with a rounded end.'

As he left the room to search the garage again, she wondered whether to make out that she'd somehow come out of her trance. About to stand up and pull her skirt over her buttocks, she heard Barry close the back door. Her heart racing, her hands trembling, she desperately tried to stand, but her muscles seemed to lock. *I must have cramp!* she thought as she tried again to bring her body upright.

'Now then!' Barry grinned as he parted her bottom-orbs to reveal her small hole. 'Let's give this a try!' Stretching her buttocks further apart, he presented the rounded end of a screwdriver handle to her brown portal. Pushing and twisting to the accompaniment of Marianne's whimpers, he realized that he'd never drive the shaft deep into her bowels without a lubricant.

Opening the fridge door, Barry plunged the screwdriver handle into the butter dish. 'That should do it!' he cried as he splayed her taut buttocks again. Easing the handle past her defending muscles, he grinned as he slipped inch after inch into her trembling body. 'It's not bloody thick enough!' he moaned, slipping the shaft out.

Please, God, no! Marianne prayed as Barry opened a cupboard and took out a huge Christmas candle.

'This is more like it!' he enthused, thrusting the waxen shaft into the butter. 'It's a good two inches in diameter with a perfectly rounded end!'

Tensing her muscles as Barry pushed the end of the candle past her tight anal ring, she gasped as her hole opened, slowly stretching to accommodate the progressively thickening shaft. 'This is ideal!' Barry cried, watching her brown tissue yield as he pushed the candle in further.

Her eyes squeezed shut, Marianne gritted her teeth as the cone-shaped end of the candle disappeared into her tight bottom-hole, her brown tissue now expanding fully to take the smooth, two-inch-thick shaft. 'I reckon you could take three inches!' Barry tormented the girl as he pushed the candle deeper into her stretching rectal sheath. 'Or four, even!'

Gasping, grimacing, as the solid candle sank further into her bowels, Marianne was amazed by her heightening arousal. The lewd sensations were heavenly, she had to admit, as Barry twisted and turned the waxen phallus, pushing it ever deeper into her defenceless young body.

'This sort of thing will sell my dirty videos!' he laughed, standing back and gazing at the thick candle emerging from between the girl's inflamed buttocks. 'Yes, the more perverted, the better! And now for your cunt!'

Taking a wine bottle from the fridge, Barry knelt behind Marianne and parted her bulging cuntal lips, exposing the glistening pink flesh surrounding her wet vaginal entrance. 'Yes, I reckon your cunt can take a wine bottle!' he laughed, presenting the thick end of the bottle to his vulnerable girlfriend's gaping hole.

Her bottom-sheath painfully stretched, Marianne couldn't believe what Barry was trying to do as her vaginal lips rolled along the wine bottle as it entered her sex-cavern. The filling sensation within her young pelvis was incredible, and she gasped and writhed as the bottle finally pressed against her cervix.

'My God!' Barry breathed. 'I've never seen anything like that before! I wouldn't have believed it unless I'd seen it with my own eyes! This is great for the videos. They'll sell like fucking hot cakes!'

Grimacing, Marianne couldn't believe it, either! She thought she'd split open as Barry began thrusting the bottle in and out of her bloated vagina. Her clitoris massaged by the wet bottle, she quivered as her orgasm rose from her womb and erupted from her solid pleasure-bud.

'Coming!' she wailed as her climax rocked her young body. Her anal sphincter gripping the candle, her vaginal muscles rhythmically tightening around the bottle, she reached hitherto unknown heights of sexual ecstasy, crying out her pleasure, shaking uncontrollably in her new-found obscenity.

Thrusting the candle in time with the bottle, Barry fucked her love-holes, jolting her body as he drove the phalluses between her legs, delighting at the lewdness of his wanton act of abuse.

Finally slowing his rhythm as Marianne shuddered in the wake of her incredible climax, Barry gazed at her sensitive brown flesh stretched tightly around the candle. Wondering whether she could take a larger phallus or not, he slipped the bottle from her inflamed vagina. Twisting and gently pulling on the candle, he withdrew the wax shaft from her tight hole as she gasped with sheer sexual bliss.

'How about having the wine bottle up your arse?' he quipped. Marianne could take no more, let alone the wine bottle! Rolling off the chair, she lay on the floor, her legs wide, her holes sore, aching from the crude thrusting. Her breathing slowing as Barry ordered her to stand up, she prayed that her ordeal was finally over.

'Sort your knickers out and pull your skirt down,' he ordered her, clearing away the evidence of his debauched act before sitting at the table, wondering when to start filming. Following his instructions, Marianne adjusted her clothing and sat opposite, opening her eyes as he clicked his fingers.

Her anal duct aching, her vaginal juices decanting into her bulging panties, she tried to make herself comfortable on the chair as she gazed into Barry's dark eyes. 'I feel strange,' she said, wriggling on the chair. 'I must go to the doctor for a check-up.'

'What's the problem, love?' he asked, feigning concern.

'I don't know. I feel funny, between my legs, inside my bum.'

'Perhaps you've been sitting on damp grass or something. Anyway, I'm going out to the garage to . . . to tidy up. It's a right mess out there!'

'Oh, by the way, I'm thinking of going out this evening – you'd nothing planned, had you?' Marianne asked as he neared the back door.

'Er . . . Actually . . . Where are you going?'

'I thought I'd go and see Jill.'

'Why not ask her round here? I'm going out to see a client so I won't be in your way.'

'All right, I'll do that.'

'Good. I'll go and clear the garage up. See you in a while.'

Alone at last, Marianne massaged between her legs, desperate for her holes, her stretched muscles, to return to their original size. Standing up to ease the discomfort, she tried to formulate her plan, her plan to leave Barry.

But how do I ensure that I can still play my games with Jill and Lydia? she wondered. Word must never get out that she'd been conning everyone! 'Decision time!' she breathed, opening the back door. 'Barry!' she called, walking round the side of the house. Finding him working at the bench in the garage, she took a deep breath. 'Barry, I want to talk to you!' she said sternly.

'What about?' he asked, trying to conceal whatever it was he was constructing.

'I want to talk to you about us, our relationship,' she began.

'Our relationship?' he echoed, his dark eyes frowning. 'Our relationship's OK, isn't it?'

'Things have changed, Barry. I don't want to carry on the way we . . .'

'Juxtaposition.'

Her heart racing, her stomach churning, Marianne desperately tried to move her body, to put an end to the ridiculous farce – but she couldn't move. Her muscles wouldn't respond, she was unable to speak. To her horror, the trigger word seemed to have worked!

'Our relationship is fine,' Barry smiled, staring into her glazed eyes. 'There's nothing to worry about, you're perfectly happy with me – and you want to stay with me. You're desperately in love with me, Marianne, remember that! Now, I'll bring you out of the trance and you can go and make me a sandwich and a cup of coffee.'

As Barry clicked his fingers, Marianne's power over her

body returned immediately. Stunned, she said nothing as she left the garage. Closing the back door behind her, her heart pounding, her legs sagging, she leaned on the kitchen table to steady herself. 'No, it must have been my imagination!' she tried to convince herself. 'The word doesn't really work! It can't!'

As Barry entered the kitchen, Marianne turned to face him, praying for him to say the word again, desperate to prove to herself that it *had* been her imagination. 'I'll make you a sandwich,' she smiled, her legs still shaking, her palms wet. 'What are you up to in the garage?'

'Juxtaposition!'

Her arms hanging limply by her sides, again, Marianne had no control over her young body. Her thoughts swirling, she realized that now the word actually worked. Although her thinking was clear, she was in some sort of hypnotic trance.

'I'm making some devices, sex-toys and the like, for the filming sessions,' Barry said as he squeezed her firm breasts and kissed her cheek. 'We're going to be in the money!' he laughed. 'And the beauty of the whole thing is that you'll know nothing about it! Just think, you'll be a porn queen, watched by hundreds, thousands of men – and you'll know nothing about it!'

Unable to speak, to protest, Marianne could do nothing to halt Barry as he knelt before her and lifted her skirt. Pulling her panties down, he gazed at her hairless, swollen vaginal lips, her neat dividing groove, her emerging inner petals.

'Mine, all mine!' he said triumphantly, planting a kiss on her warm mound. 'Your cunt, your whole body – all mine to do with as I wish, when I wish! Going on that hypnosis course was the best thing you ever did! And to think that I moaned about the money it cost! It was the best few hundred quid I ever spent!'

Her mind racked, her body completely immobile, deprived of her defences, Marianne gasped as Barry pushed a finger between her vaginal lips. Delving deep into her tightening pussy-sheath, he massaged her inner flesh, delighting at the power he had over the girl.

'The vibrator!' he suddenly cried. 'Come upstairs to the bedroom, and you can masturbate while I watch!' Slipping his finger from her tight hole, he stood up. 'Up you go, you dirty slut!' he ordered excitedly. 'I'm really going to use you, your beautiful cunt!'

Seemingly having a mind of their own, Marianne's legs automatically climbed the stairs and carried her to the bedroom. 'Take all your clothes off,' Barry instructed, grabbing the vibrator from the bedside drawer. Her hands mechanically removing her top, unclipping her bra and freeing her pert breasts, Marianne couldn't halt her disrobing. 'Right, now lie on the bed with your legs wide apart!' he demanded as she slipped her skirt and panties off.

Her naked body vulnerable, she lay on the bed with her legs outstretched, her pinken girl-crack wide open. 'Now use the vibrator and bring yourself off!' Barry directed his sex slave, passing her the pink plastic phallus as he sat on the edge of the bed. 'This will be a trial run, a rehearsal before the filming.'

Switching the device on, Marianne peeled her vaginal lips apart, exposing her glistening flesh, her stiffening clitoris. Pressing the buzzing tip of the vibrator against her pleasure-bud, the sensations immediately transmitting deep into her womb, she gasped. 'Ah, ah, God! God, my cunt!' She had no control over her uncharacteristic words – all she could do was listen to herself as she breathed her appreciation for her young body. 'That's good! Ah, yes! I love masturbating! God, how I love the vibrator against my clit!'

'Perfect!' Barry cried. 'You're going to be a movie star! And I'm going to be fucking rich!'

Her fear and confusion slipping away as the vibrator made her throbbing clitoris swell, Marianne reached beneath her thighs with her free hand and slipped two fingers into her drenched vagina. Thrusting her fingers in and out of her tight hole as the vibrator played on her ballooning clitoris, she began to writhe and pant as her orgasm approached.

Wailing as her climax gripped her, Marianne shook uncontrollably. 'God, I'm there!' she cried, her stomach rising and falling, her firm breasts heaving. 'God, I'm coming!' Watching the amazing spectacle, Barry massaged his huge bulge, wondering in which hot orifice to deposit his sperm. Unzipping his trousers, he positioned his rock-hard penis, his bulbous purple knob close to Marianne's gasping mouth and ordered her to suck.

Opening her full red lips wider, she took his solid knob inside her hot mouth, licking his silky-smooth glans as the vibrator sustained her multiple orgasm. Mouthing like a babe at the breast, her wet lips tightly closed around his throbbing crown, she brought out his sperm, savouring the salty fluid, swallowing hard as her cheeks filled.

Her own climax declining, she moved her head back and forth, taking Barry's knob to the back of her throat and withdrawing the solid glans again. Drinking the last of his jetting come, she suddenly realized that she was back in control. She had the free will to move, to command her limbs. As she slipped Barry's spent knob from her mouth, she frowned. *I must have convinced myself that the word really works!* she thought surprisedly, gazing up at the satisfaction so obviously depicted in Barry's expression.

Barry finally climbed off the bed, zipping his trousers

and gazing at Marianne's dripping vaginal crack, the creamy lubricant smeared over her smooth pussy lips. 'That's enough for now,' he said. 'We'll have some fun this evening. Did you ask Jill round?'

'No,' she breathed, happy to be in control again, but still perplexed as to what had happened.

'Do it the minute you get downstairs. I'll postpone Dave. Shame, really, he'd offered me fifty pounds for a couple of hours with you. Right, get dressed and come downstairs.'

As Barry left the room, Marianne smiled. Whatever had happened to her during the frightening time she'd been unable to exert her conscious will wouldn't happen again, she was sure. *A quirk, a fluke,* she decided as she dressed. *My subconscious playing tricks on me.*

This wasn't the time to walk out on Barry after all, she thought as she dressed. Apart from having nowhere to go, why *should* she leave her home? *If anyone's leaving, it should be him – the bastard!*

'All right, love?' Barry smiled congenially as Marianne entered the kitchen.

'Yes, fine,' she replied, aware of her silk panties caressing her hairless pussy lips. 'Except for one thing.' *Might as well get it over with.*

'Oh, what's that?'

'I don't quite know how to tell you this but . . . Well, you'll never believe me, Barry, but . . . my pubic hair has all fallen out!'

'Fallen out? What *are* you talking about? Show me.'

Lifting her skirt and pulling the front of her panties down, Marianne revealed her full, naked pussy lips to her boyfriend. Her vaginal crack still wet from her masturbation session, her engorged inner lips peeping out at Barry, Marianne pulled her wet panties down further, revealing her full naked glory to his wide eyes. Feigning astonishment, his only comment was that it could be due to worry.

'That's ridiculous!' Marianne laughed, suddenly having the answer. 'Worry doesn't cause your pubes to fall out!'

'Why did you shave?'

'I didn't shave!'

'Then you must have some weird sort of problem!'

'Actually, I did shave!' she laughed. 'What do you think?'

'Sexy! Yes, very sexy!'

'I knew you'd like it!'

'But, what on earth made you . . .'

'I did it for a laugh! They'll soon grow back. I read about it in a magazine somewhere. Quite a few women shave their pubes off these days.'

'I'm glad you did! You look like . . . you look like a schoolgirl! It's really good, Marianne – really good!'

'It feels rather strange. My silk knickers rub my lips as I move about – it's quite a turn-on!' Suddenly recalling Barry's instruction, Marianne grinned. 'I'll give Jill a ring and ask her round for the evening.'

'Good idea! As I said, I'll be out, so you'll have some time alone together to chat about girlie things – shaving fannies and the like!'

'Yes, it'll be nice.' *Well, that's the problem of my shaved pubes dealt with!*

Wondering how Barry intended to hide in the dining room and spy through the serving hatch without giving the game away, Marianne picked up the hall phone and rang Jill. 'I'd love to come round!' came the girl's excited reply. 'Er . . . the thing is, Lydia's with me, so . . .'

God, not Lydia! Marianne thought fearfully, recalling the girl's words: '*I'll give her a bloody good thrashing.*' Lydia was a strange one, she mused. Radiating an uncanny air of decadence, she frightened Marianne. Jill was soft, gentle, loving. But Lydia!

'That's OK, bring her along,' Marianne finally conceded.

'Great! Er... will Barry be there?'

'No, he's got to go out for a few hours. Something about seeing a client, I think.'

'Oh, right. About seven, if that's OK?'

'Fine. I'll see you later.'

Wandering into the lounge, Marianne sat in the armchair, contemplating the incredible situation. 'So much for decision time!' she sighed as the back door slammed shut. Barry was obviously off to construct some weird and wonderful sexual gadgets in the garage. *God, is this what I really want?* she wondered, imagining playing the role of a tart. 'A tart in a trance!' she giggled.

Suddenly having an idea, Marianne dashed upstairs to the bedroom. 'OK, Barry, you bastard – I'll play along with you for a while! But, I promise you, very soon now the whole thing will backfire in your bloody face!' Slipping her wet panties off and taking a large can of hair spray from the dressing table, she sat on the edge of the bed and peeled her vaginal lips wide apart. 'I'll beat him at his own debauchery!' she asserted wickedly, pressing the end of the can between her rubicund sex-folds.

Her idea was to see how big an object she could insert into her tight pussy-hole. She wanted to be one step ahead of Barry's perversity – to shock him with her own perversity! The huge can slipping into her opening sex-duct, she gasped, gazing at her full outer lips tightly encompassing the can. 'It must be almost three inches across!' she exclaimed, pushing the can deep into her young vagina. 'Well, that didn't present a problem!' she giggled, easing the can in to the hilt.

Slipping the wet can out of her inflamed vagina, she

scanned the room, looking for something larger, thicker. 'Ah, yes!' she breathed in her abandonment, discarding the can and taking a long, cylindrical plastic container of wet-wipes from the dressing table. 'This must be over four inches in diameter!'

Try as she did, painfully stretching her vaginal lips, she couldn't insert the container into her fiery cuntal sheath. Disappointed, she grabbed a bottle of baby lotion and smeared the creamy liquid over the plastic container. 'I've got to get it in!' she declared in her frightening sexual arousal, peeling her outer lips wide apart and pushing the container against her fleshy hole. Suddenly realizing the lewdness of her act, she wondered what the hell she was trying to do to her young body, and she decided that she was nowhere big enough to take the massive container.

'Ah, God!' she cried as the container was suddenly sucked deep into her vagina. 'Ah, ah, no! What have I done?' Her outer lips now taut rolls of flesh, her clitoris forced from its pinken cover, she gazed in amazement at the plastic container protruding from her abused vagina. 'God, it's . . . it's so . . . so big! My poor cunt!'

Gazing at the thrilling spectacle in the dressing table mirror, she reclined, opening her thighs as far as she could, imagining the video camera running, recording her obscene act of wanton self-abuse. Turning her head to one side, she noticed the vibrator lying on the bed. Her arousal running feverishly high, she grabbed the device, switching it on and massaging her erect clitoris with the pink tip.

Her nostrils flaring, her mouth open, gasping, she could barely believe the incredible sensations emanating from her bloated cunt, her swollen pleasure-bud. Squeezing her eyes shut, she tossed her head, writhing as her clitoris stiffened fully, sending electrifying sensations of crude sex through her inflated pelvis. 'God, no!' she cried as her vaginal muscles gripped the plastic container, trying to crush the mammoth phallus as her climax erupted, gripping her very being in its velvet hand.

Her body rigid, her breasts heaving, her nipples solid, her areolae a dark chocolate colour in her sexual arousal, she prayed for her shuddering climax to recede. 'No, no!' she murmured, her muscles locked, her hand unable to move the vibrator away from her bursting clitoris.

Finally releasing her young body, her orgasm subsided, leaving her perspiring, panting, shaking uncontrollably, her long blonde hair matted, dishevelled. 'God! Never in all my life . . .' Relaxing now, she tugged on the plastic container, gently easing it from her gripping cuntal sheath, managing to pull against the powerful suction effect of her wet sex-cylinder and slip it from her body. 'Argh, God!' she gasped as her vaginal sheath suddenly closed, the creamy walls slapping together, filling the void.

Marianne lay resting on the bed, her abused vagina aching, her pussy lips inflamed, swollen, dripping with girl-come. Examining the wet container, she was amazed that she'd been able to push it into her youthful sex-duct. But the idea spurred her on and, recalling Barry's words, she wondered about her bottom-hole. *I reckon you could take three inches!*

Taking a roll-on deodorant bottle from the dressing table, she pondered on the penis-like shape, the bulbous knob-like cap. *The manufacturer had feminine needs in mind when designing this!* she thought, smearing baby lotion over the plastic cap.

Lying on the bed with her knees up to her chest and her thighs wide, she reached down and presented the rounded cap to her tightly-closed brown hole. Pushing, twisting the bottle in her bizarre state of arousal, she managed to open her private portal, pressing half the cap into her anal sheath. 'Ah, that's nice!' she gasped, pushing the cap further into her tight duct.

Gently but firmly, she pushed on the bottle, opening her rectal sheath as the shaft drove deeper and deeper into her body. *It's not bloody thick enough!* Barry's lewd words drifted in her mind, tantalizing, teasing, goading. Slipping the bottle out of her stretched duct, she sat upright, scanning the room for something more suitable, something longer, thicker.

'Ah, yes!' she grinned, taking a perfume bottle from the dressing table. 'Six inches long, almost three inches in diameter – perfect!' Although her perverted thoughts were beginning to disturb her, she wasn't going to be swayed from scoring over Barry on the debauchery front. 'I know I can do it!' she asserted, lying back on the bed and raising her knees to her chest again.

The rounded end of the bottle well-lubricated, she offered the impromptu phallus to her oily anal portal. Gently pushing, persuading her brown ring to yield, she was determined to ease the bottle deep into her hot bowels. Her clitoris throbbed in response as her sphincter muscles surrendered to the huge phallus, opening three inches to allow the gigantic intruder access to her bowels.

'Oh, my God!' she cried as the bottle suddenly slipped deep into her rectal sheath. 'Oh, oh! God!' Her eyes rolling, she'd never experienced such heavenly sensations from her sadly neglected bottom-hole before. Lying dormant for years, she wondered why she'd never allowed her fingers to cross the short bridge of flesh between her vaginal opening and her rectum to discover her paradisiacal anus. The electrifying sensations her stretched bumhole brought her permeated her very being, and she swore to pay regular intimate attention to her newly-discovered pleasure haven.

The bottle firmly in place, tightly gripped by her velveteen rectal tube, she grabbed the discarded hair spray can, offering the metal phallus to her gaping vagina, wondering whether she could fill both holes to capacity.

Slowly, gently, she eased the can into her vaginal canal, stretching the inner flesh, opening her pussy-duct to accommodate the long, thick shaft. *If Barry were to come in now!* she thought in her mischief, imagining him standing in the doorway eyeing her blatantly abused love-holes. Her clitoris suddenly pulsating, she pushed the can fully home, the metal cooling her cervix, and took the vibrator from the quilt.

'Oh, my God!' she wailed as she pressed the vibrating pink tip to her ballooning clitoris. 'Ah, God, that's . . .' Her body writhing, contorting as if in agony, Marianne had never experienced such shuddering peaks of sexual pleasure. She felt the fire of passion deep within her pelvis, a burning desire between her splayed thighs. Her entire being centred deep within her cunt, her tight anal-tube, her throbbing clitoris. Barely able to endure the colossal orgasmic waves as they erupted from her pleasure-bud, sending incredible shock waves through her quivering body, she held her breath, her eyes rolling in her sexual euphoria.

At last, the orgasmic waves receded, leaving Marianne exhausted in their wake. Panting for breath, her holes desperately trying to eject the massive phalluses, she lay quivering, for the moment unable to move or to extract the huge shafts from her painfully bloated sex-ducts.

Managing to straighten and spread her legs, she reached between her thighs and gently but firmly pulled the can from her gripping vaginal sheath. As the metal cylinder slipped out, she gasped. The sensations causing tremors deep within her womb, she rested before attempting to remove the bottle from her rectum. 'What have I done?' she cried as her vagina closed, sealing the entrance to her womb once again. 'Christ, what have I become?'

Pulling, twisting, she finally managed to slip the large bottle from her bottom-hole, allowing her creamy anal tube to deflate, return to its former size, leaving a strange empty sensation within her young pelvis. Bringing her body upright, she sat on the edge of the bed and gazed between her parted thighs. Her outer vaginal lips red, sore, swollen, her girl-come pouring in torrents from her hot hole, pooling on the quilt, she quivered, praying that Barry was still in the garage – unaware of her disgusting act of self-abuse.

Slipping her panties up her legs and covering her inflamed holes, the once most sacrosanct regions of her very femininity, Marianne decided to go for a walk, to think, to contemplate her new-found sexual deviancy. Creeping downstairs, praying that Barry wasn't in the house, she slipped out of the front door and through the garden gate into the street.

Still wondering why she'd had no power over her actions, no free will, when Barry had used the trigger word, Marianne made her way to the park. Was the word really beginning to work? she pondered. Autosuggestion was a very real thing, perhaps that's what was happening? Whatever it was, she assured herself that it wouldn't happen again. She'd fight it if it did!

Sitting on a bench by the pond, Marianne reflected on the recent events. No pubic hair. Anal intercourse. Oral sex. Swallowing sperm. Lesbian sex. Whipping. Bondage. A candle, a hair-spray can, a perfume bottle, a deodorant bottle, a huge plastic container, a vibrator . . . 'My God!' she breathed, wondering where the old Marianne had gone.

There seemed to be nothing left to discover – she'd charted all the areas of her young body, sounded all the depths.

Whatever Barry came up with, whatever strange devices he was constructing, there was nothing she'd not already endured – was there?

Aware of her wet panties, she glanced around the park. There was no one nearby, no prying eyes as she slipped her panties off and leaned back with her thighs open. The summer breeze cooling her burning vaginal lips, she smiled, examining the crotch of her red panties – the white stains, the creamy wetness. Slipping her hand beneath her short skirt, she toyed with her distended inner lips, eliciting pleasing sensations from the soft, warm flesh, inducing her girl-come to flow from her spasming vagina.

Moving her fingers up her drenched valley to her stiffening clitoris, she closed her eyes, massaging her sensitive budling, breathing slowly, deeply, as the sensations permeated her quivering womb. Squeezing her nipple through her flimsy top with her other hand, she quickened her rhythm, rubbing her swollen clitoris faster, increasing the electrifying sensations.

A yapping dog at her feet suddenly disturbing the intimate pleasuring emanating from her erect nipple, her throbbing clitoris, Marianne quickly adjusted her skirt, covering her feminine nakedness as she scanned the park for the animal's owner.

'Go away!' she hissed at the dog. 'Bloody dog! Go on, bugger off!' Jumping up and snatching her panties from the bench in its jaws, the dog ran off towards a man walking some distance away. 'Oh, shit!' she breathed as the man took her panties from the dog's mouth and began strolling towards the bench.

'I'm so sorry,' he smiled as he approached Marianne. 'Are these yours?' Her face flushing as he held out her wet panties, Marianne returned his smile, wondering what to say, how to explain herself.

'Er... no, they're not mine!' she laughed awkwardly, gazing into his dark eyes.

In his mid-thirties, tall, slim and very good-looking, Marianne wondered what he'd do to her in the park, to her young body under the hot, summer sun, if he knew about the trigger word. Lowering her gaze to his bulging jeans, she sensed her insatiable clitoris stir between her pouting vaginal lips.

'I think your dog found them on the grass, over there,' she said, pointing behind the bench.

'Well, someone must have left the park feeling rather chilly!' he laughed as he sat beside her, dropping the panties beneath the bench. 'Don't mind if I join you, do you?'

'No, not at all.'

'He's not my dog, by the way – he belongs to a very good friend of mine. I bring him here for a walk when she's working.'

Marianne's stomach sank. *A very good friend of mine. When she's working.* But what was she thinking? she asked herself. She could hardly be jealous, she didn't even know the man! *It was a neighbour's dog,* she hoped.

'Do you come here often?' he asked.

The cliché brought a smile to her face. *What's a nice girl like you... What's a filthy whore like you...* 'Yes, quite often,' she replied.

'Always alone, or with your boyfriend?' he probed.

'Always alone. I don't have a boyfriend,' she lied, brushing her long blonde hair from her pretty face. 'Not at the moment, anyway.'

The words, the lies, tumbled from her mouth without her thinking. Eyeing his bulging jeans again, she wondered what he'd think if he knew that she was naked beneath her skirt – naked and hairless.

'Your *very close* friend, is she a...' Marianne began hesitantly.

'No, no, she's only a friend. I'm single,' he replied, obviously reading her thoughts, her body language.

'Oh,' she smiled, her heart fluttering. 'Do you live very far away?'

'See that house there, on the edge of the park?'

'What, that big place with the tall chimneys?'

'Yes – that's my house.'

'Nice! I live . . . I have a small house. Nothing special, but it's home.'

'Fancy coming back for a drink?' he asked, lowering his appreciative gaze to her shapely thighs. 'I usually have a scotch after walking the dog.'

Her stomach somersaulting, she thought of Barry. He'd wonder where she was, where she'd gone. *So what?* she reflected. *He doesn't own me!* Imagining the man between her thighs, licking, sucking on her girl-flesh, his tongue stiffening her clitoris, she realized that she didn't even know his name – and she was about to go to his house!

'I'm Marianne,' she introduced herself, holding her hand out as she stood up.

'Oh, sorry . . . My name's Rod,' he smiled, standing and shaking her hand. 'It suits you, your name. You remind me of Marianne Faithfull.'

'Do I?'

'Yes, your hair, your mouth. So, would you like to come back for a drink?'

'Yes, all right. I don't have a great deal of time, but I'd love to see your house.'

Following the yapping dog towards the large house, Marianne spoke of the hypnosis course she'd been on. 'I was thinking of setting up as a hypnotherapist, but I flunked the course!' she said despondently.

'Hypnosis is an interesting subject,' he replied as they

neared the house. 'But it can be dangerous if not used properly.'

'Dangerous?' she queried.

'Yes. In the wrong hands, hypnosis can be very dangerous. Delving into the subconscious, suggestion and all that, can be very dangerous indeed.'

Following Rod through a wooden gate and along the garden path to the back door of the house, Marianne wondered how to mention the trigger word without giving the game away. *What would he do if he knew the word?* she thought excitedly, her clitoris stirring again, her stomach swirling, her vaginal juices flowing down her inner thighs.

'Come through to the lounge,' he invited, locking the dog in the kitchen as she wandered into the hall. The lounge was big and expensively furnished. The walls lined with books and paintings, the red carpet thick, plush, it was more like a luxurious private study.

'What would you like to drink?' Rod asked, opening an antique cabinet as she sat on the sofa.

'Er . . . vodka-and-lime, please. As I was saying, I flunked the course but . . . Well, perhaps I shouldn't tell you about it.'

'Tell me what?'

'The lecturer was taken ill on the last day. He'd placed what he called a trigger word in my subconscious and . . . it's boring, let's talk about something else.'

'And the trigger word is still there, is that what you were about to say?'

'Well . . . yes, it is. Oh, thanks,' she smiled as he passed her a glass.

'I told you that messing around with hypnosis can be dangerous.'

'No, there's no danger. No one knows the word so . . .'

'What is the word? Sorry, I didn't mean to . . .'

'That's OK. My telling you won't do any harm. As long as you promise not to make me do a dance or sing or something!'

'Of course I won't!' he laughed. 'I'm just interested, that's all.'

'The word is *juxtaposition*,' she enlightened him trustingly.

'At least it's not likely to crop up in conversation!'

'No, hopefully not!'

Watching Rod sit opposite, Marianne wondered what the hell she was doing in a stranger's house, her pussy knickerless beneath her very short skirt – admitting to having had a trigger word planted in her subconscious! *I must be mad!* she thought, sipping her drink.

But it would be nice to get to know someone – to get to know a man other than Barry. *A clandestine relationship,* she mused, the thought exciting her. Rod probably lived alone, she reckoned, gazing around the room, imagining leaving Barry and moving in with Rod. *I am mad!*

'You're not aware if the word's been used, are you?' he asked. 'I mean, if someone had mentioned the word and sent you into a hypnotic trance, you'd remember nothing about it afterwards, would you?'

'No, not at all. The course lecturer used it and told me that I was standing at the sink doing the washing up. Apparently, everyone had a good laugh watching me wash nonexistent dishes!' she giggled. 'And, when he clicked his fingers, I had no recollection whatsoever! I didn't even know that I'd been hypnotized!'

'I've seen it done on TV, but I'd always thought it to be an act.'

'Oh, no! It's real enough!'

Placing his glass on a low table, Rod moved forward in his chair. *Come on, come on!* Marianne urged in her mind, her pussy lips swelling, her clitoris ripening, her vagina wetting. Perhaps all men *weren't* the same as Barry and John, after all?

Despondency setting in as she watched him pick his glass up, Marianne wondered whether to make her excuses and leave. *It must have crossed his mind to send me into a hypnotic trance and have his wicked way with me!* Perhaps, if she were to call and see him again, he'd use the word and . . .

'Juxtaposition!'

Staring blankly across the room, Marianne smiled inwardly as her stomach somersaulted at the prospect of having sex with a stranger. *What will he do?* she wondered. *Ask me to strip? To open my legs and show him my pussy?* Her sexual arousal reaching dangerous heights, she waited, praying that he'd bury his face between her legs and suck an exquisite orgasm from her yearning clitoris.

'They *were* your knickers, weren't they?' Rod asked, his voice soft but firm.

'Yes, they were,' she replied, monotonizing her words to bring authenticity to her hypnotic trance.

'Why had you taken them off?'

'I was masturbating,' she confessed, her vaginal muscles tightening, her clitoris insatiable in its yearning.

'Do you always masturbate in the park?'

'Yes, I do.'

'Aren't you afraid that someone might see you?'

'No. The thought of being caught excites me. I love being watched.'

'Has anyone ever watched you masturbating?'

'Yes, many times. Last week, there was a man in the park. He was behind some bushes, watching me.'

'And did you come?'

'Yes, several times.'

'So, you're not wearing any knickers, then?'

'No, I'm not.'

'Show me how you masturbate.'

Her heart banging hard against her chest, her womb contracting, Marianne parted her legs as wide as she could. Moving her buttocks to the edge of the sofa, she lifted her skirt up over her smooth stomach, revealing her shaved pussy-slit, her soft mound, to the stranger's gaze.

'Why have you shaved?' he asked, moving across the room and settling between her feet.

'I prefer it that way, it looks good, feels good. It excites me to see my fanny naked, like a young girl's.'

'You look very sore, what have you been up to?'

'Using a can of hair spray. Pushing it into my cunt and masturbating.'

'You're a very attractive girl. I can hardly believe my luck!' he grinned as she parted her inflamed cunny lips and massaged the soft flesh surrounding her vaginal entrance. 'The chances of meeting a nymphomaniac in the park are slim enough, but to meet one who has a trigger word! The implications are incredible!'

His words exciting her, Marianne continued her female masturbating, her blatant self-abuse, as he watched the amazing spectacle. Suddenly aware of his hot breath on her inner thigh, she moved her buttocks further forward, opening the centre of her young body, offering her vaginal entrance to his mouth, his tongue.

'Ah, yes!' she gasped as his hot, wet tongue swept up her sex-valley. 'Ah, God!' Vigorously frigging her clitoris as Rod's tongue snaked its way into her vagina, Marianne was coming ever nearer to her desperately-needed orgasm. Suddenly, Rod's finger delved deep into her bottom-sheath, the delicious sensations of depravity lifting her higher to her sexual heaven. 'Coming!' she gasped as her body shook and writhed.

Moving her hand aside, Rod engulfed her throbbing clitoris in his hot mouth, licking, sucking, sustaining her incredible orgasmic pleasure. Her lustful sensations heightened by her wickedness, her trickery, Marianne could barely endure the waves of orgasm crashing through her young body. On and on she rode the crest of her climax, quivering, wailing her appreciation, almost forgetting her *hypnotic trance*.

'Don't stop!' she cried as his finger delved deeper into her tightening anal sheath. 'Oh, God – don't stop!' His tongue sweeping over her pulsating crown, Rod elicited the final orgasmic palpitations, leaving the girl drained, her vaginal juices flowing from her hungry cunt.

'You enjoyed that, didn't you?' Rod asked as he slipped his finger from her tight rectum.

'Yes, yes!' Marianne gasped appreciatively.

'You'd like me to fuck you now, wouldn't you?'

'Yes, please – fuck me! Fuck my wet cunt!'

Her vaginal cavern aching for his solid penis, Marianne's stomach somersaulted as he unzipped his jeans. *God, make it good!* she prayed as she opened her legs as wide as she could, offering her girlishness to the stranger.

'Damn it!' Rod cursed as the front doorbell rang. 'I forgot he was coming round!' Leaving Marianne aching for sex, Rod zipped his jeans up and told her to compose herself. 'You'll come and see me again, do you understand?' he said firmly.

'Yes, I'll come and see you again,' she replied.

'Tomorrow morning, come here tomorrow morning and I'll fuck you, Marianne.'

Clicking his fingers, he stood up to answer the door. 'Sorry about this,' he smiled as the bell rang again. 'I forgot that a friend was coming to see me.'

'Oh, that's all right,' Marianne smiled as she climbed

to her feet. 'I'd better be going, anyway.'

Seeing her out through the back door, Rod eyed her shapely thighs as she wandered down the garden path. 'We'll meet again, I hope!' he called as the doorbell rang once more.

'I expect so!' she replied, opening the gate and escaping into the park, her vagina urgent in its craving for satisfaction.

Another conquest, she mused, wandering back to the bench. The evening breeze cooling her swollen vaginal lips, she sat down, gazing at the ducks drifting around the pond. *I've got an evening of sex to endure,* she thought, wondering what Barry had constructed, what hideously beautiful device he intended to use on her young body.

Unaware of the time, she relaxed in the early-evening sun, contemplating her new way of life, her blatant debauchery, her trickery. Whichever way her relationship with Barry went didn't matter now that she'd found Rod. *Sod Barry!* Closing her eyes, picturing the stranger licking between her legs, she fell asleep – her body exhausted, her mind awash with sex.

Finally arriving home at ten, Marianne found Barry in the lounge. 'Where the hell have you been?' he asked angrily, looking up from his armchair. 'I was worried about you!'

Worried about your ruined evening, more than likely! she thought, sitting on the sofa.

'Well, where *have* you been?'

'Walking,' she replied, her thoughts swirling with images of Rod, her secret master.

'Bloody hell, Marianne! You could have told me that you were going out! Jill and her friend came round to see you. They were very upset!'

'Were they? Oh well, there's always tomorrow evening.'

'That's not the point! You can't invite friends round and then go off out! What took you so long?'

She suddenly realized that, if the word worked and Barry

sent her into a hypnotic trance, she would reveal her clandestine relationship and ruin everything. Thinking quickly, she smiled.

'Actually, I ran into a girl I was at school with. We had a drink, chatting about the old days, and I completely lost track of the time.'

'Oh, I see. Well, you'd better apologize to Jill.'

'Yes, I'll ring her in the morning. So, how was your client?'

'Client? Oh, yes. Er . . . I didn't bother in the end. I was worrying about you so . . .'

'You don't have to worry about me, Barry! Anyway, I'm going to bed – I don't feel too well.'

'I'll come up, too.'

'No, let me get to sleep first. I feel awful!'

Climbing the stairs, praying that Barry wouldn't follow and force her to endure hours of perverted sex, Marianne slipped her clothes off and climbed under the quilt. Closing her eyes, her fingers toying between her full vaginal lips, she fell into a deep sleep, dreaming about her conquests – and her future exploits.

Chapter Five

Barry had left the house by the time Marianne half-opened her eyes, her naked body stirring as another day began. Thanking God that he'd gone, she checked the time – nine–thirty. What would today bring? she wondered as she climbed out of bed and drew the curtains. What indeed?

Slipping into her dressing gown as she descended the stairs, her heart leaped as the doorbell rang. Pulling her gown tightly across her firm breasts, praying that it wasn't John calling for early-morning sex, she opened the front door.

'Oh, hi, Natalie!' she greeted her young neighbour. 'Come in!'

'Thanks. I haven't seen you since you got back from the hypnosis course and I was wondering how you got on?'

'Come through, I'll put the kettle on and tell you all about it,' Marianne replied, leading the girl into the kitchen.

Sitting at the table, Natalie rested her chin on her fist, gazing at Marianne in anticipation. Her blonde bob framing her pretty face, her full red lips curling into a smile, her blue eyes sparkling, she urged Marianne to tell her everything.

'I've gone and done something very silly,' Marianne confessed, switching the kettle on and joining her friend at the table.

'Really?'

'Yes, really. I got back from the course and . . . I failed, by the way!'

'That's a shame! All that money wasted!'

'It's all right – it was Barry's money! Anyway, I pretended that the lecturer had implanted a trigger word in my subconscious. It was a joke, just a bit of fun I thought I'd have with Barry, that's all. But the whole thing's got completely out of hand. Barry's friend John came round the other evening. Like a fool, Barry went and blurted out the word to show John how easily I could be hypnotized.'

'What did he get you to do, jump up and down on one foot?' Natalie laughed.

'No, but I wish he had! Anyway, Barry had a phone call and had to go out to see a client. John was finishing his coffee and . . . John said the trigger word.'

'God! What happened?'

'Not wanting to spoil the game I'd started with Barry, I faked a hypnotic trance. And then . . . well, John told me to take my clothes off.'

'You didn't strip off in front of him, did you?'

'Yes. But there's more – I allowed him to have sex with me.'

'My God! You should have told him to bugger off!'

'No! He'd have told Barry that I was conning him, don't you see?'

'Yes, I do, but . . . being unfaithful to Barry just for the sake of a silly game is ridiculous!'

'That was nothing! I did something far worse than that. I had sex with two girls.'

'Two girls?' Natalie gasped. 'Why? Are you a . . .'

'No, I'm not a lezzie! This girl, Jill, a lesbian friend of mine, would have told Barry that I'd been fooling him.'

'So what? You can't go around having sex with people

just to keep a ridiculous game going with Barry!'

'I realize that! I suppose, with Jill and her friend, I was intrigued. You see, I was completely innocent, in their eyes, anyway. It was strange, being ordered about, being told to do this and that. I quite enjoyed the game, it was fun. Anyway, that was my first lesbian experience and I . . .'

'You call that fun? Did you enjoy having sex with two girls, then?'

'No, not really. Well, I suppose it was . . . The thing is, I've also had sex with a man I met in the park,' Marianne confessed, wondering why she was telling her neighbour her most intimate secrets.

'What, a stranger?'

'Yes. Actually, I didn't have full sex with him – he used the trigger word and got me to masturbate in front of him.'

'You're mad, Marianne! I've never heard anything so . . . You must come clean, tell Barry that you were conning him! And as for the man in the park! Why tell a stranger about the trigger word?'

'I fancied him.'

'What, so every man you fancy, or girl, for that matter, you have sex with before you've even got to know them?'

'No, it wasn't like that!'

'Then what *was* it like?'

'I'm not telling you all this just so that you can condemn me, Natalie! Anyway, I can't tell Barry the truth because he'd know that I'd had sex with John and that I'd been completely aware of what I was doing – I'd be admitting infidelity!'

'Does Barry know that you and John . . .'

'Does he know? Christ! Barry set it up!'

'Set it up? Bloody hell, this is crazy!'

'You're telling me! I want to leave Barry but there's the house, the furniture and everything. I've discovered the horrifying extent of his evil side. Thinking that I was under hypnosis, he told me about his plans, plans to sell me to men for sex, to earn money by prostituting me.'

'Barry? I can't believe that!'

'It's funny how you think you know people, and then you discover that you don't know them at all! It's also funny how you think you know yourself and then . . .'

'I'm stunned, Marianne – completely stunned!'

'There's more, I'm afraid!' Marianne sighed. 'There's another reason that I have to leave Barry. The word – he used it a couple of times and . . . and it actually worked.'

'It can't have done!'

'Well, it did! I lost all control over my body, my actions.'

'Autosuggestion, that's probably what it was. I've read quite a bit about self-hypnosis.'

'Whatever it was, what the hell do I do now?'

'God only knows! Why are you telling *me* all this, anyway?'

'I suppose I needed to talk to someone, someone I know and trust.'

'You needn't worry about me hypnotizing you and having sex with you! *I'm* not a lesbian!'

'I didn't think I was that way . . . I know you're not a lesbian, Natalie!'

Leaving the table and pouring the coffee, Marianne wondered whether it had been a good idea to confess to Natalie. But she'd needed to tell someone, to ask someone for help with the terrible mess she'd got herself into.

'Had Barry not used the word to prove to John that it worked, none of this would have happened!' Marianne groaned. 'He made me lift my skirt and pull my panties down to prove that I was hypnotized!'

'He should never have done that!'

'No, and he should never have set me up with John! And

I should never have played the bloody stupid game in the first place!'

'I'll tell you what to do. Leave Barry, which you're going to do anyway, and tell your girlfriends that . . .'

'I can't reveal that I was conning them! I don't want people thinking that I'm a lezzie, that I was a willing participant!'

'But you were!'

'Yes, but no one knows that! Anyway, how can I tell Barry that I'm leaving him, that I'm just up and going without a reason – and taking my share of the house with me? If he knew that I'd deliberately been unfaithful, he'd do his utmost to make sure that I don't get a penny from the house! What the hell can I do?'

'I don't know, Marianne – I honestly don't! What's the trigger word?'

'I can't tell you. Too many people know as it is!'

'You can trust me, Marianne!'

'Yes, but what if you told Ian about it and he . . .'

'My husband wouldn't . . .'

'Wouldn't he? As I said, you think you know people, and then you discover that you don't know them at all!'

'But Ian wouldn't . . . God, you've got *me* thinking now! I'd love to pretend to have a trigger word and have some fun with him!'

'No, you wouldn't. We all have a darker side, Natalie. Ian might have secrets, things you're better off knowing nothing about.'

'I'm sure he hasn't!'

'Think about this. Is there anything you'd rather he didn't know about you, about your past?'

'No, nothing! Well . . . I've never told anyone this before but . . . There was a friend of Ian's who helped us move into the house just before we were married. He . . . let's just say that I see your point.'

'You had an affair?'

'No, not an affair, exactly. Ian had to go away for a week, a sales conference, and I went and did something I've regretted ever since. I had sex with his friend.'

'There you are, then! Ian might have been having sex with someone while you were screwing his friend, so I wouldn't feel too guilty about it!'

Natalie's face dropped as the horrifying thought sunk in. It had never crossed her mind that Ian might have been unfaithful. Her own guilt was bad enough, let alone the thought that he might have been sleeping with another woman in his hotel room!

'I suppose you can't trust anyone, not one hundred per cent, anyway,' Natalie reflected. 'But this is incredible, Marianne! The things you've done are . . .'

'Yes, yes, I know! But what I don't know is what the hell to do! I've nowhere to go. Well, apart from . . . But worse than that is the fact that I'm beginning to enjoy sex with different people!'

'God, you need help! Why not get onto the course lecturer and tell him what's happened?'

'He'd probably use the trigger word and screw me!'

'No, he wouldn't! I could always come with you.'

'Yes, and he'd use hypnosis and screw *you*!'

'Not if he's a professional man, he wouldn't!'

'He's a *man*, Natalie!'

'Yes, I suppose he is. We've got a spare room if you need somewhere to stay for a while.'

'Thanks, but no. I'll work something out. The only real problem is Barry bringing men home to screw me. If the trigger word works, I'll have no power to . . . I might go and stay with my mother for a few weeks.'

'Look, I really must be going,' Natalie sighed as she walked to the door. 'We'll talk about this again, Marianne, when I've more time – I've got an appointment with the hairdresser this morning. Thanks for the coffee. And don't worry! I'm only next door so, if you need help, just shout.'

'Thanks, Natalie,' Marianne smiled, opening the front door and seeing the girl out, eyeing her slender thighs, her short skirt. 'I'll keep you posted, OK?'

'Yes, you do that!'

'By the way, the word is *juxtaposition*,' Marianne enlightened her, gazing at her rounded breasts, her nipples pressing through her tight T-shirt.

'I thought you weren't going to tell me?' Natalie grinned as she turned and walked down the path.

'I trust you! Bye!'

Grabbing the Christmas candle from the cupboard and wandering out into the back garden, Marianne sat on a patio chair and opened her gown. The sun warming her young body, her pert breasts, she relaxed. Her fingers toying with her hairless pussy lips, her stirring clitoris, she eased the huge candle deep into her moistening vaginal sheath.

The sensations permeating her quivering pelvis, she slowly slipped the wet candle in and out of her tight pussy, imagining Natalie naked. Massaging her swelling clitoris with her fingertips, she closed her eyes, wishing she'd grabbed the vibrator from the bedroom – wishing Natalie had used the trigger word.

Pondering on the dreadful situation she was in, she wondered again what to do. Her clitoris, now awake after many virtually dormant years, would demand her attention daily, she knew. Her entire body had awoken, her nipples become alive, her vagina insatiable in its yearning for tongues, fingers, candles – penises.

As her clitoris throbbed slightly, sending a quiver up her spine, she thought of Rod, wondering whether to take a stroll through the park and visit him. But no, before she did anything, she had to conceive a plan. Her fingers leaving her clitoris, her hands by her sides, she wallowed in the beautiful sensations the massive candle was bringing her.

'Juxtaposition!' Barry's voice bellowed from the open back door. Her heart racing, Marianne lay still. *Pretend to be sleeping,* she thought, slowly closing her thighs to conceal the candle. 'Marianne, are you sleeping?' Barry asked as he stood before her. 'Juxtaposition!' he repeated. 'I don't know if it's worked or not, Dave – I'm not sure whether she's asleep or in a trance,' Barry said, shocking Marianne.

'She's got a beautiful pair of tits!' his friend laughed.

'She's got a beautiful cunt, too! Let's see if the word has worked. Marianne, open your legs and show Dave your shaved cunt.'

Her heart pounding, banging hard against her chest, her hands trembling, Marianne froze. Barry would realize that she was sleeping and wake her up, she was sure, but what could she do? *The whole thing has gone too far!* she thought, glad that the trigger word hadn't really worked and that she was still in control of her actions.

'Wake up, Marianne!' Barry ordered irritably, shaking her shoulder. Stirring, she opened her eyes and pulled her gown over her young breasts. 'This is Dave,' Barry introduced, turning to the young man by his side.

'Oh, hi! I'm sorry, I was sleeping. Er . . . want some coffee?' Marianne asked, rising to her feet.

'No, there's no time for coffee,' Barry grinned, winking at his friend. 'I've brought Dave round to show him something,' he added. 'Something special!'

Standing with her thighs squeezed together to keep the

candle in place, Marianne tried to formulate a plan. Was Dave the first of many paying customers? she wondered, eyeing his tight blue jeans. Or did Barry merely want to show him the power he had over his girlfriend?

Scrutinizing the young man, Marianne smiled. He was tall with dark hair and deep-set eyes. In his early twenties, clean-shaven and masculine, he'd make a good catch! *Not bad-looking at all!* she mused.

'Juxtaposition!' Barry said loudly. Motionless, Marianne waited in anticipation, praying that the phone would ring or that someone would call round. Her thoughts swirling, she wanted the young man to use her for sex, but her conscience nagged her. This was wrong, she knew, but her arousal was beginning to win the battle raging in her racked mind.

'Right, she's all yours,' Barry quipped, turning to the young man.

'I can't believe this!' Dave laughed, reaching for his wallet. 'I've never seen anything like it!'

'Believe it or not, she's completely under your control! You can do what you like with her. Order her to . . . well, I'm sure you have a good enough imagination!'

'Better than good enough! God, just think – a beautiful young girl who'll do anything I ask of her!'

'You're right there – she'll do absolutely anything!'

'This is too good to be true! There's fifty, as agreed.'

'Thanks, Dave. I'll slip this under the floorboards along with my mags and see you later.'

Watching the money change hands, Marianne's stomach somersaulted, her clitoris stirred, her vagina tightened around the candle. Wasn't Barry going to watch? she wondered as he walked to the back door.

'Enjoy yourself!' he called, stepping into the kitchen.

'I will! Believe me – I bloody well will!' Dave replied

enthusiastically. 'Now, Marianne, I'm going to enjoy an hour or so with you, with your beautiful shaved cunt and your lovely tits! This is a secluded garden, so let's start with you taking your dressing gown off.'

Hearing the front door slam shut, Marianne swore to get her own back on Barry. To leave her alone and vulnerable with another man was despicable! she thought. And to take fifty pounds from him, to sell her to another man for sex, was sickening! But, she consoled herself, she was still in control. Although there was little point in being in control if she could do nothing to stop Dave from using her! The only way was to make out that the word hadn't worked, to begin moving about, asking where Barry had got to and . . . But did she really want to put an end to the game?

'Come on, take your gown off!' Dave instructed. 'I've paid good money for you, and I want my money's worth! Barry tells me that I'm the first to pay him for using you. He also told me that he's lined up several other men. He should do well at fifty quid a time!'

The horrifying words resounding through her mind, Marianne opened her gown and slipped it off her shoulders. If she were to have sex with a stranger for fifty pounds, then she'd take the money from Barry's hiding place – the money *she*'d earned, she decided. At least she'd discovered where the dirty magazines were. *Beneath the floorboards in which room?* she wondered as Dave knelt before her, scrutinizing her naked body.

'You've a nice cunt!' Dave praised, parting her swollen pussy lips, exposing her distended inner petals. 'I love shaved cunts – you can see all a girl has between her legs when there's no . . . Christ!' he exclaimed. 'What's this?'

Slipping the candle from her tight vagina, he examined the wet waxen shaft, grinning as he looked up between her elongated nipples at her pretty face. 'Been having a quick frig-off in the garden, then?' he laughed. Remaining silent, Marianne decided not to say one word, no matter what he did or said. 'Fancy that! You've been bringing yourself off with a bloody great candle!'

The incredible situation sending electrifying sensations of lewd sex through her naked body, she began to relax. Looking down at the stranger kneeling before her naked body, examining the glistening flesh between her inflamed vaginal lips, sent a quiver up her spine, a bolt of desire through her young womb. This was so wrong – so wonderfully wrong!

Kissing her soft mound, Dave breathed in her girl-scent. 'Mmm, you taste nice!' he said, licking the length of her open sex-groove. 'Worth every penny, in fact!' he added, slipping two fingers between her swollen labia and easing them into the heat of her saturated vagina.

Her legs weakening, Marianne sighed as her master drove his fingers deeper into her tightening sex-duct, stretching her creamy sheath wide open as he massaged her inner flesh. Her clitoris swelling beneath his lapping tongue, she found herself longing for his cock. *Will he get me to suck him and swallow his sperm?* she wondered. *Or will he fuck me?*

'Barry's a lucky man, having a sex slave!' Dave remarked. 'Mind you, I wouldn't sell someone as beautiful as you to another man! Still, that's Barry, I suppose. He's had so many girls on the side, behind your back, that I'm surprised you've never caught him out!'

Her stomach churning, her heart sinking, Marianne was discovering even more about Barry the bastard. *So many girls on the side, behind your back . . .* The stunning revelation haunting her, she swore to get Barry out of her life, to get as far away from him as possible.

Rod, she mused as Dave slipped a third finger into her hot love-mouth, opening her girl-flesh further, fully exposing her erect clitoris to his snaking tongue. *Rod would have me live with him, given half the chance, I'm sure!* But would he use her as Barry had? Would Rod use her as . . . Rod had already used her!

'OK!' Dave said eagerly, slipping his wet fingers from the girl's vagina and sucking her juices from them as he stood up. 'For your first trick, I want you to get on all fours, on the grass, and stick your bum high in the air.'

Following her master's instructions, Marianne felt a pang of desire course through her quivering pelvis as she took her position on the lawn. Kneeling behind her, Dave parted her taut bum-cheeks, peering at her small hole nestling above her distended vaginal lips. Her body open, blatantly on display to a stranger, she was overwhelmed by a terrific sense of corruption – evil. She desired anything and everything in the name of cold sex. *The more perverted, the better!* she found herself thinking as Dave toyed with her anal entrance.

'Very nice!' he praised, yanking her buttocks further apart and gently sliding two fingers deep into her tight bottom-sheath. 'There's nothing I like more than fucking a young girl's tight bum-hole!'

Resting her head on the grass, projecting her rump up further, Marianne breathed deeply as the lewd sensations emanated from deep within her hot rectum, slowly creeping over her tingling flesh, stiffening her clitoris. Hearing his zip open as Dave slipped his fingers from her tightening hole, she grinned. She knew nothing about the man, she'd never even seen his penis, and yet he was about to drive the organ concerned deep into her most private portal and fuck her there – fill her bowels with his gushing sperm.

The thought exciting her beyond belief as she recalled the money changing hands, she waited for the anal fucking to begin. Taking the money from Barry's hiding place would cause him to suspect her, but he could do nothing, say nothing. *The tables will turn yet!* she mused as Dave's bulbous knob stabbed at her brown hole.

Pressing his solid knob against her sensitive portal, he managed to drive the head past her defeated muscles and into the fiery heat of her accommodating rectum. 'Ah, God!' he gasped. 'God, you're tight!' He drove his knob further into her hot bottom-sheath, opening her, filling her with his rock-hard organ until he'd impaled her completely.

Manoeuvring her head, Marianne gazed between her firm breasts at her master's huge balls as he gently withdrew his organ and pushed it home again into the forbidden depths of her anal cavern. Swinging, gently slapping her bloated pussy lips with his slow fucking motions, the sight of his heavy balls excited her.

She craved sex now, sex with anyone and everyone – male and female! – she reflected. But her bottom-hole was her new-found pleasure centre, bringing her a certain lewdness, a perversity, that she relished in. The beautiful experience of a massive penis driving deep within her hot bum-hole delighting her, she imagined Jill positioning her open vagina beneath her face, begging for Marianne to lick her cunt as Dave fucked her from behind. *God, there's so much more to experience!* she mused, picturing Jill's open cunt, her dripping sex-folds, her erect clitoris throbbing in orgasm.

Imagining Barry slipping his penis into her mouth and demanding her to suck as Dave shafted her bum-hole, Marianne quivered. *Three men, three hard cocks!* she thought in her ever-rising arousal – her ever-deepening depravity. *Three or four men – and two girls!* The immoral picture forming in her mind as Dave began thrusting with a vengeance, Marianne closed her eyes, revelling in the obscenity of her forbidden coupling.

Recalling the old Marianne, the Marianne who would never dream of even looking at another man, let alone allowing a stranger to slip his penis into her anal-tube, she wondered, yet again, at her incredible transformation. *Perhaps all women harbour a nymphomaniac deep within their subconscious,* she thought. All men were perverts – she'd learned that much! – she reflected as Dave quickened his rhythm.

'God, this is heaven!' he cried, grabbing her hips and shafting her for all he was worth. Her naked body jolting, her sensitive nipples brushing against the grass, heightening her arousal, she wondered what vulgar act her master would instruct her to commit next.

'Coming!' Dave suddenly gasped as his penis swelled, stretching her tight arse open further. Driving his throbbing knob deep into her rectal sheath, rocking her young body, he fucked her as hard as he could, taking her ever-closer to her own climax. His sperm jetting, lubricating the illicit union, Marianne grimaced as her neglected clitoris swelled and throbbed. Reaching between her open thighs, she massaged an exquisite orgasm from her pleasure-bud, gasping as the electrifying sensations shook her naked body.

Her cuntal sheath void, yearning to grip on the candle, Marianne imagined two penises thrusting into her young holes, fucking her, pumping her full of sperm. The picture forming in her mind, sustaining her orgasm, she rubbed her clitoris harder, faster, as Dave thrust his last thrust and stilled his trembling body.

His penis absorbing the inner heat of her bowels, he lay panting over her back as she brought out the last tremors of orgasm from her solid clitoris. Finally slowing her masturbating rhythm, she sensed his penis shrinking within her anal sheath. *Two cocks!* she thought, picturing the massive members driving into her inflamed holes. *Three cocks!* she laughed inwardly, her taste buds rousing at the thought of salty sperm gushing into her mouth, bathing her tongue.

Slipping his spent penis from her quivering body, Dave sat back on his heels, gazing at his slave's inflamed anal ring, the sperm oozing, running down her bottom-crease to her open vaginal entrance. Feeling uncomfortable with her face pressed against the grass, Marianne awaited her next instruction, wondering whether her master was into spanking or not.

'Roll over and lie on your back,' he instructed her as he stood up. Wondering what he was up to as he walked across the lawn to the garage, Marianne lay beneath the hot morning sun, her limbs spread, her hairless pussy lips swelling, her vaginal juices flowing.

Returning from the garage clutching several lengths of rope, a mallet and four short pieces of wood, Dave settled on the grass beside Marianne, grinning wickedly. Hammering the lengths of wood into the ground, he spread her limbs further and bound her wrists and ankles to the stakes. Her arms outstretched above her head, her legs wide, her naked body was totally defenceless, vulnerable to his every perverted whim.

Slipping his jeans off, Dave moved between Marianne's thighs, stabbing his once more solid knob between her gaping vaginal lips. 'Ah, that's good!' he murmured as his shaft drove deep into her tight, wet vagina. 'You're a bloody good fuck!'

Shafting her young body, ramming her cervix with his pistoning glans, he gazed longingly at her firm, rounded breasts, her elongated nipples. 'I've a surprise for you!' he gasped. 'A nice surprise in a minute!' Marianne felt her clitoris throb as her master leaned over her and sucked her nipple into his hot mouth. Biting her brown milk bud, thrusting deep into her spasming vagina, she knew he was near to his second climax as her clitoris swelled against his massaging shaft. Wondering what he had in store for her as he bit harder on her nipple, she gasped as he suddenly withdrew his penis and knelt astride her breasts.

Positioning his girl-wet glistening shaft in her cleavage, he squashed her pert breasts together, crushing his hard penis. Rocking his hips, his wet organ sliding between her warm mammary spheres, his sperm jetted, spraying her neck, her chin. Lifting her head, Marianne opened her mouth, gasping at the sight of his purple glans throbbing in orgasm. Catching the male come with her tongue, she swallowed, licking her lips, savouring the salty liquid, praying that he'd move closer and thrust his knob deep into her hungry mouth.

Sensing her yearning, he moved up her body and pushed his jetting glans into her hot mouth. Closing her lips around her prize, Marianne licked and sucked, swallowing the last of his orgasmic spend as her master gasped and shuddered in his ecstasy. Running her tongue around his glans, Marianne prayed that he'd suck her clitoris into his mouth and bring her to her desperately needed climax. She craved orgasm now, the relief of sexual satisfaction, and almost begged him to masturbate her to a beautiful climax.

Withdrawing his penis, he sat beside his slave, admiring her breasts, gazing at his sperm glistening in the sunlight as it trickled down her chin, her neck. 'I expect you'd like to come,' he said, slipping his finger into her drenched pussy-hole and dragging her juices up her sex valley. Massaging her clitoris, stiffening her budlette, he grinned as she began to gasp. 'You want to come, don't you?' he asked, rubbing her erect nodule faster. 'You want your cunt to spew out your girlie-come and your clitty to pulsate with orgasms, don't you?' His words exciting her, taking her even closer to the summit of her sexual pleasure, she quivered, tossing her head from side to side as her tethered body became rigid with sex.

As her orgasms rose from her quivering womb and erupted in her throbbing clitoris, Marianne cried out, wailing as the waves of pure sexual ecstasy rolled through her tethered body, bathing her mind with lust. On and on the incredible waves crashed through her trembling flesh, bringing her the desperately needed sexual relief she craved.

'Don't stop!' she cried involuntarily. 'Please, don't stop!' Massaging faster, bringing out her pleasure, he grinned, gazing at her flushed face, her gasping mouth.

'Worth every penny!' he laughed as her climax began to decline, leaving her quivering, panting. 'I'll be back for more – once a week, I think!'

Her long blonde hair veiling the satisfaction on her pretty face, her nipples erect, aching to be sucked, her areolae a deep brown, Marianne lay staked to the ground in the wake of her beautifully enforced multiple orgasm. But she wanted more more anal intercourse, more orgasms. She craved to be spanked, to have her taut buttocks whipped, her young body abused again and again.

Releasing her naked body – to Marianne's disappointment – Dave ordered her to get up and slip into her dressing gown. Buckling his jeans, he cleared away the evidence of bondage, storing the stakes and rope in the garage for his next visit. Seating her on the patio chair, he slipped into the kitchen, clicking his fingers and ordering her to wake up before dashing through the hall and making his escape through the front door.

Wandering into the house, her neck still wet with her master's sperm, Marianne took a flannel from the bathroom and cleansed herself, saddened that her exquisite sexual ordeal was over so soon. *But he'll be back!* she thought happily, drying her chin with a towel. *He'll be back for more and more! Hmm . . . under the floorboards*, she mused, grinning as she thought of grabbing the fifty pounds she'd earned. With fitted carpets throughout the house, she wondered where to start. *I can't rip the carpets up!* she thought, wandering downstairs to the kitchen.

The kitchen floor looked promising, she decided, peeling a corner of the cushion flooring away from the wall. Discovering two loose boards, she grabbed a knife and prised them up. Her eyes smiling as she peered down the hole, she pulled out several magazines and a metal cash box. Placing her find on the table, she sat down, opening the box to take her hard-earned wages.

'Five hundred pounds!' she gasped, counting out the crisp notes. 'That'll do nicely!' Flicking through the magazines, she was disgusted, and simultaneously highly aroused, by the sight of three naked men with their penises firmly implanted in a young girl's orifices – her mouth, her vagina, her rectal sheath. Turning the page, she scrutinized the glossy, close-up photograph of a girl squatting over a man with his penis embedded in her vagina. Another man crouching low behind her had driven his solid member deep into her anal sheath, filling the girl's pelvic cavity.

Her womb fluttering at the obscene sight, Marianne prayed that she'd be 'hypnotized' and forced to endure such an incredible experience. 'Five hundred pounds!' she breathed, returning the magazines and replacing the boards. Stuffing the money into her dressing gown pocket, she wondered what Barry would think, what he'd do when he discovered the theft. 'That's his problem!' she laughed, climbing the stairs.

After a shower, Marianne dressed in her tight miniskirt and T-shirt, wondering how to spend the rest of the day as she made herself a ham salad. *Better not go on a shopping spree!* she mused, slipping the money into her bag as the phone rang.

'Hallo,' Marianne said, brushing her hair back and pressing the receiver to her ear.

'Marianne, it's me – Jonathan Brooke-Smith.'

'Oh, hi, Jonathan!'

'I was wondering whether you'd given any consideration to my proposal?'

'Er . . . Actually, I've been rather busy so . . .'

'Do you have a car?'

'A car? Er . . . Barry has but I haven't.'

'There you are, then! A Mercedes, how does that sound?'

'It sounds great but . . .'

'Come over to my offices now and we'll talk about money.'

'Well, I . . . I really don't know.'

'I'll send a cab to get you – about ten minutes, OK?'

'Yes, all right.'

'See you soon, then.'

'OK.'

Replacing the receiver, Marianne's heart leaped. *A Mercedes!* she thought, imagining Barry's face when she told him the news. But Brooke-Smith would want more than a personal assistant in return for a car like that, she was well aware.

Slipping her panties off, she grabbed her bag and waited outside the house for the cab to arrive. The breeze cooling her naked vaginal lips, she grinned, picturing herself taking dictation with her pussy-crack on display. Brooke-Smith would enjoy fucking her shaved pussy as she lay across his desk! Her juices coursing down her naked thighs, her stomach somersaulted as she pictured herself being screwed to orgasm by her boss.

The cab journey only took ten minutes. Marianne looked up at the huge office block. *Quite a set-up!* she thought as she walked across the car park and entered the building. Asking the receptionist to tell Brooke-Smith that she'd arrived, she couldn't believe that he owned such a business. *Plenty of money!* she thought happily.

Lifting a phone, the receptionist announced Marianne's arrival. 'Please take a seat,' she said, replacing the phone. 'Mr Brooke-Smith will be down in a minute.' Making herself comfortable in a huge armchair, Marianne thought of Barry, wondering what he'd say if he knew that she was visiting Brooke-Smith – knickerless!

Wearing a pin-striped suit, pale blue shirt and old school tie, Brooke-Smith walked over to Marianne. Grinning, his hand outstretched as she rose to her feet, he eyed her firm breasts ballooning her tight top. 'This way,' he said warmly, taking her hand and leading her through a door. Climbing the stairs, aware of her naked pussy, Marianne followed her potential boss, her potential master, to his office.

'A drink?' he asked, closing the door behind her.

'Thank you,' she replied, looking around the huge room. 'You have a very nice office,' she said admiringly, gazing at the expensive furnishing. 'More like a lounge!'

'Spending most of my life in this room, it's nice to have pleasant surroundings. Sit down,' he invited, waving his hand at a leather Chesterfield. 'There you are,' he smiled. 'Vodka and lime – that is right, isn't it?'

'Yes, you have a good memory!'

'And you have a very beautiful body, if you don't mind me saying so,' he complimented her, his gaze transfixed by her shapely thighs.

If only he knew the word! she thought as she sipped her drink. 'You're very flattering, Jonathan!' she giggled, her blue eyes sparkling.

'No, I mean it! Marianne, Barry came to see me this

morning,' he enlightened her as he sat beside her. 'Things aren't good between you two, are they?'

'Er... Well...'

'I probably shouldn't say anything, but I can see that you're not happy.'

'I'm happy enough, I suppose.'

'When I came to dinner, I told you that I was married. Actually, I'm divorced.'

'Why are you telling *me?*' she asked, aware of her clitoris swelling, her vaginal juices flowing as she parted her thighs a little.

'I don't want you thinking that I'm... Anyway, as I said, Barry came to see me. He was talking about you, Marianne. I know that he's always after contracts, but I would never have imagined that he'd go so far as to... He offered me an hour with you in exchange for...'

'Yes, I thought he'd do that before long!' she sighed.

'So, you know what he's been doing?'

'Yes, I know *exactly* what he's been doing.'

'Do you know that he's been using your trigger word?' he asked.

'There *is* no trigger word,' she confessed. 'The whole thing started as a joke. I led Barry to believe that there was a word that would send me into a hypnotic trance every time I heard it. I thought it would be fun! But, it seems, Barry has things other than fun planned for me!'

'So, you've been fooling him all the time?'

'Yes, I have.'

'But he told me that you'd been with another man, and with two girls, and that...'

'I can't explain it all, it's far too complicated. The reason I did what I did was because I didn't want Barry to discover that I'd conned him. If he ever finds out that I was fully aware of what I was doing, that I cheated on him . . .'

'I won't tell him, if that's what you're thinking! Look, Marianne, I don't offer contracts to companies in return for sex! What Barry proposed is . . . well, it's not the way I do things – it's not the way I work. Not that I'm saying that I don't find you sexually attractive, because I do – very much so!'

'Why didn't you use the trigger word and . . .'

'As I said, it's not the way I work. I might be a ruthless businessman, but I don't *use* people, young women!'

'It's nice to know that there are some decent men around!' she smiled, somewhat disappointed that he wasn't going to use her for cold sex. 'Why are you so desperate for me to work for you?'

'Because I like you very much, I find you sexually attractive and . . .'

'But you're contradicting yourself, surely?'

'Why do you say that?'

'Because, on the one hand you're saying that you don't use people, and on the other hand you want me to work for you because you're sexually attracted to me! Don't you want me to work for you because I have the capability, the skills you require?'

'Yes, I do. But that doesn't mean to say that . . . Look, Marianne, I'll be honest with you. I've known Barry for some time – and Saunders, his boss. Barry is about to get the big E – he's about to lose his job and I . . .'

'Lose his job! But why?'

'I don't know the ins and outs of it. Anyway, I don't want to see you suffer because Barry's out of work.'

'I'm suffering already, what with the way he's using me!'

'Yes, that's what I mean! Anyway, I don't know why you're so worried about cheating on him – he has one affair after another. He's used you all along, Marianne. I shouldn't be telling you this, but when we met the other evening and I saw your . . . when I noticed that you weren't wearing any knickers, I knew that Barry had put you up to it to help him secure the contract.'

Her face flushing, Marianne closed her thighs, wondering what else Brooke-Smith knew about Barry. But she was to blame, she reflected. She'd deliberately flashed her pussy, delighted in exposing her feminine intimacy to Brooke-Smith.

'It's not all Barry's fault,' she sighed. 'I knew full well what I was doing, so I'm as much to blame. Anyway, I know that he's been having affairs, someone told me all about Barry when they thought I was under . . . The whole thing's ridiculous! I wish I'd never played the stupid games, I wish I'd never invented a trigger word!'

'But you wouldn't have discovered that Barry had been . . .'

'That's true. The thing is, I can't walk out on Barry. We own the house jointly, and the furniture, and if he discovered that I'd been with men, and girls, with my eyes wide open, so to speak, he'd . . .'

'You'll have to do something! Unless you want to carry on the way things are.'

'I don't know what I want. You see, I've changed, Jonathan. I'm not the person I used to be. I enjoy . . . well, let's just say that I've discovered another side to me, as well as another side to Barry!'

'You're happy with the way things are, then?'

'I wouldn't say I'm happy. Anyway, about the job – I'll need time to think it over. Until I decide what I'm going to do with my life, I can't really give you an answer.'

'Fair enough. I'm glad you came, Marianne. I'm pleased that we've talked about this, about Barry.'

'Yes, so am I. Thanks for the drink. I'll . . .'

'Let me get you a cab.'

'No, no, I'll walk – it's not far,' she smiled, rising to her feet.

Shaking his hand as he stood before her, Marianne left the office and made her way outside, wondering about Brooke-Smith – and why Barry was going to get his marching orders from Saunders. But Barry had already said that he was thinking about giving his job up, so he probably wouldn't be bothered – especially as he thought he had Marianne's illicit earnings to live on!

Walking through the park, Marianne sat by the pond, gazing across the expanse of freshly-mown grass to Rod's house. Contemplating her ever-changing life, she thought about Rod, wishing she'd never mentioned the trigger word to him. *There's no chance of a proper relationship there!* she mused sadly, deciding not to visit him that day as he'd asked her to. *Maybe tomorrow, I don't know.*

Turning her thoughts to Brooke-Smith again, she couldn't work him out. *Why on earth tell me all about Barry?* she wondered. *And why not use the trigger word?* There was more to Brooke-Smith's job offer than met the eye, she thought, wishing she hadn't confessed, told him of her trickery. He was probably trying to gain her confidence – get Barry out of her life and move in, ease his way into her life and . . . 'Sod them all!' she sighed. 'I'm making money from prostitution, and I don't care!'

Leaping to her feet, Marianne made her way home. Whatever the trigger word had or hadn't done, she'd had her eyes opened, realized not only the beautiful sensations her body had to offer but the money she could earn. 'No, I won't leave Barry!' she asserted. 'He thinks he's using me, but *I'm* using *him*!'

Walking down the street, she felt happy, happier than she had for a long time. Her amazing transformation was complete, she thought. The old Marianne was no longer. *Out with the old, in with the new!*

Ringing Jill the minute she arrived home, Marianne decided to invite her round for the evening – and Lydia. 'Sorry about last night,' Marianne began as Jill answered. 'I was held up and couldn't get to a phone.'

'That's OK. We chatted to Barry for a while and then went to a pub for a drink so the evening was all right.'

'What about this evening? Come round this evening.'

'All right, I'll do that. Will Barry be there?'

'Why do you ask?'

'I . . . I just wondered.'

'I think he'll be going out. Yes, in fact, he did say this morning that he'd be out until quite late tonight,' Marianne lied, knowing that Barry would pretend to go out and then hide in the dining room.

'Oh, good!' Jill replied excitedly. 'Er . . . what I mean is, it's good that us girls will be alone together.'

'Yes, it is. Anyway, about seven, if that's OK?'

'Yes – see you at seven. I'll bring Lydia.'

'Oh, right. Yes, bring Lydia. OK, Jill, I'll look forward to it. Bye!'

Replacing the receiver, Marianne sat in the lounge imagining Jill and Lydia ordering her to strip. Picturing Lydia enjoying thrashing her taut buttocks, a quiver running up her spine, Marianne grinned. 'Not a bad day, so far! Five hundred pounds, the offer of a Mercedes, sex on the lawn with young Dave – and Barry's losing his job! Not a bad day at all!'

Again, her thoughts turned to Rod. Wishing she'd taken his phone number, she leaped from the armchair and bounded upstairs. *I need to get some practice in for Rod*, she mused, taking the mirror from the landing wall and carrying it to the bedroom. Placing the mirror on the floor, she slipped her miniskirt and T-shirt off and grabbed the plastic container from the dressing table.

Grinning as she squatted over the mirror, she lubricated the container with baby lotion and parted her taut buttocks, gazing at the reflection of her tightly-closed anal portal. Twisting and pushing the container, she was delighted as it slipped into her anal sheath with ease – stretching her sensitive inner flesh, filling her pelvic cavity.

'God, I'm getting good at this!' she giggled, slipping the container deeper into her bowels, crudely forcing open the once sacrosanct entrance to her inner core. 'Tomorrow, I'll use something even bigger!' she decided. Gazing into the mirror at her yawning vaginal crack, she grinned. 'God, how I love my body!' she laughed, imagining men's eyes gazing at her there, at her crudely exposed girlhood.

Her transformation was indeed complete, she thought wickedly as she gingerly stood up. The container holding her firm buttocks apart, she turned to look at the lewd sight in the full-length mirror. 'I never thought I'd be doing anything like this!' she gasped as the plastic phallus suddenly shot across the room like a bullet. Her rectum deflating like a punctured balloon, she gasped. 'God, that was nice!'

Her rectal sheath still sending electrifying sensations deep into her pelvis, she decided that enough was enough – for the time being, at least! Looking forward to her evening of lesbian sex, she lay on the bed to rest for a while, to conserve her energy. She'd have many multiple orgasms that evening, she was sure. And she'd delight in licking and sucking between the young lesbians' pussy lips – bringing them to their shuddering sapphically-induced climaxes.

Imagining a six-inch-diameter phallus inserted deep in her bottom-hole, she pulled the quilt across her abused naked body and finally drifted off into a deep sleep, dreaming her lewd dreams of lewd sex.

Chapter Six

Slipping into her miniskirt and emerging from the bedroom at seven o'clock, Marianne found Barry in the lounge talking to Jill and Lydia. 'Where have you been?' he asked dejectedly, looking up from his armchair. 'I phoned you several times today. And then I got home to find Jill and Lydia waiting for you on the doorstep. Where have you been, Marianne? I was worried about you!'

Worried about your ruined evening if I didn't turn up, more like! she thought.

Having had the previous evening's voyeurism session ruined by Marianne's no-show, Barry was obviously looking forward to watching the three girls writhing in lesbian lust. She should have waited another half-hour or so, she thought, just to torture Barry mentally! Forcing a smile, she wondered at his reaction if she were to tell him the truth about her day. But no, her visit to Brooke-Smith was her secret and, possibly, her lifeline if she were to leave Barry.

'I was asleep upstairs,' Marianne smiled, turning to the girls sitting side by side on the sofa. 'Sorry, but I was really tired,' she added, gazing at their microskirts, the small triangular patches of silky material concealing their pussies.

'That's OK,' Jill replied, tossing her auburn hair back and licking her full red lips. 'We've been chatting with Barry.'

Not about the trigger word, I hope? Marianne thought excitedly, imagining the word actually working and the three of them using her naked young body for group sex. *Two girls and a man attending my most intimate needs!* But Barry wouldn't let on that he knew about the lesbian trio, she was sure.

Recalling the trigger word working when Barry had used it, she decided that there must have been something about his voice that had sent her into a hypnotic trance. The word hadn't worked for Rod, or the girls, so it must have had something to do with his dulcet tones. *God, if the word worked for the girls, I'd have a real problem!* she mused. *Some real fun!*

'Are you off out this evening?' Marianne asked, looking at Barry as she sat in the armchair opposite him.

'Yes, I've got a client to see. Actually, I'd better get going. I'll probably be late home so don't wait up for me. Have a nice evening!' he added, moving towards the door, glancing at each young girl in turn.

'We will!' Jill grinned enthusiastically as he left the room. 'So, Marianne, what have you been up to today?' she asked accusingly. 'Anything ... er ... anything interesting?'

'I went to see my boyfriend,' she replied impishly as the front door slammed shut. 'We spent a couple of hours together in his huge bed,' she smiled, wondering when Barry was going to slip in through the back door and hide in the dining room.

'Boyfriend?' Jill echoed, her dark eyes frowning as she perched herself on the edge of the sofa.

'Yes – his name's Rod.'

'But, I didn't know that you had a ...'

'No one knows!' Marianne laughed, delighting in her game, praying that Barry couldn't hear her. 'I've been seeing him for six months.'

'But I thought that you and Barry were a permanent thing?'

'Nothing's permanent, is it?' Marianne asked cynically. 'No relationship is permanent!'

'No, I suppose not,' Jill replied, glancing at Lydia. 'I must say that you surprise me, though!' she said, turning to Marianne. 'I mean, *you*, seeing someone on the side!'

'Why not? It's fun, having a clandestine relationship! Sex with the same person all the time becomes boring! It's far too staid, don't you agree?'

'Yes, I do,' Jill reluctantly replied.

'Besides, no matter who your partner, you can never trust them one hundred per cent so it's best not to put all your eggs in one basket.'

Smiling at Lydia, Jill moved closer to her lover, her eyes longing for a reassuring smile. But, rather than a comforting smile, Lydia had a wicked glint in her eyes, Marianne detected as she poured three glasses of wine and passed them round. Marianne wasn't a threat to their relationship, she knew. She was simply their plaything, a sex object – their sex slave. But Jill was obviously suspicious, untrusting of her lesbian lover.

'Juxtaposition,' Jill breathed quietly as she turned her head, her eyes glued to Marianne.

'Sorry?' Marianne smiled, averting her gaze, noticing a large leather bag by Jill's feet. Jill looked at Lydia and frowned, thinking that perhaps Marianne hadn't heard the magical word. 'If you don't mind,' Marianne began. 'I have an awful headache – it's just come on. When you've finished your wine, I think I'll go up to bed. I'm sorry to spoil the evening but . . .'

'Juxtaposition!' Jill repeated loudly, desperate for the trigger word to work.

Her muscles locked, Marianne was unable to move, to protest. To her horror, the game was no longer a game! *The word doesn't work! It* can't *work!* she asserted mentally as the girls giggled excitedly. Desperately trying to move her limbs as she stood motionless before her audience, Marianne couldn't believe that she had no control over her vulnerable body. A battle raging in her mind, she affirmed again and again that there *was* no trigger word – that this wasn't happening.

'She can't have heard the first time,' Jill said nonchalantly as she reclined on the sofa, sipping her wine, wondering how to begin the evening of lesbian sex. 'Start at the beginning, I suppose!' she grinned. 'Marianne, remove all your clothes! We want to have a good look at your lovely body.'

Her hands working mechanically, Marianne pulled her top over her head, tousling her long blonde hair as she flung the garment to the floor in her involuntary wanton abandonment. Unclipping her bra, still desperately fighting her mental battle, she peeled the red, silk cups from her firm breasts, amazed by her elongating nipples, her darkening areolae.

'Suck your nipples,' Lydia ordered crudely, moving forward on the sofa in anticipation. Cupping her breasts in her hands, Marianne lifted her warm mammary spheres as she lowered her head. Taking each nipple into her hot mouth in turn, she sucked, stiffening her milk buds, darkening her areolae. 'Lick your tits, lick them all over!' Lydia cried in her arousal. Complying, Marianne swept her tongue over her breasts, wetting the firm flesh with her saliva.

'Take your skirt off now!' Jill instructed, eager to see the girl's shaved pussy.

As Marianne released her rounded breasts and slipped her tight skirt down, revealing her knickerless pussy to her audience, her heart leaped, her stomach somersaulting as an urgent desire coursed through her contracting womb at the thought of lesbian sex.

Marianne had no choice other than to concede to the fact that she was in some kind of hypnotic trance. How the faked trigger word had worked she had no idea. *Autosuggestion?* she wondered. Was that possible? But it didn't matter *how* it had worked, she mused as she kicked her skirt aside. The point was that it *had* worked!

Having all her faculties about her, she was well aware of the girls, of their chatter as they discussed the debauched evening ahead, what they were going to do with their naked sex slave – what they were going to order her to do to *their* naked bodies!

'Let's ask her a few things,' Lydia suggested.

'Ask her a few things? What sort of things?' Jill replied irritably, more eager to get down to the crude lesbian sex rather than have a chat with Marianne.

'Ask her about her sex life!' Lydia returned. 'About masturbation and . . .'

'Do you masturbate, Marianne?' Jill interrupted.

'Yes,' Marianne replied, the words falling from her lips without her thinking.

'What do you masturbate with, your fingers, a vibro, or what?'

'I expect she uses a cucumber!' Lydia laughed impishly.

'A hairspray can, a plastic container, a deodorant bottle, a perfume bottle, a . . .'

'What, all at once?' Lydia broke in, disbelievingly.

'No – I use the plastic container for my bum, and the hairspray can for my pussy,' Marianne admitted, desperate to halt her involuntary confession.

'Go and get them!' Jill ordered. 'I must see this!'

As her legs carried her from the room and up the stairs, Marianne again tried to regain command over her nude body. Taking the plastic container, the hairspray can and baby lotion from the dressing table, she moved to the bedroom door. Passing through the doorway onto the landing, she resigned herself to the fact that she was in a state of hypnosis. She was a slave to the girls – a sex slave!

'This should be good!' Lydia cried as Marianne placed her masturbation equipment on the floor. 'I can't believe that you put that huge plastic container up your bum! It must be at least four inches across!'

'Come on then, show us how you do it!' Jill breathed excitedly.

Lying on the floor, her legs wide apart, her femininity blatantly displayed, Marianne grabbed the baby lotion, lubricating the container in readiness for anal penetration. Reaching beneath her thigh, she pressed and twisted the rounded end of the huge phallus against her brown portal, trying to push it past her sphincter muscles as the girls watched with bated breath.

Slowly, Marianne's bottom-hole opened, yielding to accommodate the huge shaft. Further she drove the container into her abused rectal sheath, gasping as the delightful sensations permeated her quivering pelvis. Her sensitive tissue stretching, gripping the slippery plastic cylinder, she lifted her buttocks off the floor, pushing the phallus further into her hot bowels, leaving half its oily length protruding from her anal opening.

'I can hardly believe it!' Lydia gasped. 'Surely she won't be able to push that hairspray can into her fanny as well?'

'With that container up her bum, I doubt that she'd get a finger up her fanny, let alone the can!' Jill laughed as Marianne lubricated the metal phallus. 'It's at least three inches in diameter! She'll never do it!'

Peeling her hairless vaginal lips apart, exposing her juiced-up pinken hole, Marianne eased the can into her hot sex-cavern, her stomach rising and falling as her womb rhythmically contracted. Gently pushing and twisting the can, she drove it deeper into her abused body, gasping as the erotic sensations roused her inner base desires. The can fully home, pressing gently against her cervix, she lay with her arms by her sides, her legs wide open, displaying her stretched pinken flesh, her taut brown tissue.

'She's done it!' Lydia gasped, eyeing Marianne's erect clitoris, its entire length forced from its protective hood.

'Incredible!' Jill rejoined, wondering what to get the girl to do next. 'Shame we haven't got a man here, we could have watched Marianne have her mouth fucked!'

As the girls discussed their slave's naked body, Marianne again wondered about the trigger word. Under the total control of her mistresses, she was enjoying her lewd act, abusing her tight holes – but this wasn't the way she'd envisaged the game developing. If the trigger word was to really work, send her into a hypnotic trance, then she'd have no power to put an end to Barry's vile plans. She'd be used as a prostitute, a sex object – and there'd be nothing she could do about it, she thought. Apart from collect her earnings from beneath the kitchen floor!

'I'll get the rope out,' Jill said, opening her leather bag. *Rope?* Marianne thought excitedly. *What the hell are they going to do to me?* Barry, no doubt, was lurking in the dining room by now – listening, spying through the serving hatch at the obscenities. The thought of a voyeur excited Marianne as she turned her head, noticing that a vase of flowers had been placed in front of the partially open hatch. But she was completely innocent, she reminded herself, wishing, again, that she'd not opened up to Brooke-Smith.

Taking Marianne's hands and placing them over her stomach, Jill bound her prisoner's wrists together. 'And now for her legs!' she laughed, binding her ankles with rope.

'I've got an idea!' Lydia cried, dashing from the room. 'Don't tie her feet together!' she called from the hall. Returning with a garden cane, she grinned impishly. 'Tie her feet to each end of the cane. It'll keep her legs wide open – and her cunt!'

Taking the seven-foot cane, Jill bound Marianne's ankles to the ends, forcing her feet wide apart, exposing the full glory of the girl's bloated holes, her inflamed flesh taut around the massive phalluses. Marianne lay defenceless, unable to move, to conceal her girlhood, wondering what was coming next. Her legs painfully held apart, her thighs aching, she prayed for *some* mercy, at least.

'I know!' Jill cried excitedly. 'Tie some rope to the centre of the cane, and fix it to the ceiling so that her legs are up in the air!'

'How are we going to fix the rope to the ceiling?' Lydia asked despondently.

'Oh, that's a good point. I know! Tie a rope to the centre of the cane, and pull her legs up over her body and fix the other end of the rope to the radiator. That way, her fanny lips will be bulging between her open thighs, ready for anything!'

Quickly carrying out the girl's suggestion, Lydia stood back and admired her handiwork. Marianne's feet high in the air, her legs straight, held wide apart, the sexual centre of her young body was open to the lesbians' every perverted whim.

The end of the plastic container protruding between her splayed buttocks, Marianne grimaced as Jill tried to force it deeper into her bowels. Pushing, twisting the massive phallus, Jill wouldn't give up her debauched quest. 'Help me!' she ordered Lydia. 'Pull her bum cheeks as far apart as you can. I want to see whether she can take the entire length!'

Her sensitive bottom-crease stretched, her small hole painfully forced open, Marianne gasped as her rectum yielded, allowing the phallus to slip deeper into her bowels. 'You've done it!' Lydia screeched as Jill slipped the container further into the girl's anal-duct. 'My God, look at it! Look at her bum-hole! You'd better not push it any further – you might lose it!'

'I told you I'd do it!' Jill replied, sitting back on her heels. 'I wouldn't mind trying it myself!'

'Strip off and I'll shove the wine bottle up your bum!' Lydia laughed.

'Later, perhaps. It's Marianne we're having fun with this evening!'

'Yes, and are we going to have some fun with the bitch!'

Marianne imagined the sight her lesbian friends had of her taut bottom-hole, her crudely stretched vaginal lips. The sensations bringing her a mixture of pain and incredible pleasure, she wondered at her next enforced feat. There was nothing left to do to her young body! Or so she thought as the girls moved either side of her and tweaked her long nipples.

'I honestly thought it would be physically impossible to get it that far up her bum!' Lydia said, her hand moving down over Marianne's smooth stomach to the girl's exposed clitoris.

'A girl I used to know said that she'd seen a dirty video where a woman had a fist up her fanny and, at the same time, another fist up her bum!'

'God! I can't believe that!' Lydia laughed, her fingers massaging Marianne's swollen clitoris.

'Well, it's true. Do you realize, if Barry were to discover the trigger word he could have a field day?' Jill said pensively. 'He could do anything and everything he wanted!'

'Yes, I'd been thinking about that earlier,' Lydia smiled.

'Perhaps we should tell him?'

'Whatever for?'

'I don't know. Anyway, I'm going to get our pretty little sex slave to give me a good licking!'

Slipping her panties off, Jill lifted her microskirt and knelt astride Marianne's head. Lowering her open sex-groove over the girl's face, she settled her full pussy lips over her mouth and ordered her slave to push her tongue out.

'Ah, that's good!' Jill gasped as Marianne's tongue lapped between her open cunt-folds.

'Mind your head on the cane!' Lydia said, gently slipping the phalluses from Marianne's young body, leaving her holes gaping, her juices flowing in torrents. Licking the wet flesh between Marianne's inflamed vaginal lips, Lydia pushed two fingers deep into the girl's bottom-sheath, opening her there, bringing her wonderful sensations of debauched sex.

Swallowing Jill's flowing cuntal juices, Marianne lost herself in the three-way coupling, delighting at the thought of Barry watching as she heard movements coming from the serving hatch. Was he wanking himself off? she wondered as Lydia inserted a third finger into her tight bottom-hole and sucked her solid clitoris into her hot mouth.

'Ah, yes!' Jill cried. 'Faster! Lick my clitty faster!' Working her tongue over Jill's throbbing clitoris, Marianne elicited the girl's shuddering orgasm, sucking hard on her pulsating nodule, delighting at the thought of another girl coming in her mouth. 'More! Don't stop!' Jill ordered, writhing above her slave, grinding the open centre of her quivering body hard against Marianne's wet face.

As Marianne's clitoris exploded in orgasm in Lydia's wet mouth, she spluttered on the copious flow of vaginal juice, desperate for air as Jill forced her cunt harder into her mouth. The orgasmic shock waves rocking her young body, her hands tied, her legs held apart, Marianne shook uncontrollably as her climax subsided, only to rise and grip her in lust again.

With Lydia's fingers thrusting deep into her anal-sheath, Marianne could barely stand the incredible pleasure she was deriving from her abused body. Her mouth full of cunt flesh, she gasped as Jill slipped her sex valley from her face. Panting for air, crying out her lewd pleasure as her multiple orgasm took her even higher to her sexual heaven, she rolled her eyes and tossed her head – completely and utterly lost in her sexual delirium.

At last, the waves of pure lust receded, leaving her trembling, her smooth stomach rising and falling, her firm breasts heaving. 'I'll come in her mouth now!' Lydia cried, slipping her panties down her long legs.

'I thought you wanted to spank her?' Jill giggled, untying the rope from the radiator.

'All right, I'll come in the whore's mouth after I've given her the spanking of her life!'

'Not too hard, Lydia!' Jill laughed, gently lowering Marianne's legs to the floor.

'I'll be the one who decides how hard!' Lydia snapped. 'You can't roll her over with the cane between her feet,' she ruminated, removing the cane. 'There, now we'll roll her onto her stomach and both give her a bloody good thrashing!'

As her naked body was rolled over, Marianne's tethered hands were squashed against her full vaginal lips. Her fingers toying with her wet, pinken girl-crack, she smiled as the girls kissed her taut buttocks. Each licking her sensitive orbs, wetting her with their saliva, the girls pulled her buttocks apart, exposing her used anal hole. A tongue snaking its way into her crease, licking around her brown tissue, Marianne quivered, delighting in her enforced depravity.

'OK!' Jill said, squeezing one of Marianne's buttocks as she sat up. 'I'll take this one, and you can have the other!'

'What about using the cane?' Lydia asked.

'We'll spank her with our hands first, just to warm her up – and then you can give her the thrashing of her life with the cane!'

Whimpering, grimacing as she imagined the cane swishing through the air and landing across her taut flesh, Marianne shuddered, sensing, for the first time, a frightening cold fear. The tea towel whipping her naked buttocks had brought her pleasure, the length of rope had been amazingly arousing, stinging her pale orbs – but a long, thin bamboo cane? Would the pain turn to pleasure? Or would the pleasure turn to pain?

As the girls began spanking her tensed buttocks, Marianne tried to push all thoughts of the cane out of her mind and enjoy the immense pleasure she was receiving. Each slap becoming progressively harder as her mistresses found their rhythm, Marianne felt her clitoris stiffen and pulsate beneath her massaging fingertips.

Thrashing their slave, the girls gave her no mercy as Marianne began to writhe with the beautiful sensations of pain and pleasure. The stinging slaps jolting her naked body, she caressed her clitoris faster, stiffening her sex-nodule fully. Harder, the girls thrashed her crimson buttocks until Marianne's orgasm erupted and she cried out in her sapphic coming.

'Ah! More! Coming! Ah, God, my cunt!'

'She loves it!' Jill squealed. 'The dirty little bitch really loves it!'

'Let's see if she loves *this*!' Lydia returned threateningly as she grabbed the cane. 'Get out of the way, Jill!'

'Don't hurt her!' Jill pleaded as she moved aside.

'Hurt her? I'm only going to thrash the bitch!'

The first blow of the cane jolted Marianne's naked body, causing her to cry out in terror. Driven by an uncontrollable craze for sadistic lesbian lust, Lydia brought the cane down again, flogging the girl's taut flesh, delighting as pink weals fanned out across her crimson posterior.

Squeezing her eyes shut, biting her lip as blow after blow landed across her stinging bottom, Marianne could do nothing to halt the flagellation. Her fingers still pressing against her swollen clitoris, she sensed her budling swelling as the stinging pain permeated her scarlet bottom-cheeks, transmitting deep into her pelvis. What was Barry thinking? she wondered as her clitoris throbbed, sending ripples of pleasure to mix with the pain running through her racked body.

'Not too hard!' Jill cried as Lydia quickened her pace, bringing the cane down again and again, seemingly lost now in her wanton act. 'Lydia! Not too hard!'

'Why, what's the matter?' she asked, halting the thrashing and turning to her friend.

'I've never seen you like this before! It's as if you're possessed!'

'Don't be stupid! All I'm doing is caning her!'

'Yes, but . . .'

'I'll cane *you* unless you shut up!' Lydia warned angrily.

Sitting on the sofa, Jill watched as Lydia resumed her thrashing of Marianne, wondering at the girl's new-found obsession. The lesbian couple had enjoyed spanking sessions before, but only in fun during their lovemaking. Never had Jill seen her lover's darker side emerge before, and she began to wonder fearfully whether the cane would become a regular part of their sexual games.

'I want her bum high in the air!' Lydia cried, discarding the cane and pulling Marianne's hips up. 'Come on, bring your knees up and stick your bum out!' she ordered her slave. Marianne obeyed, bringing her knees up and pushing her burning buttocks out. 'That's good!' Lydia praised, grabbing the cane. 'Now I'll *really* thrash you!'

'Lydia! Don't you think she's had enough?' Jill gasped as the cane struck Marianne's jutting bottom-orbs.

'I'll be the judge of that! What's the matter with you, Jill? Don't you want to have some fun?'

'I . . . I just think that she's had enough. What she'll think when she sees her bum, I don't know!'

'And I don't care! If you don't like it, why don't you go home and leave me to enjoy myself?'

'No, I wouldn't leave you alone with her! God knows what you'd do!'

'I'll come round on my own and really give it to her! Yes, I'll visit the bitch without you and really give her a good seeing-to!'

'No, you mustn't, Lydia!'

'You do want me to move in with you, don't you?'

'You know I do!'

'Well, shut up, then!'

Marianne *was* a threat to their relationship, she thought, realizing the extent of Lydia's dominance. But why was Jill going with a girl like Lydia? Love? she wondered. Lesbian love? If Lydia moved in with Jill, she'd take the flat over, control Jill, her life. But that wasn't Marianne's problem.

Wondering why Barry hadn't emerged from his hide and saved her, put an end to the punishment, Marianne knew that she couldn't take much more of the cane. As the thin bamboo struck home again, she winced, praying that Lydia would show her some mercy. *Lydia doesn't know the meaning of the word!* she thought as the cane swished through the air and struck her buttocks with a loud crack.

Watching the punishment in silence, Jill knew that she had no control over her lesbian lover. Wishing that she'd never introduced Lydia to Marianne as she turned her head away from the gruelling flogging, she caught sight of Barry spying through the hatch. *My God!* she thought, wondering what to do as Marianne cried out in her agonized pleasure.

'Lydia!' Jill whispered loudly. 'Lydia, come here for a moment!' Frowning, the girl sat by Jill's side, asking her what was wrong this time as Jill whispered in her ear. 'Barry's watching! Don't look now, but he's hiding behind the serving hatch!'

Rising to her feet, Lydia ordered Marianne to stand up. Freeing her hands, she instructed her to dress, wondering what Barry was up to, why he'd not burst in and put an end to the thrashing. *Perhaps he knows about the trigger word?* she mused, watching Marianne slip into her miniskirt and T-shirt as she cleared away the rope and pushed the cane beneath the sofa.

Dressed, her hair brushed, Marianne was ordered to sit in the armchair. 'Right, I'll take her bottles and things upstairs,' Jill said, grabbing the masturbation equipment. Returning to the lounge and sitting beside Jill on the sofa, she clicked her fingers, praying that Marianne wouldn't feel too much pain from her burning buttocks and start asking questions. But what questions could she ask? Jill wondered.

'Shall we have some more wine?' Jill asked as Marianne looked about her.

'What? Oh! Er . . . yes,' Marianne replied as Barry entered the room. 'Oh, Barry – you're back early!'

'It didn't take as long as I thought it would,' he smiled. 'Here, let me pour the wine.'

Trying to make herself comfortable, Marianne did her best not to show that she was in pain. Her buttocks burning a fire-red, she pondered the situation. As far as she knew, the girls had no idea that Barry had been watching the merciless thrashing. Barry had no idea that Marianne and the girls knew of his voyeurism. But the games were out of Marianne's control now. The trigger word sending her into a hypnotic trance, she was powerless to stop her abusers living out their corrupt fantasies.

'So, what have you all been up to?' Barry asked, filling the wine glasses.

'It's odd, but I have no recollection!' Marianne breathed, catching Barry's eye.

'We've been chatting and guzzling wine!' Jill laughed. 'You're not pissed are you, Marianne?'

'Of course I'm not! It's strange, but I really don't remember anything about this evening!'

'You were dozing earlier,' Lydia smiled. 'You slept for a while so . . .'

'Ah, that explains it,' Marianne said. 'I've been feeling really tired recently. I wonder whether I'm coming down with something?'

'We'd better go,' Jill said, gulping down her wine as she caught Barry's accusing gaze.

'Already!' Marianne asked, checking the time. 'God, I must have slept for ages! What must you think of me, inviting you both round and then falling asleep?'

'Don't worry!' Lydia laughed. 'Come on, Jill, let's leave these two in peace.'

Seeing the girls out, Marianne returned to the lounge. Her body aching, her love-holes burning, she settled her stinging buttocks on the sofa, wondering what Barry was thinking. His thick black hair falling over his face, his dark eyes reflecting his base desires, she wondered in which direction her relationship would go now that he'd changed so much – now that *she*'d changed so much.

'Had a good evening?' he asked, adjusting his bulging trousers.

'Very good, apart from my falling asleep!' Marianne

laughed, pondering on the magical trigger word. 'How did you get on?'

'Not too bad. Although, to be honest with you, I've just about had enough of working for Saunders.'

'You're not thinking of leaving, are you?' she asked, realizing that he was forging ahead with his plans to act as her pimp.

'Yes, it's crossed my mind.'

'But . . . what would we do for money? Until I'm earning, I don't think you should leave, Barry!'

'I've one or two money-making ideas up my sleeve, so don't worry – we won't starve!' he quipped.

'I wish I could start earning,' Marianne sighed. 'There must be a way of earning some real money! I don't mean a poorly-paid job, but *real* money.'

'That reminds me, I must ring a friend about something. I won't be a minute,' he said, leaving the room.

After watching the lesbian trio, Barry must be aching for sexual relief, she mused. Unless he'd wanked himself off, spurted his seed all over the dining room carpet! Hearing his muffled voice, Marianne moved to the door, listening to his conversation, wondering what he was up to.

'Is that all you want?' Barry asked, his voice almost a whisper. 'Well, it's up to you, Alan. But I'd have thought that you'd want . . . All right, whatever you say. Twenty pounds, OK? It doesn't matter whether it takes five minutes or an hour, a blow job will cost you twenty! A hundred and forty a week? What are you talking about? Every evening? Christ, Alan! All right, seventy quid a week, paid in advance. No, that's your problem! If you don't turn up, you lose your money! Come over now, if you want to. Yes, seventy up front. OK, see you soon.'

Barry was going to earn a small fortune from pimping,

Marianne mused, wondering who Alan was. But she'd take the money, unless he decided to hide the cash somewhere else when he discovered the theft. *I don't need Barry!* she reflected as he entered the room. *I can sell my body for sex without his help! I don't need him!*

'Alan's coming over in a minute,' he smiled, moving to the window.

'Who's Alan?'

'Alan, from down the road.'

'Not Christine's Alan?' she gasped.

'Yes. He wants to borrow... ah, here he is now. Juxtaposition.'

Again, the word had actually worked! Unable to move, Marianne listened as Barry opened the front door and explained the procedure. 'She'll act as a sex slave,' he said. 'She won't say anything or do anything without you instructing her. Just tell her what you want her to do, and she'll do it.'

'How long has she been into prostitution?' Alan asked.

'For some time. It's the only way the useless whore can earn a decent living!' Barry laughed.

'And you don't mind?'

'No, not at all! There's nothing between us now. It's a business relationship – I bring her clients, and she services them!'

'God, you must be making a fortune! There's the seventy pounds.'

'Thanks. I don't know about a fortune, but I'm thinking of giving up my job and living on Marianne's earnings.'

'A pimp! Bloody hell, Barry! Talk about no scruples!'

'Scruples don't come into it! She's a whore, and I'm earning money from her. Right, in you go. I'll be in the kitchen.'

As Alan entered the lounge and closed the door behind him, Marianne pondered on Barry's hurtful words. But she was becoming used to his cruelty. If anything, his actions only served to strengthen her determination to turn the tables. Deciding to contact the course lecturer and confess, she stared blankly at her client's bulging trousers as he stood before her.

Moving forward on the sofa, following his orders, she unzipped his trousers. *A cock's a cock!* she consoled herself as she tugged his trousers and boxer shorts down to reveal his stiff penis. There was no need to look up to his face, to acknowledge the owner of the solid penis, she mused as she pulled the loose skin back to unveil his purple knob. She was now a real slave, having no choice other than to follow her master's instructions.

'Suck it!' Alan demanded. 'Hurry up, I haven't got much time!' No, he probably hadn't, Marianne thought. Christine, Marianne's friend of several years, would be waiting for her unfaithful husband to return home. 'That's good!' he cried as she engulfed his bulbous knob in her hot mouth. 'Ah, God! If only Chris would do this!'

So that was the reason for his infidelity. That was why he only demanded oral sex. Marriage vows broken, shattered, Marianne mused – and all because his wife wouldn't agree to use her mouth as she would her vagina and allow her husband to fuck her there. *Some marriage!* she thought, wondering how many men, how many clients, Barry would round up.

'Wank me while you're sucking!' Alan ordered crudely, thrusting his hips forward. Moving her hand up and down his veined shaft, Marianne licked and mouthed his glans, eagerly awaiting his sperm, wondering how many men she'd be told to suck to orgasm. 'That's good!' he enthused as his shaft twitched and his knob swelled. 'Don't stop! I'm . . . God, I'm coming!'

Gushing, bathing her tongue, his male cream filled her

cheeks, running down her chin as she fervently slurped on the orgasming fountainhead. On and on the product of his climax flowed, sustained by Marianne's snaking tongue around his pumping fountainhead. Thrusting his organ deep into her mouth, his glans jetting sperm down her throat, he grabbed her head. 'Drink it, you dirty cow!' he bellowed. 'Ah, yes, yes! God, you've got a beautiful mouth!'

His flow of sperm finally slowing to a trickle, he gently rocked his hips, sliding his glans over her pink tongue, watching her lips roll along his wet shaft. 'God, I needed that!' he murmured as he slipped his knob from her mouth. 'Lick me, clean me,' he instructed, gazing at his sperm glistening on her full red lips. Holding his organ in her hand, she moved her head forward, lapping up the globules of come, cleansing his penis – the penis that rightfully his betrayed wife had exclusive rights to. Would he go home and fuck her? she wondered. Would he fuck his wife and picture Marianne's mouth encompassing his throbbing glans?

Pulling away and tugging his trousers up, Alan moved to the door, not even glancing at Marianne as he told her that she'd be drinking from his cock every evening. Muffled voices came from the hall as Alan closed the lounge door behind him. That was it, she'd done her job, played the role of a tart – sold herself for crude sex.

The front door slammed shut and Barry entered the lounge. The client had gone – spermed in her mouth and gone home to his loving wife, she mused as Barry clicked his fingers and ordered her to wake up. Looking around the room, the taste of sperm lingering, she forced a smile, wondering again at the powerful trigger word.

'When's Alan coming round?' she asked, licking her lips.

'I don't know,' he replied. 'It wasn't a definite arrangement. Marianne, have you been out today?'

'Why?'

'There's something missing from the kitchen.'

'Something missing? What?'

'Er... just a book. Did you go out and leave the back door open?'

'No, of course not! You've probably left it upstairs or somewhere. Which book was it?'

'It doesn't matter,' he sighed, his forehead lined, his expression pained.

So, he's discovered that his five hundred pounds has gone missing! she laughed inwardly. *Poor Barry, all that money – gone!* And there was nothing he could say about it! But, she suddenly realized, if he were to use the word and question her, she'd not be able to stop the truth from falling from her pretty lips.

'Juxtaposition!' he bellowed as he stood before her. This was it, she thought anxiously, realizing that the word had worked, yet again. To her relief, Barry unzipped his jeans and offered his hard glans to her mouth. 'Now you can suck *me* off!' he chuckled, seemingly forgetting about the missing money.

As she took his knob into her mouth, Marianne guessed that he'd not question her about the money because he thought that she had no knowledge of his hiding place. There was little point in asking her about something she knew nothing of. What conclusion he'd come to, she didn't know, or care – she was five hundred pounds the richer, that was all that mattered!

'I liked watching you suck Alan's cock and drink his sperm,' Barry murmured as he pushed his organ-head further into her accommodating mouth. 'And watching you being thrashed by those lezzies was something else! Christ, the way you shoved that plastic pot up your arse was brilliant! Tomorrow we'll start making the videos! And I'll tell you something else, Marianne – I'm going to have you used and fucked by so many men that I'll be on a grand a week! Now, suck me off, you slag!'

Her fate seemingly sealed, Marianne endeavoured to regain control over her actions. Trying to pull away, to slip Barry's penis from her mouth, she realized the full extent of the strange trance she was in. Her head actually moved forward as she involuntarily took Barry's knob further into her mouth. Licking, sucking, she obediently complied with her master's demands and wanked his fleshy organ.

As his sperm jetted, filling her hot mouth, Marianne savoured the salty liquid, comparing the taste with Alan's, wondering again how many men would use her, fuck her mouth and drain their heavy balls. Swallowing Barry's sperm, she was surprised as he suddenly slipped his solid shaft out. Rubbing his throbbing glans against Marianne's lips, her face, he pumped his sperm over her youthful skin. Desperate to swallow more of his jetting come, Marianne engulfed his knob again, sucking, drinking from his massive cock. Her face drenched, dripping with the creamy product of his orgasm, she lost herself in her enforced act of debauchery, taking his cock-head to the back of her throat and swallowing hard.

'Keep still now!' Barry gasped. His knob absorbing the wet heat of her mouth, Marianne remained motionless. Slowly slipping his penis in and out, he shuddered in the aftermath of his climax as the last of his sperm bubbled from his cocktip slit and ran over her pink tongue. 'That was good! You did very well!' he commended as he slid his wet cock from her mouth and zipped his jeans.

Sitting opposite, he ordered Marianne to wipe her mouth on the back of her hand before clicking his fingers and bringing her out of her hypnotic trance. Again, Marianne was in control of her young body, and she gazed at Barry, wondering once more what sort of man he really was.

'I've been offered a job,' Marianne announced.

'Really? Where?' he asked surprisedly.

'Brooke-Smith,' she replied, deciding to annoy Barry, to piss him off.

'Brooke-Smith!' he echoed angrily. 'When was this?'

'Today. He offered me a company car – a Mercedes.'

'You can't work for *him*! I don't want you . . .'

'Why can't I work for him? It's a very good job, Barry. I'd be his personal assistant and . . .'

'Yeah, and I know what sort of personal assistant he wants! I forbid you to take the job, Marianne!'

'Forbid me? Do you own me now?'

'No, I didn't mean . . . I care for you, love. I don't want you working for a randy old bastard like Brooke-Smith.'

Care for me? Marianne thought angrily. Barry was more than a bastard, she reflected – he was a hideous monster! 'I'm going to bed!' she snapped. 'Don't come up and annoy me, I'm tired!'

Barry had spent the night on the sofa, leaving for work before Marianne had woken, much to her relief. Still fuming, she washed and dressed and nibbled on a sandwich, wondering about her next move. Grabbing her diary from her handbag, she flicked through the pages as she wandered through the hall to the phone.

'Mr Ducante?' she asked as a man answered.

'Speaking.'

'My name's Marianne, I was on the hypnosis course you ran.'

'Oh, yes – Marianne! How are you?'

'I'm fine, thanks. I wanted to ask you something, if you can spare me a few minutes.'

'Yes, of course – what's the problem?'

Marianne explained her predicament to her mentor, but he was reluctant to discuss the matter over the phone. 'All I can say is that never in all my life have I heard of a trigger word being implanted in the subconscious by autosuggestion. It's just not possible for a subject to implant a trigger word in his or her own subconscious, Marianne!'

'But it's happened!' she insisted despairingly.

'Well, there's a first time for everything, I suppose. Look, I'm not calling you a liar, but . . . Why not come up and see me and we'll discuss it further?'

Not wanting to travel the long distance to visit him, she hung up, wondering why he'd not helped her, talked about it properly – why he'd even *mentioned* the word liar. Deciding to go to the park on the off-chance of bumping into Rod, Marianne left the house, ignoring the ringing telephone as she closed the front door. *I'll bet that's Ducante!* she thought as she walked down the street. *I'll bet he wants to use the trigger word and have his wicked way with me!*

The sun was already hot in the clear blue sky, too hot, Marianne thought as she crossed the park. Flopping onto the bench, she sighed, again wondering what her next move should be. Gazing at Rod's house, she decided to visit him, just to talk, to get to know him a little better. She'd pretend that the trigger word didn't always work, she mused as she neared the house. Should he mention the word, unless it *really* worked and sent her into a trance, she'd just smile and ask him what he'd meant by 'juxtaposition'.

Finding the back door locked, Marianne wandered around the house to the front door. Ringing the bell, she gasped as she read the words engraved on a brass plate. *R.D. Bewick. Hypnotherapist.*

Dashing around the side of the house at the sound of someone in the hall, she ran through the back gate and out into the park, her heart beating wildly as she recalled masturbating on Rod's sofa. *He must have thought, or known, that I was faking it!* she reflected anxiously, recalling Ducante's words. *God, what must he have thought of me?*

Sitting by the pond, despondency set in. Her heart sinking at the thought of never being able to visit Rod again, she wondered why he hadn't mentioned that he was a hypnotherapist. *It's all going wrong!* she thought sadly. Her relationship with Barry was all but over, she hadn't seen John for a while, not that she really wanted to – and now she felt that she couldn't face Rod again. 'But the trigger word really *does* work!' she breathed in her rising confusion, leaping up and returning to Rod's house.

'Marianne!' he smiled as he opened the front door.

'Hi, Rod. Why didn't you tell me about this?' she asked accusingly, pointing to the brass plate.

'Because I . . . Come in and we'll talk about it.'

Sitting on the familiar – intimately familiar – sofa, Marianne recalled masturbating in front of Rod. *But I was innocent!* she consoled herself as he sat in the armchair. *I was completely innocent!*

'I didn't tell you my profession, Marianne, because I didn't believe your story about the trigger word. No one in his right mind would place a trigger word in a subject's subconscious, and leave it there.'

'But the lecturer was taken ill before he . . .'

'Then why hasn't he contacted you and removed the word? He would never . . .'

'All right, I'll be honest with you. I faked the word to have some fun with . . . Anyway, the word, after faking it several times, actually worked.'

'Do you recall what happened when you were here the other day?'

'Yes, I do.'

'Do you remember what you did?'

'We talked, and then I left.'

'Marianne, when a subject is under hypnosis, he'll later recall everything that had happened during that time.'

'Yes, so what?'

'I used the word when you were here and you . . .'

'That proves it, then! I have no recollection whatsoever!'

'But that can't be true, Marianne! Look, I'm only a hypnotherapist. I help people who want to give up smoking and the like – I'm not an authority on hypnotism. But I do know that subjects recall all that happened to them during hypnosis. OK, I'll accept that the trigger word really does work, but you must accept the fact that, whatever happens during hypnosis, the subject will recall everything afterwards.'

Marianne averted her gaze as Rod rose to his feet and opened the drinks cabinet. She'd have to admit to recalling her wanton masturbation if she were going to have Rod help her. Building up her courage, she took a deep breath.

'All right, I do remember,' she confessed, lowering her head as he passed her a drink.

'And now will you admit that the word doesn't really work?' he asked, much to her surprise.

'No! It *does* work, Rod! You have to believe me!'

'Is there a drink or a certain food that you don't like?'

'Scotch – just the smell of it makes me feel sick! Why, what are you getting at?'

'Juxtaposition.'

Pouring a glass of water, Rod passed it to Marianne. 'It's neat Scotch – drink it!' he instructed. Again, the trigger word had worked. Unable to stop herself, holding her breath, she downed the drink in one.

'How do you feel?' he asked, taking the empty glass.

'Sick!' she breathed, holding her hand to her mouth.

'Wake up, Marianne.'

Gazing at Rod, Marianne frowned. 'You made me drink Scotch!' she complained. 'I couldn't stop myself from drinking it! Argh! I feel sick!'

'It was only water!' Rod laughed.

'It was Scotch, I could taste it!'

'It was water! That shows the immense power of the mind, I think you'll agree? Anyway, it proved that you *are* able to recollect all that happens during hypnosis. Look, I have a client due in a few minutes. I'll accept that your word works, and I might be able to help you. I might be able to erase it from your subconscious, but not now. Can you come back after lunch?'

'Yes, I can.'

'Right, I'd better get ready for my client – he's another one who wants to give up smoking!'

'OK, I'll see you later. Is it all right if I go out the back way?'

'Of course it is – I'll see you out.'

Wandering down the garden path, Marianne sensed a great relief. If Rod could rid her subconscious of the word, then she'd be able to fake it again, have her fun, enjoy her sexual conquests. Turning to wave goodbye, she smiled, happy that she was getting to know Rod. 'See you later!' she called, opening the gate.

'OK! Oh, by the way – a subject under hypnosis won't do anything he or she doesn't want to do. Remember that, Marianne!'

Walking through the park, Marianne pondered on Rod's words. 'God, he meant that, hypnotized or not, I *wanted* to masturbate in front of him!' she sighed as she walked home. 'Shit, he must think me a right tart! I *am* a right tart! I didn't want to drink Scotch – I wanted to drink his sperm!'

Chapter Seven

Marianne ignored the ringing phone as she ate her lasagne. Whoever it was would call later, she thought, finishing her meal and clearing the table. But when the doorbell rang, she felt compelled to answer.

'Oh, Lydia! Er... come in,' she greeted the pretty girl cautiously, praying that she wouldn't use the word and spend the afternoon forcing wine bottles up her bottom-hole! 'I'm just off out. I have an appointment, but I have a few minutes.'

'Thanks,' Lydia smiled as she walked passed Marianne, her short skirt revealing her firm, shapely thighs.

God, I want her! Marianne found herself thinking. 'Go into the lounge. Where's Jill?' she asked, fighting temptation.

'She's gone shopping. I came to see you because... Juxtaposition.'

Again, the word had actually worked. This was the one time Marianne would have feigned an illness, anything to keep her date with Rod! But, her body now completely under Lydia's control, Marianne could do nothing to get rid of the girl. Desperately, she tried to move, to protest, but she had no command over her body or her speech.

'I can't stay for long, unfortunately,' Lydia began, slipping her hand up Marianne's short skirt and massaging her silk-covered girl-crack. 'I want to try something out, test this hypnosis business. Now, listen carefully, Marianne. You're to meet me this evening. I saw you sitting in the park earlier, and it gave me an idea. You'll meet me, alone, in the park at seven o'clock this evening. Do you understand?'

'Yes,' Marianne answered automatically.

'Good. Tell no one where you're going. If Barry asks, tell him that you're going to see Jill. Your cunt feels hot, Marianne! I'd love to stay for a while and finger your hot cunt, lick your hard clitoris to orgasm, but I don't have the time. But this evening, in the park, I'll bring you some of the best orgasms you've ever had! And I'll thrash your beautiful buttocks with a tree branch until you come! Right, let's adjust your skirt, that's it. Now, wake up.'

Would she be able to stop herself from going to the park? Marianne wondered. Without anyone mentioning the trigger word, she'd have the power to stay at home at seven o'clock, surely? There'd have to be more than the hands on the clock to prompt her to act!

'I was only passing,' Lydia smiled. 'I was wondering whether you'd like to come out for a drink with Jill and me one evening?'

'Oh, that would be nice!'

'OK, I'll let you know when. I've got to arrange it with Jill, so one of us will give you a ring.'

'I'll look forward to it! Anyway, I'd better get going.'

'Yes, I must dash. I'll be in touch.'

Seeing the girl out, Marianne gave a sigh of relief. *Thank God she didn't hypnotize me and stay for hours!* she thought. Grabbing her bag, she realized that, if Rod were able to erase the word from her subconscious, then perhaps Lydia's hypnotic suggestion to meet her at the park at seven would also be erased. Deciding to meet Lydia and enjoy some beautiful lesbian-induced orgasms, no matter what happened, Marianne left the house and made her way to Rod's.

'Right!' Rod said authoritatively as he opened the door. 'Come through and sit on the sofa and we'll try and rid your subconscious of this trigger word!'

Following him into the lounge, Marianne sat down, praying that he could help her. But he wanted to know all that had happened to her since she began playing her games with her fake trigger word before he did anything.

'Nothing's happened to me,' she replied. 'Can't you just hypnotize me and erase the word?'

'I'll try. I don't see why it shouldn't work. Right, here goes – juxtaposition. Now, Marianne, you will no longer respond to the word, "juxtaposition". You will not fall into a hypnotic state when you hear the word, do you understand?'

'Yes, I understand.'

'OK, wake up.'

Gazing at Rod, Marianne smiled. Her blue eyes sparkling, she sensed a pang of sexual desire course through her pelvis as she recalled Rod sucking her clitoris to orgasm. *God, I need him!* she thought, aware of her swelling clitoris, her tightening vagina. *I need his cock coming in my mouth!*

'There all done!' he said triumphantly, returning her smile.

'Are you sure?' Marianne asked, praying that she really was free at last – free to fake her hypnotic trances and enjoy crude sex in apparent innocence.

'Let's try it out. Juxtaposition. There, you see, you're not hypnotized!'

To her horror, the word *had* sent her into a trance. Trying to move her hands, endeavouring to speak, her stomach sank as she wondered whether she'd ever be free.

'Marianne! Marianne, stop playing around!' Rod laughed. 'All right, if you want to play games, then take your knickers off and eat them!'

Slipping her panties down her long legs, Marianne pulled them over her shoes and began to chew on the red silk. Tearing a strip of material off with her teeth, she was about to swallow it when Rod stopped her.

'Wake up!' he cried, his expression reflecting his concern.

'I couldn't stop myself!' she complained, spitting out the shredded silk and stuffing the remains of her panties into her handbag. 'It hasn't worked, Rod!'

'God, I don't believe this! I don't know what to do, I really don't!'

Trying again, Rod failed to free the girl of the trigger word.

'Can't you implant a suggestion in my subconscious that will wake me up the minute I fall into hypnosis?' Marianne asked.

'No! You can't play around with the subconscious like that. You can't implant words to counteract other words! No one really understands the subconscious, Marianne. The power of the mind is incredible. For example, it's a well-known fact that, when a subject is in a hypnotic state, you can place the end of a pencil on the back of his hand, telling him that it's a burning cigarette, and a blister will form. The power the mind has over the body is incredible!'

'Yes, and the power other people have over *me* is incredible! What am I going to do?'

'Other people? Who knows about the word?'

'Barry, my . . . my soon-to-be ex-boyfriend.'

'But you told me that you didn't have a boyfriend.'

'Soon-to-be-ex.'

'What does he get you to do when he hypnotizes you?'

'He . . . nothing much, but I don't want him to have power over me.'

'In that case, make him your ex-boyfriend now, today, and keep well out of his way.'

'There's someone else,' Marianne admitted softly, wondering whether to be honest and tell Rod everything or not. 'A girlfriend of mine, she . . .'

'She'll be all right, won't she? I mean, she won't use the word to . . .'

'I'd better tell you everything, Rod,' she sighed melancholically. 'It's a long story – but I'd better tell you everything.'

Listening intently, Rod could hardly believe Marianne's incredible confession. Gasping now and then, shaking his head in disbelief, he finally interrupted the girl.

'Your boyfriend had perverted sex with you, and then his friend visited you and did the same thing?'

'Yes. I know that I . . .'

'This is incredible! Your boyfriend actually arranged for his friend to visit you, and then he watched you being whipped and . . . I've never heard anything like it!'

'There's more,' Marianne sighed. 'You haven't heard the half of it! A girlfriend used the word and she . . .'

'Don't tell me that she had sex with you, too!'

'Yes, and her friend, another lesbian.'

'My God! This is a phenomenal story!'

'It's not a story, it's true!'

'No, I didn't mean . . . The thing is, Marianne, as I told you earlier, under hypnosis, people would never do anything that they didn't want to do. Did you enjoy the lesbian sex?'

'Well . . .'

'You must be honest with me.'

'Yes, I suppose I did enjoy it.'

'And the whipping and anal intercourse, did you enjoy that?'

'Rod, I . . .'

'Did you, Marianne?'

'Yes, I did.'

'I've never... anyway, please, do go on.'

Revealing that Barry had sold her to men friends for perverted sex sessions, Marianne finally came to the end of her amazing story. Gazing into Rod's disbelieving eyes, she fearfully awaited his reaction. *People would never do anything that they didn't want to do.* The horrifying words swimming in the murky depths of her racked mind, she wondered why Rod was saying nothing. *Probably too disgusted with me to speak!* she thought sadly.

'I must say, Marianne, that I am completely stunned! I've never heard such an incredible story! There's been a lot of research into hypnosis, into the subconscious, but I don't think anyone realizes the frightening depths of the mind! I really don't know what to say. I honestly don't know what to make of it all!'

'Then, say nothing. Look, I'd better go – I should never have told you...'

'No, don't go – you can't!'

'Why not?'

'The cigarette burn factor... if some joker were to use the trigger word and tell you that your heart was about to stop... Christ! There's no telling what would happen! You could die, Marianne!'

'Oh, my God! Can't you help me?'

'I've tried, for Christ's sake! Look, I have a friend... well, not a friend, he's just someone I know. Anyway, he might be able to help you. He's heavily into hypnosis, he knows far more about it than I do!'

'Ring him now!'

'He'll be working. I'll have to ring him this evening. In the meantime, keep away from the people who know about the word. Stay here for a few days and...'

'Rod, I've more to tell you.'

'Christ! There can't be more, surely?'

'I've changed. I used to be prudish and now... I've experienced sex, real sex, crude sex, and I... I seem to have discovered another side to myself, a side that I would never have dreamed existed. I've also discovered another side to my boyfriend! But *my* other side...'

'What sort of man is he? To use you like that, what sort of bastard is he?'

'Exactly that – a bastard!'

'We all have a darker side, Marianne. Who knows what lurks in the mire of the subconscious?'

'Evil monsters, that's what! Can I ask you something?'

'What?'

'If, under hypnosis, I was told to meet someone at a certain time, would I be able to stop myself from going?'

'God knows, Marianne! I mean, I thought I knew a fair amount about hypnosis, but what with the things you've told me! Planting a trigger word in your own subconscious like that is amazing!'

'So I'd not have the power to ignore the command and stay at home, then.'

'I suppose, if you were aware of the time, it might trigger something. For example, if the arranged time was six o'clock, then you might see a clock and... Just keep away from clocks and watches, as well as all those who know about the word! There's the phone, excuse me for a minute.'

Closing the lounge door behind him, Rod left Marianne to ponder, to reflect. Wishing that Rod had used the word to screw her as she felt her clitoris throb, she thought about her future. *God, I've really messed up any chance of a relationship with him!* she mused sadly. *He must think that I'm nothing but a slag!*

There were too many people involved, and the way Barry

was carrying on, there'd be dozens more jumping on the bandwagon – jumping on Marianne! She could cope with the nymphomaniacal girls, they wouldn't present a problem. But the evil Barry was a different matter! And when he lost his job, he'd work her so hard that she'd probably end up dying from sheer sexual exhaustion!

'Sorry about that,' Rod smiled as he entered the room. 'So, who's used the word and asked you to meet them?'

'One of the girls I told you about.'

'Where and when?'

'I . . . I'd rather not say.'

'Oh, all right. Look, I've another hour or so before my next client – do you fancy a walk in the park?'

'No, no, thanks. I'd better be going. I'll come and see you again, if you'd like me to, that is.'

'I'd like to see you every day, Marianne!'

'You . . . you don't think I'm a tart, then?'

'No, of course not! Under hypnosis, you've discovered sex, that's all. Mind you, it's just as well all women haven't discovered sex the way you have – the world would be full of . . . anyway, as I said, I'd like to see you every day.'

'I might call round in the morning, if you're in?'

'Yes, I'll be in. Should I be with a client, I won't answer the front door, so come in through the back way and make yourself at home.'

'OK, thanks. There goes your phone again, I'll see myself out. Goodbye, Rod. And thanks again.'

Now what do I do? Marianne wondered despondently as she strolled across the park, her vaginal lips naked beneath her short skirt. *Christ, I nearly ate my panties!* Had she not been so concerned, she'd have laughed, but the thought of someone playing around, telling her that her heart was about to stop, worried her.

Sitting on the bench, she was pleased that she'd told Rod everything. *Perhaps I should tell Barry everything?* she mused. But no, with the word still working, he'd still have power over her and there was no telling what he'd do! Even if she were to leave him, he'd find her and use the word to force her to return. He could end up controlling her life completely!

Spending the rest of the afternoon on her bed meticulously going through her course notes, Marianne again wondered about implanting a trigger word in Barry's subconscious. 'If only I could master hypnotism!' she breathed. 'I *will* master it if it's the last thing I do!'

The time nearing five, Marianne cleared her notes away and left the house before Barry returned from work. Her pussy still naked beneath her skirt, she wandered past the park and into town. Although she'd wanted to meet Lydia for an evening of crude lesbian sex, she decided that she'd keep well away from the park, and from Lydia, until she was able to rid her subconscious of the trigger word.

Window shopping, Marianne decided to spend some of the money she'd stolen from Barry. Eyeing a tartan minidress, she imagined herself wearing the skimpy garment, turning the men's heads as she walked down the street. *God, I feel sexy!* she mused. *I feel horny!*

Without thinking, Marianne inadvertently glanced up at the town hall clock as she crossed the road. 'Ten to seven.' The words reverberating around her mind, she turned and started walking towards the park. *No!* she screamed inwardly as her legs carried her faster towards Lydia and her inevitable fate.

Making her way across the park towards the bench, she noticed the young lesbian by a clump of trees. The girl was waving, beckoning Marianne to join her. Hopelessly trying to change direction, to walk away, Marianne approached the girl and obediently stood before her.

'So it *did* work!' Lydia grinned, squeezing Marianne's firm breasts. 'This hypnosis thing is brilliant! I could even phone you, mention the word, and demand that you come round and attend my pussy! You're mine, Marianne, mine to play with as and when it takes my fancy! Now, follow me, I've found a nice spot in the woods where we can spend the evening together – an evening to remember!'

Following her mistress though the long grass surrounding the clump of trees, Marianne felt her clitoris throb in anticipation. Emerging into a small clearing, she looked about her. A fallen tree lay on the soft grass where Lydia had placed her equipment – lengths of rope, a small branch with awesome-looking twigs fanning out from the main shaft, three monstrous-sized vibrators, one at least twelve inches long, tubes of KY gel, and a roll of sticky tape. This was, indeed, going to be an evening to remember!

Lifting her short skirt and bending over the tree, Lydia ordered her slave to kneel behind her. 'Lick my bottom,' she said, spreading her legs wide, revealing her shaved cunny lips nestling below her anal entrance. 'Come on, lick me all over!'

Parting the girl's bottom-orbs, Marianne pushed her tongue out and began licking the warm, soft hillocks. 'My bottom, lick my bottom!' Lydia gasped. Moving to the yawning crease, Marianne tentatively ran her tongue over the brown tissue surrounding her mistress's private portal. 'Ah, yes, that's it! Keep doing that!' Lydia breathed in her rising arousal. 'Keep licking my bum-hole, slave!'

Her taste buds rousing as she licked the bitter-sweet anal iris, Marianne pulled the girl's buttocks further apart, opening the small entrance to her bowels. Her tongue snaking its way into the dank heat, she closed her lips over the sensitive chestnut flesh, French kissing her mistress's derrière.

Lost in her crude act of anilingus, Marianne sucked and mouthed Lydia's bottom-hole, delighting in her new-found lewdness, ignoring her mistress's instructions to attend her pussy-hole. 'My cunt!' Lydia gasped. 'Lick my cunt now!'

Pushing her tongue further into the girl's tight anal entrance, Marianne breathed heavily though her nose, moaning her debased pleasure. 'Do as you're told!' Lydia admonished. 'Lick my cunt or you'll have the thrashing of your life!'

Moving her attention down as Lydia projected her bottom, Marianne lapped between the girl's drenched sex-folds, savouring her girl-come, swallowing the aphrodisiacal nectar. 'Push your tongue right up my cunt!' Lydia gasped. 'Pull my fanny wide open and tongue-fuck me!'

The crude instructions resounding around Marianne's mind, she complied, yanking the girl's hairless pussy lips apart to reveal the wet, pinken entrance to her cuntal sheath. 'My bum!' Lydia wailed, her whole body quivering. 'Finger my bum! Push two fingers into my bum!'

Locating the girl's anal portal, Marianne forced two fingers deep into her rectum, opening the tight duct, waking sleeping nerve endings there, causing Lydia to fill the wood with her cries of wanton lesbian lust. Thrusting her fingers in and out of Lydia's tight anal tube, Marianne forced her tongue deep into the girl's open vaginal sheath, inducing a torrent of pussy cream to flow.

'God, that's good!' Lydia gasped, bending further over the fallen tree and parting her legs as wide as she could to expose her intimacy to her slave. Her rectal sheath gripping the intruding fingers, her vagina spasming in response to Marianne's darting tongue, she shuddered, deliberately leaving her clitoris neglected, unattended – intentionally teasing, torturing herself.

Her body shaking violently, Lydia could barely hold back her impending orgasm. Swivelling her hips, positioning her erect clitoris dangerously closer to Marianne's hot mouth, she finally wailed her instructions. 'Now! My clitoris . . . Suck it now!'

Immediately obeying, Marianne engulfed her mistress's throbbing nodule in her wet mouth, sucking the most exquisite multiple orgasm from the pulsating protuberance. 'Three fingers!' Lydia sang, her crude demand reverberating through the wood as she recalled Marianne's bottom-hole yielding to the invading plastic phallus.

With ease, Marianne slipped a third finger into the girl's anal tunnel, distending the velveteen walls, causing Lydia to shake uncontrollably as she rode high on her seemingly perpetual climax. Thrusting her fingers deeper into her mistress's rectal sheath, lapping at her clitoris, Marianne had found her sexual heaven. All she wanted now was sex, and more sex.

Sucking and licking the final ripples of pleasure from Lydia's aching clitoris, Marianne grinned as she was ordered to leave her mistress. Slipping her fingers from the girl's bottom-hole and sitting back on her heels, Marianne gazed at her open holes, the creamy girl-come oozing from her inflamed vaginal opening, the saliva covering her anal crease glistening in the evening sun.

'You did well!' Lydia enthused, dragging her perspiring body from the tree trunk and collapsing on the soft grass beside Marianne. 'Give me a few minutes to recover, and I'll return the pleasure!' she grinned. 'While you're waiting, you can remove your clothes. I want you completely naked, Marianne. Stand over me so that I can watch you unveil your feminine beauty.'

Marianne stood with her feet either side of Lydia as the girl reclined, gazing up between her slave's long legs. 'You're not wearing any panties!' she hissed. 'You'll wear panties in the future so that I can watch you pull them down! Now, remove your clothes!'

Tugging her skirt down and stepping away from Lydia as she kicked the garment aside, Marianne retook her position, her girl-crack open, directly above her mistress's wide eyes. Pulling her T-shirt over her head, she thought of Barry, grinning inwardly as she imagined Alan arriving for his prepaid blow job to find that his slave wasn't there to attend him.

'And now your bra!' Lydia demanded, gazing up at Marianne's pouting vaginal lips, her inner labia protruding invitingly from her open cuntal valley. Unclipping her red lace bra and peeling the cups away from her pert young breasts, Marianne felt a pang of sexual excitement surge through her womb. Her sensitive nipples lengthening, becoming fully erect, she prayed that her mistress would suck them, bite them.

'OK, now kneel down with your wet cunt above my face.' In her anticipation, Lydia breathed the licentious demand huskily. 'I want to lick your wet cunt.' Marianne knelt, aware of her pinken slit opening as the feminine centre of her obedient young body neared Lydia's hungry mouth. 'That's it, knees further apart so that your cunt presses against my face!'

Settling her swollen vaginal lips over the girl's open mouth, Marianne gasped. The two female orifices locked in lesbian lust, their lips kissing, Lydia licked Marianne's inner flesh, caressing the tongue-like folds with her tongue. Her eyes rolling, Marianne looked up to the trees, the evening sun filtering through the canopy of leaves high above.

'Ah! Ah, I love my cunt!' she cried to the heavens. 'God,

how I love my cunt!' Her clitoris swelling, throbbing as her mistress's tongue swept over its sensitive tip, Marianne reached down and stretched her vaginal lips wide apart, exposing the full length of her cumbud to her lover's caressing tongue. The sensations of imminent orgasm building within her contracting womb, she gyrated her hips, sliding her wet sex valley back and forth over Lydia's mouth.

Shuddering, decanting her girl-juices, Marianne finally reached the summit of her orally-induced pleasure. Her crown swelling, throbbing, pumping out its orgasmic pulses, she rocked her hips faster, grinding her open cunt into her mistress's hungry mouth. Riding the peak of her debauchment, sustaining her climax, she pulled her cunny lips open further, painfully stretching the pink inner flesh, forcing her clitoris further into Lydia's hot mouth.

Slowing her swaying hips, Marianne closed her eyes and tossed her head back again as Lydia's tongue massaged her nodule, eliciting the waning orgasmic pulses from her sexual nucleus. Her naked body finally motionless, Marianne allowed her young mistress to drink from her hot hole. Lapping the flowing girl-come, swallowing the fruits of Marianne's orgasm, the girl drained her slave's cuntal sheath, cleansed her vaginal folds.

'I enjoyed that!' Lydia gasped, pushing Marianne away and licking her juice-covered lips. 'Mmm, you taste good! Now I want you to lie over the tree so I can get to your bum!'

Her legs sagging as she climbed to her feet, Marianne laid her naked body over the fallen tree. Her buttocks high, her feet wide apart, the very core of her femininity lay bared to her mistress. As Lydia moved behind her, Marianne again thought of Barry. He'd be fuming by now, having to return a portion of the money to Alan for failing to deliver the goods.

As her buttocks were crudely yanked apart, she smiled, imagining Alan having to return to his deceived wife, his balls full, aching – his knob yearning for a hot female mouth.

Smearing KY gel between Marianne's bottom-orbs and grabbing a vibrator, Lydia worked silently, presenting the tip of the buzzing phallus to her slave's anal portal. Gasping as her sphincter muscles relaxed, allowing the cylindrical monster to delve deep into her rectal sheath, Marianne realized again the immense pleasure her tight bottom had to offer. *It's like having two cunts!* she mused gratefully as the vibrations transmitted deep into her pelvis.

'You look great with the vibrator sticking out of your bum-hole!' Lydia giggled, twisting the end of the device and increasing the vibrations. Breathing heavily, her quivering body doubled over the rough bark of the fallen tree, Marianne sank her fingernails into the soft grass as her womb contracted, sending urgent waves of desire surging though her spasming vagina.

'Please . . . my cunt!' she gasped, desperate for her mistress to fill her empty vagina with another phallus. Her tormented body jolting as another vibrator slipped deep into her sex-sheath, Marianne whimpered as the beautiful sensations mingled. The melodic vibrations harmonizing, transmitting their music deep into her uterine cavity, Marianne had never known such sexual pleasure.

Taking a length of sticky tape, Lydia reached between Marianne's legs and pressed one end to her quivering stomach. Pushing the vibrators fully home, she ran the tape over the protruding ends and stuck it to the girl's lower back.

'There, now the vibros will stay in place during your thrashing!' she shrilled, grabbing the tree branch. 'This will teach you, not wearing your panties!' Marianne grimaced, tensing her buttocks as she awaited her inescapable gruelling punishment. 'In the future, you'll wear your panties for at least three days and then offer them to me, your mistress. I want them well-juiced, Marianne, nicely perfumed with your cunt juice! Do you understand?'

Her body now aching for sexual relief, Marianne said nothing as she sensed the tree branch gently scratching at her taut buttocks. *The waiting is worse than the punishment*! she thought anxiously as the spidery twigs ran down her inner thighs – teasing, tantalizing her youthful skin.

The vibrations seemingly increasing, her neglected clitoris swelling, yearning for massaging fingers, a caressing tongue, Marianne squeezed her eyes shut as the branch played around the sticky tape in her bottom-crease. When was the thrashing to commence? she wondered as the twig-ends clawed at her tender skin, running around the protruding vibrator, lingering there, torturing the tight brown tissue.

The branch scraping up her inner thighs again, clawing at her vaginal lips, those lips forced to balloon either side of the tape running through her sex valley, Marianne's anticipation – her fear – heightened. The sharp twig-ends would lacerate her taut flesh, she suddenly realized to her horror. Like a dozen fingernails scratching at her youthful skin, the branch toyed with her buttocks again.

'Want it now?' Lydia asked in her husky voice. Marianne couldn't reply. Her vocal chords seized as she opened her mouth to beg for mercy – she could do nothing to halt the cruel beating. 'I'll use the rope to whip you,' Lydia added, discarding the branch. Breathing a sigh of relief, Marianne relaxed, turning her concentration to the beautiful sensations the vibrators were bringing her.

The first lash of the rope caused her naked body to jolt, her erect nipples to rub painfully against the rough tree bark. Before the stinging pain had left her buttocks, another lash cracked across her taut skin. With her love-holes crudely invaded by buzzing vibrators and a rampant lesbian whipping her blatantly exposed buttocks, surely these were the lowest depths of depravity? She couldn't slip any deeper into the mire of corruption, she thought as the rope again cracked loudly across her crimson buttocks.

Biting her lip, Marianne took her punishment, whimpering as the thrashing pushed her close to the limits of sexual pain and pleasure. Her clitoris rock-hard, craving the alleviation only possible from orgasm, she prayed that her mistress would pay intimate attention to her ballooning nodule. 'Come . . .' she wailed. 'Want to . . . want to come!'

The rope flogging her now-burning buttocks, Marianne knew she could take no more. The birds fleeing the trees as her sobs filled the wood, she gasped her relief as Lydia finally halted the punishment and discarded the rope. Her perspiration-drenched body quivering as the vibrations deep within her pelvis permeated her clitoris, she cried out as, at last, her orgasm exploded.

'Ah, my cunt, my cunt!' she wailed as her clitoris sent powerful shock waves of sexual bliss through her trembling body. Sustaining her slave's climax, Lydia groped between the girl's legs, massaging her solid nodule through the strip of sticky tape, taking her even higher to her sexual paradise, deeper into the vile swamp of her depravity.

As the sensations receded, leaving Marianne trembling, panting, but tranquil in the aftermath of her desperately-needed climax, she tried to lift her aching body from the tree trunk. Helping the girl, Lydia steadied Marianne's naked body, peeling the tape from her sex-groove, allowing the buzzing vibrators to shoot from her inflamed holes like small torpedoes.

Clinging to Lydia as Marianne's girl-come gushed down

her inner thighs, she slowed her breathing, her eyes rolling, her head lolling to one side in her near-semiconscious state. 'You enjoyed that, didn't you?' Lydia giggled, tweaking Marianne's sore nipples. 'You'll be pleased to hear that your ordeal is far from over, my girl! The night is but young, as they say! Now, I want you to straddle the tree, sit on it with your legs either side as if you're riding a horse.'

Marianne desperately needed rest, but her body moved automatically, mounting the tree trunk without her thinking. Her full vaginal lips gaping, her glistening inner flesh pressing against the rough bark, she tried to make herself comfortable, manoeuvring her hips to alleviate the painfully chafing bark.

'Rock backwards and forward,' Lydia ordered. 'Rub your clitty against the trunk.' Having no control over her somatic nervous system, Marianne could do nothing to prevent her muscles rocking her naked body, rubbing her swollen clitoris, her pink inner flesh, against the craggy bark. 'Lie down now,' Lydia said. 'Lie down and cling to the tree so that I can get to your holes.'

Complying, Marianne laid her naked body across the tree, her limbs hanging either side of the trunk, her nipples, her soft mons painfully pressing against the gnarled surface. 'Ah, that's good!' Lydia exulted, eyeing the girl's yawning sex groove, her bottom-hole, completely unveiled by her spread buttocks. 'And now for my next trick!'

Hearing the buzzing vibrator, Marianne held her breath, wondering which of her two inflamed love-holes the phallus would sink into as Lydia moved behind her. Forcing the vibrator between Marianne's vaginal lips and the tree trunk, Lydia made her final adjustment, ensuring that the pink cylinder reached to the top of the girl's sex-groove, pressing hard against her yearning clitoris.

Standing back, Lydia watched as Marianne began to writhe, clinging to the tree as the vibrations swelled her clitoris. Gasping as the sensations infiltrated her inner core, Marianne began to swivel her hips, sliding her yawning vaginal crack along the wet vibrator shaft. Her bottom high, her buttocks crudely parted, she shuddered as Lydia slipped two fingers deep into her anal sheath, adding to the delicious sensations emanating from her clitoris.

'This will be *our* tree,' Lydia whispered as she thrust her fingers in and out of Marianne's tight bottom. 'We'll come here again and again to enjoy the tree. Now I want you to come, squirt all your beautiful cunt juice over the tree – christen the tree.'

Marianne's orgasm erupted quickly, causing her naked body to shudder uncontrollably, her nipples to chafe against the rough bark, adding a thrilling sense of obscenity to her inconceivable climax. Stretching her slave's bottom-sheath wider as she inserted a third finger into the creamy duct, Lydia thrust as hard as she could, finger-fucking the girl's tight rectum, bringing her lewd sensations of perverted sex.

'God, no more!' Marianne sobbed. 'I can't take any...'

'I'll be the judge of that!' her mistress returned in her wickedness as Marianne's climax receded, leaving her trembling, exhausted in her sexual gratification. 'All right, I'll show you some mercy,' Lydia grinned, slipping her fingers from her slave's rectal duct and removing the vibrator. 'Rest for a while, and then I'll *really* make you come!'

Leaving the girl lying over the tree trunk, Lydia sat on the short grass, dreaming up her next perverted act, wondering how many multiple orgasms Marianne could endure. Toying with the ten-inch vibrator, she lay back on the grass, running the buzzing tip up and down her girl-crack, emitting low moans as her clitoris responded. Reaching beneath her leg as she brought her knees up, she presented the rounded tip of the vibrator to her bottom-hole. Teasing the sensitive brown tissue, slipping the tip of the plastic phallus into her tight hole and withdrawing it again, she began to gasp.

'Come here, slave!' she ordered, watching as Marianne dragged her sated body from the tree trunk and obediently stood beside her mistress. 'Come down here and use the vibrator on my bottom-hole!' she ordered the girl, passing her the pink cylinder and opening her legs wide. 'Push it into my bum and fuck me there with it!'

Settling on the grass, Marianne pressed the device to her mistress's small hole, twisting the shaft as she drove it into the girl's rectum. Manoeuvring her hips, Lydia grinned as the shaft sank further into her velveteen anal duct, gasping her instructions as the vibrations permeated her very being. 'More! Further!' she cried as Marianne managed to force at least six inches into her mistress's quivering body. 'More!' Lydia gasped, to Marianne's amazement. 'Go on, do as I tell you and push it right in!'

Watching the thick shaft gliding into the girl's tight anus, Marianne managed to drive all but an inch of the awesome phallus into her bowels. Writhing on the grass, Lydia placed her hands behind her knees, pulling her legs up and apart until her knees almost touched her ears. Her pussy lips bulging, her girl-crack yawning, her bottom-crease barely perceptible as her flesh tautened, she lay with the very centre of her young body flagrantly exhibited to Marianne's wide eyes.

'Now put one in my cunt!' Lydia murmured. Marianne grabbed a second vibrator, switching it on and slipping it between the girl's swollen cunny lips and driving it deep into her vagina. 'Ah, that's good! Now fuck my holes with them!' Lydia instructed in her lewdness. 'Fuck my holes really hard!'

Grabbing the ends of the vibrators, Marianne began her thrusting, withdrawing the shafts and then ramming them deep into the girl's abused holes. The incredibly shameless act arousing her, Marianne gazed in amazement at the shafts as they emerged and disappeared again and again. Recalling her fantasy, she imagined two penises there, fucking her mistress's love-sheaths, sperming into her spasming sex-ducts.

Marianne had become sex-crazed, lust-struck, she mused. Her hunger for lust now insatiable, she imagined being instructed to take part in a lewd orgy in the woods. She'd be ordered to drink the gushing sperm from several orgasming knobs, to lick out pussy-slits, to open her body, her orifices to men, and receive their massive cocks. The incredible picture vivid in her mind, she thrust the vibrators into Lydia's lust-ducts with a frightening vengeance.

'Ah, ah! I'm coming!' Lydia gasped as she tossed her head from side to side, her long black hair veiling her flushed face as she pulled her knees further apart, opening the pinken epicentre of her femininity to her sex slave. 'God, fuck me, fuck my holes!' she cried in her abandonment as her muscles gripped the pistoning shafts.

Lydia finally ordering her slave to slow her rhythm, Marianne wondered what her next wanton act of lesbian debauchery would be. As her mistress lay quivering on the soft grass, Marianne pondered on her life, her new life since her games had begun. Was this what she really wanted? A life devoted to debased sex, both lesbian and heterosexual – was that what she really wanted? Even if Rod were able to rid her subconscious of the enslaving trigger word, could she now give up her insatiable quest for sexual gratification?

'Leave me now!' Lydia gasped as Marianne gently pressed the plastic shafts deep into the girl's ardent sheaths. 'Enough!' she cried as she brought her legs down and squeezed her thighs together to conceal her indecently exposed, abused girlhood. The vibrators still in place, causing Lydia to convulse spasmodically, she ordered Marianne to dress hurriedly and leave.

Obeying, Marianne covered her aching body with her miniskirt and top and left the wood. Walking through the park, she wondered at which point she'd regain control of her actions – if at all! The orange sun low in the evening sky, she walked the streets until she arrived at her house. As she slipped the key in the lock and opened the door, she realized that she was back in control. But she wondered why Lydia had sent her away. Perhaps she'd arranged to meet someone else in the woods?

'Where the fuck have you been!' Barry demanded angrily as he emerged from the lounge and stood in the hall with his hands on his hips.

'Oh! Er... Barry, I...'

'Well, where the fucking hell *have* you been?' he repeated, his dark eyes afire with rage.

'Hey, hey, hey – wait a minute!' Marianne stormed uncharacteristically, raising her hand to shut him up as she entered the lounge. 'What do you mean, *Where the fucking hell have you been*? What is it with you, Barry? Do you own me now or something, for fuck's sake? I don't want to walk through the door to be confronted by you hurling expletives at me! I'm not a piece of shit, I'll have you know!'

Visibly stunned, Barry gazed open-mouthed at Marianne as she flopped onto the sofa. Never before had she lost her temper, never until now had she raised her voice in anger. But now? Gazing into the fire reflected in her usually misty blue eyes, Barry began to wonder whether he really knew her or not.

The tables are turning! Marianne mused, reading Barry's

thoughts as he tentatively offered his apology by way of a pathetically weak smile. *The bloody tables are turning!* Although she knew only too well that it was she who was still ultimately under his control. But, there again, she wondered why he was offering his apologetic smile. Why not just use the magical word and admonish her, whip her, tell her never to leave the house again?

'I've been worried, Marianne,' he said softly, sitting down opposite. 'You keep going out and I never know where you are or when you're coming back.'

'It's summer, Barry. I enjoy the sun, going for walks in the park. *You* should get out more, exercise more.'

'I phoned several times today and there was no answer. You must have been for a hell of a long walk! Have you contacted Brooke-Smith and turned down the job offer yet?'

'Turned it down? Why would I turn it down?'

'I told you – I know what sort of personal assistant Brooke-Smith wants! Anyway, I've had some bad news.'

'Oh, what's that?'

'Saunders has fired me.'

'Oh, no! But why?'

'It's a long story. He gave me a month's notice but I decided to . . .'

'In that case, I need Brooke-Smith's job now more than ever!'

'There's more bad news, I'm afraid. I had five hundred pounds stashed away, and it's gone.'

'Five hundred? You didn't tell me!'

'I . . . I was keeping it for the honeymoon.'

'Where did it come from?'

'Here and there, fiddles, things like that.'

'Where was it?'

'In the kitchen, well out of sight.'

'God, has anything else been taken?'

'No, fortunately!'

'I'll *have* to work for Brooke-Smith now!'

'No, you won't. I've one or two ideas up my sleeve, so we'll be all right, financially. I've been planning to set up my own business for some time now.'

'What sort of business?'

'Er . . . as an advertising consultant. I've several clients already.'

Yes, I know you have! 'I saw Christine on my way home this evening,' Marianne grinned – she lied.

'What's that got to do with it?'

'She said that Alan had popped out for a while and had come back in a foul mood! Apparently, he'd been to see someone, something to do with business, and they'd let him down. Perhaps you could ask him if he needs . . .'

'I've already spoken to Alan about it. He's very interested.'

'It's a competitive world, Barry. If you let people down the way Alan was let down, you'll get nowhere.' *If only he knew that I knew that he . . .*

'I realize that!'

'Apparently, he'd paid up front for a business service of some sort, and whoever it was didn't come up with the goods. Christine was saying that Alan was about to send several other people along to his business contact, but now he's in two minds about it.'

Wincing, Barry checked his watch. Marianne glanced at the wall clock, wondering whether Barry would ring Alan and tell him that the goods were now available. 'You shouldn't leave money lying around the house, Barry. Five hundred pounds! Anyway, no doubt you'll soon be able to replace it.'

'Yes, and sooner than you think! I'm going to change the locks, just in case someone's got a key.'

'No one would have a key! They probably got in through a window or something. Anyway, I'm going to have a bath,' she announced as she stood up. 'I won't be long.'

Lurking on the landing, Marianne grinned as Barry lifted the phone and rang Alan. 'She's here, come round now,' he whispered. 'Yes, I know – I said that I was sorry Alan! Yes, she's definitely here now. Of course she won't go out, it's half past ten! All right, ten minutes.'

Leaving the door unlocked and running her bath, Marianne slipped out of her clothes and immersed her naked body in the hot water, wondering what Barry would do when Alan arrived only to discover that she was in the bath. Shaving the stubble from her mound, her soft vaginal lips, her mind swirling, she thought about locking the door and lying with her head under the water. She'd not be able to hear the magical word, and Barry wouldn't be able to get in. Alan would storm out of the house, let down yet again!

'Juxtaposition!' Barry called as he opened the bathroom door. 'There she is, all ready for you!' he laughed, showing Alan in.

'God, she's got a good body!' Alan said, admiring her gentle feminine curves, her crevices. 'She's shaved her fanny!'

'She likes it that way! She's a right tart, I'll tell you! Is it still only her mouth you want, or has the sight of her schoolgirl cunt tempted you to pay for more?'

'Only her mouth. I don't have much time, what with Christine waiting for me. Tomorrow evening, I might be persuaded to slip my knob up her tight cunt, though! Christine's going out with friends, so I'll have plenty of time.'

'I'll work out a price for you. Anyway, I'll leave you to it.'

As Barry closed the door, Alan stood by the bath and ordered Marianne to kneel. Sitting up and positioning her naked body before her master, she awaited the inevitable.

Unzipping his jeans, he presented her with his erect penis, pulling the loose skin back to expose his solid glans to her misty blue eyes.

'Suck it, whore!' he ordered crudely. Taking his shaft in her wet hand, she opened her mouth and engulfed his knob, running her tongue over the silky-smooth surface to the accompaniment of his gasps. 'Ah, that's good!' he breathed, slipping his knob deeper into her hot mouth and withdrawing again. 'Keep still!' he instructed. 'Keep your head still and I'll fuck your mouth!'

His hips swinging back and forth, his knob gliding in and out of her hot mouth, over her pink tongue, he clung to her head. 'You're a dirty little whore!' he gasped. 'I'm going to spunk over your tongue. I'm going to . . . Ah, God, that's good!'

Clinging to the side of the bath as his thrusts jolted her naked body, Marianne eagerly awaited his male come, impatient to savour the product of his orgasm. Her breasts bouncing as he rammed his knob harder against the back of her throat, she felt her clitoris swell, desperate for relief.

'Coming!' he cried as his shaft inflated and his knob throbbed. Spurting his jism into her mouth, bathing her tongue, splattering the back of her throat, he grimaced, thrusting his pulsating organ even harder. Almost choking on the salty liquid, Marianne breathed through her nose, her eyes open wide as her master gripped her head harder, using her mouth as if it were her vaginal sheath. His seemingly never-ending cascade of sperm filling her cheeks, running down her chin and dripping onto her pert breasts, Marianne felt sexually exhilarated.

Although she desperately wanted control over her young body, to fake her hypnotic state, she was deriving immense pleasure from servicing Alan. As his orgasmic flow ceased, again, she reminded herself of her innocence. Here she was, taking another man's knob into her mouth, swallowing his jetting sperm – but she was completely innocent.

'Now lick me clean!' Alan demanded, slipping his wet knob from the heat of her abused mouth. Taking his shaft in her hand, she pushed out her tongue, licking, cleaning the purple bulb, lapping up the residue of sperm from his veined tool. Without so much as a word of thanks, of appreciation for her part in the lewd act, Alan zipped his jeans and left the bathroom.

Still under the hypnotic spell, Marianne couldn't move, couldn't immerse her young body in the hot water to rinse away the sperm glistening on her firm breasts, her erect nipples. Barry finally entered the room and ordered her to lie down before bringing her out of her trance. Sitting on the stool, he smiled as she looked about her.

'What's that?' he asked, pointing to the jellyfish-like sperm clinging to her breasts, swirling in the water as if alive, waiting for passing food.

'Soap, I expect,' she replied, gazing at the mother-of-pearl creature spiralling in the lapping water. Taking the soap, Marianne cleansed her breasts, washing away Alan's sperm as Barry looked on.

Would *he* demand her mouth now, she wondered as he gazed longingly at her young body. Would he pump his sperm deep into her mouth? Or was he waiting until she went to bed before using and abusing her? *Two knobs coming in my mouth would be fun!* she found herself thinking as she savoured the remnants of Alan's come lingering on her tongue.

'So you're out of work,' she said, catching his amorous gaze as she parted her fleshy pussy lips and massaged soap between her pinken folds.

'Yes, I am. But I'm going to earn a hell of a lot of money! I've made something, in the garage.'

'Oh, what's that?'

'I'll show you tomorrow – it's to do with my new business.'

'What is it?'

'I'll show you tomorrow!'

'Well, whatever happens, I'm going to accept Brooke-Smith's job offer.'

'He'll be all over you, trying to get his hand into your knickers and . . . I really don't understand you, Marianne!'

'You don't understand yourself, so how can you expect to understand me?'

'What *are* you talking about?'

'Understanding people.'

'What do you mean, I don't *understand* myself?'

'Where's your life taking you? Where do you *want* it to take you? Where's your relationship with me taking you?'

'What do you mean? What *is* all this?'

'Do you have a conscience, Barry?'

'Of course I do!'

'What sort of man are you, *really*?'

'I don't understand . . .'

'No, you wouldn't.'

'I'm going to bed!'

'OK, I'll join you shortly.'

As Barry left, Marianne closed her eyes. The warm water lapping between her legs, caressing her distended inner cunt lips, she grinned, wondering where Barry's new hiding place was, where he was stashing money. Fondling her erect clitoris, she thought about her young body, the money she could earn from sex-starved men – and women! 'I don't know about Barry!' she giggled, climbing out of the bath. 'But *I'm* going to be rich!' *What's he been up to in the garage?* she thought, imagining him strapping her to some horrendous sexual machine.

Climbing into bed, she was relieved to find Barry sleeping soundly. *Another day over!* she reflected as she pulled and twisted her protruding inner pussy lips, caressed her stiffening clitoris. Her free hand beneath her leg, her finger toying with her sensitive anal entrance, she wondered what tomorrow would bring. *Sex, sex and more sex!*

Chapter Eight

Reading through her hypnosis notes whilst having her early morning coffee, Marianne sighed. She was desperate to learn the technique of hypnotism, to learn how to send Barry into a hypnotic trance and implant a trigger word in his subconscious. 'I *will* do it!' she affirmed, leaving the kitchen and wandering out into the garage.

Pulling a tarpaulin aside, Marianne stood with her hands on her hips, amazed – and disgusted – by Barry's handiwork. *He said he was going to make a pillory!* she mused. *But this is ridiculous!* The craftsmanship perfect, the wooden pillory comprised the usual holes for the neck and wrists, but more, they were attached to a low frame. Rather than stand, Marianne would have to kneel astride a central plank of wood to align her head and hands with the holes. Her stomach would rest on the padded plank, affording some comfort, at least, she surmised. Ropes attached to the frame were obviously for securing her knees, effectively keeping her legs apart, exposing her buttocks, her vaginal entrance, to her abuser.

There were several attachments that Marianne couldn't work out – small weights hanging from chains and various clamps and straps – but she'd soon discover their purpose! 'He *has* been busy!' she breathed, pulling the tarpaulin over the awesome device and returning to the kitchen to hear the phone ringing.

'Hallo,' she panted, having dashed through the hall.

'Marianne, it's Jonathan.'

'You don't give up, do you?' she laughed.

'No, I don't! Listen, I was wondering whether you'd like to have lunch with me?'

'What, today?'

'Yes, why not?'

'Well . . . er . . . I'm not sure what's happening today. Barry's been fired and, rather than take a month's notice, he left there and then.'

'Yes, I'd heard that he'd left.'

'He'll be back shortly, he's just gone into town for something.'

'Do you have to get the OK from him before you do anything, then?'

'Well, no. Look, ring me later, after I've spoken to Barry. The pips are going, there's someone trying to get through – I'll talk to you later.'

Replacing the receiver and lifting it at the first ring, Marianne frowned to hear Rod's voice. 'How did you get my number?' she gasped in her puzzlement. 'You don't know my surname!'

'Ah, ha!' Rod laughed. 'I have my ways! No, seriously, I rang the chap who lectured on your hypnosis course. We had quite an interesting chat. Anyway, eventually I mentioned you, and he came out with your surname.'

'You're lucky the phone's in my name and not Barry's! So why are you ringing me?'

'I was worried, Marianne. Thinking about the incredible things you told me, I thought I'd better see how you are. What happened at seven o'clock last night?'

'Nothing, nothing happened. I went to town and walked around the shops so . . .'

'I know that you're lying to me, Marianne! Has your soon-to-be-ex-boyfriend used the word again?'

'I'm not lying! No, he hasn't used the word again, not yet, anyway,' Marianne replied, biting her lip as she recalled kneeling in the bath and sucking on Alan's throbbing knob, swallowing his gushing sperm.

'Look, you really do need my help. Yesterday, you said that you might come over. Are you still going to?'

'I really don't know what I'm doing today, Rod. I seem to be having people coming at me from all directions. And I don't mean that type of coming!'

'What *do* you mean, then?'

'A friend keeps pestering me to work for him, Barry's due back from town soon, and now you're . . .'

'I wouldn't hang around if Barry's due home!'

'God, that's a thought. Knowing him, he'll bring half a dozen men back!'

'Come and stay with me, as I suggested yesterday. You'd be safe here and . . .'

'I've been thinking about that. It's no good running away, Rod. I must stay and deal with this myself.'

'How *can* you deal with it? The only way to deal with it is to keep out of Barry's way!'

'I'm determined to master the art of hypnosis. If I had a trigger word to use on Barry, I could get my own back, use *him* as *my* slave and . . .'

'You shouldn't be thinking along the lines of tit-for-tat, Marianne! This is a serious business! I thought that you realized the severity of the situation.'

'Yes, I do, but I'm *not* going to run away!'

'All the time you're there, with Barry, you're open to abuse!'

'Oh, Barry's just walked in through the back door. I might see you later this morning, I don't know.'

'If I were you, I'd come over here right now! Come here before he has the chance to . . .'

'I've got to go, Rod. Thanks for ringing, it's nice talking to you. See you later.'

Entering the kitchen with a fixed smile, Marianne wondered when Barry was going to place her in his pillory and use her naked body to satisfy his perverted lust. *At least he's come home alone!* she mused as she filled the kettle, imagining half a dozen men using her tethered body, half a dozen solid penises pumping sperm into her tight holes.

'You're quiet,' Barry said. 'Is there anything wrong?'

'No, I'm fine,' she replied, a quiver running up her spine as she pictured six hard penises sperming over her naked body, her elongated nipples. 'Want some coffee?'

'Yes, thanks. It's strange, not having to go to work.'

'Tell me about it! So what are you going to do today?'

'I've bought some new locks. Before I do anything, I'm going to fit them.'

'Good! I don't like the idea of someone searching my home, it gives me the creeps!'

'What have you got planned?'

'Nothing, really. I'll probably go out to the park later.'

'You're always going to the park! What is it about that place?'

'I like it there, it's relaxing. Is anyone coming round?'

'What, here?'

'Yes, any of your friends?'

'Er . . . no, not as far as I know. Why do you ask?'

'I just wondered whether you needed me to be around or not.' *Whether you needed my body to earn you some money!*

'What do you mean? Why would I need you to be around?' he asked, his dark eyes frowning.

'I don't know, I just wondered. Oh, by the way – I need some money, do you have any cash?'

'Er . . . yes, how much?'

'Fifty.'

'What do you need fifty pounds for?'

'This and that.'

'Right, well, I'll have to go and get it.'

'Where from?'

'Juxtaposition.'

And now to discover the new hiding place! Marianne thought as she fell into a hypnotic trance. Surprised that Barry was still keeping his cash in the same place as he pulled the vinyl floor covering back, she decided to buy the tartan minidress she'd seen in the shop window the previous evening. Parading around the park in the tight dress would turn the men's heads, she thought wickedly.

'An experiment,' Barry said pensively as he replaced the floor covering and stuffed fifty pounds into his pocket. 'I've been thinking about this hypnosis thing. I'm going to tell you to do something and see if, when I bring you out of your trance, you'll be aware of what it is you're doing. OK, take your clothes off, Marianne. When you wake up, you'll not realize that you're naked. You'll think that you're fully dressed, even if we have visitors. You'll go about the house and garden completely unaware that you're naked.'

Her hands mechanically removing her clothes, Marianne was sure that Barry's suggestion wouldn't work. If it did, she pondered, then he'd have frightening power over her. If, even in her waking state, she didn't realize that she was naked, the implications would be horrifying! Imagining Barry inviting several friends round to a dinner party, she pictured herself as the naked hostess. *Oh, my God!* she thought as she slipped her skirt and panties down. *I hope he doesn't think of the idea!*

Finally standing naked before her master, she watched as he gathered up her clothes and stuffed them into a Tesco's bag. 'Right, this should be interesting!' he laughed, placing the bag in a cupboard. 'Talk about the king with no clothes! OK, Marianne – wake up!'

The strange hypnotic state leaving Marianne, she was relieved as she looked down to her pert breasts, fully aware that she was completely naked. *So, it hasn't worked!* she thought as Barry walked to the kitchen door. But she'd pretend that it had!

'Come and have a look at the front garden,' he said, leaving the room.

'What for?' she asked, following him through the hall, realizing that this was a test. 'I thought you were going to get me some money?'

'Yes, in a minute. I want to ask your opinion. I've been wondering whether to pave a small area of the lawn.'

As Barry opened the front door and stepped outside, Marianne was horrified as she followed, walking into the front garden in full view of anyone who might pass by. The hypnotic suggestion hadn't worked inasmuch as she knew only too well that she was completely naked, but her awareness didn't bring the embarrassment she'd normally feel. Walking across the lawn, to her surprise, she felt no humiliation whatsoever. She felt as comfortable, as secure, as she would have had she been fully clothed.

'I was thinking about paving that section of lawn, under the window there. I thought we could stand a row of flower tubs beneath the window. What do you think?'

'Yes, I think it's a good idea,' she replied, wondering why she wasn't in the least worried that someone might see her. 'Anyway, if you give me the money, I'll go into town.'

'OK,' he smiled, pulling the notes from his pocket. 'What

are you going to wear into town?' he asked, handing her the money.

'I'll go as I am,' she said, now half believing that she was fully clothed. 'I'll get my bag and go now.'

Following Marianne into the house and closing the front door, Barry gazed at her, her pussy-slit, her full vaginal lips, amazed by the power he had over her. His mind teeming with ideas, he decided that today he'd start making his dirty video tapes – and earn a small fortune!

'I'll be a couple of hours,' Marianne said, slipping the money into her handbag as the doorbell rang.

'Will you get that?' Barry asked, his excitement rising as she placed her bag on the table and made her way to the front door. 'I'm just nipping out to the garage.'

Her mind confused, almost convincing her that she was fully clothed, she opened the front door to find John standing on the step. 'Hi, John – come in!' she smiled as he stared open-mouthed at her shaven pussy-slit. 'Come in, John!' she repeated, standing back and opening the door wider. 'Or are you going to stand there all day?'

'Oh, yes, right,' he replied hesitantly, stepping into the hall.

'Barry's in the garage – come through. What's the camera for?' she asked, gazing at the Pentax hanging from his neck.

'I've just picked it up, it's been repaired.'

Leading John into the kitchen, her curvaceous body blatantly exhibited to her guest, she poured three cups of coffee. 'I'm just going into town,' she said, passing John a cup. 'I've seen a nice dress I want. You're not at uni today, then?'

'Er... no, not today,' he replied, placing his camera on the table and sitting down, his gaze transfixed on the weals fanning out across her taut buttocks as she bent over to put the milk in the fridge. 'I've finished my thesis.'

'Oh, that's good. That must be a weight off your mind.'

'Yes – yes, it is.'

'I really don't know what Barry's up to out there. He's making something, but I don't know what,' she said, standing up and leaning with her buttocks against the worktop.

'He's not at work today, then?'

'No! Haven't you heard? He's been sacked!'

'Sacked? Oh, will he be here every day, then?' he asked despondently. 'What's he going to do for money?'

'He's starting up some sort of consultancy thing. Why don't you go out to the garage and see him?'

'I . . . I'll have my coffee first,' he smiled, toying with the teaspoon, obviously wondering what the hell Marianne was playing at as she stood with her feet apart, seemingly unaware that she was blatantly displaying her gaping pussy-slit.

'Right, I must finish my coffee and get going!' Marianne said, taking a brush from her bag and grooming her long blonde hair.

Now virtually convinced that she was clothed, she moved about the kitchen, unashamedly displaying her taut buttocks, her vaginal crack, her erect nipples. Dumbfounded, John wondered whether Barry had used the trigger word and told her to strip, and then left her in a hypnotic trance. But no, he decided, she was acting perfectly normally. Rising to his feet, his penis solid, straining within his tight jeans as he glimpsed her inner petals protruding between her full vaginal lips, he moved to the back door.

'I will have a quick word with Barry,' he smiled, opening the door. 'I won't be a minute.'

'OK,' Marianne replied, packing her brush into her bag. 'Tell him his coffee's here, will you?'

'Yes, I will.'

Opening the garage door, John was surprised to find that Barry wasn't there. Wondering what on earth was going on, he returned to the kitchen just in time to catch Marianne before she left for town.

'Barry's not out there,' he said as Marianne slung her bag over her shoulder.

'That's odd! Perhaps he's popped out for something. Anyway, I'm off to town, do you want to wait here for him?'

'Are you going into town like that?'

'Like what?' she asked, looking down at her firm breasts. 'Is there something wrong?'

'Juxtaposition.'

Standing motionless, Marianne suddenly realized that she was naked. *What's happening to me?* she wondered as John took her bag and placed it on the table. Suddenly remembering all that had happened, recalling strolling around the front garden in all her naked glory, she silently cursed Barry, wondering where he was, why he was going to allow her to walk into town without a stitch of clothing.

'Marianne, why are you naked?' John asked.

'Barry told me to strip,' she replied mechanically.

'Why?'

'I don't know.'

'Didn't you realize that you were naked?'

'No, I thought I had my clothes on.'

'It must have been hypnotic suggestion.'

'Yes, it was.'

'You'd better dress before you go into town otherwise you'll get yourself arrested! I don't know what the hell Barry thinks he's playing at!'

'He put my clothes in there,' she said, her finger automatically pointing to the cupboard. 'In a plastic bag.'

Opening the cupboard and grabbing the bag, John placed

her clothes on the worktop. 'Before you dress, I might as well have a little fun,' he breathed, running his finger up her pinken pussy-crack. 'I was hoping that Barry would be out. I thought we'd have a photo session. Is that nice?' he asked, slipping his finger into her hot vaginal sheath.

'Yes, it is,' she replied, closing her eyes as he gently massaged her inner flesh.

Standing with her feet apart, Marianne recalled meeting Lydia in the park, having automatically walked there at the appointed time. She also recalled parading her young body in the front garden, answering the front door while naked, and she now realized that Barry could have permanent control over her. She felt more like a slave now than ever before. Her body belonged to Barry, it was his to do with as he wished. The power of suggestion was frightening, she pondered, wishing now that she'd taken Rod up on his offer and moved into his house for a while.

'You've a lovely cunt,' John breathed, inserting another finger into her creamy sex-duct. 'I would have come round sooner, but I've not had the time. But I've been thinking about you, Marianne. Every day, I've thought about you, your cunt. From now on, I'll be visiting you every day, when Barry's not around. Right, I'm going to take some photographs of you. I'm rather short of cash, you see. I'll get a good price for the pictures on the campus.'

Slipping his wet fingers from her tightening vagina, John grabbed his camera. Praying that Barry would walk in and save her as John fiddled with the flashgun, Marianne patiently awaited her instructions. 'OK, feet wide apart and bend over the table,' he finally ordered. Taking her position, Marianne jutted her taut buttocks out as John knelt behind her and focused on her distended vaginal lips. 'That's good!' he praised. 'I see you've had a good thrashing! Who did that?'

'A girlfriend.'

'Really? You are a naughty little girl! You'll have to introduce me to her. Now, reach behind your bum and pull your cunny lips wide apart.'

Obediently complying, Marianne parted her fleshy vaginal lips, exposing the pinken entrance to her drenched sex-duct. Her arousal rising as the camera clicked and whirred, she stretched her sex-cushions further apart, revealing the inner walls of her pussy-sheath.

'Just a couple more,' John murmured, taking another shot. 'And then we'll have you on your back across the table doing the splits. The lads will love the pictures – they'll pay well to get close-up shots of a nice juicy cunt!'

Taking the last shot, John moved closer to Marianne and lapped up the love-juice seeping from her vaginal entrance. 'You taste good!' he breathed appreciatively. 'I like the taste of a young girl's cunt!' Her clitoris ripening as her master's tongue snaked between her swelling pussy lips, Marianne began to breathe heavily.

But she desperately needed to be in control. Her arousal causing her naked body to quiver, she longed to turn the clock back and feign hypnosis rather than be a real slave to her abusers. What had started out as a joke, a laugh, she reflected, had now turned into slavery!

'I might fuck you in a minute,' John said as he stood up. 'Fuck you and spunk up your cunt! OK, get up and lie on your back across the table.' Taking her position, Marianne lay with her long legs spread, her buttocks over the edge of the table, her swollen vaginal lips bared.

Ordering Marianne to peel her cunny lips back as he took several close-ups of her intimacy, John finally placed his camera on the table. 'I need something . . . Ah, that's it!' he cried, grabbing the vacuum cleaner from the corner of the kitchen.

Standing the upright cleaner on the floor between Marianne's legs, he parted her buttocks and presented the handle to her tight brown hole. 'This will sell the pictures!' he laughed, easing the thick plastic handle past her sphincter muscles. 'Just relax! I'm going to push the handle deep into your bum.'

Her rectal sheath expanding as the handle drove deep into her bowels, Marianne felt her clitoris throb and her vagina spasm. The lewd pictures *would* fetch a good price, she knew! But would anyone recognize her? Many students from the university gathered in the park during their lunch break, someone was bound to recognize her!

'You do look a sight!' John laughed as he stood back and gazed at the obscene spectacle. 'Well, that's one way to vacuum the floor!' Taking several photographs, he put the camera aside and unzipped his jeans. 'Might as well fuck you before I go!' he laughed, standing astride the vacuum cleaner and presenting his swollen glans to her vaginal opening. 'The vacuum cleaner handle up your bum, and my cock up your cunt! You *are* a lucky girl!'

Marianne gasped as John's solid shaft drove deep into her tight vaginal sheath. Her rectum bloated, her sphincter muscles tightening around the phallus as her pussy inflated, she grinned inwardly. *It's like having two cunts*, she remembered herself thinking when Lydia had forced a huge vibrator deep into her bottom-hole. But she still hadn't realized her dream – two penises between her spread legs, driving deep into her tight holes, pumping their sperm into her shuddering body. *And one in my mouth!* she mused.

'Having your bum shafted really tightens your cunt up!' John gasped as he drove his knob in and out of Marianne's wettening sex-duct. 'I'll have to bring a mate round. We'll fuck both your holes at once!'

The words heightening Marianne's arousal, she squeezed

her anal sphincter muscles, rhythmically gripping the plastic handle. Delicious sensations emanating from her abused anal canal, she whimpered as John pressed his thumbs into her fleshy vaginal lips, pushing them hard against her pubic bone as he opened her sex valley, exposing her solid clitoris.

'Like being used, do you?' he asked, quickening his rhythm. 'Like having your tight holes fucked and your clitty massaged, do you?' Marianne didn't answer as John began rubbing her swollen cumbud. The sensations building deep in her quivering pelvis, she didn't want to speak. All she wanted was to wallow in her lewdness – her enforced lewdness.

'God, I'm going to come!' John grimaced, ramming her cervix with his ballooning cock-head. 'God, you're a bloody good fuck!' Sensing his sperm jetting deep into her vagina, Marianne opened her mouth, gasping as her own climax gripped her shuddering body, coursing through every nerve ending, tightening every muscle. 'You're a dirty little tart!' John breathed, sliding his glistening, girl-wet shaft back and forth, gazing at her inner lips rolling along the veined surface of his solid cock.

Her orgasm receding, gently lowering Marianne from the dizzy heights of sexual pleasure, she licked her dry lips, wondering what beautiful sexual act she'd be forced to endure next. Stilling his spent penis, John breathed heavily, gazing down at his slave's open crack, her inner lips enveloping his sperm-soaked shaft. He, too, was wondering what obscenity to commit, what to force his slave to do next.

Slipping his flaccid organ from Marianne's trembling body, John steadied himself, leaning on the table, grinning at her tongue sensually snaking over her full lips. Moving around the table, he turned her head to face him. 'Suck me!' he ordered. 'Come on, lick my spunk and your cunt juice from my cock!'

Taking his knob into her hot mouth, Marianne rolled her eyes, savouring the heady male-female flavour of sex. Pushing his length into her mouth, resting his knob at the back of her throat, John tweaked Marianne's nipples. 'We'll have to make use of these,' he said, pulling on her milk buds, stretching the sensitive brown tissue. 'When I come round tomorrow, we'll have some real fun with your titties!'

Rhythmically sucking on her master's swelling penis, Marianne wondered again where Barry had got to. Imagining him hiding in the bushes, gazing at his young girlfriend, the vacuum cleaner handle buried deep within her bowels, her yawning vaginal crack dripping with sperm, she wondered when he'd next use her.

'OK, that's enough for now,' John said, slipping his penis from Marianne's mouth. Moving between her legs, he gently eased the vacuum cleaner handle from her bottom-hole, grinning as her muscles tightened, closing the entrance to her dank bowels. 'Now I think you'd better get dressed, Barry might walk in at any moment,' he said, standing the vacuum cleaner in the corner of the room and zipping his jeans.

As Marianne dressed, covering her dripping pussy-crack with her tight red panties, John stopped her. 'I'll try something, seeing as Barry seems to have been successful with his hypnotic suggestion. Take your panties off. You'll never wear panties again, do you understand? Never will you wear panties from now on. Now, carry on dressing.'

Slipping her wet panties down her long legs, Marianne finished dressing, wondering whether John's suggestion would work as well as Barry's had. Imagining her shaved pussy permanently naked beneath her short skirt, she wondered what she was becoming, what she was turning into.

'Right, wake up,' he ordered, slipping her panties into his pocket as she finished dressing and stood obediently before him. 'I'd better get going. It doesn't look as if Barry's going to come back,' John smiled.

'OK,' Marianne replied, aware of sperm trickling down her inner thighs. 'I'm off into town now. That's odd, where *has* the time gone!' she gasped, gazing up at the wall clock. 'It's far later than I thought it was!'

'I didn't realize it was that late, either. Anyway, I'll see myself out. I might call round tomorrow, if that's OK?' he grinned as he turned in the doorway.

'Yes, whenever. See you, John.'

As the front door closed, Marianne took two sheets of kitchen roll and dabbed the sperm from her inner thighs. 'No panties,' she breathed, lifting her skirt and wiping her girl-crack. 'If these hypnotic suggestions carry on, I'll become someone else. I'll completely lose my bloody identity!'

As Barry wandered in through the back door, Marianne decided that he must have been hiding in the garden, watching her session of enforced sex. 'Where have you been?' she asked. 'John came round to see you and you'd disappeared!'

'Sorry, I nipped out for something. I thought you were going into town?'

'Yes, I'm just about to.'

'You're not going out this evening, are you?'

'Why?'

'I've got some friends coming over. I thought it would be nice if you were here.'

'When did you arrange that?'

'A little while ago. You will be here, won't you?'

'What, to serve you and your friends?'

'Serve us?'

'With tea and coffee, or beer.'

'Oh, I see. No, no, I didn't mean that.'

'I will be here, yes. Right, I'll see you later,' she said, grabbing her handbag.

'OK. How long will you be?'

'I don't know! I'm not going to *time* myself, Barry! I'll see you when I see you. Bye.'

Walking down the street with a light breeze cooling her inflamed cuntal lips, Marianne thought again of the tartan minidress. Her pussy knickerless, she'd only have to sit with her thighs slightly parted or bend over a little and her femininity would be on display. The thought exciting her, causing her stomach to somersault, she decided she'd call into a coffee shop on her way back and *inadvertently* expose her girl-crack to an unsuspecting man. *A man sitting with his wife!* she thought wickedly.

'Would you like to try it on?' the shop assistant asked, handing Marianne the dress.

'Yes, thank you,' Marianne smiled.

'I'm sure it's going to be too small for you. I could order your size, if you'd like me to?'

'No, I think this will be just right, thanks anyway.'

Taking the garment into a cubicle, Marianne slipped her skirt and top off. Holding the dress up and standing naked before the mirror, she grinned. 'It's going to be *far* too small for me!' she giggled, Slipping the dress over her head, she tugged it down her naked body, squeezing her hips, her breasts into the tight material. Finally managing to pull the zipper up her back, she gazed into the mirror again. Leaning backwards, her hairless pussy lips peered out between her thighs. Turning round, she leaned forward a little, gazing back at her swollen vaginal lips in the mirror. 'Perfect!' she breathed, grabbing her clothes and leaving the cubicle.

As Marianne had expected, the men's heads did turn as

she walked down the street. Several wolf whistles came from a group of teenage boys across the road, and Marianne turned to look in a shop window, bending over slightly, exposing her buttocks, her girlishness to the boys' wide eyes. 'Look at that girl!' an elderly woman said to her friend as they passed by. 'It's disgusting, going around like that!'

Grinning, Marianne walked briskly down the street to the coffee shop, praying there'd be someone she could sit opposite and shock. *All this began as a joke*, she reflected, wondering again at the incredible change she'd been through. Even without hypnosis, she was enjoying her body, and she began to wonder whether the constant sex had somehow re-educated her subconscious, woken her sleeping sexual desires. Virtually nymphomaniacal now, she was beginning to think of nothing other than sex. Her life focused between her legs, between her pouting vaginal lips.

The coffee shop was fairly busy. Sitting at a window table, Marianne scanned the pale faces – drawn housewives taking a break from shopping, a young couple holding hands across the table, and a middle-aged man and his wife sitting in silence. Moving her chair, Marianne parted her thighs, knowing that the man would see her blatant exhibitionism beneath the table if he were to look in her direction.

Ordering a coffee from the waitress, Marianne waited, her heart fluttering, her stomach somersaulting as she parted her thighs further, knowing that her pussy-crack was grinning at the man. His looked past his wife and gazed into Marianne's misty blue eyes as she proffered a slight smile. His eyes lowering, lighting up as he focused between her legs, he quickly averted his lustful gaze.

Marianne sensed that she wasn't in control as she placed her hand between her legs and massaged her swelling clitoris with her fingertip. The man watching her blatant public masturbation from the corner of his eye, Marianne felt a rush of desire course through her contracting womb. Her eyes darting between the other customers, she opened her legs wider, peeling her shaved pussy lips back, exposing her pink inner flesh to her astounded spectator. *I can't come in here!* she thought as her clitoris responded to her gentle caress. *God, what am I doing?*

Somehow, her subconscious had been trained, her character altered. The sex she'd experienced with men and women, the bondage, the whipping, the incredible orgasms, had melted her sense of morality. But more, she was driven by a perpetual desire for sexual satisfaction, a wicked craving to shock. Even if she were to rid herself of the trigger word, the old Marianne was lost forever.

Virtually unaware of anyone other than her male voyeur, Marianne rested her elbow on the table, her eyes rolling as she massaged her clitoris faster. Her face serene, angelic, she closed her eyes as her orgasm rose from her feminine depths and exploded in her clitoris. Shuddering, her mouth open, gasping, she gazed at her voyeur through her lashes. Visibly stunned, he stared in disbelief at the blatant obscenity, the beautiful sight of a young girl masturbating her clitoris to orgasm.

Her bottom-hole void, yearning for a massive phallus, her vagina spasming, decanting its hot girl-come as Marianne sustained her climax with her vibrating fingertip, she wished she'd brought the Christmas candle with her. *Next time*, she decided as her orgasm waned, leaving her trembling. Lowering her head, trying to disguise her obvious pleasure as the waitress passed her table, Marianne slipped her finger into her drenched vagina.

Her body calming now, she massaged her inner flesh, bringing out the last gentle waves or orgasm. Raising her head, she smiled at the dumbfounded man as she slipped her finger from her tight sex-duct and sucked it, savouring her girl-come, provocatively running her pink tongue over her lips.

'May I borrow the sugar?' he asked as he walked over to her. Marianne smiled her affirmation as he took the sugar bowl and dropped his card on the table. He was fairly tall with brown, well-groomed hair. His suit, collar and tie gave him an air of professionalism. Clean-shaven, his face tanned, Marianne imagined him between her legs, his tongue snaking round her throbbing clitoris.

Closing her legs, concealing her inflamed vaginal lips, her yawning girl-crack, she looked down at the card as he returned to his unsuspecting wife. *Christopher Davies, accountant.* Looking up, she grinned at her potential conquest and held her clenched fist to her ear, indicating that she'd ring him. As his wife turned to face her, Marianne sipped her coffee, innocently gazing at a painting on the wall above the woman's head.

Her husband's penis would be stiff, bulging his trousers as he flashed Marianne a smile before his wife turned to face him. *How easy!* Marianne mused. *How easy to take another woman's man!* As the couple left, Marianne decided to take a stroll in the park. She'd ring Christopher Davies later. Give him a chance to return to his office and then call him, talk dirty to him, ask him what he thought of her cunt. He had no idea who she was, so she could say whatever she liked over the phone. *Perhaps he'll wank while I'm talking to him,* she thought as she paid for her coffee and left.

Passing a church as she neared the park, Marianne was suddenly overwhelmed by a wicked yearning to commit an evil act. Opening the church door, she entered the cold building, wondering where the vicar was. Walking down the aisle, her vagina oozing with her juices of lust, she climbed the carpeted steps to the altar. *Dare I?* she wondered, running her hands over the tapestry covering the altar. Eyeing two candlesticks standing at either end of the altar, Marianne grinned. Climbing onto the altar, she moved to one end, her heart racing, her stomach somersaulting. *The devil's daughter!* she mused.

Made from brass, the candlestick held a long candle, the rounded tip a good three feet high. Standing on her toes, her pussy-crack above the candle, she lifted her new minidress up over her stomach and eased the wax phallus between her swollen cunny lips. Gently lowering her body, she threw her head back as the waxen shaft glided into her tightening vagina.

'God, it's big!' she cried, her profane words resounding around the church as she completely impaled herself on the solid shaft. Gyrating her hips, bobbing up and down, she gasped as her vaginal muscles tightened, gripping the slippery shaft. Her mind bent on committing the most evil and depraved act she could imagine, she raised her body, slipping the candle from her hot pussy-hole. Dragging the other candlestick across the altar, she positioned it by the first, giggling as she manoeuvred her young body, aligning her yearning love-holes with the two rounded tips.

Gently lowering the open centre of her young body, she eased the candles into her holes, gasping as her sheaths stretched, opened to accommodate the holy offerings. 'God, it's beautiful!' she cried as the shafts slipped deeper into her young body, bringing her incredible sensations in her sacrilegious obscenity. *You gave me my cunt*, she thought blasphemously, throwing her head back and looking up to the church roof. *You gave me my holes, my beautiful cunt and my tight bum – so I'll use them!*

Massaging her clitoris as she bounced up and down, double-fucking herself with the phallic symbols, she brought out her orgasm, wailing her pleasure as her young body shuddered uncontrollably. 'God, this is good! Ah, God, my cunt! My beautiful bum!' On and on her climax rolled, taking her ever-closer to her sexual heaven, ever deeper into the mire of her new-found evil. Her girl-come streaming down the waxen shaft as she bounced on the love-poles, she finally slowed her rhythm, gently caressing her pulsating clitoris, gasping in her wanton abandonment.

'Jesus Christ!' a man in a cassock cried as he stood before the altar looking up at Marianne's swollen pussy lips, taut around the massive candle. 'What do you think you're doing?' Marianne looked down at the vicar, her blue eyes sparkling. She felt no remorse, no embarrassment as she grinned at the man's ashen face – only a sense of satisfaction at the shock, the disgust, so obviously depicted in his expression. 'What are you doing, girl?' he repeated angrily, his eyes transfixed on her exposed clitoris.

'Fucking your candles!' she giggled, aroused more than ever now.

'Come down from there! I have never...'

His words tailed off as Marianne raised her trembling body, easing the shafts from her abused holes. He could only stare in disbelief as she peeled her cunny lips open, exposing her swollen clitoris, her pinken vaginal entrance, her girl-cream flowing in torrents, running down her inner thighs. As she climbed down from the altar, she deliberately opened her legs wide, virtually doing the splits, revealing her tight brown hole to the vicar's wide eyes. Standing before him, her minidress still high over her stomach, she grinned.

'Don't mind me using your candles to bring myself off, do you?' she asked. His mouth hanging open, he said nothing as she tugged her dress down, concealing her blatantly violated femininity. 'I was just passing your church and felt like a frig. When I saw the candles, I just couldn't help myself!' she giggled.

As she left the church, she turned to face the man of God. 'I'll *come* again, if it's all right with you?' she giggled. He gazed at her, her dishevelled blonde hair, her breasts ballooning her tight dress, her shapely thighs. 'Is it all right?' she asked again. 'You don't mind me fucking your candles?' Unable to voice his evil affirmation, he nodded, a slight smile furling his lips as he looked up to the roof. 'When I'm passing again, I'll come in – and come! You can give me a hand!' she called as she walked out into the summer sun, leaving him to contemplate the blasphemous act.

Sitting on the park bench, Marianne gazed at Rod's house, wondering whether he was with a client or not, whether to visit him – enjoy an hour of debauched sex with him. *No, I mustn't!* she suddenly thought, realizing that her clitoris was beginning to rule her life. *My God, I did it in a church – on the bloody altar!* Recalling the candles, her incredible orgasm, she wondered what she was becoming, what had possessed her to commit her blatant act of sin. Walking home, she knew that she had to fight, to change her ways, or she'd be sucked deeper into the mire of her own debauchery. *Unless I stop now, I'll never be able to stop!*

Calling Barry as she walked out into the back garden and neared the garage, she wondered what horrendous devices he'd attached to his pillory. She wondered, too, how to end her enslavement. Covering his creation with the tarpaulin as she entered the garage, Barry frowned. 'You've been a long time!' he scolded, eyeing her tartan minidress. 'Is that what you spent the money on?'

'Yes,' she smiled. 'Do you like it?'

'It's several sizes too small for you!' he laughed. 'It certainly shows your body off! Yes, I like it very much!'

'What have you been up to? You're spending more and more time out here. What are you doing?'

'Making something. You'll see it before long, it's a surprise.'

'Oh, you've carpeted the floor! I hadn't noticed!'

'Yes, this is going to be my den. I've moved the junk out of the way, and I'm going to put a sofa out here. I'll work out here, use it as my office.'

'What's the video camera set up for?'

'Er... well, the before and after. I'm videoing the transformation.'

'Oh, I see. Well, I'll leave you to it.'

'Come back soon, Marianne, and I'll show you what I've made.'

'All right. I'm going to ring Jill.'

Returning to the house, Marianne took the Christmas candle from the cupboard. She grabbed the card from her bag and dialled the number, wondering what to say to the lucky accountant. 'Christopher Davies,' he answered.

'Chris, it's me – the girl from the coffee shop,' Marianne replied, her stomach somersaulting as she massaged her clitoris.

'Oh, hi! I was wondering when you'd ring.'

'Enjoy your coffee, did you?'

'That was the best cup of coffee I've ever had!' he laughed. 'What's your name?'

'You can call me Sarah.'

'No, your real name.'

'That would be telling! Did you like my cunt?' she asked wickedly.

'God, yes! You're some girl!'

'I'm frigging my clitty at the moment. I'd like your cock up my bum. Would you like to fuck my bum?'

'Christ, you're beautiful! I'd love to fuck your bum!'

'Are you alone?'

'Yes, in my office at home – I work from home.'

'Why don't you have a nice wank? Get your cock out and wank while I tell you what I'm doing to my cunt.'

Marianne paused, listening as he shuffled in his chair. She imagined him pulling out his stiff penis as she slipped a finger into her perpetually drenched vagina. What she was doing this for, she had no idea. Just another step down the road to her complete and utter debasement, she mused. She'd call at the church again, she decided. Call on the vicar, wank him off, splatter his seed on the stone floor of the church.

Her mind becoming increasingly hungry for sin, she slipped her finger from her vaginal cavern and grabbed the candle. Easing the waxen shaft into her young cunt, she gasped. 'Ah, that's feels good!'

'What are you doing?' her partner in masturbation asked.

'I've just pushed a huge candle up my wet cunt. Are you wanking?'

'Yes, yes, I am. I'm really stiff. I'd like to come up your cunt.'

'Perhaps you will, one day. I'm pulling the candle out now. I'm squatting, trying to force it up my bum. Can you picture me, picture my cunt, hanging wide open, dripping with my come? Picture my bum-hole as I twist the candle. I'm pushing it . . . Ah, ah, God! It's in! Yes, I've got it in! Now I'm . . . Ah, ah! Now I'm easing it right up my bum. Further, further. Are you going to come?'

'Ah, God! Yes, soon! I want to shove it up your arse!'

'Perhaps I'll let you do that one day, too. Now the candle's right in. I'm standing again. God, my buttocks are wrapped around the end of the candle. I'm fingering my tight cunt now. Three, no, four fingers. God, I'm drenched! I need a stiff cock in my mouth! Would you like me to suck your cock and swallow your sperm?'

'Yes ... yes ... Coming! Ah, coming. My sperm, it's running over my balls! Ah, I want your mouth, your bum, your cunt!'

'I'm ... I'm coming, too! God, my cunt's coming! Ah, my cunt, my beautiful cunt!'

Gasping their orgasmic sounds down the phone, Marianne and her unseen partner in lust finally slowed their massaging. 'God, I needed that!' he breathed.

'And so did I!' Marianne laughed as the back door closed. 'Look, I've got to go!'

'I'll ring you, Sarah.'

'You don't know my number!' she giggled, squatting and tugging the candle out of her rectal sheath.

'I'll do the dial-back and get your number.'

'No, you won't. I'm not stupid, I dialled one-four-one before your number. Sorry about that. You'll hear from me soon. Bye!'

Hiding the candle beneath the hall table, Marianne adjusted her dress and wandered innocently into the kitchen. 'Juxtaposition,' Barry breathed as she walked to the back door. The word had worked again. Stopping, she turned to face her master, her hands limp by her sides, her expression blank, wondering what he was going to demand of her. 'As I told you earlier, I'm having some friends over this evening. I want you to wear your new dress, and no knickers or bra. You're going to entertain my friends, Marianne. The garage is now a sex den where you'll receive my friends and earn me money. There are five of them, and they've each paid me forty pounds for the pleasure of your body for the evening. Make sure you're here this evening, Marianne. They're arriving at seven, so you'll be here, ready and waiting, Do you understand?'

'Yes, I do,' Marianne replied.

'Good. Now, go and take a shower. And shave the stubble off your cunt, I want it baby-soft. OK, wake up.'

Wondering what would happen if Lydia rang and used the trigger word to invite her to the park, Marianne strolled out into the garden. *Who would win?* she mused, praying that her dream was going to come true that evening. Imagining five solid penises using her tethered body, a quiver ran up her spine. She decided not to answer the phone should it ring. Lydia could wait, but the throbbing penises couldn't!

Sitting on the lawn with her dress riding high and the soft grass caressing her bulging pussy lips, she decided that she'd really enjoy the men that evening. After what was sure to be an incredible experience, she'd leave Barry – only to return when she'd mastered hypnosis. She couldn't spend her life serving Barry and his perverted friends. But she could spend the rest of her days using Barry as a slave. 'I will do it!' she asserted as she lay back beneath the hot summer sun. 'I will do it!'

Chapter Nine

Waking at five to discover that she'd fallen asleep on the lawn, Marianne climbed to her feet and made her way to the bathroom. Barry was hammering and sawing in the garage, probably constructing some instrument of torture for the evening of depraved sex, she mused. Slipping her minidress off, she stepped into the shower, tossing her head back and squeezing her eyes shut as the hot water rained over her sun-tanned face.

Barry would use his video camera to record the debauchery, no doubt keeping his friends' faces out of frame as they drove their penises deep into her naked body. *Change the names to protect the guilty*, she mused wryly. But, Marianne consoled herself, she'd grab the money – her hard-earned money!

Taking the shower nozzle from the wall, Marianne parted her fleshy vaginal lips, opening the entrance to her sticky pussy-hole. Pressing the nozzle against her pink inner flesh, she gasped as the hot water quickly filled her sex-cavern. 'Ah, that's nice!' she breathed as her vagina swelled and overflowed, the hot water streaming down her legs as she shuddered with delight. Again, her clitoris stirred, and she wondered how much sex she could take, how many beautiful orgasms she could endure. John, Alan, Barry, David, the girls, candles, vibrators . . . And whatever the evening held in store for her! *God, I love sex!* she reflected.

Squatting, her vaginal lips distended, Marianne positioned the shower nozzle between her splayed buttocks, directing the hot water onto her anal ring. Her small hole yielding to the water pressure, her bowels suddenly ballooned. 'Ah, ah!' she breathed, her head lolling forward, her eyes rolling, as the water suddenly overflowed, gushing past the nozzle and flooding her feet.

Massaging her erect clitoris with her other hand, she elicited a shuddering orgasm, writhing as her bowels bubbled with hot water and her clitoris pulsated in ecstasy. 'Oh, my God!' she gasped as the beautiful sensations caused her young body to shake violently. 'Oh, my cunt! God, my cunt! My clit!'

The sensations finally subsiding, she leaned back against the tiled wall and dropped the nozzle to the floor, the water spraying up from the snaking nozzle, showering her firm breasts. 'How many times can I come?' she whispered as she climbed unsteadily to her feet. 'God, how many times?'

Dragging her thoughts away from her insatiable clitoris, Marianne stepped out of the shower and walked across the landing to her bedroom. Standing before the full-length mirror, she grinned. *No need to shave the stubble off*, she thought, gazing at her pouting cunt lips, still smooth and soft after shaving them in the bath the previous night. Eyeing the hairspray can on the dressing table, she wondered whether Barry had had the insight to line up a row of candles or plastic bottles for the men to plunge into her young body, her two love-holes. *Knowing Barry, he's bought several bloody great candles!* she laughed inwardly as she slipped into her tartan minidress, squeezing her firm breasts into the tight garment.

Opening the dressing table drawer, she pulled out a pair

of red silk panties, wondering about John's hypnotic suggestion. Stepping into the garment, she was unable to pull them up her long legs. Her muscles wouldn't respond as she tried again and again to conceal her intimacy. Discarding the panties, she realized that she was wide open to suggestion when in a hypnotic trance – any suggestion! *Where will this all end?* she wondered fearfully – excitedly.

Noticing a pair of Barry's trousers folded over the back of the chair, she discarded her panties and slipped her hands into the pockets, wondering whether he'd hidden the cash his friends had given him beneath the floorboards yet. 'Yes!' she cried victoriously, pulling out a wad of notes. 'Two hundred!' Hiding the money behind the wardrobe, she sat at the dressing table brushing her long blonde hair. She'd now collected seven hundred pounds from Barry, she mused, applying her lipstick – stolen seven hundred pounds! 'You're doing well, Marianne!' she giggled, gazing at her reflection in the mirror.

As she peered deep into her own misty blue eyes, she wondered again at the old Marianne, where she'd gone. Never had she dreamed that she'd stand on a church altar and lower the open centre of her young body onto two huge candles and masturbate. But her new way of life pleased her. It was bringing her money and more than enough sexual satisfaction. Or was it? she wondered. Her clitoris stirring between her full cunny lips again, her girl-juice flowing, lubricating her sex-sheath in readiness for penile penetration, the cold reality of her situation hit home.

Again, Marianne swore to learn the art of hypnosis, to turn the tables and pay Barry back for all he'd done. She also thought about John, the photographs he'd taken of her. *He's another one who'll have his comeuppance!* she asserted. But for now, she had the evening to look forward to, and she wandered downstairs to await the arrival of her abusers.

As the time neared seven, Barry became nervy, jittery as he paced the lounge floor, checking his watch every few minutes. 'What's the matter?' Marianne asked, looking up from the sofa and brushing her blonde hair away from her pretty face.

'Nothing,' he replied, gazing out of the window. Turning to face her, he breathed the magic word, grinning as Marianne's eyes gazed blankly across the room. 'Right, they'll be here any minute now!' he said excitedly, taking her hand and pulling her to her feet. 'Follow me – I'm taking you to my sex den!'

Following Barry, Marianne was having second thoughts about the evening. As she entered the garage and gazed at the pillory, she wished that she'd gone to the park or into town – anywhere to get away from Barry and his perverted friends! At least the garage was comfortable, she thought, gazing at a sofa. A long padded bench catching her eye, she imagined having her naked body intimately examined by her masters. Lengths of rope hung ominously from the corners of the bench and, noticing a whip and bamboo canes, she quivered, picturing herself tied down, her naked buttocks exposed for a thrashing.

Several vibrators, candles and plastic bottles of various sizes lined a wall-shelf, and Marianne wondered now not only at Barry's darker side, but the unfathomable depths of his evil mind. More lengths of rope hung over the pillory standing in the middle of the garage and a host of grotesque metal devices lay on a small table. Barry had certainly done a good job transforming the garage into a sexual torture chamber, she thought fearfully as he patted her taut buttocks.

'OK!' Barry grinned, switching on the bright spotlights positioned above the pillory. 'I want you posing provocatively when they arrive, a sort of welcoming sight, if you get my meaning! Now, hoist your dress up above your waist and lie on the bench, on your stomach.'

Tugging her dress up, exposing her bulging, hairless cunt lips, her gaping pussy-crack, Marianne sensed her arousal, and her fear, rapidly rising. *Five men!* she mused as she climbed onto the bench and obediently awaited her next instruction. *Five penises!*

'Right, legs apart, that's it – wider! Now I'll secure your ankles and wrists with the ropes. What a welcoming sight this will be!'

Pulling her legs as wide apart as he could, Barry secured her ankles, tying the ropes fast before moving to the top of the bench. Her arms outstretched, he secured her wrists and stood back, admiring his handiwork. 'Oh, I forgot this!' he said, forcing a huge pillow beneath her tethered body. Her buttocks high in the air, Marianne imagined the view – her shaved cunt lips open, revealing her pinken inner girl-flesh, her small brown hole blatantly displayed, nestling within her open bottom-crease. *There's no escaping now!* she thought fearfully as Barry left the garage to answer the front door.

Hearing voices, Marianne took a deep breath. *Five men*, she thought again. *My God, five men – five cocks!* Her mind racked, she wondered why she'd ever let things get out of hand. Even though the trigger word worked, she could have prevented this incredible situation, she reflected. *I should have gone to stay with my mother!*

'Come in,' Barry invited his eager guests. 'She's all ready for you.'

'God, what a beautiful sight!' a male gasped. 'Christ, she's shaved her cunt! Do you mind if I . . .'

'Do what you like, she's all yours!' Barry laughed. 'All of you, do what you like to the bitch! After all, you've paid for the pleasure!'

As fingers groped between her legs, exploring her most intimate places, crudely violating her vagina, Marianne pondered on Barry's debased wickedness. *Selling his girlfriend's body to five men for sex!* she thought angrily as a finger delved deep into her rectal sheath. Although this was her dream come true, she hated Barry for what he was, for the way he treated her. Tomorrow, she'd leave him, and only return when she'd mastered hypnotism.

'Let's take her dress off!' someone suggested, untying her hands. Marianne closed her eyes as the tight garment was tugged up her body and over her head. She didn't want to see her abusers, the evil lust mirrored in their eyes, their wicked grins. As hands ran over her buttocks and up her inner thighs, she quivered, wondering what it would be like to have five men screw her, taking it in turns to fill her defenceless holes with their jetting sperm.

'Who's going first?' someone asked.
'Who's *coming* first, you mean!' came the laughed reply.
'I'll take her arse!'
'We'll all do her cunt first, and then her arse.'
'Let's turn her over.'
'OK, and after we've all fucked her cunt and her arse, we'll put her in the pillory and give her a bloody good thrashing!'

As Marianne's feet were released and her naked body rolled over, she felt her clitoris throb in anticipation. She was nothing but a sex object, a slave to the men, the strangers who were discussing her as if she were a brainless blow-up doll. As she was positioned with her buttocks over the edge of the bench, her vagina open, defenceless, hands groped her breasts, twisting and pinching her nipples, sending messages of lewd sex through her quivering womb.

The group remained silent as the first penis drove deep into Marianne's vagina, unashamedly violating her once monogamous sheath. Thrusting with a vengeance, the invading male organ jolted her young body, the knob battering her cervix as fingers painfully stretched her pussy lips apart and hot mouths sucked on her hardening nipples. Through her eyelashes, she watched Barry behind his video camera, making his first dirty movie, recording the wanton abuse, delighting at using his girlfriend's young body to earn money. *But I've got the money!* Marianne consoled herself as a finger located her bottom-hole and crudely drove deep into the dank heat of her anal sheath.

The stranger between her splayed thighs suddenly gasped, driving his solid weapon harder into her tightening pussy-hole. Marianne sensed his sperm gushing, lubricating the enforced union, filling her spasming cuntal sheath. 'That's the first load!' someone chuckled as the thrusting penis pumped out its come. Her cunt gripping the solid organ shaft, sending electrifying sensations of sex through her sated body, Marianne whimpered her appreciation in the form of incoherent words, delighting at the gift of the gushing male come filling her tight sex-cavern.

'Quickly, move over! Let's keep the fucking going!' came the urgent call from one of the men. As the wet penis slid out of her drenched pussy, another solid member took its place, driving deep into her quivering body, taking her closer to her climax. *Men lining up waiting to fuck me with their hard cocks*, she mused wickedly as her body rocked with the second penile hammering.

'Come on, suck this and prepare me for my second fuck!' demanded the man turning Marianne's head. Gazing through slitted eyes at the dripping knob, she opened her mouth and engulfed the purple plum. Savouring her cuntal juices and the remnants of the stranger's sperm, she rolled her tongue over the silky-smooth glans. *That's two cocks in me at once!* she thought in her lewdness. *And a finger up my bum. But I want three cocks!*

Her vagina stretched by the huge pistoning organ, she felt her clitoris swell and her womb contract as the beginnings of her orgasm rolled through her pelvis. The penis in her hot mouth swelling, stiffening for the next fucking, Marianne rolled her eyes, her mind awash with images of five penises splattering her face, her tongue, with torrents of sperm. 'Here comes your second lot!' the man between her legs gasped as he gripped her hips and repeatedly thrust his knob against her cervix.

The sperm jetting into her drenched sex-duct, Marianne's own climax erupted, the waves of pure sexual debauchery crashing over her young body, bringing her more satisfaction than she'd ever imagined possible. Her anal sphincter muscles rhythmically contracting, squeezing the thrusting finger, she was almost delirious with sexual pleasure. Mouthing on the now-solid penis filling her mouth, she moaned through her nose as another succession of orgasmic waves spiralled through her trembling pelvis. *More!* she begged in her mind as the knob within her mouth gently slipped to the back of her throat. *More cocks, more sperm!*

The orgasming penis driving into her inflamed cunt making its last thrusts, Marianne shuddered as her climax began to recede, leaving her trembling uncontrollably in its wake. The organ withdrawing from her brimming vagina, her stomach rose with the force of the third penis as it penetrated her used sex. As the third fucking began, the penis within her accommodating mouth was hurriedly replaced by a fresh one. Again, she savoured the aphrodisiacal blend of cuntal cream and sperm, snaking her tongue over the smooth knob, sucking out the remnants of male come and swallowing hard.

The intruding finger still massaging the velveteen walls of her rectum, Marianne's body was alive with sex, her mind seething with lust. Tongues snaking round her erect nipples, licking her smooth stomach, her exposed clitoris, she had never known such incredible arousal. Her vagina spasming, rhythmically massaging the thrusting cock, she became lost in her depravity, praying that Barry would bring more and more men home to use her for perverted sex.

'The third lot!' the man thrusting into her tight cunt cried as his sperm flooded from his throbbing knob. The products of three male orgasms pouring from her hole and coursing between her buttocks to lubricate the pistoning finger, Marianne recalled the immense pleasure her rectal sheath, her *second cunt*, had brought her. She craved anal intercourse now, yearned for a hard cock to thrust deep into her tight bottom-hole and fill her bowels with sperm.

The third fucking virtually over, Marianne gobbled on the stiffening penis filling her wet mouth, wondering whether the men would have enough orgasmic cream left for her to drink before they'd finished their evening of filth. The incredible vaginal ramming slowing, the spent penis slipped out of her cunt-hole, only to be hurriedly replaced by another. This was the biggest yet! she thought happily as the massive shaft drove into the sopping depths of her inflamed honeypot. Again, a revived knob slipped from her mouth to be exchanged for a semi-erect dripping shaft.

Her taste buds alive as she lapped up the heady blend of intercourse, she wondered how long her cunt could take the repeated fuckings. The men she'd revived with her mouth stood awaiting their second fuck, and she prayed that this time they'd slip their huge members deep into her bowels. *One up my bum and one up my cunt!* she thought as the fourth screwing commenced. Again, her abused body took the sexual pummelling, her cunt gripping the male organ like a vice as her muscles spasmed. *Perhaps Barry will bring the score to six*, she mused, glimpsing him through her lashes as he panned in with the video camera on the wet penis driving into her mouth.

The men moving around the bench, fucking her vaginal sheath in turn, reviving and cleansing their knobs in her mouth in readiness for another fucking, she wondered how long they'd last. *The pillory!* she thought fearfully, imagining the whip thrashing her taut buttocks while the men recovered from their second coming. The night was far from over, she knew only too well as the fourth orgasming knob filled her aching vagina with sperm.

The thrusting knob hammering her cervix, spurting its spunk deep into her ravished body, she imagined Jill and Lydia joining in the debauchery. Picturing Lydia's open cunt folds above her face, she prayed for the opportunity to drink from the girl's sex-hole again, to bring her clitoris to orgasm with her sweeping tongue. But, the thought suddenly struck her, she'd never seen Barry fuck another girl. Perhaps Jill or Lydia would allow him the pleasure – and force Marianne to watch.

Last but not least, she mused as the spent knob slipped from the heat of her fiery vagina and yet another solid shaft entered her. 'Musical knobs!' Barry laughed as Marianne was forced to suck on the fourth organ and cleanse it for the next round. The fifth penis swelling, stretching her vaginal sheath wide as its sperm gushed, Marianne wondered again whether Barry would join in with the debauchery. Or would he wait until the others had done with her and give her the fucking of her life?

'God, I needed that!' the man between her thighs gasped as he made his final thrusts before withdrawing his spent penis. 'Bloody hell, I couldn't hold back! My turn for the whore's mouth now!' he laughed, moving around the bench as the revived penis slipped from Marianne's mouth. As she mouthed and sucked on the last knob, swallowing the bubbling sperm, the group discussed Marianne's next ordeal.

'I say fuck her arse!' came one crude suggestion.

'Let's fill her mouth with spunk!'

'No, I second her arse.'

'And me!'

'Her arse it is! Come on, get your cock out of her mouth and we'll roll the little tart over!'

The solid knob leaving her mouth, Marianne's perspiring body was lifted from the bench. Standing her with her feet wide apart, she was bent over the bench. Her buttocks splayed, her bottom-hole exposed in readiness, her hands were tied with rope to the far corners of the bench.

'OK, who's having the whore's arsehole first?'

'Let's toss for it!'

'Toss when we've got this tart to fuck? You must be joking! Let's keep the same order as before. Brian, you go first.'

Brian, Marianne mused: *The first time a name has been mentioned.* But names, identities, didn't matter – especially Marianne's! Wondering whether Barry had told his friends what the trigger word was, she imagined them calling at the house whenever they wanted to use her for perverted sex, using the trigger word to abuse her young body. A quiver running up her spine at the idea, her body jolted as a hand scooped up the sperm pouring from her inflamed vagina. 'Drink this!' she was ordered as the cupped hand neared her mouth. Lapping up the orgasmic blend like a cat at the cream, she was forced to drink the contents of her vaginal cavern until she was dry.

'Here goes!' her first anal abuser cried, parting her taut buttocks and stabbing at her tight brown ring with his solid knob. Slowly, her sphincter muscles yielded, allowing the bulbous purple glans to enter her tight rectal tube. Gasping as the veined shaft sank into the dank heat of her bowels, she squeezed her eyes shut, praying for her throbbing clitoris to receive intimate attention. Further the organ drove into her bowels, stretching her sensitive brown tissue until she sensed heavy balls resting against her outer cunt lips and a warm belly gently pressing on her taut buttocks.

'It's in to the root!' her partner in lust gasped triumphantly. The audience gathering round to gaze at the lewd spectacle, Marianne slowly gyrated her hips, massaging her bowels with the solid rod, satisfying her craving for debased sex. Her buttocks suddenly yanked apart, the pistoning began. Slowly, the solid penis slipped out of her bottom-hole and then drove in again, the heavy balls gently slapping her glistening cunt lips as the beautiful anal fucking drove her wild.

'Pull her bum-cheeks wider apart!' Barry ordered as he focused the video camera on the pistoning cock. 'I want to get a good shot of this!' Grimacing as unseen hands painfully stretched her bottom-orbs further apart, Marianne clung to the sides of the bench, her young body jolting with every hammering thrust of the stranger's penis. 'Give the tart a real good fucking!' Barry chuckled, heightening Marianne's determination to get her own back.

As two hands grabbed her inner thighs, forcing her legs wider apart, opening the very centre of her girlhood for all to see, Marianne felt her master's body shudder and become rigid. His sperm suddenly gushing, bathing the lewd union, she gasped as a huge vibrator sank deep into her vaginal sheath, the buzzing tip playing on her cervix. 'God, I can feel it vibrating my knob!' the man cried as he drove his penis deep into her anal duct. 'Ah, God! Christ, that's good!'

The vibrations transmitting through the soft walls of her vagina and caressing her pulsating clitoris, Marianne's climax suddenly erupted, causing her spasming love-holes to convulse and grip the intruding shafts. Whimpering her appreciation as her bottom-sheath filled with sperm, she lifted her head to see two men standing before her, their penises solid, stiff in readiness for her rectum. *God, I don't think I can take them all!* she thought fearfully, gazing at the swollen purple knobs, the broad veined shafts.

Her love-ducts bloated, her womb rhythmically contracting, her clitoris pulsating in orgasm, Marianne imagined two knobs buried deep within her hot bowels, the shafts stretching her brown ring, both organs pumping out their sperm, using and abusing her defiled body. Her mind swimming with obscene thoughts, she imagined four cocks, two up her bum and another two driving into her stretched cunt-hole. *What's happened to me?* she wondered, realizing that her craving for perverted sex was riding dangerously high.

The exquisite anal fucking finally over, the wet penis slipped out of Marianne's inflamed bottom-hole, leaving her shuddering with the vibrations deep within her cuntal sheath. 'Leave the vibro up her cunt while I fuck her arse!' the next man laughed as he presented his solid knob to her sperm-drenched brown hole. 'Ah, that's good!' he cried, forcing his tool past her defeated muscles and deep into her quivering body. 'You've lubricated her well! Now *I'll* lubricate the little bitch's arsehole!'

Her anal tube still aching from the first crude fucking, Marianne winced, biting her lip as the second penis began its cruel shafting. The video camera still running, she wondered how to get a copy of the tape, the idea of watching herself on television being anally fucked by five men delighting her. *Better still, grab the original tape!* she thought. Barry wouldn't know what the hell was going on, what with his two hundred pounds gone missing, and then the video tape.

Although Marianne wasn't in control of her actions, she

was, at least, making more money than ever before. *If I carry on like this*, she mused. But no, Barry's suspicions would soon rouse if she were to continually take money from him. *I could always work on my own as a prostitute*, she thought, wondering where her morals, her sense of right and wrong, had gone. *Earn a fortune as a common slut!*

'She's got a fucking good arse!' her abuser gasped as he thrust his knob deep into her bowels. 'We'll have to give her a double-shagging before we've finished with her! One up her cunt and one up her arsehole!' The divine words of pure corruption lifting her to incredible heights of sexual ecstasy, Marianne's clitoris swelled again. The vibrator sending electrifying sensations through the route of her clitoris to erupt in the sensitive tip, she thanked God for her beautiful young body – for her sweet cunt. Her body shaking violently as her anal sheath took the incredible shafting, she gasped, wondering how much more sexual abuse she could endure – how much more sexual abuse she *needed* to satisfy her rampant lust.

As the knob buried deep within the dank heat of her bowels exploded in orgasm, pumping another load of male come into her quivering body, Marianne cried out in her own coming. 'Ah, yes, yes! Fuck me! Fuck my arse!' Her lewd words echoing around the garage as someone thrust the vibrator in and out of her convulsing pussy-sheath, she knew now that she'd sunk to the lowest depths of depravity. Her anal muscles gripping the pistoning penis like a vice, her vagina rhythmically contracting, squeezing the vibrator, she panted for breath as her clitoris sent another series of incredible orgasmic shockwaves through her pelvis.

'Enough! Please, enough!' she cried as the thrusting into her bowels continued. But her cries only served to increase the force of the penile thrusting, the solid knob ramming into her bottom-hole with such impact that her naked body rocked violently. At last, the penis withdrew, leaving Marianne panting, gasping, her body perspiring, her long blonde hair matted, concealing her flushed face. Squeezing her cuntal muscles, she managed to eject the vibrator, sending it to the floor with a dull thud. Her girl-come flooding from her gaping vaginal hole, pooling on the carpet, Marianne stilled her quivering body, slowed her breathing, praying now that she'd be saved from another anal fucking.

'Now it's my turn!' a gruff male voice bellowed as Marianne's buttocks were yanked apart to expose the inflamed entrance to her bowels. Squeezing her eyes shut and biting her lip as the third bulbous knob eased its way past her tight brown ring, she clung to the bench, her body tense in anticipation as the shaft slipped easily into her hot sperm-drenched tube. Hands gripping her hips as the thrusting began, her young body rocked, jolting with the anal pounding, taking her closer to yet another orgasmic summit. Her vaginal lips dripping with her girl-come, slapped by the heavy balls, she began to wonder now whether she really wanted two men using her, driving their penises deep into her tight holes.

'No, please, I can't take . . .' Her words drifting around the garage unheard, the men gathered round her aching body, gazing at her bottom-ring, the taut brown flesh gripping the sliding shaft. 'Please, stop now!' she begged as hands groped beneath her young body and squeezed her firm breasts, painfully twisting her erect nipples. Again, the buzzing vibrator was forced deep into her tight vaginal canal, taking her ever nearer to incredible orgasm. 'No . . . Can't come . . . Can't come again! Please, I can't come again!'

As her climax erupted nonetheless, sending violent waves of lust through her abused young body, she felt the penis within her anal sheath swell and eject its sperm. The thrusting harder now, she wailed her painful pleasure, her head rolling from side to side, perspiration stinging her eyes as her very core shook ferociously with the beautiful anal pounding.

'Please, no more!' she begged again as her orgasm began to subside.

'We'd better give her a rest,' Barry said as his friend thrust his knob into the girl's bowels for the last time and slipped his wet penis from her inflamed anus.

'No way!' another objected. 'We've paid for the bitch, and we're going to have her!'

At least Barry had *some* compassion, Marianne thought as the vibrator slipped from her fiery cunt and dropped to the floor. But, compassion or not, she was shown no quarter. The fourth solid glans defeating her weary muscles, penetrating her hot bowels, the heavy balls resting against her swollen cunt lips, Marianne gripped the sides of the bench and held her breath in preparation for another gruelling anal fuck.

Her rectum hot, inflamed, brimming with sperm as the fourth knob began its rectal fucking, Barry focused the video camera between Marianne's buttocks, recording her gruelling ordeal as she was cruelly screwed with the hurried urgency of an inexperienced schoolboy.

'God, this is the first time I've ever fucked a tart's arse!' the man cried as he thrust harder into her rectal sheath.

'Take it easy!' Barry cried. 'It's not her cunt you're fucking! You'll rip the whore open if you're not careful!'

'Course I won't! The slag can take it! She'll *have* to take it!'

The cold words of crude sex echoing around Marianne's racked mind, she jolted as three fingers drove deep into her vagina, massaging her drenched inner flesh as she lay bound by her wrists in her strange hypnotic state – unable to halt the evening of sexual torture. Suddenly, she thought of Jill's gentle touch, her caressing tongue, her massaging fingers. But, she had to admit, she craved both the cruel male attention and the gentle female. Not that Lydia, the rampant lesbian, had been particularly gentle!

Her face rubbing against the padded bench-top, her hair matted with the perspiration of frantic sex, Marianne took the fourth anal pummelling, the violating vaginal exploration. *One more*, she thought as the man behind her grunted, his sperm gushing into her exhausted young body. *One more and then . . . and then what? The pillory? The whip? What else will they subject me to?* Surely she was worth more than forty pounds for an entire evening of depraved sex, she mused. Barry the bastard should have charged them at least fifty each, if not more!

Virtually delirious now as the spent penis slipped from the furnace of her rectal sheath and the fifth solid cock-head drove past her fatigued muscles, she whimpered, her tears flowing, pooling on the soft padding. Fingers still massaging her cuntal sheath, drawing out her slippery sex-cream, Marianne felt her clitoris swell, ripe for orgasm yet again.

The penis pumping out its sperm, draining the heavy balls slapping her distended cunt lips, Marianne gasped as her climax erupted, sending a succession of pulsating sensations through her aching pelvis. *No more! No more!* she screamed in her racked mind as the flow of sperm stopped and the pistoning penis stilled. Soaking up the inner heat of her bowels, the bulbous knob rested, the root of the massive shaft enveloped by her taut brown ring as she lay quivering in her climax.

The sticky fingers leaving her vagina as her orgasm subsided, Marianne wondered about her future. She'd definitely leave Barry and only return when she'd mastered the fine art of hypnosis. And then she'd be in complete control, use *him* for cold sex, use *him* as her slave. *If I can survive this evening, I'll be all right*, she thought as the fifth penis stirred again inside her aching rectal sheath.

The fifth and final knob withdrawing and then stabbing once more between her tensed buttocks at her sperm-drenched brown hole, Marianne grimaced. Inch by inch, the huge shaft entered her bottom-hole, bloating her pelvic cavity, but she knew now that her dream wouldn't come true. She'd desperately craved three penises in her female orifices, filling her young body with sperm, but the men wouldn't have the staying power to realize her dream. The fifth penis ejaculating again, creaming her rectal sheath, she gave a sigh of relief.

Her anal ordeal was almost over. The final knob spurting the last of its come into her aching bottom, she convulsed as the organ withdrew, leaving her body brimming over with orgasmic spend, aching, yearning for rest. *Ten times*, she pondered as her hands were released and her aching body brought upright. *I've been fucked ten times!* Clinging to the bench as she stood on her sagging legs, her inner thighs flooded with sperm.

'God, she's in a right state!' Barry laughed, focusing the camera on her inflamed cunt lips, her drenched thighs. 'So, what do you want to do to her next?'

'I know!' one laughed as he lay full length on the couch. 'Get her to squat over me and I'll fuck her cunt. And then, someone else can kneel behind her and fuck her arsehole!'

'OK, do it, Marianne!' Barry ordered. 'This'll be great for the video!'

'We'll all get a copy of the tape, I hope?'

'Of course you will, you're the movie stars! A friend of mine is going to make copies, he's got the equipment. You'll each have a copy in a few days.'

Time to grab the original, Marianne mused as she mechanically climbed upon the bench and knelt astride the man's erect penis. Lowering her body, she sensed her vaginal sheath expand as the huge member drove deep into her young body. Her cunt lips settling around the broad base of the penis, she rested on her elbows, her buttocks high, splayed, the portal to her bowels exposed. Suddenly, a bulbous knob was there, between her taut buttocks, pressing hard against her tight anal ring.

Her pelvic cavity already full, she gasped as the knob drove into her bottom, only stopping when the base rested against her sensitive brown tissue. Completely impaled on two cocks, she gasped as someone slapped her buttocks, causing her to jolt, her pelvic muscles to grip the intruding male organs.

'Let the whore do the fucking!' Barry laughed. 'Marianne, rock your body back and forth, you can do all the work – slave!' Complying, Marianne began to rock, the penises withdrawing and entering her abused holes in unison. The sensations delighting her, she grinned inwardly, imagining the lewd sight. The pain from her sore anal duct now outweighed by insurmountable pleasure, she opened her mouth wide as a man turned her head and presented his purple knob to her full red lips.

Three penises! she thought in her rising wickedness. *Three at once!* But would they all manage to come in unison, to fill her female orifices with their gushing sperm simultaneously? As she took the silky-soft glans in her mouth and gently sucked, her rocking body impaled her on the two shafts entering her holes between her legs, and then on the solid member within her mouth. The knob driving to the back of her throat and then withdrawing, she quivered, her body electric with shock waves of pure sexual lust.

The man beneath her pulling and twisting on her erect

nipples, her entire being became alive, glowing with sex as Barry focused his camera on the two penises driving into her tightening holes. Fingers massaging her clitoris, bringing out another incredible orgasm, Marianne became rigid, every muscle locked, every nerve ending tingling with lust as the three penises exploded in orgasm, filling her mouth with gushing sperm, bloating her aching bowels, filling her vaginal cavity. On and on she rode the crest of her shuddering climax, her naked body drinking the male offerings, perspiring in the crude four-way coupling.

Finally the men stilled their cocks, gasping as their slave's body convulsed, twitched, sending pulses of lust through their knobs. 'Perfect!' Barry cried, moving around the bench with his video camera. 'Bloody perfect! OK, what next?'

'What next?' the man with his penis rooted deep within Marianne's bowels asked. 'Christ, I need a rest! I'm all out of spunk!'

'And me!' the man beneath Marianne rejoined.

'That's a shame!' Barry complained. 'Oh well, if you're all knackered, then . . .'

'*We*'re not!' the pair standing by the table chuckled, much to Marianne's horror. 'You lot have come three times, and we've only come twice!'

'Great!' Barry replied excitedly. 'So, what's it to be?'

'How about her mouth? Both in her mouth together?'

'Yes, that's good! I like that! OK, do it!' Barry ordered.

As the penises withdrew from Marianne's racked body, and she climbed off the bench, she was ordered to kneel before her masters. Eyeing the two purple knobs wavering before her flushed face, she prayed that this was it, the last debauched act, the last gruelling test of endurance. Opening her full red lips and taking the pair of knobs into her mouth, she ran her tongue over the silky glandes, imagining two loads of sperm gushing, filling her cheeks to capacity. As she sucked, fingers probed between her buttocks, her cuntal lips. Her inflamed rectal opening yielding as two fingers slipped into her sperm-drenched duct, she moaned deeply through her nose, delighting in the enforced act. More fingers slipped deep into her cunt, stretching her sex-duct wide, delving, exploring, as she took the two knobs further into her hot mouth.

Cupping each pair of heavy balls as she mouthed on her masters' knobs, she felt their penises twitch, their glandes swell. Four fingers now embedded within her anal tube, painfully stretching her delicate tissue, she quivered as her clitoris was vigorously massaged. Her body shuddering as her climax gripped her very being, she licked and sucked, swallowing her masters' jetting come as the knobs exploded within her mouth, filling her cheeks with spunk.

Like a babe at the breast, she mouthed on the knobs, drinking as the sperm flowed. This was her role in life now, she mused. This was the role she was destined to play, the role of a wanton tart – unless she could master hypnosis. 'Swallow our spunk, slave!' one of the men towering above her gasped as he thrust his knob deep into her mouth. The other man following suit, Marianne could barely accommodate the pulsating knobs, but she could do nothing to stop her body obediently responding, her mouth opening wider. Control over her actions had been lost, possibly forever.

'Christ, that was bloody good!' came the satisfied voice from above as one knob finally withdrew.

'We'll do this again!' the other man said, slipping his dripping glans from Marianne's mouth. 'Again and again!'

The fingers finally withdrawing from her sex-sheaths, Marianne remained still. Sperm running down her chin and dripping onto her pert breasts, her inner thighs drenched with male come, she could take no more. Eyeing the pillory through her lashes, she prayed that she'd not be whipped, thrashed before the men finally left her to collapse in a heap of exhausted trembling limbs.

As the men left the garage, Marianne fell to the floor, her naked body sprawled out across the carpet, aching, convulsing from the enforced sex. Without so much as a word of appreciation, they'd gone, discarded her. *They could have at least made me comfortable on the bench*, she thought as she rolled onto her back and stretched her aching limbs. But slaves weren't to be made comfortable! They were to be used, fucked and abused.

'Good!' Barry chuckled as he returned to the garage. 'That was bloody good! Stand up and let's have a look at you!' Marianne dragged her aching body up and stood trembling before her master, praying that he'd not use her to satisfy his own perverted lust as she clung to the bench to steady herself. 'Shame we didn't get to use the pillory. Still, there's always next time!' he laughed, tweaking her sensitive milk buds. 'There's always tomorrow! Right, go into the house and get something to clean the bench with. There's sperm and cunt juice everywhere! Go on, don't just fucking stand there, bitch!'

Returning to the garage with a sponge and a bowl of soapy water, Marianne washed the padded bench in readiness for her next session of crude sex. 'Come on, we haven't got all bloody night!' Barry complained. 'Before you have a shower and wash your cunt out, you can make me some sandwiches. I'm meeting the others in the pub, so fucking well hurry up! And take your dress with you!'

Returning to the house, sperm coursing down her slender thighs, glistening on her chin, her brown nipples, Marianne placed her dress over the back of a chair and stood at the worktop making her master's sandwiches, wondering at his cruelty. Not only his sex slave, his prostitute, she was also his housekeeper – his charlady! she thought sadly, recalling the nights spent together making love. The nights before she'd introduced the trigger word and feigned hypnosis – the distant nights.

As Barry sat at the table eating his sandwiches, he looked up at Marianne's flushed face and grinned. 'Well, that's two hundred you've earned me this evening, but it's not enough! The lads are going to put the word around that there's a dirty tart for hire so, hopefully, we'll have a regular flow of men ready and willing to pay for an evening of perverted sex with you.'

Standing by the table, Marianne's tears flowed down her cheeks as Barry's cruel words sank in. 'Bastard' wasn't a strong enough word for him, she thought as she watched him eat. Determined more than ever now to retaliate, to repay him, she resolved to learn the art of hypnosis if it was the last thing she did. Her cunt oozing sperm and girl-come, her anal portal dripping with the products of five male orgasms, she desperately wanted to climb the stairs and cleanse her abused body in the shower. But Barry had other plans for her.

'Right, lie on the floor!' he demanded as he stood up. Obediently following his instructions, she lay down, her arms by her sides, her naked body defenceless, vulnerable. Unzipping his trousers, he stood astride her firm breasts and pulled out his solid penis. Looking up at the huge member towering above her face as he massaged the loose skin over his purple knob, she could hardly believe that she'd once been in love with this monster.

Gasping as he wanked, he looked down at Marianne, her sperm-drenched pretty face, her pert breasts. 'Never seen me wanking before, have you?' he grinned. 'And you've certainly never seen me wank all over your face!' As his sperm suddenly gushed, splattering Marianne's face, her long blonde hair, she squeezed her eyes shut. 'Ah, that's good!' Barry breathed, running his hand up and down his veined shaft, spraying his slave with his spunk. The white liquid splattering her cheeks, her mouth, her long blonde hair, Marianne prayed for him to go out and leave her to cleanse her abused body and rest. She prayed for the incredible day to end, for the night to come.

If this was the way Barry was going to treat her, as nothing more than a common slut, she'd have no choice but to leave there and then – walk out the minute she was back in control of her young body. As the last of his spunk landed on her forehead and ran down her temples to her ears, he stepped aside and zipped his trousers. That was it, the final degrading act of the evening, she thought thankfully as he ordered her to stand before him.

Facing her master, his sperm coursing down her face, she awaited his next instruction, praying for the trigger word to leave her subconscious. 'I'm going to meet the lads now. You'll clear up the kitchen when I've gone and then wash your cunt out in the bath and go to bed. I don't need you any more this evening, but tomorrow... Well, you'll see! You'll come out of your trance when you hear the front door close. Do you understand?'

'Yes,' she replied softly as he left the room.

'Oh, and I want a decent breakfast tomorrow! I don't want the usual crap, you'll cook me a bloody good breakfast and bring it to me in bed at eight o'clock! Get up at seven and bring me breakfast in bed at eight!'

As the front door slammed shut, Marianne breathed a sigh of relief. Her body now under her complete control, she flopped onto a chair and massaged her aching limbs. Although she'd enjoyed the sex, the throbbing penises, her incredible orgasms, she wanted to be rid of Barry. Again, she told herself that she didn't need his help to sell her body for sex – she was more than capable of doing that without a pimp! *I'll have to get my own place*, she mused, rising to her feet and wiping the sperm from her face.

Climbing the stairs, Marianne ran a bath and immersed her aching, sperm-drenched body in the hot, soapy water. Wondering what had happened to Alan, the arrangement he'd made with Barry to have Marianne suck him to orgasm every evening, she lay back with her head beneath the water, the sperm floating, clinging to her hair like jellyfish tendrils. *I've been here before!* she thought, turning her head and focusing on the drifting spirals of male come.

Reaching beneath her thigh, she slid a finger into her rectal sheath, bringing out the sperm, cleansing her rear sex-duct. 'My second cunt!' she breathed, massaging the inflamed inner walls of her anal canal. Fingering her sperm-flooded cunt-sheath with her other hand, she cleansed her love-holes, wondering about her evening of depravity. *The pillory!* she suddenly thought as images of her naked body bound to the horrendous device filled her mind. 'God, where will it all end?'

Her body clean and fresh, Marianne climbed out of the bath and towelled herself dry before powdering her youthful skin with talc. Her femininity was still there, she thought happily, breathing in the scented powder. 'Barry can call me what he likes, do what he likes to me, but I'm still feminine!' *Face it, Marianne, you're a common slut!*

Stepping out of the bathroom, she thought about Barry's cooked breakfast. 'I'll cook him bloody breakfast and take it to him in bed, all right!' she hissed. 'I'll mix my cunt juices with his scrambled egg and watch him eat it! I'll stuff the sausages up my cunt before lovingly placing them on his fucking plate!'

Beneath her quilt, Marianne closed her eyes, recalling the evening's events, picturing Barry in the pub, laughing, joking with his perverted friends. *The video tape!* she suddenly recalled. *Must go and find the tape!* As she raised her naked body on one elbow to climb out of bed, she collapsed, her head flopping onto the pillow. *Must . . . must find the tape.* Sleep engulfing her, calming her aching body, she drifted into her dreams of controlling Barry, using him, enslaving him. Revenge will be sweet!

Chapter Ten

Her body clock waking her at seven the following morning, Marianne dragged herself from her bed, glaring at Barry sleeping soundly. *Bloody breakfast in bed!* she cursed inwardly, wondering whether she'd have the power to leave the house and walk to the park without making his breakfast.

Wandering naked downstairs to the kitchen and slipping into her tartan minidress, she remembered that she'd not be able to conceal her swollen pussy lips with her panties. *Too many subconscious suggestions*, she thought angrily, mechanically breaking two eggs into a glass bowl. 'Shit, I can't stop myself from making his bloody breakfast!' she gasped as she took the milk and butter from the fridge. 'But I can do this!' she giggled, sprinkling half a pot of pepper into the bowl.

The food ready on a tray at seven-thirty, she grinned. 'Eight o'clock, he said. Shame, it'll be stone-cold by then! Still, I have to stick to the instructions – eight o'clock!' Wandering out into the garden, Marianne sat on the lawn with her knees up to her chin, wondering what the day would bring. The soft blades of grass tickling her bulging pussy lips, she sighed, reaching beneath her thigh and toying with her pink inner petals.

The constant sex *had* re-educated her subconscious, she

mused, slipping her finger into her hot vagina. Pressing against the soft cushioned walls of her sex-duct, she wondered whether to go to the garage and borrow a vibrator. *Perhaps a quick one before I take the food up*, she thought as her insatiable clitoris swelled in expectation.

As she slipped her finger from her tight vagina and stood up, the front doorbell rang. 'Who the hell's that at this time?' she hissed, dashing into the house. 'Oh, Rod!' she gasped as she opened the door to the good-looking young man. 'How on earth did you find my address?'

'Don't worry about that now. Listen, Marianne, I can't stop, but I've some news for you. Come over to my place later this morning, say ten o'clock, and I'll teach you how to use hypnosis.'

'But why didn't you do that before? I've been through . . . Never mind what I've been through. Why didn't you suggest that before?'

'I didn't like your idea of tit-for-tat. Hypnotizing your boyfriend and . . .'

'Soon-to-be-ex.'

'Yes, right. Anyway, I didn't like the idea of you getting your own back on him, playing silly games like that. But now, well, unless you do something about your situation, you'll find yourself sucked so deep into all this that you'll never be free. I've been reading up on trigger words and the like – they can be bloody dangerous! But more, there's auto-suggestion. When you're in a trance, you're completely vulnerable to suggestion. You could end up as your boyfriend's permanent slave! That reminds me, you *were* lying to me when I rang you, weren't you? He had used the word again, hadn't he?'

'Yes, I was lying. I'm sorry, Rod. Look, I'll be over later, about ten.'

'Good. We'll sort this thing out once and for all!'

'How come you're up and about so early?'

'I always get up early. I'll see you later, Marianne. And don't let me down because all you'll be doing is letting yourself down – and sealing your own fate!'

'I'll be there, I promise – unless, that is . . .'

'Juxtaposition! Now, Marianne, you'll be at my house at ten, or as soon you can make it. Do you understand?'

'Yes, I understand.'

'This will override any other suggestions. You will be at my house at ten o'clock or before. Wake up!'

'I know what you've just done!' she giggled. 'I have no choice now, have I? I'll see you later. Bye, Rod.'

'I'll look forward to it. Take care!'

Closing the door, Marianne wandered into the kitchen, aware of her clitoris throbbing, her cuntal juices flowing, as she thought again about using one of Barry's vibrators. *After I've taken him his breakfast*, she decided, stepping through the back door and making her way to the garage. 'God, he's careless!' she gasped, noticing the video camera on a shelf. Grabbing the camera and removing the cassette, she grinned. 'Like taking candy!' she giggled, replacing the camera. 'He's got no money, and now no video tape!'

Returning to the house, she hid the cassette in a kitchen cupboard and took the breakfast tray upstairs to Barry. 'Here we are!' she smiled, placing the tray on the bed. 'Breakfast in bed!'

'Oh . . . er . . . yes, right, thanks,' he yawned as he sat up. 'This is nice, what made you do it, love?'

'Why shouldn't I bring you breakfast in bed? Anyway, I'm going out shopping, I'll see you later.'

'I don't want you to go out, Marianne, I have something planned for this morning.'

'In that case, I'll stay in!' she smiled. 'I'll go and make you a coffee.'

Leaving the room, Marianne knew that this was her only chance to get out of the house, away from Barry and his trigger word. Quietly closing the front door behind her, she slipped down the path and out into the street, breathing in the warm summer air as she almost skipped down the road. Her minidress doing nothing to conceal her smiling pussy-crack, she grinned. *Soon, I'll be in control! Not only of my own body, but of Barry's!*

Sitting on the park bench, Marianne imagined Barry's face when he took his first mouthful of scrambled egg. Stone cold and spicy hot, he'd curse her, call for her and curse her again when he discovered that she'd gone out without his permission. 'His slave's escaped!' she laughed, watching a man walking his dog. Thoughts of Rod looming, she recalled their first meeting, the dog running away with her wet panties.

She desperately wanted to see Rod, to talk to him, to tell him of her beautiful night of sexual horror. But was it wise to tell him about the men, the five throbbing knobs? Walking towards his house, not wanting to arrive too early, she decided to lie on the grass by his back gate, sunning herself – her pussy-crack. As she sat on the grass, to her horror she noticed Barry striding across the park towards the pond. 'Christ, he's come looking for me!' she gasped, leaping to her feet and dashing into Rod's back garden.

Running around the side of the house, she hammered on the front door, hoping that he was in. 'You're early!' he beamed as he opened the door. Saying nothing, Marianne pushed past him and walked through the hall to the lounge. 'What's up?' Rod asked as he followed her. 'Marianne, are you OK?'

'He's out there, in the park!' she panted. 'My soon-to-be-bloody-ex, he's come looking for me!'

'You're safe enough here! Calm down, Marianne! Sit down, and I'll make some coffee. Then we'll get straight into your hypnosis lesson, OK?'

'The sooner the better!' she smiled, flopping onto the sofa, her exposed girl-crack grinning at Rod. 'Sorry,' she giggled, tugging her skirt down to conceal her femininity.

'Please, don't apologize! You look wonderful!'

'I wouldn't normally go around like this, but I can't wear panties!' she complained. 'Subconscious suggestion and all that. I can't pull panties up my legs – my hands just won't allow me to do it!'

'All right, wait there and I'll bring the coffee in. And then we'll get you sorted out.'

Placing the coffee on the table, Rod settled on the sofa beside Marianne. 'Now, what I intend to do is this,' he smiled, passing her a cup. 'I'll send you into a hypnotic trance, and then I'll teach you how to use hypnosis. As you failed the course, you're obviously not an easy one to teach but, under hypnosis, you'll take everything in. It's a bit like sleep learning.'

'You're not going to use the trigger word, are you?'

'No, no! I'll use my own methods to hypnotize you. I've been trying to think of the best way out of this problem and, hopefully, I've found the answer. All you'll have to do is hypnotize your boy— *ex*-boyfriend, and then tell him that the trigger word has changed. Erase the word jux . . . oh, I'd better not say it! Tell him that the trigger word is chandelier, candelabra, anything! You see, he'll then start using the new word, and you'll be able to feign hypnosis.'

'But I want the trigger word erased from my subconscious, Rod! Too many people know about it! It's not only Barry!'

'Yes, well, it's impossible to remove the word from your subconscious – as we discovered the other day! I can't erase the word – God knows why, but I can't do it! The point is, by telling him that the word has changed and erasing the real one from his memory, you'll be free.'

'At least I'll be in control where Barry's concerned.'

'I wouldn't try hypnotizing too many people, Marianne. It's not good to . . .'

'I'll plant a trigger word in Barry's subconscious! I don't care what you say, I'm going to do it!'

'Well, that's up to you – I can only advise you not to do it. Anyway, put your cup down and relax. That's it, lie back, hands loose by your sides. Now, close your eyes and listen to me.'

All too aware of Rod's words, Marianne couldn't believe that she was under hypnosis as he rambled on. 'It hasn't worked,' she complained.

'Relax, you're under hypnosis now, as I speak,' he assured her before continuing his monotonic instructions. 'It's in the eyes and the voice – and the faith you have in yourself, the faith to hypnotize. You'll look into your subject's eyes and use *your* eyes, and your calming voice to bring about a state of hypnosis.'

Marianne sat in silence until her lesson was finally over and Rod snapped his fingers. 'There, all done,' he smiled as she turned to look at him.

'But nothing happened!'

'Didn't it? You now know how to use hypnosis, Marianne. It might take a while for you to master it completely, but you can do it well enough to give your ex a false trigger word and make him forget the real one.'

'I've no idea how to hypnotize him!'

'It's all in your subconscious. Just sit your subject down and make sure he's comfortable, that he has no distractions. Tell him that he feels sleepy, that his eyelids are heavy and . . .'

'God, it sounds ridiculous! Heavy eyelids and all that crap!'

'Just try it when you get home.'

'OK, I will. But I'm sure it won't work – it can't!'

'Go home now. Come back later this morning, and I guarantee that you'll be telling me you've successfully hypnotized your ex. Unless he's one of the very few who are so strong-willed that nothing will get through to them!'

'That sounds like Barry!' Marianne sighed. 'He's a strong-willed bastard, all right! May I try it on you, Rod?'

'No. Sorry, but no. Try it, as you put it, on your ex. Now, off you go.'

'I'll come back later this morning. I . . . I'd like to see you again, Rod,' she smiled as she finished her coffee.

'Yes, and I'd love to see you again. Go on, off you go. You've got work to do!'

'OK. Wish me luck!'

'You don't need luck. Go out the back way, and I'll see you later.'

Waving as she walked through the gate and out into the park, Marianne couldn't believe that she now had the power to use hypnosis. Although a nagging voice deep within her subconscious told her that she could do it, she found the idea impossible. Praying that she would at last get her own back on Barry, she made her way home only to find that he was out. 'The bastard's probably still searching for me!' she hissed, climbing the stairs to her bedroom.

Lying on her bed wondering what to do, she thought about hypnotically suggesting to Barry that he should tell his friends that Marianne had left, that there was no more fun to be had in the garage. But she was torn. Although her gruelling evening of debauched sex had brought her immense satisfaction – *too much satisfaction!* she reflected – she wanted to be in complete control, instructing the men to do this and that to her naked body. Playing the submissive role was something she no longer wanted. Or was it? she wondered. 'I really don't know what I want!' she sighed as the front door slammed shut. She wanted the debauched evenings to continue, she decided – but without Barry!

'Marianne!' Barry bellowed from downstairs. 'Marianne, where the bloody hell are you?'

'Up here, in the bedroom!' she replied, sitting on the edge of the bed, praying that she'd be able to hypnotize him as he burst into the room.

'Where the hell did you get to?' he demanded.

'Sit down, Barry,' she smiled, her voice soft, calm. 'I want to try an experiment.'

'What the hell are you talking about? You went down to get my coffee, having given me a stone-cold breakfast covered in bloody pepper, and then you . . .'

'Will you listen to me, Barry? Please, just relax, I have some news for you – good news. Now, sit in the chair and look into my eyes and relax. You feel calm, your eyelids are heavy . . .'

'What the hell . . .' he began as he sat down.

'Sleepy, you feel sleepy, drifting, slowly drifting. Heavy eyelids, close them now. Close your eyes, Barry.'

Watching in amazement as Barry closed his eyes, his head slumping forward, Marianne couldn't believe that she'd done it. 'Barry, stand up!' she ordered, stunned as he rose to his feet. 'Pull your trousers and shorts down.' Obediently, he followed her instruction, standing before his mistress with his penis hanging limp over his heavy balls. 'Wank for me! Come on, have a wank!' she giggled excitedly.

Taking his stiffening penis in his hand, Barry complied, moving the loose skin back and forth over his swelling knob as Marianne watched with bated breath. Gasping as his pleasure increased, he grimaced, quickening his wanking rhythm. Soon, he'd spurt his spunk all over the carpet, she knew. *The tables have turned!* she thought happily as he began to groan. 'Stop!' Marianne instructed with a wicked glint in her eye. His hands returning to his sides, his erect penis twitched, craving the last few wanking movements necessary to bring it spurting relief. 'Now, pull your trousers up. I'm not having you spunking all over the bedroom carpet!'

Unsure of herself, her ability to hypnotize, Marianne wondered whether Barry was playing her at her own game and feigning his own hypnotic trance. *Talk about the tables turning!* she mused again as she wondered how to test him. If he *was* faking and she told him that she knew what he'd been up to, that he'd sold her for sex, what the hell would his reaction be? Plunging so deep in the pool of deception, she wondered whether she'd ever be able to surface. If she revealed too much, and he wasn't hypnotized, he'd know that she knew... *God, this is ridiculous!* she thought. *He knows that I know that he knows... What a bloody confusing mess!*

'One or two people have discovered that a trigger word was implanted in my subconscious by my course lecturer,' she began. 'You know nothing about the trigger word. I'm only telling you in case you discover that Jill and Lydia hypnotized me and used me for lesbian sex. If you do know about the word, which I don't think you do, then you'll forget it, Barry – it's gone, it no longer exists. I can't remember anything about Jill and Lydia using me, but I know that they did – I worked it out for myself. I was innocent, Barry. They used the trigger word and forced me to commit lesbian acts – I was completely innocent. Anyway, I've managed to change the word to... well, I don't suppose it matters if I tell you. The word is now "candelabra". No one knows about it. I might tell you one day so that we can have some fun, but no one else will ever know.'

Still uncertain as to whether Barry really was in a state of hypnosis, Marianne ordered him to sit down. She wouldn't try planting a word in his subconscious, not yet, not until she was sure that he'd really been in a hypnotic trance. 'OK, wake up!' she ordered, clicking her fingers.

Gazing around the room in apparent bewilderment, Barry frowned. 'What . . . what happened?' he asked, focusing his bleary eyes on Marianne.

'What do you mean?'

'I feel . . . I don't know, I feel strange. Anyway, where was I? Oh yes, the bloody breakfast was awful! And where the hell did you get to?'

'I went for a walk, Barry.'

'Juxtaposition!'

Shit! Marianne cursed inwardly as she slipped into a trance. *It didn't bloody well work!* 'So, try to use hypnosis on me, would you? I'll tell you this, my girl, my filthy little slut – it didn't work! But you've confirmed something for me, something that's been nagging at me for some time. I've been wondering whether you remember the things I've put you through. I was pretty certain that you remembered nothing, but there was always that nagging doubt. Now that you've told me that you remember nothing, I've no need to worry. I can use you for even more perverted sex, make as much money as I can from your cunt, and you'll know nothing about it! You've no idea what I've put you through! Five men, five cocks, Marianne! You know nothing about that, do you? Candelabra, my arse! Now, wake up!'

Sighing as she gazed at Barry, Marianne was close to tears. She would never escape this monster, she was sure of that. *Rod and his bloody hypnosis!* she thought angrily. *Some bloody guarantee!*

'So, you've been for another of your walks, have you?' Barry asked.

'Yes, is there anything wrong with that? I mean, I am my own person, Barry. If I feel like taking a walk, I'll take a walk. Anyway, I need some money. There's the shopping to be done and . . .'

'All right, all right! I've got some cash in my other trousers. How much this time?'

'Another fifty, if you have it.'

'No problem!' he laughed, taking his trousers from the back of the chair. 'I'm doing well. I've several clients who have paid in advance and . . .'

His face turning pale, Barry hurriedly searched his trouser pockets, cursing under his breath as he realized that the cash had gone. Frowning, he left the room and dashed downstairs. *To check beneath the kitchen floor*, Marianne thought. Grinning, she stood up and walked to the window, gazing out into the back garden. 'So, he uses me, and I use him!' she giggled, wondering what he'd think when he discovered that he'd not put the money beneath the kitchen floor.

'Marianne!' he called up the stairs. 'Marianne, have you seen any money lying around?'

'No, I haven't!' she replied, bounding down the stairs to the kitchen to be greeted by his angry face. 'You've not lost any, have you?'

'I thought I had some in my trousers, but there's none there! I don't understand it! Five hundred was stolen, and now . . .'

'How much did you have?'

'Two hundred quid, for fuck's sake! Two hundred bloody quid, and it's gone!'

'You're terrible with money, you really are!'

'I haven't lost it, it's been taken!'

'You've changed the locks, so how can it have been taken? When did you last see it?'

'Last night, it was in my trousers – I'm sure!'

'I don't know, Barry – I really don't! So there's no cash, then?'

'No, there's no ready cash, but only temporarily! Believe me, only temporarily! I'm going to make a quick phone call,' he said, his mouth twisting into a grin as he closed the kitchen door behind him.

Realizing that he was going to offer her young body to someone for sex, Marianne grabbed her bag and slipped out of the back door. Creeping around the side of the house again, she made for the safety of the street. But what to do? Where to go? She could hardly spend all day in the park! Deciding to go next door and have a coffee with Natalie, she stole down the path and rang the bell.

'Hi, Ian – is Natalie in?' she asked as the good-looking young man opened the door.

'I'm afraid she's out, Marianne. Do you want to come in and wait?'

'Yes, if you don't mind.'

'Juxtaposition.'

Stunned as she fell into a trance, Marianne stood on the door step, her hands trembling, her heart racing as she fell into a hypnotic trance. Natalie, obviously, had told her husband about the trigger word. *No one can be trusted*, she thought fearfully, wondering what Ian was going to do as he invited her into the house. Following him into the lounge, she stood in the centre of the room, her short dress catching Ian's eye as he sat in an armchair gazing at her.

'So, the trigger word *does* work!' he smiled. 'When Nat told me all about it, I laughed. I thought you were having her on with all this hypnosis stuff. Anyway, she trusts me. She told me that she trusts me – poor cow! I told her that I'd never be unfaithful to her. I said that I'd never mention the word to you and do anything underhand. It's funny how things turn out. She's away for the day and I was just thinking,

Wouldn't it be great if I could get hold of Marianne and use the trigger word! Anyway, your timing's perfect! There's a sink full of washing-up, the house needs vacuuming and dusting, the bed has to be made, and there's a pile of ironing to be done ... Nat told me to do it all while she's out, but you can do it for me!'

Wondering why he was only going to use her as a housekeeper, Marianne bit her lip, praying that the day would come when she was free of the word – free of the people who only wanted to use her for their own satisfaction. 'There is one thing,' Ian began. 'I like my chargirls to go about their chores naked. Take your clothes off, Marianne!'

Her hands mechanically slipping her minidress off and her feet kicking her shoes aside, Marianne stood completely naked before her young master. 'You've shaved your cunt!' he gasped in disbelief. 'My God, you've shaved your cunt. Come here and show me.' Walking towards Ian, Marianne stood with her feet apart, her full pussy lips smooth and hairless, her pink inner lips protruding unashamedly. 'You look like a bloody schoolgirl! You must be a dirty little bitch, shaving your cunt like that! I'm going to enjoy today. In fact, this is going to be the best day of my life! Before I fuck you, get on with the housework. Start with the washing up. I'll follow you around, watching you as you do the work, watching your tits, your tight bum – your schoolgirl cunt. OK, into the kitchen and get started – slave!'

Walking through the hall to the kitchen, Marianne stood at the sink, confronted by a pile of dirty dishes and plates. Beginning her first chore as Ian stood behind her, cupping and squeezing her taut, smart buttocks in his grasping hands, she thought of Barry. He'd be cursing again, whining, not knowing that his girlfriend was next door, naked. As Ian's finger slipped between Marianne's thighs and toyed with her bulging pussy lips, she gasped. Her insatiable clitoris stirring yet again, she desperately needed the relief that orgasm brought. *God, I'm a filthy whore!* she thought as her womb contracted and her elongated nipples hardened.

She'd been aware of her clitoris, her flowing cuntal juices, since she'd first thought of masturbating with one of Barry's vibrators earlier that morning. Now, as Ian's finger penetrated her tight sex, she craved orgasm. 'The sooner you've done the housework, the sooner you can have my cock up your wet cunt,' Ian breathed in her ear as he kneaded the cushioned walls of her wet vaginal sheath.

All men are the same! Marianne decided as Ian massaged a breast, twisting and pulling on her erect milk bud. But Marianne herself was as bad! Delighting at using her young body for sex, she was as bad, or as good, as any man! Slipping his finger from her tight cunt-hole, Ian turned Marianne round. Facing her master, her hands wet and soapy, she remained still as he cast his eyes over her pert breasts.

'You've a good body!' he breathed, his eyes lowering to the slight swell of her stomach. Gazing at her shaved mound, her swelling cunt lips, he grinned. 'Let's not worry about the housework now. You've got all day for that! But I can't wait all day for your tight cunt. Now, where shall I have you? Yes, over the kitchen table! Natalie would never allow me to do her over the table! For that matter, she won't allow me to do her anywhere! OK, bend over, my lovely, and bare your cunt in readiness for the fucking of your life!'

Following her master's instructions, Marianne bent over the table, her pussy lips bulging below her rounded buttocks as she rested her head on the tablecloth. 'I wish Nat was more into sex!' Ian complained. 'Bloody hell, if I could get her to do this sort of thing, I wouldn't be screwing her sister on the side!'

There's a turn-up for the books! Marianne thought as Ian slipped his stiff penis out and ran his knob up and down her wet cunt-crack. *I could always blackmail him!* But, she realized, all the time Ian was able to use the word, she was under his power. There was no point in blackmailing her master! He'd put her through sexual hell if she were to try to blackmail him! Sexual bliss, more like!

Poor Natalie! Marianne mused as Ian's bulbous knob slipped between her pouting cunt lips and sank into the welcoming warmth of her tight vaginal canal. But, she reflected, while Ian was away, Natalie had screwed his friend! *They're as bad as each other!* she concluded as Ian's knob came to rest against her creamy-wet cervix. *And I'm worse than the lot of them!*

'Ah, that feels good!' Ian breathed as he began his slow fucking motions. 'You like my prick up your tight cunt, don't you, Marianne?'

'Yes, I do,' she whimpered as her clitoris throbbed.

'Where else would you like my prick? In your mouth, perhaps?' he asked.

'Up my bum,' she replied – to her astonishment.

'Really? You're into that, are you?'

'Yes, I love it! I love having my arse fucked!'

Her words seemed to come from nowhere, bubbling from her pretty lips without her thinking. *What the hell am I saying?* she wondered as Ian slipped his penis out of her vagina and presented his wet knob to her anal entrance. *Oh, my God! I'm no better than a dirty little slut!* Her vile confession echoing around the murky depths of her racked mind, she grimaced as Ian slid his knob past her sphincter muscles and into the fiery heat of her rectal sheath.

'Ah, God!' Ian gasped as he drove his shaft deep into Marianne's anal canal. 'It's right in! Christ, if only Nat would let me fuck her arse! If only you could see your bum! God, your pretty brown hole's stretched wide open! Even Nat's sister won't let me fuck her arse! You must be a right little whore if you love having your bum fucked!'

I am a right little whore! Marianne reflected. Having had five penises sperming up her bum the previous evening, she was hungry for anal sex, craved the sensation of an orgasming knob buried deep within her hot bowels. Again, she wondered where it would all end. Her new way of life had taken her to the very depths of sin. *I'll burn in the eternal fires of hell!* she thought fearfully, recalling the candles buried deep within her lust-holes as she had squatted on the church altar. *Is this selling my soul to the devil?*

'Ah, I'm going to come!' Ian cried as he thrust his solid organ into her anal-sheath. 'God, I'm come . . . coming! Oh, God! You're so tight, hot . . . ah, coming!'

Marianne felt the gushing sperm deep inside her pelvis as the anal shafting continued. Her body quivering uncontrollably as she reached between her thighs and massaged her glowing clitoris, she cried out in her coming. 'Harder! Fuck my arse harder!' Grabbing her hips, Ian drove his fleshpole into her tight tube, filling her bowels with his jetting spunk, using her naked body to satisfy his evil lust.

Hearing the front door close as the last of his sperm shot into Marianne's inflamed anal sheath, he quickly slipped his penis out of her luscious arse and zipped his trousers. 'Quick, get up!' he whispered loudly, pulling Marianne from the table. 'Fucking hell, she can't be back already! Get in there! Get in the cupboard and don't make a sound!'

Stepping into the large cupboard, Marianne remained silent as Ian quickly closed the door and greeted his young wife. 'Hallo, love! What . . . er . . . what are you doing back?' he asked, his voice shaky, riddled with guilt.

'I missed the train,' Natalie replied, dumping her bag on the table. 'The next one wasn't due for over an hour, so I decided to go another day.'

'Oh, I see. Er . . . why don't you go upstairs and change?'

'Change? What for?'

'Well, you don't want to wear your best clothes around the house, do you?'

'No, I suppose not. Are you all right, Ian? You look nervy, uneasy. Is everything all right?'

'Yes, of course it is! Go and change and I'll make you some tea.'

'All right. I won't be a minute.'

Dragging Marianne from the cupboard the minute Natalie was upstairs, Ian marched her into the lounge and ordered her to put her dress and shoes on. 'Hurry up, for fuck's sake!' he grunted as Marianne slipped into her dress and stepped into her shoes. 'Quick, get out of the house and don't come back!'

Walking to the front door, Marianne decided to come back as soon as she was in control of her body. She'd have coffee with Natalie, sit at the table gloating over Ian's guilt, delighting at his predicament as she dropped the odd hint. She couldn't be blamed, she mused. Natalie knew all about the trigger word, about the hypnosis – the blame would lie squarely on Ian's shoulders.

Opening the door and pushing Marianne outside, Ian told her to return to her normal waking state as soon as she heard the door close. He had no idea how to bring her out of her trance – all he could do was hope that she'd wake up and go home. Grinning as the door closed, Marianne waited for several minutes before ringing the bell, delighting at the prospect of dropping Ian in the shit.

'Oh, you're back! Hi, Natalie!' Marianne greeted her

neighbour as the pretty girl opened the door.

'Marianne! Yes, I've just this minute got home. Come in,' Natalie beamed, her blue eyes frowning as she glanced down at Marianne's thighs, the minidress barely concealing her girlhood.

'Thanks. Don't mind me popping round for a coffee, do you?'

'No, of course not! Come through to the kitchen,' she replied, leading the way through the hall. 'I like your dress. It's rather short, though.'

'Yes, it's too small for me, really. I was going to take it back but . . . Hallo *again*, Ian!' Marianne grinned as she entered the kitchen.

'Er . . . oh, Marianne! Er . . . how are you?' he stammered, his face flushing with guilt.

'I got locked out,' she said as she sat at the table.

'Locked out?' Natalie echoed. 'Have you lost your key?'

'No, locked out of *your* house! I came round to have a coffee with you earlier but you were out. Ian invited me in and . . . he was putting the kettle on, and then . . . I don't know what happened after that. I found myself out in the front garden so I rang the bell and you answered the door.'

'But I've only just got in!' Natalie frowned. 'You weren't in the garden when I arrived!'

'I'm just going up to the loo,' Ian said, moving quickly to the door and leaving the room.

When he'd gone, Natalie sat opposite Marianne and gazed into her wide eyes. Marianne knew what Natalie was thinking as she smiled at her friend – she knew that she'd ask about the trigger word.

'Did Ian use the trigger word?' Natalie asked outright.

'Trigger word? No, no, he didn't! Why do you ask?'

'Do you recall the things that you do while you're hypnotized?'

'Normally, yes. But not always – why?'

'I think Ian used the word, Marianne. You said that you came here to see me, and Ian let you in.'

'Yes, that's right. He was going to make the coffee and . . . well, the next thing I knew, I was standing in your front garden!'

'How do you feel?'

'What do you mean?'

'Your . . . your body. Do you feel anything?'

'Actually, my bum really hurts, and . . .' Her hand between her thighs, Marianne frowned. 'And I'm soaking wet!'

'What, your *bum*?' Natalie gasped, the colour draining from her cheeks.

'Yes! God, what's that white stuff coming out of my bum?' Marianne breathed, examining her sticky fingers. 'God, what the hell is it?'

'*I* know what it is, Marianne! It's sperm! Ian's sperm! The fucking little bastard!'

'Ian's . . . but . . . the word, you told him about the word, didn't you?'

'Yes, but I didn't think that he'd . . . I'll kill him!'

'And so will I! I'm going home to wash, Natalie. God, he must be some kind of pervert to . . . I'm going home!'

Leaving the house, Marianne concealed her wicked grin, imagining the row, Ian's futile denials, Natalie's hysterically screamed accusations. Natalie had seen the proof with her own eyes, she'd seen the sperm dripping from Marianne's fingers – her husband's sperm! Ian was a dead man! *And it serves him right!* Marianne thought as she walked down the street towards the park. *And it serves him bloody right!*

Sitting on the bench by the pond, remorse flooding her mind, Marianne sighed. *I should never have done it!* she thought. *I should never have told Natalie!* But, she consoled herself, she was innocent. Ian had used the word, and then used Marianne for debased sex. Natalie had a right to know if her husband was screwing around behind her back! And as for screwing his wife's sister! *Cheating bastard!*

But Marianne's innocence trip was wearing thin. Her recent acts of debauched behaviour had been committed under the influence of hypnosis – but *she*'d started the deceit, the lies, the incredible hoax. She'd been the one who'd faked hypnosis purely to have sex with anyone, male or female. 'Basically, I'm to blame for everything,' she sighed. 'But not for Natalie's husband screwing her sister!'

'I thought I'd find you here!' Barry bellowed as he approached the bench from behind and stood before Marianne. 'I'm fed up with your bloody disappearing acts, Marianne! What the hell do you think you're playing at?'

'I'm not playing at anything, Barry! If anyone's fed up, it's me! I'm fed up with you wanting to know where I've been all the time! And I'm pissed off with you following me! I saw you this morning, skulking around the park looking for me! What is it with you?'

'What is it with *you*, you mean! You're always wandering off, disappearing without so much as a goodbye! I don't know where you're going to be from one fucking minute to the next!'

'I'm leaving you, Barry!' Marianne announced. 'I've made my mind up, I don't want to be with you any more.'

'Why? Why are you leaving me? Is there someone else?'

'No, there's no one else. It's just that I've had enough! I want to be free. I want to find myself. I want to work for Brooke-Smith without having to worry about you and what you think. I want to run my life my own way. I want to . . .'

'Juxtaposition!'

Her heart racing, Marianne knew that she could never escape Barry. As he ordered her to walk towards the trees, she recalled her time with Lydia, the incredible lesbian sex, the vibrator – but what had Barry planned, what was he up to? Why take her into the trees? *Sex*, she mused as they entered the wood. *He wants to fuck me in the woods!*

'Stop here!' Barry ordered as they emerged into the small clearing. The fallen tree brought more memories flooding back to Marianne – the rough bark, the thrashing, the incredible orgasms. 'Take your dress off, you fucking little whore! I'll teach you to keep wandering off! And if you think that I'll allow you to walk out on me, you've got another think coming! You're my meal ticket, Marianne! You're going to earn me a fortune! And when I've enough money, I'll dump you! I'll discard you like the piece of shit you are!'

Slipping her shoes off and pulling her dress over her head, Marianne stood naked before her cruel master, quivering as she awaited her inevitable punishment. But, to her astonishment, Barry clicked his fingers and ordered her to wake up. Gazing down at her pert breasts, she feigned disbelief.

'What . . . what am I doing here? Why am I naked?'

'You're going doolally!' Barry scorned. 'You tell me to come into the woods with you, then you strip off and ask me what you're doing naked! You need psychiatric help, woman!'

So *that* was his game, she mused. Make out that she was falling out of her tree, send her over the edge with his tricks. *Christ, he'll try to have me certified next!* Grabbing her dress and pulling the garment over her head, Marianne said nothing as she stepped into her shoes. What Barry was playing at now was despicable. To try to have her believe that she was going over the edge was evil!

A last-ditch attempt! she decided, taking a deep breath and gazing into his dark eyes. Her determination was incredible as she looked deep into his eyes, staring into his very soul as she mouthed her hypnotic words. 'You're feeling sleepy. Your eyelids are heavy. You're falling under my spell.'

Frowning as Barry closed his eyes and stood motionless with his arms hanging limply by his sides, Marianne ordered him to strip naked. Kicking his shoes off and slipping his trousers and boxer shorts down, he unbuttoned his shirt and tossed it to the ground. As he pulled his socks off, Marianne sat on the fallen tree, praying that, at long last, she'd mastered the art of hypnosis.

'Tell me, Barry, what were you doing in the garage last night?'

'My friends came round. I hypnotized you and took money from my friends and they fucked you,' he replied to her sheer delight. 'I made a videotape of them fucking your arse and . . .'

'Yes, all right – I know the rest. Now, you'll forget the word, "*juxtaposition*", do you understand?'

'Yes, I understand.'

'In future, when you want to hypnotize me, you'll use the trigger word "*delta*". You'll remember nothing of this conversation when I bring you out of your trance. Also, you'll fall into a hypnotic trance and do exactly as I tell you whenever you hear the words, "*time for sex*". You'll remember nothing, unlike me, of what happens to you during hypnosis. Do you understand?'

'Yes, I understand.'

'Repeat all that I've just said so that I know you understand completely.'

'When I want to hypnotize you, I'll say the trigger word "*delta*". When I hear the words "*time for sex*", I'll fall into a hypnotic trance and do exactly as you say. I'll remember nothing of what happens to me during hypnosis.'

'Good, that's very good! And now for a test. Ian, our

neighbour, has just fucked my bum. His sperm keeps oozing between my buttocks. I'll bend over, and I want you to lap up his sperm, lick my bum clean. Do it now!'

Lifting her skirt and bending over, Marianne grinned as Barry knelt behind her and licked her small hole. 'Suck me!' she ordered. 'Suck Ian's sperm from my arse!' Sucking, bringing out the sperm, Barry followed Marianne's orders to the letter. 'That's good, Barry! For a fucking bastard, you're doing very well! Now, hurry up and finish cleaning me because I want to watch you wanking.'

Licking the last of the male come from Marianne's bottom-hole, Barry stood up. 'Right,' Marianne giggled as she pulled her dress down and stood grinning at her slave. 'I'll sit on the tree and watch you have a wank. Go on, off you go!'

Standing naked in the clearing, his stiff penis in his hand, Barry began his wanking. His eyes closed, he moved his hand up and down his veined shaft, groaning as his climax approached. 'Keep going!' Marianne urged. 'Come on, spunk for me!' His sperm suddenly jetting, landing on the soft grass, Marianne shrieked with glee. 'I've got you under my spell now, you bastard! Just look at you, wanking yourself off in the woods! You're pathetic! Look at your sperm flying through the air!' As he finished masturbating, his legs sagging, his breathing unsteady, Marianne put him to the final test. 'Kneel down and lick your sperm up!' she ordered.

Falling to his knees, he lapped up the white liquid splattered all over the short grass, swallowing his come until Marianne grew bored. 'OK, get dressed and we'll go home! I have plans for you, Barry – great plans! Now, hurry up and get dressed, and remember – you'll not be able to recall anything that happened!'

Watching him dress, Marianne's stomach somersaulted. She could do anything and everything now, she thought

happily. At last, Barry was her slave! *The tables have turned!*
'OK, wake up!' she instructed him once he'd dressed. Walking through the trees, she turned to look back at him. 'Aren't you coming home?' she called.

'Yes, I am,' he replied, following her out into the open, clueless about the events in the wood.

As they walked across the park, Marianne wondered whether she'd really succeeded in hypnotizing Barry. *He could have been faking it*, she mused. Would he lap up another man's sperm from her tight bottom-hole in an effort to trick her? *Yes!* she decided, Barry would do *anything* to con anyone! But what would he gain from pretending to be under hypnosis? Then again, he was a devious bastard! No one would ever know how his mind worked, she concluded.

As they neared the house, Marianne turned and smiled. 'Time for sex!' she said loudly and clearly. Barry stopped in his tracks, his face blank, his hands limp. 'There'll be no great test to see whether you're faking it or not,' she said. 'I'll test you over a period of a few days. You'll start by running me a bath. While I'm relaxing, you'll cook the dinner. After dinner, you'll attend my pussy, lick me to a wonderful orgasm, and then I'll go to bed – I need an early night. Oh, yes – you'll sleep on the sofa tonight. I don't want you in my bed, Barry – you'll sleep on the sofa tonight. Wake up!'

Entering the house, Barry suggested that he run a bath for Marianne. 'You have a nice long soak, love, and I'll cook the dinner,' he said as he climbed the stairs to the bathroom. Was he faking it? she wondered as she slipped out of her dress and climbed the stairs. Only time would tell.

Chapter Eleven

Waking to find herself alone in bed, Marianne grinned as she stretched her limbs and kicked the quilt to the floor. Wondering how well her slave had slept, she summoned him. 'Barry! Barry, are you there?' She'd have to feign hypnosis should he use the new trigger word and order her to suck his knob, to drink his sperm – but she'd be in control! *Things are going to be completely different from now on!* she thought happily. 'Barry, where are you?' she called again, deciding to use her word and order him to bring her a cup of tea – and then to bring her to orgasm with his darting tongue.

Opening the door, Barry smiled. 'Hi!' he said as he sat on the edge of the bed. 'I slept on the sofa, I hope you don't mind. I just thought that you could do with a good night's sleep.'

'Oh, I wondered where you'd got to,' she replied, her stomach somersaulting as she thought of ordering her slave to masturbate her to orgasm.

'Alan rang just now, he's coming over for coffee.'

'Alan? Oh, Christine's Alan. What's he want?'

'Nothing much, just a chat and . . . You're not going to do your disappearing act again today, are you?'

'I might go for a walk in the park, I don't know,' she grinned. As she was about to breathe her word and order her slave to bring her a cup of tea, Barry stood up and moved to the window. *Poor thing*, she mused. *I'll have my tea and then order him to lick between my pussy lips, drink my early-morning come.*

'Juxtaposition!' Barry said firmly as he turned to face Marianne.

Stunned, Marianne fell into a hypnotic trance, wondering why he'd not forgotten the word. Her head spinning, she couldn't believe that she'd been taken in by Barry. *But why would he run my bath, cook a lovely meal, lick my clitoris to orgasm, and sleep on the sofa?* she wondered. What would he gain by running around after her, by treating her as his mistress? Her mind swimming, she listened to his familiar words.

'You'll not go out this morning!' he bellowed. 'First of all, Alan's coming over to use your mouth – to fuck your pretty mouth. God knows, I've let him down enough as it is! This afternoon, another friend of mine will be visiting us. He's paying me fifty pounds to fuck you. He wants you in the pillory so you'll remain at home today – naked and ready for my clients!'

God, not Alan again! Marianne thought, pondering the inexplicable situation. Lying naked on the bed, her young body was, once again, defenceless, vulnerable. Her stomach sank as she gazed at her master through slitted eyes and thought about the pillory. The happiness she'd felt, the power she'd thought she had over him had all gone. *Back to square one!*

'OK, get up and wait in the kitchen for Alan!' Barry ordered. 'He wants sucking off, Marianne, so you'll suck him off – *and* you'll make a good job of it! I don't want to lose Alan, he's a bloody good client.' Her body automatically rising from the bed, she made her way downstairs to the kitchen and sat at the table. Desperately trying to work out what had gone wrong, why Barry had seemed to fall into a genuine hypnotic trance, she sighed. *He* was *hypnotized!* she reflected as he filled the kettle. *So what's gone wrong?*

'Right, I'll bring you out of your trance,' he grinned. 'You'll believe that you're fully clothed, Marianne. When Alan gets here, I'll hypnotize you again and you can earn me some money. Remember, you're fully clothed. Wake up.'

Resting her elbows on the table, it didn't occur to Marianne that she was naked as she decided to try her word again. 'Are you making coffee?' she asked.

'Yes, want some?'

'Mmm, please. Oh, Barry... Time for sex!'

Motionless, Barry seemed to be in a hypnotic trance, but Marianne couldn't be sure. *How to test him?* she wondered as she stood before him. 'Barry, where do you hide your magazines?' she asked.

'Beneath the floorboards, over there, in the corner,' he replied without hesitation.

'Do you love me?'

'No.'

'Did you ever love me?'

'Yes, I think so.'

'What happened? What went wrong?'

'Christine, she... I've been screwing Christine.'

'What, Alan's wife?' Marianne gasped.

'Yes, I've been screwing her for several weeks.'

'When are you seeing her again?'

'This morning. She's coming round later this morning.'

'So why do you want me to stay in the house? I would have thought that you'd want me to go out if she's coming round!'

'I told her about the hypnosis. We're going to have some fun with you, get you to watch us screwing.'

'I can't believe that of Christine! OK, I'll stay in and you can have your fun. But you must forget the word "*juxtaposition*", Barry! Erase it from your memory. The new word is "*delta*". Do you understand?'

' "*Delta*" – yes, I understand.'

'Good, now wake up.'

Barry continued to make the coffee, seemingly unaware of what had happened as Marianne thought about Christine. *I'd never have guessed!* she mused, picturing Barry's erect penis entering the girl's cunt. Strangely, she felt no jealousy, no sadness. Barry didn't love Marianne anymore. *And my love for him has gone too*, she reflected as the doorbell rang.

'Juxtaposition!' Barry breathed as he left the room. *God, it's worked again!* Marianne thought, unable to take control of her naked body as Barry led Alan into the kitchen. *What the hell's going on with this hypnosis stuff?*

'Well, there she is!' Barry laughed. 'Naked, and ready and waiting for you.'

'Good. I haven't got much time so . . .'

'Given her cunt any more thought? Twenty pounds extra, and her cunt's all yours.'

'I haven't got the time right now. This evening, perhaps.'

'OK. Well, I'll leave you to it. The kitchen's all right, is it? I mean, go up to the bedroom if you want to.'

'She's fine where she is. Sitting down, her mouth's at just the right height to suck me off!'

'Right, well, I've some things to do in the garage. Let yourself out when you've done and I'll see you this evening.'

As Barry left the kitchen and closed the back door behind him, Alan unzipped his trousers and pulled his stiff penis out. 'There we are!' he chuckled. 'All stiff and ready for your hot mouth! Suck it, bitch! Lick me, suck me and swallow my come!'

The situation was incredible, Marianne mused as she

engulfed Alan's silky-smooth glans in her mouth. If only Alan knew about Christine and Barry! If only Christine knew about Alan and Marianne! 'Wank me!' Alan ordered as he pushed his knob deeper into her mouth. 'Come on, I haven't got much time!'

Complying, Marianne gripped his solid shaft in her hand and quickly moved it back and forth. Her tongue snaking around his knob, she eagerly awaited his sperm, wondering what Christine would say if she were to see the beautiful coupling. 'Coming!' Alan suddenly gasped. 'Lick, suck . . . Coming!'

His sperm bathing her tongue, Marianne savoured the male nectar. Her taste buds rousing, her clitoris stirring between her moist cunt lips, she desperately wanted the throbbing penis buried deep within her hot cunt, deep within her bottom-hole, pumping sperm into her bowels.

'Ah, that's good!' Alan breathed, looking down at Marianne's full red lips, taut around his broad shaft. 'Yes, yes . . . ah, keep licking, bring it all out! Ah, God! Drink from my cock, whore! That's it, suck, lick . . . ah, swallow my come, drink my sperm!'

Swallowing the jetting come, Marianne closed her eyes, her stomach somersaulting as her clitoris pulsated, craving attention, desperate for orgasm. As Alan's knob slipped out of her mouth, leaving sperm trickling down her chin, she decided to masturbate, to go upstairs and masturbate with her perfume bottle pushed deep into her bowels, the plastic container stretching her vagina wide open.

'That was good!' Alan gloated as he zipped his trousers and left the room. 'I might be back this evening for some more!' he called as he opened the front door. As the door closed, Marianne wondered when Barry would return and bring her out of her trance. She also wondered when Christine was due to come round for sex with Barry. *Alan arrives and sperms in my mouth, and then his wife's arriving to fuck Barry – amazing!*

Marianne pictured Barry again, his long penis driving into Christine's hot cunt, his sperm jetting, bathing her cervix as they writhed on the floor, locked in their illicit lust. Would the sight arouse her? she wondered as Barry entered the kitchen and ordered Marianne to lick the sperm from her lips and wake up.

'I've got a funny taste in my mouth,' she said, licking her full lips. 'I wonder what it is?'

'I've no idea,' Barry replied. 'You didn't have your coffee.'

'Oh, thanks,' she smiled as he passed her a cup. 'So, what's happening this morning? Anything interesting?'

'You could say that!' Barry laughed. 'Actually, no, nothing's happening this morning. I'm going to be working in the garage for a while so . . .'

'Time for sex!'

Again, the trigger words had worked. Gazing blankly across the room, Barry leaned on the worktop, his cup of coffee in his hand, his face expressionless. 'Put your coffee cup down and go and get a vibrator from the garage,' Marianne ordered. Obediently leaving the kitchen, Barry returned with a huge vibrator and stood before his naked mistress. Reclining with her buttocks over the edge of the chair, her thighs wide apart, her cunt lips swollen, gaping, Marianne grinned.

'Kneel between my legs and use the vibrator on my clitoris. Make me come, Barry - vibrate my clitoris and finger my cunt and my bum until I come,' she breathed huskily. Taking his position, Barry switched the vibrator on and opened Marianne's sex-groove, exposing her already solid clitoris. Slipping a finger into her tight cunt and another into her hot rectum, he gently pressed the buzzing tip of the vibrator against her cumbud. 'Ah, ah, yes!' Marianne gasped as the sensations transmitted deep into her young womb. 'Ah, that's nice! I'm going to get you to attend my pussy whenever I feel the need to come! Ah, that's it! God, that's good! Whenever I want to come, you'll masturbate my clitty, vibrate my little spot and satisfy me!'

Her orgasm quickly building within her quivering pelvis, Marianne opened her legs further, allowing Barry's thrusting fingers deeper penetration. 'Coming!' she wailed as she tossed her head back, her long blonde hair flowing, her cheeks flushed with sex. 'Keep it still! Keep it against my . . . ah, my beautiful clit!'

Her cunt muscles gripping Barry's fingers like a vice, Marianne shuddered as her climax permeated her trembling body, reaching out and bringing life to every nerve ending. The seismic waves finally subsiding, leaving Marianne panting, shaking violently, she pushed the vibrator away. 'Keep fingering my holes!' she gasped as the ripples of orgasm slowly faded. 'That's nice, keep fingering my wet cunt, my arse.'

Looking down at her hairless pussy lips stretched around Barry's pistoning finger, Marianne grinned. 'You did very well,' she commended him. 'Now take your fingers out of my beautiful holes and drink my come, lap it all up until I'm clean,' she ordered her slave. Leaning forward as he slipped his fingers from her drenched sex-cavern, her hot anal sheath, he pushed his tongue out and cleansed her gaping crack. 'That's it, lick it all up like a dog!' she giggled, watching his tongue sweeping up her inflamed sex-groove.

As Barry worked between her glistening pussy folds, Marianne pondered on the trigger words. Barry seemed to be hypnotized, but why couldn't she erase the word *juxtaposition* from his memory? And why had Rod been unable to remove it from Marianne's subconscious? *Now we've both got trigger words!* she laughed inwardly. At least they were now equal – equally using each other. It was a matter of who breathed their word first, she thought, wondering again what time Christine was coming round.

'OK, that's enough,' she instructed. ' Go and put the vibrator back and then stand over there where you were.' Slipping into her minidress, concealing her pinken pussy-slit, Marianne waited for Barry to return. 'Go and stand over there!' she ordered as he entered the kitchen and closed the back door. 'What time's Christine coming round?' she asked.

'Half past nine,' he replied mechanically.

'God, it's quarter past now! Right, wake up,' she instructed as he leaned against the worktop.

Innocently gazing out of the window as Barry sipped his coffee, Marianne's thoughts turned to Christine. How could a girl like Christine, seemingly happily married and, if anything, extremely shy, ever agree to performing with Barry while Marianne watched? *You think you know someone, and then you discover that you don't know them at all!* The familiar words echoing around her mind, she turned to face Barry.

'I must go out into the garage and see what you've been working on,' she said, wondering at his reaction.

'No, don't go out there. It's a surprise,' he said, checking his watch. 'When did you put your dress on?'

'When? When I got up, why?'

'Er . . . no reason. Shall we have our coffee in the lounge?'

'Yes, if you want to,' she replied, following him into the hall. 'Time for sex!' she said loudly as they entered the lounge. Standing motionless in his hypnotic trance, Barry gazed at the wall. 'Now then, slave!' Marianne grinned wickedly. 'When you begin your fun with Christine, you'll keep calling her a slut, a tart, a whore and a fucking little bitch. Do you understand?'

'Yes, I understand.'

'When you're fucking her, you'll tell her that she's nowhere near as good a fuck as I am. You'll tell her that my cunt is much tighter than hers, that my tits are bigger, firmer. You'll tell her that I give far better blow jobs than she does. Mind you, according to Alan, she's not into sucking cocks! You'll continually praise my body and condemn hers and be nasty to her. OK, wake up.'

Sitting on the sofa as the doorbell rang, Marianne grinned. Breathing the trigger word and sending her into a trance, Barry left the room and opened the front door. *If it works and Barry says all those things to her, that'll be the end of their relationship!* she thought happily as she patiently awaited her visitor – patiently awaited the fun and games.

'Well, here she is!' Barry said triumphantly, leading Christine into the room.

'She really *is* hypnotized, is she?' Christine asked, tossing her long black hair over her shoulder as she gazed at Marianne.

'Yes, really! I told you, I can put her into a trance whenever I want to simply by mentioning the trigger word. Watch, I'll prove it to you. Marianne, lift your dress up and open your legs and show Chris your shaved fanny.'

'Shaved fanny?' Christine echoed. 'Did *you* shave her?'

'No, she did it herself.'

'Are you sure there's nothing between you two?'

'Yes, of course I'm sure! Our relationship's over.'

Her hands moving automatically, Marianne exposed her naked pouting pussy lips to the astonished girl. Gasping, Christine fell to her knees and scrutinized Marianne's crack, tentatively prodding her hairless girl-lips with her fingertip. Peeling the fleshy sex-cushions apart and peering into her vaginal entrance, she turned to Barry. 'God, I've never touched another girl!' she giggled. 'I've never seen another girl's pussy, let alone a shaved one!'

'Push your finger into her fanny, you might like it!' Barry laughed.

'I'm not a lesbian, Barry! But I suppose it'll be an experience.'

Marianne felt the girl's finger slip between her swelling cuntal lips and enter her vaginal sheath. Exploring the hot wet depths of Marianne's love-hole, she turned to Barry again, her deep green eyes frowning. 'Will she remember anything afterwards?' she asked, her eyes reflecting her concern. 'I don't want her knowing that I fingered her pussy!'

'No, she'll remember nothing. That's the beauty of it, she won't have a clue!'

'This is amazing!' Christine giggled, slipping her finger out of Marianne's hot hole and wiping it on the girl's dress. 'Wait a minute . . .' she began as she stood up. 'If you have this amount of control over her . . . You don't have sex with her, do you, Barry? You said that your relationship with her is over. That is true, isn't it?'

'Yes, of course it is, Chris!'

'You're still going to leave her, as you said you would? I don't want to leave Alan just to find that you . . .'

'Yes, I'm going to leave her, I promise you! I'm only doing this to show you how the hypnosis works, Chris.'

'You said that you wanted to make love to me while she watched us. Why bother to do that? I mean, what's the point?'

'Just for fun! I thought it might turn you on, having Marianne watch me being unfaithful to her.'

'Well, if you're sure that she'll remember nothing about it.'

'I'm not sure, I'm positive! Now, shall I help you out of your clothes, or would you like Marianne to undress you?'

'No, you do it. I told you, I'm not a lesbian!'

'We might as well have her naked, too. Marianne, take

your dress off! Now, Christine, my little angel, let me help you out of your skirt and knickers!'

As Marianne stood up and slipped her dress off, she hoped that Christine would ask Barry whose tits he preferred, who had the better figure. Sitting on the sofa again, her rounded breasts in full view, her thighs parted, exposing her girl-crack, she watched the illicit disrobing. Christine's breasts tumbling from her bra cups as Barry removed the garment, her chocolate-brown nipples grew, standing proud from the dark discs of her areolae. Her hairy pussy coming into view as Barry peeled her red panties away from her mound, Marianne gazed longingly at the girl's full vaginal lips. *God, I'd love to lick her!* Christine had a pretty good body, she mused – curvaceous, feminine, lickable. But not nearly as good as Marianne's!

'There, now you're both naked!' Barry chuckled excitedly.

'And what about you?' Christine, giggled, tugging at Barry's jeans. 'Come on, clothes off!' she demanded, turning to scrutinize Marianne's naked body, her pert breasts.

'All right, all right!' Barry replied, unbuckling his belt. 'You can't wait for it, can you?'

'No, I can't! I hope you're big and stiff for me!'

'Well, take a look for yourself!' he laughed as he dropped his jeans and shorts, his penis catapulting to attention before the girl's wide eyes. 'Big and stiff enough for you?'

'Oh, yes!' she gasped, dropping to her knees and admiring his organ. 'Well, aren't you going to fuck me?' she asked, reclining on the floor and spreading her slender legs.

Moving between her thighs, Barry ran his solid knob up and down her girl-crack, lubricating his glans before driving it deep into Christine's yearning cunt. 'Ah, yes, that's big and stiff enough!' she gasped, turning to look at Marianne again. 'It's strange having her watch us, isn't it?'

'Yes, it is. God, your cunt's tight!'

'Tighter than hers?'

'No, she's got a much tighter cunt than you have!'

'Oh, thanks a lot, Barry!'

'No, I didn't mean . . . Ah, you're hot, wet . . .'

'What *did* you mean? You'd rather be screwing me, wouldn't you?'

'She's a better fuck than you are, Chris – you fucking little bitch.'

'Oh, brilliant! You really know how to turn a girl on!'

'I didn't mean . . . I don't know why I said that!'

'No, neither do I, Barry! You told me that she was no good in bed. You said that her tits were . . .'

'She's got better tits than you, you slut! They're firmer, bigger. What the hell am I saying?'

'You're saying that her tits are better than mine – and that I'm a slut!'

'Ah, God, I want to come inside you!' Barry gasped as he rammed his penis deep into the girl's vagina. 'God, I'm nearly there already – you fucking whore! Shame you don't give blow jobs – Marianne's brilliant at cock sucking!'

'Right, that's enough, get off me!'

'God, I'm . . . I'm coming! Coming up your cunt, you fucking little tart!'

'Get off me, Barry! Obviously you would rather be with . . .'

'I'm there! Coming up your slack cunt, you fucking slut!'

Satisfaction creeping across Marianne's face as she watched Christine desperately trying to push Barry off, she wondered at the power of hypnotic suggestion. As Barry pumped his sperm deep into the girl's young vagina, Marianne's mind flooded with ideas. *I could tell him that, whenever he sees a pussy, he won't be able to get a hard-on!* she thought wickedly. *That would fuck him right up!*

'If you've quite finished using me, will you please get off?' Christine blasted as tears welled in her green eyes.

'Yes, I've finished using your cunt, you fucking slag!' Barry replied, stunned at his words as he slipped his penis from the girl's pussy-hole. Hurriedly dressing as Barry lay shattered on the floor, Christine swore that their relationship was over. 'It's done with!' she sobbed. 'I . . . I never want to see you again, Barry!'

'But, Chris! I didn't mean what I said!'

'You didn't mean it? Then why say it?'

'I can't explain. I don't know why . . .'

'If it's some kind of joke, then it's not very funny! Do you prefer her body to mine or not?'

'I've got to be honest, Chris – she's got a damn sight better body than you have, you fucking old slag!'

'Right, that's it!' Christine stormed as she finished dressing and stomped towards the door. 'Goodbye, Barry. And good bloody riddance!'

'But, Chris!'

As the front door slammed shut, Barry rose to his feet and stood before Marianne. 'Put your dress on,' he sighed despondently. 'I really don't know why I said those things to Chris. I don't know what came over me!' Pulling her dress over her head, Marianne couldn't wait to get at Barry's subconscious and fill it with suggestions. This was the beginning, she thought – the beginning of a new era! Bringing her out of her trance, Barry sat in the armchair, his forehead lined, anxiety mirrored in his dark eyes. Obviously confused, he shook his head and sighed.

'God, I don't know!'

'What don't you know?' Marianne smiled.

'Nothing.'

'Time for sex!'

Mesmerized, Barry reclined in the chair, his face serene, his hands limp in his lap. 'So, you've fucked up your relationship with Christine!' Marianne laughed as the doorbell rang. 'Wait there,' she said, leaping to her feet and dashing to the door. 'Oh, Natalie!' she gasped as she opened the front door. 'How are things?'

'Awful!' the girl complained as she followed Marianne into the kitchen. 'My marriage is over – Ian's left me for my sister, would you believe?'

'Sit down, Nat,' Marianne smiled, sitting opposite the girl. 'Look into my eyes and relax. You feel sleepy, your eyelids are heavy. Sleepy, sleepy.'

Amazed as the girl's head slumped forward, Marianne ordered her to stand up. 'This is incredible!' she giggled. 'I've got two people under my control now! So, Natalie, do you masturbate?'

'Yes, I do,' the girl replied, much to Marianne's delight.

'Tell me all about it – where you do it, how often you do it, how you do it.'

'Normally, I masturbate in the bath. I open my legs and rub my spot.'

'What about your pussy-hole? Do you finger yourself?'

'Yes, sometimes. I often use the shampoo bottle. I push it into my nest, all the way in, and then frig my clitty.'

'And what about your bum? Have you ever fingered your bum?'

'No, I never touch myself there.'

'We'll have to change that! Your bum can bring you wonderful feelings! How often do you masturbate?'

'I try to come at least once every day.'

'Really? Where else do you do it, apart from in the bath?'

'Sometimes in bed in the mornings, after Ian's got up. And in the garden, if the weather's good – on the sun bed.'

'What about your tits, do you play with them?'

'I like sucking my nipples. I can just reach to suck them.'

'What about other girls? Have you ever touched another girl?'

'Yes, at school I used to. I used to sit next to Diana Kingsley. We used to put our hands down each other's knickers and frig each other.'

'Did she ever lick your cunt?'

'No, but we used to suck each other's nipples after school in the woods behind the playing field. I was only fifteen and my tits were very small, but hers were big, very big.'

'I think you need to discover your bum, Nat – you don't know what you're missing! Come into the lounge, there's something I want you to do. You'll remember nothing afterwards, nothing at all!'

Following her mistress through the hall, Natalie obediently stood in the centre of the lounge. 'Barry!' Marianne said, turning to her boyfriend. 'Come here and remove Natalie's clothes. We're going to have some fun with her.'

Relaxing on the sofa, Marianne pondered on her wickedness, realizing for the first time the full potential of her incredible power. As Barry unbuttoned Natalie's blouse and slipped the garment over her shoulders, revealing the girl's straining bra, Marianne grinned, wondering what to get the couple to do, what wickedly sinful act she should order them to commit. As Barry unclipped Natalie's bra, her heavy breasts tumbling out of the red silk cups, Marianne gazed at the girl's large, deep brown areolae, her huge wedge-shaped nipples.

'Suck her tits!' she ordered Barry, moving forward on the sofa. 'Go on, suck her lovely nipples!' Bending, Barry complied, taking the girl's erect nipple into his hot mouth. 'Suck it really hard!' Marianne trilled excitedly. 'Suck her really hard, Barry!' Grimacing, Natalie screwed her eyes shut as he sucked on her milk bud, squeezing her ballooning breast with both hands, bringing the girl a mixture of pain and pleasure. 'OK, now take her skirt off – and her panties!'

Neglecting Natalie's distended nipple, Barry knelt on the floor and tugged her skirt down to her ankles. Eyeing the swell of the girl's red panties, Marianne felt a pang of arousal course through her contracting womb. She'd instruct Natalie to lick between her full vaginal lips, to commit the beautiful act of lesbian oral sex, she decided as she lifted her dress and toyed with her wet pinken sex-folds. As Barry peeled Natalie's panties away from her mound, exposing her well-trimmed black pubes, her deep girl-crack, Marianne grinned. Reclining on the sofa, her buttocks well over the edge of the cushion, her thighs spread wide, her cunt open, she instructed Natalie to kneel before her. 'Between my legs,' Marianne said softly. 'Kneel on all-fours before your beautiful mistress – slave!'

Her pretty face between Marianne's thighs, her mouth close to her mistress's open vaginal slit, Natalie projected her buttocks, her gaping cunt lips. 'Barry, kneel behind her and fuck her cunt!' Marianne ordered in her wanton wickedness. 'Natalie, I know that you're not a lesbian, but you'll lick my cunt, my clitoris, and make me come while Barry fucks you. You'll lick my cunt as if you're really enjoying it! You never know, perhaps you *will* enjoy it!'

Slipping his jeans off, Barry grabbed his rock-hard penis and slipped it between Natalie's swollen cunt lips, driving his bulbous knob deep into her young body, pushing the girl forward, thrusting her face into Marianne's shaved crack. 'Your first taste of cunt!' Marianne giggled impishly. 'Go on, lick me out!' Her tongue running up Marianne's open sex-groove as Barry thrust his weapon into her quim from behind, Natalie obediently followed her instructions. 'Ah, that's nice!'

Marianne breathed as the girl's tongue swept over her stiffening clitoris. 'Barry, you're not to come! Don't come until I tell you to!'

Closing her eyes, Marianne relaxed as her new slave attended her femininity. Wondering whether she'd be able to hypnotize Jill and Lydia, she decided that it was time to pay them a visit. She'd expected Lydia to ring and breathe the magical word down the phone and order Marianne to meet her at the park for an evening of lesbian sex. *Probably been too busy licking each other's cunts!* Marianne decided as Natalie's tongue snaked into her vaginal sheath, seeking out the hot girl-come.

'Stop now, Barry!' Marianne ordered. 'Take your cock out of her cunt and sit on the sofa.' Once he'd seated himself, his penis solid, pointing skyward, Marianne ordered Natalie to move away. 'This should be fun!' she giggled, sitting on Barry's lap with her legs open wide. Settling her vaginal entrance over Barry's hard knob, she gently lowered her body, his shaft sinking deep into her hot cunt, impaling her completely. 'Get yourself between our legs and lick my clitty!' she ordered Natalie.

Gazing below her smooth stomach, Marianne grinned. Her swollen cunt lips tightly encompassing Barry's massive shaft, her clitoris exposed, she shuddered as Natalie's tongue began its intimate licking. Gyrating her hips, Marianne massaged her inner cuntal flesh with Barry's solid cock, inducing her girl-juice to flow in torrents from her inner nectaries. 'Keep licking my clitty!' she gasped, grabbing Natalie's head and forcing her open mouth hard against her pinken flesh. Gasping as he managed to swivel his hips, Barry was close to orgasm. 'Natalie wants your sperm!' Marianne breathed, lifting her body and slipping his cock from her vagina. Lowering her body again, Marianne sat with his penis nestling between her open pussy lips, the massive head close to her clitoris. 'Now lick us both until we come!' she ordered Natalie.

Gazing at Barry's swollen knob resting between her vulval lips, at Natalie's tongue repeatedly sweeping over the silky surface, Marianne peeled her girl-flesh apart, presenting her clitoris to the girl's pink tongue. Suddenly, Barry's sperm jetted from his knob, spraying Natalie's face, her tongue, bathing Marianne's open sex-groove. Mouthing and licking the orgasming knob, Natalie swept her tongue over Marianne's clitoris, bringing her mistress to her climax in unison with Barry.

'God, that's nice!' Marianne gasped as she watched her clitoris throb against Barry's pulsating knob. 'Lick me, girl!' she breathed. 'Use your tongue to massage his sperm into my clit!' Lapping her mistress's sperm-drenched crack, her pulsating clitoris, Natalie was, indeed, a fine sex slave, Marianne thought. Her orgasm beginning to subside, leaving her gasping, trembling, Marianne instructed her slave to suck Barry's knob, to lick it and cleanse it. Taking his cock-head into her hot mouth, Natalie moved her head back and forth, sucking, licking, swallowing the remnants of his sperm as she mouth-fucked the huge organ.

Watching the arousing sight, Marianne laughed. 'It looks as if it's my knob!' she said. 'Sticking up between my thighs, it looks as though I've got a fucking great cock!' Toying with her clitoris as Natalie restiffened Barry's penis, Marianne lost herself in her evil wickedness. 'Want him to fuck your bum?' she asked the girl. Still mouthing, sucking on the purple plum, Natalie said nothing. 'Natalie, stop doing that, he's hard enough now. Kneel by the sofa with your bum sticking out.'

Taking up her position, Natalie rested her head on the sofa and jutted her taut buttocks, exposing her small brown portal. Climbing off Barry's lap, Marianne ordered him to kneel behind the girl. Grinning wickedly, Marianne took his solid shaft in her hand and presented his knob to Natalie's virginal brown ring. 'Push, Barry!' she demanded, holding the girl's buttocks wide apart as she watched her vestal portal yield. 'Go on, push, Barry – it's going in!'

Watching Barry's knob disappear into Natalie's rectal sheath, Marianne recalled the five penises driving deep into her own anal canal. Her craving for anal sex climbing to frightening heights, she imagined two solid cocks driving into her bottom-hole, fucking her there, filling her bowels with their jetting sperm. *I managed to get the perfume bottle up my bum*, she reflected. *So why not two cocks?*

As Barry's shaft entered Natalie's rear sex-sheath, his heavy balls resting against her bulging vaginal lips, Marianne ordered him to begin his fucking. His shaft withdrawing and thrusting into the girl, Marianne longed to have her own bottom fucked. 'God, it's a beautiful sight!' she gasped, her eyes transfixed on Barry's pistoning penis. 'You're no longer a virgin, Natalie! But it's a shame that you're not conscious. I'd love to see your face, watch your expression as Barry fucks your bum!'

Grunting, his body becoming rigid, Barry was nearing his climax. His powerful thrusting into Natalie's anus jolting the girl's young body, he suddenly grimaced, his sperm pumping, jetting deep into her bowels. 'Really give it to her!' Marianne shrieked as she yanked Natalie's buttock-orbs wide apart. 'Go on, fuck her tight little arsehole like there's no tomorrow!'

Relishing her shocking words of corruption, Marianne reached beneath Natalie's rocking body and parted her wet cunny lips. Massaging her erect clitoris, she took the girl to a shuddering orgasm, wondering what to put her slaves through next as the girl whimpered and writhed in her obvious ecstasy. As Barry stilled his thrusting penis, his knob absorbing the heat of Natalie's bowels, Marianne ordered him to slip his organ out and lick his sperm from the girl's tight brown hole. Quivering in the aftermath of her climax as Barry slipped his penis from her bottom-sheath, Natalie buried her face in the sofa cushion, emitting low moans of pleasure as Barry began his anal licking.

'That's it, drink your sperm from her bum-hole!' Marianne instructed, slowing her clitoral massaging. Pulling Natalie's buttocks wide apart, Marianne ordered Barry to push his tongue into the girl's inflamed bottom-hole. 'Go on, you can do it!' she giggled, stretching the tight hole open with her fingertips. 'Shit, there's the doorbell! Who the hell's that? Keep licking her there, Barry. I'll be back in a minute!'

Dashing into the hall and opening the front door, Marianne was pleased to see John standing on the step – but she didn't dare invite him in! 'I've got visitors, John,' she smiled. 'Was it Barry or me you wanted to see?'

'Both of you,' he replied. 'I'll come back later if . . .'

'On second thoughts, come in for a minute, John. Barry might want to have a word with you.'

As John stepped into the hall, Marianne closed the front door and gazed into his blue eyes, her stare penetrating his very soul as she intoned her words of hypnosis. Frowning at first, John soon began to relax, his face losing its smile, his expression blank. Taking his hand and leading him into the lounge, she ordered him to slip his clothes off.

'Hurry up, John!' she said eagerly. 'You and Barry are going to realize a fantasy of mine. You're both going to fuck my bum – simultaneously!' Dashing upstairs as John undressed, Marianne grabbed the bottle of baby lotion from her dressing table and returned to the lounge. Pulling her dress over her head, she stood naked before John, admiring his solid penis, his heavy balls.

'Barry, stop licking Natalie's bum and stand up,' she

ordered, wondering how to position herself so the men could both push their solid knobs deep into her bowels. Smearing baby lotion between her taut buttocks, around her anal entrance, she ordered Barry to lie on the floor. Lubricating his knob with the lotion, she turned to John and smeared the cooling cream over his purple plum.

Kneeling astride Barry, grinning as she gazed into his misty eyes, she instructed Natalie to push Barry's knob into her bottom-hole. 'Come on, Natalie, push his cock right up my bum!' she giggled, projecting her buttocks, exposing her well-oiled brown hole. Taking Barry's penis, Natalie pushed the solid head against Marianne's tight hole, managing to force it past her defeated muscles and deep into her bowels. 'Ah, that feels good!' Marianne breathed, slowly settling on the huge penis. 'Now, John, kneel between Barry's legs and Natalie will push your cock into my bum.'

John's huge penis wavering as he knelt between Barry's legs, Marianne prayed that he'd be able to slip it alongside Barry's cock, stretching her rectal sheath wide to give her a double anal fucking. The thought exciting her, she sensed her cuntal juices streaming from her neglected vagina as Natalie pressed John's bulbous knob between her quivering buttocks.

'Use more baby lotion!' Marianne gasped as Natalie tried to force the knob into her already stretched hole. The lotion cooling her inflamed brown ring, Marianne grimaced as Natalie tried again to force John's solid knob past her tight muscles. 'Go on, you can do it, Natalie!' she gasped. 'That's it, push it in!'

Her taut brown ring expanding as John's knob pressed harder against her brown flesh, Marianne let out a rush of breath. Suddenly slipping into her anal duct, John's plum opened her rectal entrance, painfully stretching the delicate tissue. 'God, I can't . . . I can't take two!' Marianne cried as John drove his penis deep into her tight bottom-hole. The two huge shafts filling her to capacity, Marianne rolled her eyes, her head slumped forward, her matted long blonde hair brushing Barry's face. Her weight on her aching arms, she gently lowered her trembling body, resting on Barry as John impaled her completely on his twitching cock.

'I've done it!' Marianne gasped as she slowly gyrated her hips. 'God, I've got two cocks up my bum!' Delighted that she was now a confirmed slag, Marianne grinned wickedly as she swivelled her hips, her double anal fucking bringing her an incredible sensation of debased sexual satisfaction. 'God, it's beautiful!' she cried. 'John, start fucking me, ram your prick hard into my arse. Natalie, you can suck the spunk from my arse when they've done me!'

Thrusting his penis into Marianne's bloated anal sheath, massaging Barry's knob with his, slapping Barry's balls with his, John brought Marianne's fantasy to life. Her naked body perspiring, jolting, Marianne closed her eyes, praying that the solid knobs would spurt their sperm in unison, both fill her abused body at once. 'God, it's incredible!' she cried as John quickened his rhythm. 'God, my bum! My beautiful bum!'

The men gasping, Marianne felt their cocks swell. 'Both at once!' she ordered her slaves. 'Both spunk up my arse at once!' Their cock-heads ballooning, their sperm jetting deep into Marianne's bowels, she writhed and whimpered as her clitoris exploded in orgasm. 'Coming!' she wailed, reaching between her full vaginal lips and massaging the pleasure from her sex-nodule. 'Fuck . . . fuck me!' she wailed, as her entire body shook violently. 'Ah, my beautiful arse!'

As John's thrusting penis slowed, Marianne slowed her own massaging rhythm, eliciting the last ripples of orgasm from her inflamed clitoris. Collapsing over Barry, she rested her perspiring body, her rectal sheath tightly gripping the spent male organs, soaking up the swirling sperm. 'John, slowly, very slowly, slip your cock out of my bum,' she breathed huskily. Her rear love-sheath gently deflating, she breathed heavily, her body jolting as the knob slipped out and her brown ring closed around Barry's penile shaft.

'God, we must do this again!' she cried as she gently moved forward, sliding Barry's shrinking penis from her inflamed bottom-tube. 'Ah, ah! Ah, God!' she cried as her ring closed, sealing in the creamy products of two male orgasms. Crawling off Barry, she lay on her back, her eyes rolling, her body trembling. 'God, I've never... I've never had such a good fuck in all my life!'

Rolling onto her stomach and spreading her thighs, she ordered Natalie to lie on the floor between her legs and suck the sperm from her bottom-hole. Complying, Natalie parted Marianne's taut bum cheeks and closed her full lips around the girl's abused hole. Sucking, her tongue probing, she drew out the sperm, swallowing the nectar, cleansing her mistress's anal sheath.

Her eyes rolling again as the incredible pleasure spread throughout her quivering body, Marianne knew that her insatiable holes, her clitoris, would never bring her enough satisfaction. She wanted more and more depraved sex – more penises, more sperm, more cunts, more girl-juice. 'You two get dressed,' she ordered Barry and John as her body shuddered at the thought of *three* penises thrusting into her anal sheath. 'We'll all do this again, and you, Natalie – *you're* going to experience a double bum-fuck the next time we're all together! Ah, that's good! You've got a nice tongue!'

The anal cleansing finished, Marianne rolled onto her back and instructed Natalie to dress. 'Leave your knickers off!'

she giggled. 'I want you to kneel over my face in a minute. I'm going to lick your cunt to orgasm.' The men fully clothed, Marianne ordered them to sit on the sofa and watch Natalie's lesbian oral coupling. 'By the way, John, you can pay for the sex you've had. Take all the money you have and stuff it beneath the sofa!' she laughed, watching as he took at least three twenty-pound notes from his wallet. 'That'll do nicely! Now, Natalie, bring me your sweet cunt – I want to drink from your beautiful cunny-hole!'

Positioning her gaping vaginal crack above Marianne's face, Natalie lowered the centre of her young body, settling her girlhood over her mistress's thirsty mouth. 'Mmm,' Marianne moaned as she pushed her tongue into the girl's hot vagina and savoured her girl-come. 'You taste good!' Rocking her hips, Natalie began her gasping, her clitoris swelling as Marianne's tongue lapped up her slippery honeydew.

Her young body shuddering, Natalie leaned back, placing her arms behind her and supporting her weight on her hands. Her sex-groove opening as she threw her head back, she opened her mouth, her eyes closing as she slipped deeper into a swirling pool of pure sexual ecstasy. 'Coming,' she whispered softly. 'Coming, coming.' The words of sex falling from her pretty lips, she gently rocked her young body, delighting in the sensations emanating from her ripening clitoris.

Suddenly singing out her appreciation as her climax gripped her, she ground her open cunt hard into Marianne's hot mouth. Her slippery cunt milk decanting, flowing from her spasming pussy-hole, she lost herself in her sexual delirium. *She's going to be another regular visitor!* Marianne decided as she drank from the girl's gushing cunt. There were going to be many regular visitors – both male and female!

As Natalie's orgasm began to subside, Marianne thought

again about Barry. If she could erase the real trigger word from his memory, she'd have complete control. John also knew the word, and the girls – but Barry was the real problem. If she couldn't erase the word, she'd leave him and set herself up in a flat, she decided as Natalie collapsed to the floor, her cunt spewing out its come, her clitoris done – until the next time!

Rising to her feet, Marianne slipped into her dress and ordered John to go and wait by the front door. 'Put your knickers on, Natalie,' she said, tossing the garment to the girl. Hiding the baby lotion, she seated Barry and checked the room for evidence of her debauched group sex session. 'Right, Barry, you will wake up when you hear the front doorbell ring,' she said, leading Natalie into the hall.

'When you hear the words, "*Time for sex*", you'll both fall into a hypnotic trance,' Marianne said. 'Do you both understand?'

'Yes,' John replied.

'I understand,' Natalie said.

'Good. Natalie, you'll wake up when you get to your front door. And you'll remember nothing other than the trigger words, *Time for sex*.'

Opening the door, Marianne waited until Natalie had gone before ringing the bell and ordering John to return to his waking state. 'Come through, John,' she invited, closing the front door. 'Barry's in the lounge.'

'Thanks,' he smiled, following Marianne. 'Hi, Barry!'

'Hi, John. How are you?' Barry greeted.

'I'm fine!' he replied, obviously recalling nothing of the double anal fucking.

'I'm going upstairs for a while,' Marianne said, all too aware of sperm oozing from her inflamed bottom-hole. 'I'll leave you two to have a chat.'

Closing the lounge door behind her, Marianne made her way up to the bedroom and laid her aching body on the bed. 'God, quite a day, so far!' she giggled. 'What the hell will the rest of the day bring?' As she contemplated her new-found life, her sexuality, she thought again of what she'd become. *A fully-fledged slag!* she laughed inwardly, grabbing the bedside phone and asking the operator for Christopher Davies's number. Punching the buttons, she decided to tell him that she'd had two cocks up her bum, sperming up her bum. *That'll turn him on!* she mused as a woman answered the phone.

'Hi, is Christopher there, please?' she asked.

'No, he's out – can I take a message?' the woman replied.

'Are you his wife?'

'Yes, I am.'

'Oh, I see. I was going to tell Chris that I've just had two cocks up my bum at once, both sperming into my arse!' Marianne giggled.

'I *beg* your pardon? Who *is* this?'

'I'm Chris's girlfriend, his slag on the side – his bit of skirt. I'm the one who gives him great blow jobs and lets him fuck my arse. Poor Chris, it's a shame you're such a prude! Wouldn't you like him to fuck *your* arse?'

'You're sick!'

'No, I'm just heavily into sex! Tell him I rang, will you – my name's Sarah. Bye!'

Replacing the receiver, Marianne felt more wicked than ever. 'I feel great!' she giggled. 'Right, a couple of hours' sleep, and then it's back to my life of beautifully perverted sex!'

Chapter Twelve

Barry and John had disappeared by the time Marianne had hauled her aching body from the bed and staggered downstairs. Wondering where they were, what they were up to, she called next door to see how Natalie was feeling after her enforced sex session.

'Oh, Marianne – come in!' the girl invited as she opened the front door.

Is Barry's sperm oozing from her bum-hole? Marianne wondered. 'I thought I'd come and see how you are,' she smiled, wondering whether Natalie had realized that she'd walked into her house, before mysteriously finding herself back home – a hell of a long time later!

'Ian's gone, thank God! The bastard's gone!' Natalie announced bitterly. 'I realize now that I don't need him. I've got the house, and he's got my dopey sister, so I suppose we're all happy.'

'It's funny how things turn out, isn't it?'

'It certainly is! Come into the lounge and have a glass of wine. By the way, what happened when I came round to see you earlier? I remember going into your kitchen, and then . . .'

'And then you went home again,' Marianne replied, closing the front door behind her and following Natalie into the lounge.

'You were so distressed over Ian that I don't think you knew what you were doing!'

'I *was* rather upset. But I've come to the conclusion that I'm better off on my own. I don't need Ian – or anyone else, for that matter!'

Temptation rears its beautiful head! Gazing at the girl's long legs, her miniskirt, Marianne imagined her hot pussy, her secret – or not so secret – garden. Recalling Natalie kneeling astride her head, she quivered. The girl had tasted nice, she reflected, picturing her open sex-folds, her erect clitoris throbbing in orgasm. *God, I want her again!*

'I'm leaving Barry,' Marianne confided, wondering whether Natalie would suggest that she move in with her and they live together as lesbians.

'Leaving him? I've heard that one before!' Natalie quipped.

'Yes, I know – but this time, I mean it! All this hypnosis stuff has ... I've come to the same conclusion as you – I don't need him! I haven't told him yet, but I'm going to get myself a nice little flat. I've had a brilliant job offer with a company car – a Mercedes, would you believe?'

'God, that sounds all right!'

'Yes, and the money'll be pretty good, too.'

'But the house ... You own it jointly with Barry, don't you?'

'Yes, but there's no way Barry would sign his half over to ... Wait a minute, there is a way!'

'How?'

'I'll tell you later, Nat. I must dash, I'll tell you later! This evening, come round this evening!'

Dashing from the house in her excitement, Marianne grinned. Ringing the building society, she spoke to the manager, explaining that Barry was leaving her and that he wanted to sign his half of the house over to her. 'If you're to take on the mortgage alone, we'll need your employer's references and a statement of your earnings,' the pompous man returned.

'That's no problem! My employer will be only too happy to do that.' *Jonathan Brooke-Smith will be only too eager to help me!*

'In that case, if you give me details of your employer, I'll start the ball rolling as soon as possible.'

Ringing Brooke-Smith, Marianne explained her predicament. 'You see, Jonathan, Barry and I are splitting up, and he's going to sign his half of the house over to me. I need a reference and a statement of my earnings.'

'No problem! I'll write you a glowing reference. The thing is, when *are* you going to come and work for me?'

'I'll start next week, OK?'

'Fine! Nine o'clock on Monday morning, all right?'

'I'll be there, Jonathan.'

'And so will your car. See you on Monday, Marianne.'

'Great. And thanks – I owe you one!'

'Do you now? I'll look forward to that!'

'Er... yes, well, until Monday. Bye.'

Searching Barry's bureau, Marianne came across his bank statement. 'God!' she breathed aloud. 'Where the hell did he get all that money from? Twenty grand!' Hearing the front door open, she closed the bureau and hurriedly left the dining room. 'Hi, Barry!' she smiled, meeting him in the hall. 'Where have you been?'

'I went out with John,' he replied. 'Jux—'

'Time for sex!' Marianne interrupted before Barry could say the word.

Again, he fell into a strange hypnotic trance. 'This is getting easier!' Marianne giggled, leading him into the lounge. 'Now, Barry, where did you get the twenty-odd grand from that's in your bank account?'

'I've been stashing it away for years. A lot of it was left to me by my aunt.'

'Well, you're now going to write me a cheque – for the full amount! Go and get your cheque book.'

Returning from the bureau, Barry meekly penned a cheque out to Marianne. 'You'll never wonder why you did this, do you understand?'

'Yes, I understand.'

'You'll always think of it as a gift, a present you decided to give me. Also, you're going to sign the house over to me. And lastly, will you please forget the word "*juxtaposition*?" '

'Yes, I will.'

'You've never heard of the word, Barry. When you want to hypnotize me, you'll use the trigger word "*delta*", have you got that?'

'Yes, I have.'

'Good. Now, go and put your cheque book back and then come and sit down,' Marianne instructed, slipping the cheque behind the mantlepiece clock.

Returning to the lounge, Barry sat down, gazing around the room in bewilderment as Marianne ordered him to wake up. 'So, what are you doing for the rest of the afternoon?' she asked casually. 'And when are you going to start earning some money from your consultancy business or whatever it is?'

'In about half an hour!' Barry laughed. 'I've a friend coming round to . . . well, I won't go into the details. Juxtaposition!'

God, how the hell do I make him forget that bloody word? Marianne wondered angrily as she slipped into a hypnotic trance. *How the hell do I do it?* Things would be completely different if only Barry were to forget the real trigger word. But would that ever happen? She very much doubted it!

'OK, Marianne – follow me to the garage. You're going in

the pillory, my girl! There'll be another fifty quid in my pocket when Dave gets here! Come on, take your dress off and follow me!'

Pulling her dress over her head, Marianne recalled Dave, the pervert who'd staked her naked body to the lawn and used her to satisfy his insatiable thirst for lust. If only she was in control! But, hypnotized or not, what control would she have when trapped in the pillory? she wondered as she dropped her dress to the floor and followed her master. As they entered the garage, Marianne gazed at the pillory – and the whip and canes. Wishing she'd breathed her word and ordered Barry to cancel the arrangement, her clitoris throbbed in expectation.

'Come over here and get on all fours over this plank, you fucking bitch!' Barry ordered harshly, lifting the top section of the pillory away. 'That's it, rest your neck and wrists in the cutouts and I'll drop this back into place, like this – and you're now my prisoner!' he laughed. Her buttocks projecting, her cunny lips exposed beneath her yawning bottom-crease, Barry moved her knees further apart, tying ropes around her calves and fixing the ends to the frame to secure the degrading position. 'And now for your tits, you dirty little whore!' he chuckled, clamping metal clips to her long nipples. Hanging heavy weights from the clips, he gazed at her firm breasts, painfully stretched into taut cones of flesh. 'Dave will like that! He's a right perve!'

And so are you! Marianne reflected, grimacing as the clips bit into her hardening nipples. *Come to that, so am I!* Again, Barry's cruel words reflected his inner self, the real Barry – Barry the bastard. With no respect, no thought for his girlfriend, his only concern was making money from pimping. 'The lads are coming over again this evening to use you!' he laughed, slapping her buttocks, causing her naked body to jolt. 'They're coming over to fuck your holes, to use you as the dirty little whore that you are!'

Moving to the shelf, Barry opened the video camera to remove the cassette. Frowning, he gazed at the empty compartment. 'That's odd,' he breathed. 'I don't remember taking it out.' What with the missing money, and now the cassette, he was becoming suspicious, Marianne knew. Hopefully, as far as the massive cheque was concerned, her hypnotic suggestion would work. But he was bound to think it strange that he'd given her all his money, she thought.

'I don't understand it!' Barry sighed as he placed the camera on the shelf. 'Marianne, do you know where the cassette is?'

'No,' she said softly.

'Something weird is going on! The money, and now the bloody tape! Something's going on!'

As Barry left the garage, Marianne tried to make herself comfortable. Her neck and wrists clamped, her stomach resting on the padded plank, her legs bound with rope, she could barely move. *God, my tits hurt!* she cursed inwardly as the weights swung, pulling on her sensitive nipples. Hearing voices, she wondered what Dave had in mind, what perverted act he'd planned to commit on her tethered, naked body.

'There's the little bitch!' Barry bellowed as he showed Dave into the garage. 'I'll be in the house if you need me – not that you will!'

'I've got all I need here, thanks!' Dave laughed, eyeing Marianne's exposed bottom-hole, her ripe vaginal lips.

'Right, give her a good seeing-to, and a fucking good thrashing!' Barry laughed.

'This is incredible! I mean, just look at the state of her! Christ, I wish I had a girlfriend like her!'

'The other evening, I brought five friends round and they all fucked her arse!'

'What, one after the other?'

'Yes! The fucking little tart's going to earn me a small fortune!'

'It seems strange, using your girlfriend like this. Don't you feel anything for her?' Dave asked.

'No, nothing. I used to but . . . well, I met someone else. Not that she's around anymore. What Marianne and I have now is a business relationship – and one that works very well! Anyway, enjoy yourself!'

Alone with Dave, Marianne pondered on Barry's words. *Just a whore.* When she'd started messing about with her trigger word, she'd thought his darker side was more or less normal – his male desires unleashed. But now? She'd discovered another side to herself, she reflected. Her insatiable craving for debased sex, her unquenchable thirst for anal sex . . . But Barry had more than a mere craving for sex – he was evil!

'You've a beautiful body, Marianne,' Dave enthused. 'As I said the last time I was here, if you were my girlfriend, I certainly wouldn't sell you for . . . still, it's none of my business. I suppose Barry's right, you're just a whore. I'll never forget discovering that fucking great candle stuffed up your cunt! Anyway, I've paid Barry fifty pounds for you, so I want my money's worth! You benefit from the cash he's earning from you, so what the hell?'

I've got all the money! Marianne reflected smugly as Dave knelt behind her and parted her taut bottom-orbs. *But if only I had control!* Once the house had been signed over to her, she'd chuck Barry out. She'd use her trigger word and order him to go and rent a flat – and never come back! *I could keep him on as my housekeeper!* But, she reflected, there would be little point in throwing him out so long as he retained his power over her.

'This whip looks interesting!' Dave chuckled as he slapped Marianne's buttocks and stood up. 'We'll start with a good thrashing, I think!' he laughed, grabbing the whip. The first lash of the thin leather tails causing her young body to convulse, Marianne vowed to put Barry in the stocks and give him the thrashing of his life by way of retaliation. *What a way to earn fifty pounds!* she thought as the second lash tensed her burning buttocks.

The relentless thrashing continuing, the heavy weights hanging from her aching nipples oscillated, painfully stretching her young milk buds. The lewd sensations mingling with the stinging pain spreading across her buttocks, she felt her clitoris swell and throb. Once again, the leather tails lashed her crimson orbs, the thin weals fanning out across her taut flesh. Once feminine, girlish, dainty, her blonde tresses and make-up always impeccable, Marianne knew she was now no more than a slut. But with her knickerless, shaved pussy, her minidress, her dishevelled hair, she'd discovered a new and exciting contrariness far removed from her once soft and gentle femininity.

'You little whore!' Dave cried as he brought the leather tails down again. 'After I've thrashed you, I'm going to fuck your tight little arse-hole!' The crude words sending quivers of sex through the girl's pelvis, she gasped, her young body trembling, shaking violently as the cruel tails lashed her crimson buttocks again.

Almost delirious as her clitoris pulsated, yearning for fingers, a tongue, a vibrator, Marianne gasped her confused words of sex. 'More . . . fuck . . . more! My bum! Fuck my bum! Ah, my tits! More!' Dropping the whip and grabbing a long, thin bamboo cane, Dave grinned as he struck the girl's twitching buttocks, leaving broad weals across her stretched flesh. 'More, more!' Marianne begged, her body convulsing uncontrollably, her mind awash with images of her degradingly displayed girlhood.

Wondering how to force three penises deep into her tight anal sheath as the cane landed across her twitching buttocks again, Marianne's thoughts turned to Rod. *If he could see me now!* she mused as the cane cracked loudly across her young arse-globes. *God, what would he think?* Barry knew nothing about Rod. She could stay with him if she failed to remove the real trigger word from Barry's memory – or carry on enduring the gruelling sex sessions. At least money wasn't a problem now. But there was little point in banking Barry's cheque, she realized. He'd simply use the trigger word and take the money back! And as for signing the house over...

'I'm enjoying this!' Dave chortled as he brought the cane down again, thrashing Marianne's crimson buttocks with an uncanny air of revenge. *Are all men into thrashing young girls?* Marianne wondered as Dave discarded the cane and knelt behind her tethered body, gazing at her fiery bottom-globes. *There must be some kind of Freudian psychology to explain it!* she decided, determined to get Barry in the pillory and give him a good seeing-to.

'And now I'll screw your bum!' Dave laughed as he slipped his purple knob between Marianne's bloated cuntal lips, lubricating his cock-head in preparation for the enforced anal fucking. 'Ah, your cunt's really hot! If only my wife would allow me to whip her and fuck her bum!'

Wife? Marianne echoed as he slipped his penis from her oily cuntal sheath and pressed his knob against her anal ring. *I thought he was single!* Recalling her wicked phone call to the accountant's wife, Marianne decided to ring Dave's and have some more fun.

'Straight in!' Dave gasped as he drove his knob deep into

her hot bowels. 'I'm going to fuck your arse every day, Marianne! Every day, I'll come round and spunk up your tight arse!'

The beautiful anal pounding taking her nearer to her sexual heaven with every crude thrust, Marianne recalled Natalie unknowingly surrendering her anal virginity. *God, she's coming round this evening!* she suddenly remembered – *and Alan*! If everyone arrived at the house at once, then . . . *Mass hypnosis!* she thought, imagining eight or nine naked bodies at her disposal.

Suddenly groaning, Dave drove his knob deep into her hot bowels, spurting his spunk into her trembling body, draining his heavy balls. 'That's good!' he cried, thrusting into her tight hole again as he grabbed her hips. 'Ah, yes! Take that!' he gasped, ramming his weapon in to the root as his sperm gushed. 'Take that! And that! And that!'

His pistoning finally over, he slowly slipped his spent rod from the girl's inflamed anal sheath, leaving her trembling, her clitoris throbbing, desperate for orgasm. 'Right, I'll leave Barry to release you,' he imparted, zipping his trousers. 'I'll see you tomorrow for another session of whipping and bum-fucking!'

As Dave left the garage, Marianne thought about the evening. She'd ring Jill and Lydia, she decided. Make one last attempt to remove the trigger word from her abusers' memories. Ian wasn't a problem, he'd gone off with Natalie's sister. Christine? There was no way she'd come along – not after Barry's cruel words! *Better get John round, too*, she decided as Barry arrived.

'That's another fifty in the bin!' he laughed, releasing Marianne. 'Come on, stand up! I want you cleaned up ready for this evening! The lads are coming over – all five of them!' Marianne shivered. Her anal sheath sore, the last thing in the world she needed was five orgasming penises driving into her tight bottom-hole! Or was it?

Following Barry into the house, she retrieved her dress from the lounge and slipped the garment over her aching body. Obediently sitting at the kitchen table as Barry clicked his fingers, her plans for the evening in ruins, she decided to spend the night at Rod's house.

'My bum really hurts!' she complained as Barry leaned on the worktop, gloating over her predicament. 'I can't think what I've done, but it really stings!'

'You're always complaining about your bum!' Barry snapped.

'See for yourself!' she returned, lifting her dress and bending over. 'It looks as if I've been caned!'

'How come you're not wearing any panties?'

'I must have forgotten to . . .'

'Jux . . .'

'What?'

'I can't think what I was going to say,' Barry frowned. 'Jux . . . That's strange, I can't think . . .'

'You said "*jux*". What does *that* mean?'

'I have no idea! My mind's gone blank!'

'Time for sex.'

Falling into a trance, Barry gazed blankly across the room. *He's forgotten the word!* Marianne thought jubilantly. *He's forgotten the bloody trigger word!* 'Barry, what were you about to say?' she asked, praying that, at last, she was in complete control.

'I can't recall the trigger word,' he replied mechanically.

'What about the new word?'

'New word?'

'Don't you remember? I told you to use another trigger word, can't you remember it?'

'No, I can't recall the trigger word.'

'Perhaps it's just as well. I don't need you to help me earn money. I can sell myself for sex without your help!'

Wondering why Barry should suddenly forget the original trigger word as well as the false one, Marianne instructed him to ring his five friends and cancel the evening of debauched sex. Making herself a cup of coffee as he walked through the hall and rang each friend in turn, she pondered on the future. There were still too many people who knew of the word – too many people who would use her for sex. *If I can hypnotize Barry, John and Natalie, then I can hypnotize anyone!* she decided.

'Now ring Dave and tell him that tomorrow's off,' she ordered Barry as he entered the kitchen. 'I'll decide who comes round, and when! Oh, and call John – tell him to come over this evening.' *That's Alan, Natalie and John coming round*, she mused. *Mass hypnosis!*

Obeying Marianne as he returned to the kitchen, Barry sat at the table. With a spring in her step, her heart fluttering, Marianne dashed to the phone and rang Jill, inviting the girl and her lesbian friend over for the evening. 'Come round for drinks,' she said eagerly. 'Barry will be out, so we'll down a few bottles of wine and have a chat.'

'Great!' Jill replied enthusiastically. 'Lydia will be pleased. She was asking when we were going to see you again.'

'Was she now? OK, I'll see you both this evening.'

Breezing into the kitchen, Marianne grinned. 'So, Barry, you can't remember the trigger word! Well now, there's a turn-up for the books! It would seem that your evil reign of abuse is finally over! You've lost your job, you've lost my love for you, you've lost your power over me, and you're losing your money and your share of the house! What do you think about that?'

'The money was a gift – I gave it to you as a present.'

'And you're going to sign your share of the house over to me, aren't you?'

'Yes, I am.'

'Good! I was going to throw you out, but I've changed my mind. I'll use you as you used me, Barry! You'll be my slave! I'm going out now. While I'm gone, you'll vacuum and dust the lounge, prepare it for this evening. And you'll never again question me, where I'm going or where I've been. You'll treat me as your mistress. Oh, and one last thing. Whenever you see a naked girl, a pussy, tits or whatever, you won't be able to get a hard-on! Whenever there's any prospect of sex, you won't be able to get it up! That way, I'll be sure of your fidelity, your loyalty to me – your mistress! I'll allow you sex on the odd occasion. I'll allow you to get it up as and when it suits me – and with whom! OK, wake up.'

Rising to his feet, Barry gazed into Marianne's misty blue eyes. 'I'll do some housework, clean the lounge,' he smiled.

'Good idea. I'm going out for a walk. I don't know when I'll be back, it might be half an hour or three hours.'

'OK, love. I'll see you when I see you.'

'Don't you want to know where I'm going?'

'Er . . . it's none of my business, really.'

'You're right – it's none of your business.'

'I'll see you later, love.'

'Yes, you will. Oh, and put some wine in the fridge, will you?'

'Yes, of course.'

Walking down the street, Marianne could barely believe the incredible U-turn the situation had taken. *It's not only the tables that have turned – it's my whole world!* she thought happily as she neared the church. Entering the building, she grinned. 'Hallo again, vicar!' she called. Turning away from the altar, the phallic candles, the ashen-faced man half-smiled, gazing at the girl's beguiling thighs as she walked towards him. 'I said I'd be back, didn't I?' she giggled devilishly.

'Yes, you did,' the cleric replied. 'Er... come into my office,' he invited hesitantly, his eyes darting around the church as if looking for prying angels.

'You're a man, a normal man, aren't you?' she asked, following him into a small side room.

'Normal?' he echoed, his brown eyes frowning.

'Yes, normal. You like sex, don't you?'

'Er... well, you see...'

'Do you know who I am?'

'No, I don't.'

'You've probably heard of me – I'm the devil's daughter!'

'Please, this is a church! You mustn't...'

'Mustn't what? Mustn't show you this?'

Leaning with her buttocks against the desk, Marianne lifted her dress up over her stomach, grinning wickedly, delighting at the mixture of horror and lust reflected in the man of God's wide eyes as he gazed at her hairless, swollen vaginal lips, her gaping sex-groove. Taking his hand, she pressed his fingers against her warm, fleshy sex-cushions. 'Like it?' she asked impishly. 'Do you like my cunt? Satan's daughter's hot, wet cunt – do you like it?'

'My God! I... Please, you can't... Yes, *yes*, I like it very much!' he gasped, giving in to the angel of lust and kneading Marianne's soft hillocks.

'You may kneel before me, before your false goddess, and kiss my beautiful cunt,' she invited in her evil wantonness.

Kneeling, he kissed her warm mound, breathing in her girl-scent as he pushed his tongue out and tasted the milky globules of nectar clinging to her distended inner lips. 'Like licking out young girls' cunts, do you, vicar?' Marianne asked, gazing down at his protruding tongue exploring her yawning sex-groove. Silently, he worked between her cunny lips, licking, tasting, lapping up her vaginal offering as if he'd never savoured a girl's honeydew before. 'My clitoris, vicar!' Marianne ordered, peeling her pink sex-folds wide apart to expose her erect budling to his sweeping tongue. 'Ah, God, that's it – lick me just there and I'll come in your mouth!'

Her cries of sexual ecstasy resounding around the church as the vicar took her to heaven, she clung to his balding head, gasping her blasphemous expletives. 'God, lick my cunt! Oh, God! Drink the come from my beautiful cunt!' On and on her orgasm rolled, her clitoris throbbing in response to the vicar's snaking tongue. 'Please, finger my cunt!' she begged as her young vagina spasmed. Slipping three fingers into the girl's love-duct, the vicar began his thrusting, bringing out her girl-come, tightening her convulsing muscles, sustaining her multiple orgasm.

Her dishevelled blonde hair concealing her pretty face as her head lolled forward, Marianne panted, her body trembling uncontrollably as her pleasure slowly subsided. 'No more!' she gasped as the vicar's tongue caressed her sensitive sex-button. 'No . . . no more!' Moving back, the man of God slipped his girl-wet fingers from her tight sex-sheath and looked up at her flushed face.

'Did you enjoy that?' he asked as he rose to his feet, licking his cunny-wet lips.

'God, yes!' Marianne exclaimed. 'You're good at eating pussy! Do you lick your wife's cunt out?' she asked, toying with her engorged inner lips.

'I'm not married.'

'Oh, you must have to wank a lot!' she giggled, dropping to her knees and lifting his cassock. 'Allow me to save you the trouble!' she grinned, tugging his boxer shorts down, exposing his erect staff. Gasping as Marianne pulled his foreskin back, the vicar watched as she engulfed his purple knob in her hot mouth.

'Ah, ah! This is wrong!' he gasped as she ran her tongue over his silky-smooth glans. 'This is so very... please, don't stop!'

Wanking his hard shaft as she mouthed and sucked on his bulbous glans, Marianne's stomach somersaulted as she brought out his gushing sperm. His holy seed filling her cheeks, running down her chin, she moved her head back and forth, mouth-fucking his organ as he grimaced in his forbidden sexual paradise. 'Christ, you're good!' he cried in his new-found wickedness, rocking his hips, ramming his apoplectic knob against the back of her sperm-drenched throat. 'God, you're *fucking* good!'

Slipping his penis from her wet mouth, Marianne licked his glans, cleansing his deep purple knob, lapping up his salty sperm. 'You're big!' she observed. 'Very big! I'll let you fuck my tight cunt one day! And you can fuck my arse, I'd like that!'

'Where do you come from? I mean, who are you?'

'I told you, I'm the devil's daughter. I sold my soul – as you've just done, Vicar!'

Standing before the guilty, red-faced man, Marianne gazed into his brown eyes, wondering what he was thinking. 'I must be going,' she smiled as he adjusted his cassock. 'I'll be back, though. I promise you – I'll be back! This was only a quickie, to give you a taste of what's to come.' Turning, she left the small office, the vicar's holy seed lingering on her pink tongue as she walked through the church and out into the warmth of the evening sun.

* * *

Passing the park on her way home, she wondered whether to tell Rod of her incredible successes with hypnosis. But no, he'd probably condemn her if she were to reveal that she now had great power over Barry – and Natalie! Walking up the path to her house, her yearning vagina spewing out its slippery girl-juice, she took a deep breath and let herself in.

Barry had carried out her orders admirably, she observed, as she saw the lounge in pristine condition. 'You've done well,' she smiled as he appeared.

'I've done the kitchen, too,' he replied, gazing at her vaginal lips peering out from beneath her dress.

'How about some sexy fun? We haven't made love for ages!' Marianne giggled, sitting on the sofa with her dress high and her hairless pussy-slit gaping. Barry's eyes lighting up, he knelt between her thighs and pulled out his limp penis. 'Oh, don't I turn you on any more?' she asked dejectedly, eyeing his drooping member.

'I don't understand it!' Barry sighed miserably, looking down at his flaccid penis.

'Here, let me wank some life into it for you,' she offered, taking his fleshpole in her hand. The beast remaining lifeless, she slid off the sofa and sucked his knob into her hot mouth, licking his glans and wanking his shaft. Sighing, Barry pulled away and zipped up his jeans. 'I just don't understand it!' he complained.

'No, neither do I! That's the first time I've ever sucked you and you didn't like it! You used to ask me to suck your cock, and I never would. Now that I've changed my mind, you don't want me to!'

'I *do* want you to, Marianne!'

'Well, you're not much use to me like that, Barry! Have you been wanking?'

'No, of course not!'

Her hypnotic suggestions had worked very well, Marianne mused as she rose to her feet. She was free to do as she wished, while Barry, with his floppy penis, was unable to do anything! Walking through the hall to answer the front door, she wondered which of her visitors had arrived first – and whether she'd be able to use the power of hypnosis to have some fun. *I hope it's Natalie!*

'Oh, hi, Alan!' she greeted as she opened the door.

'Hi, Marianne. I've come round for . . . is Barry in?'

'Yes, he is – come in. Look into my eyes for a minute, Alan,' Marianne smiled as she closed the door.

'Why?'

'I want you to gaze into my eyes. Look deep into my eyes. You feel sleepy, your eyelids are heavy,' Marianne droned as Alan stared into her faraway eyes. His expression blank as she continued her hypnotic mantra, she knew that she'd succeeded. 'Now, Alan, whenever you hear the words, "*time for sex*", you'll fall into a hypnotic trance and do exactly as I say. Do you understand?'

'Yes, I understand.'

'Good. I don't know whether Barry's told you about the trigger word or not but, if he has, then you'll forget it. You've never heard of the word, "*juxtaposition*". OK, wake up.'

Leading Alan into the lounge, Marianne couldn't help grinning. 'Alan's come to see you,' she announced, facing Barry. *He's come to come in my mouth – but he won't!*

'Yes, I've come to . . . you know,' Alan said, winking at Barry.

'To what?' Barry asked.

'Our arrangement – I've come round to . . .'

'Arrangement?' Barry echoed, frowning.

'I'll put the kettle on. Coffee, Alan?' Marianne asked sweetly.

'Thanks,' he replied, making an odd facial expression at Barry as she left the room.

Things are going from good to brilliant! Marianne thought as she filled the kettle. *That's Barry, Natalie, John, and now Alan under my control!* But what about Jill and Lydia? she wondered as the doorbell rang. Would they, too, fall prey to her hypnotic words?

'Oh, Christine!' Marianne breathed surprisedly as she opened the door. 'Er . . . come in.'

'Thanks. I was walking down the road when I thought I saw Alan go into your house.'

'Yes, he's in the lounge with Barry — come through,' Marianne invited, closing the door as the girl stepped into the hall. 'I'm making some coffee, if you want one?'

'No, I won't stay.'

'Alan, Christine's here,' Marianne said, showing the girl into the lounge.

'Oh, Chris!' Alan's face flushed with guilt as he glimpsed Marianne's shapely thighs. 'What are you doing here?' he asked, averting his gaze as his wife looked daggers at him.

'I've come to see what you're up to.'

'I only wanted a quick word with Barry. I was just going. I've . . . er . . . I've got to go and see someone. I'll see you at home later,' he blustered, moving to the door. 'See you, Barry. 'Bye, Marianne.'

Showing Alan out, Marianne speculatively decided to leave Barry and Christine alone for a while. 'I'm nipping down to the shop for some milk,' she proffered, peering round the lounge door.

'OK,' Barry smiled, winking at Christine.

Creeping into the dining room, Marianne gazed through the partially open serving-hatch, wondering what Christine would say to Barry after her last encounter with him. Putting her arms around his neck, she'd obviously forgiven him for his cruelty. 'I want you, Barry!' she breathed huskily, grabbing his crotch. 'Make love to me! We've got time, Marianne will be a while yet. Make love to me, Barry!'

Kneeling, Christine unzipped Barry's jeans and pulled out his flaccid penis, gazing up at his face in puzzlement. 'What's the matter?' she asked. 'Don't you want me any more?'

'Yes, I do! It's just that . . .'

'I'll suck you. I've never done it before, but I'll suck you and make you nice and stiff for my pussy.' Engulfing his knob in her wet, warm mouth and wanking his limp shaft, Christine finally sighed and stood up. 'What is it, Barry? I thought you'd always wanted me to suck you. What's wrong?'

'I don't know! Perhaps I'm worried or something.'

'Finger me, finger my cunt. That'll make you hard. Lick me, Barry, lick my clitty and make me come. You like doing that, don't you?'

'I'd rather lick Marianne's clit. She's so much better . . . what the hell am I *saying?*'

'Roughly translated, you're saying that you no longer want me!' Christine sobbed as she dashed from the room, slamming the front door shut as she fled the house in tears.

Stifling a laugh, Marianne wondered what other evil hypnotic suggestions she could place in Barry's subconscious. *Life's getting better and better!* she mused as she walked through the hall and opened and closed the front door. 'Oh, has Christine gone?' she asked Barry innocently as she entered the lounge.

'Yes, she has,' he replied, somewhat disgruntled, she thought.

'Is everything all right, Barry? You seem . . . I don't know, you seem different.'

'I'm OK. But I don't understand . . . Why couldn't I get it up earlier?'

'God knows! Perhaps you're past it!' Marianne laughed. 'Anyway, I'm going to have a shower. Get some wine glasses out, will you? Oh, and press my new dress – it's crumpled. Jill and Lydia are coming over, I'll be down later.'

'Yes, Marianne.'

Jill bounded up the stairs to find Marianne sitting at her dressing-table mirror. 'Barry said you were up here,' she smiled. 'Lydia's downstairs.'

'Oh, good. Jill, before we go down, sit on the bed and look into my eyes.'

'What on earth for?'

'I'll tell you in a minute, just make yourself comfortable and gaze into my eyes.'

Again, Marianne droned her hypnotic words. 'When you hear the words, "*Time for sex*", you'll fall into a state of hypnosis and do anything and everything I ask of you, do you understand?'

'Yes, I do,' Jill replied dreamily.

'Good. Now, you'll forget the word, "*Juxtaposition*". It means nothing to you, you've never heard of it. Just remember the words, "*Time for sex*". OK, when I wake you up you're to go downstairs and tell Lydia to come up here and see me. Right, wake up!'

Gazing around the room, Jill frowned. Had it worked? Marianne wondered as the girl stood up and smiled. 'I'll see you downstairs,' Jill said, leaving the room. 'I'll tell Lydia to come up and see you.'

Sitting on the bed, her long black hair shining, her full red lips half open, her dark eyes mesmerized, Lydia was as easy as Jill to put under. 'You're a pretty little thing,' Marianne smiled, squeezing the girl's pert breasts. 'You've a nice body, a nice cunt. I'm going to enjoy using you more than anyone else. Lydia, when you hear the words, "*Time for sex*", you'll fall into a hypnotic trance and do exactly as I say. Do you understand?'

'Yes, I do,' the girl replied.

'Good. Wake up!'

A tidal wave of wickedness surged through Marianne as Lydia returned to her waking state. *I can do anything!* she exulted as she led the girl downstairs. *Anything!* 'Time for sex!' she decreed as Lydia sat on the sofa next to Jill. Barry's face took on a serene look, as did the girls' pretty faces. 'Right!' Marianne declared. 'You're all under my spell! What I want you to do is this. When I leave the room, you'll all want sex with each other. Barry, you'll want to fuck the girls but, of course, you won't be able to get it up! Jill and Lydia, you'll both be desperate for Barry, hungry for his cock. As he can't get an erection, you'll think him a prize wanker! OK, all wake up!'

Pouring the wine, Marianne passed the glasses round, grinning as she noticed the lust mirrored in the girls' eyes, the passion reflected in Barry's expression as he gazed at them, their long legs, their pert breasts. 'I'm just going next door to see Natalie,' she volunteered, wondering why her pretty neighbour hadn't arrived. 'I've just remembered that I promised her I'd call in. I'll try not to be too long.'

'Take your time,' Barry said. 'We'll save some wine for you.'

'OK, see you all later.'

Hiding behind the serving hatch, Marianne slipped her hand between her thighs, her fingers toying with her engorged inner pussy lips as she watched the trio. Moving towards Barry and settling at his feet, Lydia tugged his zip down, grinning up at him as she unbuckled his belt. 'Come and give me a hand, Jill,' she giggled as she pulled his flaccid penis out. 'Come and help me stiffen Barry's lovely cock!'

Slipping her skirt and top off, Jill removed her bra and panties, standing naked before Barry with a sensual glint in her eyes. 'Doesn't the sight of my cunt arouse you?' she asked, gazing at his lifeless penis.

'Yes, very much!' Barry sighed as Lydia pulled his foreskin back and engulfed his knob in her pretty mouth.

'Look, Barry, I'm fingering my cunt,' Jill giggled as she slipped three fingers between her swollen pussy lips and drove them deep into her wet vagina. 'Lydia, take your clothes off and I'll suck his cock – stiffen the beast ready for our wet cunts!'

Removing her clothes, Lydia sat next to Jill on the floor, kneading Barry's heavy balls. 'Why aren't you stiff?' she asked. His face flushing, Marianne felt sorry for him. But this was his punishment for all that he'd put her through, for the despicable way he'd treated her. As both the girls licked his purple knob, Marianne crept into the lounge and gasped.

'What the hell's going on?' she cried, gazing at the lewd spectacle.

'Oh! Er... Marianne!' Barry breathed. 'I... we...'

'So this is how you behave behind my back, is it?'

'Marianne, I...' Jill began as she rose to her feet, hurriedly dressing, covering her femininity.

'I don't blame you!' Marianne said. 'It's Barry I blame! You're bloody useless, Barry! To be honest, I was thinking of leaving you anyway. You're no good to me with a limp dick! And now this!'

'Marianne! I... Please, don't leave me!' Barry begged as the girls finished dressing and vacated the room.

'It's all right, it's not your fault,' Marianne said, following them into the hall. 'I know that Barry's a bastard – you were taken in by his charm, it wasn't your fault.'

'I'm sorry, Marianne,' Jill said, her full lips half smiling. 'I don't know what came over me! I don't understand it!'

'Neither do I!' Lydia rejoined. 'I'm not into men!'

'Don't worry about it!' Marianne smiled. 'I know Barry, I know how he charms people. I don't blame you two. Come round in the morning for coffee.'

'If you're sure that . . .' Jill began as she opened the front door.

'Of course I'm sure! I'll see you both tomorrow. 'Bye.'

Answering the phone as she closed the front door, Marianne smiled. 'Hi, Rod! How are you?'

'I'm fine. I . . . I haven't seen you for a while and I thought . . . How's the hypnosis going?'

'Great! I've hypnotized several people! I've got Barry just where I want him now.'

'Marianne, your soon-to-be-ex – has he become your ex yet?'

'No, not as such – why?'

'I want to know where our relationship is going.'

'Relationship? Oh! Er . . . come over Rod. I want to talk to you, so come over now.'

'All right. Is he there?'

'Yes, but I'll get rid of him.'

'OK, I'll come round.'

Replacing the receiver, Marianne wandered into the lounge to find Barry gazing out of the window. 'Marianne . . .' he began pensively as he turned to face her. Was he going to beg her not to leave him? she wondered as she gazed into his dark eyes. The tables certainly had turned! 'Marianne,' he repeated. 'Delta!'

Feigning a hypnotic trance, Marianne's mind swirled. *What the hell's happened?* she wondered as Barry stood before her and squeezed her firm breasts. *What the hell's going on in his subconscious?* Thanking God that he'd not used the real trigger word, she pictured Barry's friends standing round her tethered body, their penises in their hands, their sperm splashing over her pretty face. She could still enjoy his perverted friends, she decided, recalling the anal fuckings. And earn money!

'Marianne, I seem to have a problem getting an erection. I want you to suck my knob. I'm worried that something's wrong with me,' Barry continued, tugging his jeans down. 'Kneel down and suck me.'

Kneeling before her supposed master, Marianne breathed her trigger words, sending him into a state of hypnosis.

'You poor thing!' she giggled, gazing at his limp tool. 'The power of the mind, Barry, that's what it is! The power your mind has over your body! OK, I'm feeling generous – I'll allow you an erection, and an orgasm. When I suck you, your cock will stiffen and you'll come in my mouth. You'd like that, wouldn't you?'

'Yes, very much,' he replied in his trance.

'By the way, Rod's coming over shortly. You'll be nice to him, offer him a drink and make him feel at home. And you'll tell him that we're splitting up. OK, I'll feign a hypnotic trance again – wake up!'

Taking Barry's knob into her mouth, Marianne sucked and licked his silky glans, happy that his penis was stiffening. 'Wank me and drink my spunk!' he gasped as his fleshpole twitched. 'Ah, that's good! Yes, yes! Keep sucking my cock! Ah, God!' His sperm suddenly gushing into her mouth, Marianne ran her wet tongue over his throbbing glans, bringing out his male offering as he towered above her, shuddering in his ecstasy.

Moving her head back and forth, she swallowed hard,

drinking from his cock-head as his knees sagged and he clung to her head for support. *He's remembered the false trigger word. Another turn-up for the books!* she thought as she slipped his spent member from her sperm-drenched mouth. But what did she really want? she wondered as Barry ordered her to stand up. Did she want to stay with him? Or would Rod be a better choice?

'That was good!' Barry enthused as his zipped his jeans. 'That was *very* good! I don't know why I couldn't get it up before, but I now know that I haven't got a problem. Now, Marianne, you'll not leave me, do you understand? You love me and you want to stay with me. You'll never even think about leaving me. OK, wake up!'

Love you? Marianne brushed the curtain of hair from her dazed eyes. *You don't know the meaning of the bloody word!* But then, did she? *Love, lust, sex – what's the bloody difference?*

'I'm starting my new job on Monday morning,' she announced, wondering at Barry's reaction. 'I'm working for Brooke-Smith. I'll have a company car, a Mercedes. And the money will be good. You don't mind, do you?'

'No, not at all! I'm pleased that you've got a job at last. The money I've been making recently keeps disappearing so . . .'

'That'll be Rod,' she stated as the doorbell rang.

'Rod? Who's Rod?' Barry asked.

'My lover. You don't mind me having a lover do you, Barry?'

'Er . . . I'm confused. No, no, I don't mind at all, love. All I want is for you to stay with me, never leave me. I don't mind what you do as long as . . .'

'Yes, all right – don't go on! I'll go and let him in.'

Showing Rod into the lounge, Marianne wondered whether

Barry would tell him that they were splitting up. Floundering, his mind confused, there was no telling what he'd say, she thought fearfully. 'Barry, this is Rod,' she smiled as she entered the lounge.

'Hi, pleased to meet you!' Barry greeted, shaking Rod's hand.

'I . . . I hope you don't mind me . . .' Rod began hesitantly.

'Barry doesn't mind you coming round, Rod!' Marianne laughed. 'We're splitting up, aren't we, Barry?'

'Er . . . yes, that's right, we're splitting up. Would you like a drink, Rod?'

'Scotch, please.'

'Come and sit on the sofa, Rod,' Marianne smiled. 'I'll have vodka and lime, Barry.'

Holding Rod's hand as they sat down, Marianne adjusted her dress, hoisting it up to reveal her naked pussy-slit. The situation was weird, she thought as Barry passed the drinks, his gaze transfixed between her long legs. Taking Rod's hand, she placed it between her parted thighs, massaging her swollen vaginal lips with his fingertips.

'Marianne!' Pulling away, Rod frowned in disbelief.

'What's the matter?' she asked, her sparkling eyes reflecting her rising lust.

'You can't . . . I mean . . .'

'Barry doesn't mind, do you, Barry?'

'No, not at all. We're splitting up, so . . . I'll leave you alone for a while,' he said, opening the lounge door.

'Marianne, you've used hypnosis on him, haven't you?' Rod asked accusingly as Barry closed the door behind him.

'No, of course I haven't!'

'You can't fool me! Look, what is it you want? I mean, are you staying with Barry, or do you want a relationship with me? You can't have both, Marianne!'

Can't I? she mused, sipping her drink. *The devil's daughter can have you, Barry, John, Natalie, Jill, Lydia – and the vicar!* Unzipping Rod's trousers, she pulled out his stiffening penis. 'I haven't had the pleasure yet, have I?' she smiled, leaning over and sucking his knob into her mouth.

'No, you haven't. But what about . . . Ah, God! What about Barry? Ah, Marianne, that's nice!'

'*What* about Barry?' she grinned as she slipped his penis from her mouth and licked his swollen glans. 'You want me to choose? Then I choose you. I won't move in with you, Rod. Barry's leaving, so he won't be in the way. I'll come and visit you, and you can visit me and we'll make sweet love. No one has control over me now – I'm free.'

'I'd like you to live with me. God, that's nice!'

'One day, Rod – one day, I'll live with you.'

Moving her head up and down, taking Rod's glans to the back of her throat before slipping it between her rolling lips, Marianne brought out his sperm. Swallowing his gushing come, she thought about the future – money, sex, fun. And power!

'Oh! Er . . . sorry!' Barry gasped as he entered the room, gazing at Rod's huge penis filling his girlfriend's accommodating mouth.

'That's OK,' Marianne smiled, lazily relinquishing Rod's glistening cock. 'Pour us another drink will you, Barry?'

'Er . . . yes, of course.'

'Marianne!' Rod exclaimed as he concealed his penis.

'It's all right, Rod! I'll come and stay with you for the night, would you like that?'

'Well . . . er . . . yes, that would be nice.'

'Good. Barry, I'll be out for the night, I'm staying at Rod's place.'

'Yes, all right,' he replied meekly, refilling the glasses.

'Go and pack my toothbrush and things in my overnight bag.'

'Yes, OK.'

Downing his drink, Rod stood up. 'This is an incredible situation, Marianne!' he exclaimed. 'I don't think you should be doing this to Barry.'

'He's all right! I haven't used hypnosis on him, if that's what you're still thinking.'

'Then he's very understanding! Anyway, we'd better be going.'

'I'll be over in a while, Rod. You go home, and I'll see you later.'

'All right. But don't be too long, will you?'

'Don't worry, I won't.'

Seeing Rod out, Marianne wandered into the kitchen to find Barry sitting at the table, her overnight bag on the floor, packed and ready. 'Are you all right?' she asked, sitting opposite him.

'Yes, just a little confused, that's all.'

'Confused about what?'

'I don't know.'

'Why not ask some of your friends over tomorrow evening? We'll have some wine and . . .'

'Del . . .'

'What?'

'Del . . . God, I must be tired, I can't remember what I was going to say!'

'The only word I can think of is "delta" – is that what you were about to say?'

'Delta? No, I don't think so.'

'Oh well, not to worry.'

At last! Marianne thought. *I've done it – I'm in complete control!* Smiling, she felt her clitoris swell at the thought of

Barry's five perverted friends using her tethered body. She didn't need Barry – she'd get rid of him before his friends arrived. She'd be ready and waiting in the garage, her naked body spread on the padded bench. But where was Natalie?

'Time for sex,' she breathed, watching Barry fall into a trance. 'You'll give me all the money you earn, Barry. And you're signing the house over to me. I'll stay with you, but only if you treat me as your mistress! You've treated me despicably, and now the tables have turned! When I tire of you, become bored with you, I'll sell the house and go and live with Rod. Wake up!'

'Want some coffee?'

'No, thanks. Go and run me a bath, Barry. I don't know what time I'll be home tomorrow, it depends on whether Rod and I spend the morning making love or not. By the way, there's a cheque you made out to me behind the mantlepiece clock – take it to my bank first thing in the morning,' she instructed, wondering at his reaction.

'A cheque?' he queried.

'Yes, the one you gave me for twenty-odd grand.'

'Oh, right – the present I gave you. Yes, I'll bank it for you.'

'Good. Now go and run my bath. Oh, and you'll give me a lift to Rod's place. No, better still, give me your car keys!'

'Yes, Marianne.'

Answering the phone as Barry obediently climbed the stairs to run his mistress's bath, Marianne smiled to hear Rod's voice. 'You are impatient!' she giggled. 'I'm just going to have a bath, and then I'll come over.'

'Wash here,' he replied. 'I want you to come over now and . . .'

'No, Rod! Listen, I've just about had enough of being ordered around! I've been slave to Barry, to his friends, to . . .

I'm my own person now! This is my life and I'll lead it! I'll have my bath and then come over.'

'Juxtaposition!'

Her eyes glazing over, Marianne stood motionless. Her heart fluttering, her stomach churning, her mind racked, she listened in trepidation to Rod's instructions. 'You'll come over straight away! There's a sink full of washing-up to be done, there's housework, ironing . . . And, of course, there's my cock! Get yourself over here now, girl! Get yourself over here this instant – slave!'